# Constable's Apprehension

***Other Five Star Titles by Laurie Moore:***

Constable's Run
The Lady Godiva Murder

# Constable's Apprehension

*Laurie Moore*

**Five Star • Waterville, Maine**

This novel is a work of fiction. Names, characters, places and incidents are either the product of the author's imagination, or, if real, used fictitiously.

First Edition
First Printing: October 2003

Set in 11 pt. Plantin.

Printed in the United States on permanent paper.

**Library of Congress Cataloging-in-Publication Data**

Moore, Laurie.
Constable's apprehension / Laurie Moore.—1st ed.
p. cm.
ISBN 0-7862-5334-7 (hc : alk. paper)
1. Police—Texas—Fort Worth—Fiction. 2. Fort Worth (Tex.)—Fiction. 3. Policewomen—Fiction. I. Title.
PS3613.O564C65 2003
813′.6—dc21 2003052871

For my beautiful daughter, Laura . . . always for Laura.

# Acknowledgments

Many thanks to Hazel Rumney of Five Star for "discovering" me, and to my editor, Russell Davis, for sticking with my Constable novels; without their confidence in this law enforcement series, you would not be reading this. For my agent, Peter Miller, of PMA Literary and Film Management, Inc., it's a pleasure to work with you. For the Sweet Shop of Fort Worth, many thanks for providing the Fudge Love truffles for my tri-state book tour; your chocolates are world-class. And for my publicist, Bethany Hunt, you are amazing. I must also recognize members of the DFW Writers Workshop, a talented group of colleagues who listen to my chapters each Wednesday night and share my passion for writing. And finally, for my daughter, Laura, who shores up my confidence by laughing at my stories and telling me I'm not just a great mom, but a wonderful friend . . . you turned out pretty good yourself, young lady.

# Prologue

Jinx Porter woke up delighted to be getting another kiss at the pig.

In an unbelievable turn of events, the predominantly Republican Tarrant County Commissioners Court had appointed him—a yellow-dog Democrat—to fill out his ex-girlfriend's unexpired term as constable. The county judge's sister and brother-in-law had suffered a devastating financial loss in a grisly home invasion several months before, and the violent event played an instrumental role in Jinx's comeback. The Texas Department of Criminal Justice issued a blue warrant for the suspect, Odie "Straight-Eight" Oliver, but no law enforcement agency, to date, had been able to flush out the paroled convict. Getting Oliver in custody before he could harm anyone else was of paramount importance to the judge when he cast the swing vote. Since Jinx had arrested Oliver on prior occasions and knew him on sight, the former lawdog became the odds-on favorite to take over the vacant position.

In a world crawling with thugs, Jinx Porter could be one of those bad things that happened to bad people.

Jinx checked the clock.

In a few minutes, he needed to shave, shower and dress. He hadn't worn a suit since the last time the judge swore him in as Tarrant County constable, and he wanted to give the appearance of a man who deserved to reclaim his old job.

He still hadn't forgiven Raven. For sixteen years, he'd

fought tooth and toenail to hang onto his elected office; and until he stepped on the toes of Fort Worth's most powerful woman, Eleanor Thornton, he'd been happy going to work every day, enforcing the law, hunting down parole violators and serving court documents. Mrs. Thornton should've known she couldn't dodge those divorce papers forever. Then when the rich old harpie bankrolled Raven's political campaign . . . well, hell, Raven never should've run against him if she didn't plan to fulfill the four-year term.

He reminded himself not to dwell on it. The worst days of his life were over and done with. He'd left "Cowtown" for a log cabin in San Augustine, Texas; but after living the life of a hermit for a year, he returned to Fort Worth and moved back into the Château Du Roy, happy to start over.

Caesar, Jinx's five-year-old Siamese cat, landed on his chest. The ornery feline burrowed his head beneath Jinx's chin, and in seconds, emitted a low purr.

Okay, so he still had a soft spot for his ex. After all, Raven had given him the seal point; once he lost the election and the friends he could count on one hand abandoned him, only his furry old pal made life bearable. He even created a Cat-of-the-Year contest. And on the third Thursday of each December, he gathered Caesar in his lap and pronounced him the winner. He gave the cat a squeeze, nudged him aside, slung his legs over the side of the bed and sat up. Glowering, Caesar barked out a string of cat profanity and slunk over to the warm spot on the pillow.

In the bathroom, Jinx checked his reflection. Not bad for a man who had recently observed his fifty-third birthday. Bald on top, a few white hairs on the sides, in need of a new lens prescription for his eyeglasses—but he could still fire up the old jackhammer when it counted. Women didn't seem to care about good looks as long as the equipment worked and the foreman knew how to run it.

Lost in thought, he wondered if anyone would come to his swearing-in ceremony that fine Cowtown Monday.

Not his mother. Kamille Porter hadn't supported her son's venture into law enforcement eighteen years ago, and she wouldn't do so now. Ever since he first took office, she'd sat glued to CNN, waiting for breaking news that he'd met a grisly end. He thought there might be an off chance his father would show. Dan Porter only stood up to Kamille twice a year. Maybe this would be one of those times.

The way Jinx saw it, he only had three things to do once he got back to his old office. One, get rid of any doodads Raven left behind and hammer the "Dogs Playing Poker" pictures back on the walls; two, create a new computer password for himself; three, relax in his chair, put his boots up on the desk, pinch out enough snuff to make his lower lip protrude and wait for his constituents to read the newspaper article heralding his return to the precinct. Then, he'd sit back and count the minutes 'til the ladies started calling again. Don't ask why—but women loved giving cops a little stray booger.

And Jinx had one more thing to look forward to.

The county judge mentioned a nasty rumor spreading through the courthouse—that once Raven handed in her resignation, the office got so screwed up the deputies couldn't even make a decent arrest. That's how the man turned two of the four commissioners into Jinx Porter enthusiasts. Not because they liked or respected him. They needed to make a seamless transition to get the chaos under control, and Jinx Porter was the name they'd come up with.

Today, he'd take the oath. Tomorrow morning, at five o'clock, he'd shower and shave, put on a nice shirt and slacks, pull on his boots and strap on his Smith & Wesson. A dangerous felon by the name of Newton "Marble-Eye" Turner, erroneously paroled instead of another con-wise reprobate with a similar name, made the Governor's Most Wanted list. The Texas Department of Criminal Justice needed to get Marble-Eye back in the pen, and they put out a white warrant to communicate exigent circumstances.

Once Jinx took Marble-Eye into custody, he'd start looking for Odie "Straight-Eight" Oliver. Cops had a saying . . .

. . . *You may beat the rap, but you won't beat the ride.*

# Chapter One

It didn't take long for the nurses at Our Lady of Mercy Hospital to grow weary of Sid Klevenhagen.

And it didn't take tubes porcupining out of Sid's parchment hide to know that the Fort Worth police lieutenant grew weaker each day. A bedside monitor spiked lines across a monochrome screen.

The flatter the better, according to an informal polling of LPNs assigned to the third-floor cardiac unit. Most of the nurses wished Sid would go 10-42 to that big cop shop in the sky, but none seemed to want it as much as the Irish girl, a strawberry blonde with crater-sized dimples who looked after the even-numbered rooms on the cardiac wing.

A newly sworn Tarrant County constable resting uncomfortably in the bed next to Sid, overheard her lively discussions with the drill sergeant head nurse. The first exchange caused such a ruckus it roused Constable Jinx Porter from semi-consciousness. The more bitter the outcry, the more Jinx wanted to pull the curtain aside and see the menace in the next bed for himself.

For a man with barely the strength to blink, that wasn't possible.

Jinx worked his limp hand up his chest and fidgeted with a gauze pack stuck near the top of his right shoulder—the one plugging the hole hollowed out by Newton "Marble-Eye" Turner's Llama .380. Staring into the haze, he wondered if

Marble-Eye got the same ambulance ride, or whether he lay toe-tagged on the ME's slab until his next of kin could make positive ID.

Fuzzy thoughts began to sharpen. Jinx mentally reconstructed the chain of events, starting at the point he curbed the unmarked patrol car a quarter-block from Marble-Eye's. By the time he relived the part where his deputies swarmed the house, a crescendoing soprano scattered his thoughts.

"But you have to let me see Jinx. He can't die without—"

"The answer's no. If you're not a cop or next-of-kin, you cannot go in."

Jinx recognized the alto reply; it came from the head nurse.

"Let me understand this—Jinx may die and you're telling me I can't see him?"

His eyes snapped open. It sounded like—

*Raven.*

*Why would his ex-girlfriend come see him?*

"I don't care what you want to say to Constable Porter. No visitors."

"You don't understand, this is the third time—"

"No, young lady, you don't understand. Surgery was touch-and-go. He almost didn't make it."

"You have no idea what it's been like for me. I came as soon as I found out. Now you're telling me I can't go in there?"

Muffled cries seemed to make an impact on the supervising RN.

"Are you family?"

"I'm . . . his sister."

"Bullshit. We phoned his sister after we were unable to contact his parents. She told us to go fuck ourselves."

A feminine Irish voice interrupted. "There's not enough

Prozac in this godforsaken place to subject meself to that horrible Mr. Klevenhagen. He's mental!" The girl's tone turned strident. "I'd like to swap his O-Two tank for one with a skull and crossbones."

"You've never missed a paycheck. This hospital's on the verge of Chapter Eleven. Whether this organization goes bankrupt depends entirely on patients like Sid Klevenhagen. Now, go take his blood pressure."

Outside Room 302, Raven made another run at the nurse. "All right, you got me. I'm not Jinx's sister."

"Do you realize that if that was a Fort Worth police officer in there instead of a Tarrant County constable, there'd be a twenty-four-hour guard posted at the door? Nice try, young lady, but either you leave, or I'm calling security."

Voices fell to a hush.

In a way, he hoped Raven would talk her way in. They hadn't actually seen each other in what? Almost two years? They could put their bad blood behind them—maybe, in time, start the relationship over and see if they couldn't work out their differences.

Jinx let his uninjured arm drop between the bed rails. He fumbled until he reached a gizmo coiled through the railings, then pressed the button enough to raise his upper body for a look out the window. The view made the discomfort worthwhile. By craning his neck, he glimpsed past the buildings jutting up from downtown Fort Worth, and picked out the rooftop to his apartment some twenty blocks away.

The sight made him homesick for his cranky Siamese, Caesar. He imagined his best friend still positioned on the windowsill, lashing his tail in anticipation. Jinx wanted his clothes—wherever they were—and to get the hell out of Our Lady of Mercy, especially when the reflection of a homely redhead, brandishing an upraised syringe, appeared in the window.

By the time he lolled his head in her direction and saw her snarl of hair, highlighted with purple streaks, she had already injected the long tube snaking out of his good arm and floated past the fabric that separated him from the mysterious Sid Klevenhagen.

The door clicked shut, dimming the room from the harsh fluorescents of the nurses' station. Gingerly, Jinx reached for his water glass and sipped through the straw until it slurped.

"Psst."

He strained to listen.

"Psst. You awake, hoss?"

Jinx frowned. He cleared his throat and spoke in the rasp of someone who hadn't said more than two words in as many days. "You talking to me?"

"I heard slobberin'. You got somebody else over there? Maybe one a-them nurses?"

"Wouldn't do any good."

"Whatsa matter?" Sid chuckled as if he already knew. "Something wrong with the old Indian fighter?"

"You could say that. While I was knocked out, somebody rammed an arrow through the tip of it."

Sid hooted. "I know what you mean, hoss. Don't even try to have sex for at least three days after they yank it out. Be like trying to shove an eel down a coin chute."

*Thanks.*

"Not many people know it, but I got some black market Viagra that'll make you holler Geronimo. Not that I need it, nosirree. Course, you can't take it if you have heart trouble. What're you in for?"

"Got shot serving a warrant."

"Po-lice, eh?"

Only a brother officer would accent the first syllable. A

dull throb in Jinx's shoulder traveled to the middle of his back, turning his smile into a grimace. He swallowed the taste of hot copper filling his mouth.

"My name's Sid Klevenhagen."

"I'm Jinx—" A stab of pain stopped him.

"You ain't a-kiddin'."

"No, I *am* Jinx."

"Me, too. Matter of fact, I'd say everybody with the bad luck to be on this floor's cursed."

"My name's Jinx. Jinx Porter. I'm the constable."

Sid chuckled. "How long you been po-licin'?"

"Four years away from a twenty-year retirement, and not so much as a broken bone. Now, look at me." He hoped the old man would slide back the curtain. He didn't.

"How'd it happen?"

"Winged in a shoot-out."

"No kiddin'?" The lieutenant sounded tickled pink. "Why, I remember the first time I took a slug, got me right here, right in the middle of my—"

The door clicked open and a slice of light from the nurses' station played across the ceiling.

"—still got the scar. Say, little missy, wanna see somethin' big and scary?"

"Fer God's sakes, Mr. Klevenhagen, quit pushing the buzzer. What is it ye want?"

"A drink."

Sheets rustled; the LPN let out a shriek. "Get yer X-rated mitts off me before I conk ye with this bedpan. Are ye lissenin', Mr. Klevenhagen, ye filthy ol' coot?"

Footfalls padded to the door.

"Wait, nurse, come back," Sid called. "I'd like you to take a look at my dick."

"What's wrong with it?"

"Nothing. I'd just like you to look at it."

Metal hit the floor. The door banged shut, followed by muffled chatter. A feeble chuckle filtered over. The color TV, mounted in the middle of the room near the ceiling, came on in time for the Rangers to ground out at the top of the third. Through the walls, a loud proclamation tapered off to a low buzz.

"I'm Fort Worth police . . ." Sid's words distorted like a seventy-eight record slowing to thirty-three-and-a-third. "Made lieutenant and they stuck me over the jail. Some promotion."

His voice faded. For a moment, Jinx thought his roommate was speaking to someone else—

*Come inside.*

*Effective cure-all.*

*Many free ears.*

—until he fought the effects of the painkiller long enough to make sense of the gibberish.

*Homicide.*

*Detective bureau.*

*Twenty-three years.*

Eyelids fell to half-mast. The medicine kicked in, full-bore, and Jinx felt himself drift away. A swirl of sounds mingled with colors. He remembered catching Ivy's sleeve before she bounded out of the passenger seat of his patrol car and stampeded Marble-Eye's rickety front porch with the missing balusters.

*Don't do anything stupid.*

*This time, let me go first, Jinx.*

*Fat chance.*

*It's because I'm female, isn't it?*

*Cover the back with Dell.*

*How come Mickey always backs you up instead of me?*

*Ever hear of friendly fire?*

The company rep for Raven's home security system never guaranteed a home invasion wouldn't take place—only that she'd have a ten-second head start if an intruder breached the contacts.

So when she dragged in, hangdog, from Our Lady of Mercy Hospital, consumed with ugly thoughts of the RN who kept her from seeing Jinx Porter, she wrote off the blinking red light on the control panel to atmospheric conditions. The workman who installed the security system said it could happen; the Catholic sprinkling that began when she left the hospital had turned into a genuine Church of Christ downpour.

She paused at the front door and took stock of the house, then began a stealth check around the perimeter.

Nothing appeared out of order.

*What if Jinx died and she never got to tell him?*

She came full-circle, thrilled to find the doors and windows all intact.

Fifteen minutes later, the last thing she expected to see when she stepped out of the shower was the mirrored reflection of a jackbooted, ninja-dressed man seated on her bed.

Her heart leapt to her throat; her brain short-circuited. She let out a hysterical squeal, yanked a towel off the rod and cowered.

Anyone seeing her at close range would describe her with dark flowing hair, pewter-gray eyes that resembled sterling beads—or lead bullet slugs, depending on the mood—and a killer body that made *GQ* types want to whisper lewd suggestions into her ears. But this intruder with close-cropped hair, bleached platinum and moussed into spikes that gave him a dangerous look—this maniac who watched her through the cold depths of his eyes—didn't seem the least bit concerned that she stood on shaky legs because her mind had just downshifted into survival mode.

Not planning to waste an opportunity to escape unharmed, she assessed her chances of taking him. Six feet tall—that would give him an edge—one ninety; who could tell with those loose-fitting clothes whether he pumped iron? But if she could get him on the same level—say, the floor—she might equalize his brawny advantage.

Her eyes flickered to the holder mounted on the tile backsplash.

"Surely you're not thinking of attacking me with your toothbrush." The burglar shoved aside a flap of cloth, exposing the butt of a wicked automatic jutting out from his waistband. Reflexively, her gaze flickered to the closet and back.

*New plan.*

*Go for the Mossberg.*

"You're probably thinking, *If I get my shotgun . . .*"

She flinched, seeing where all this was heading. Standing on the bathmat, shivering, her voice warbled with the effort of speech. "Let me get dressed."

"I warn you, it's not there. Women are so predictable. You make these little hidey-holes . . . Honestly, Raven, those are the first places we look."

*He knew her name.*

*A stalker?*

She'd been dreading this moment, and put it off as long as possible.

"Please don't hurt me." Her voice trembled. "We'll drive to the ATM; I'll empty my checking account. Just don't hurt me." But she was thinking, *Me or you, buddy. First chance, I'll kill ya.*

He seemed to revel in her discomfort. While his gaze traveled the contours of her body, she realized the angle of the mirrored bathroom door, reflected in the plate glass mirror over the sink, permitted him a full view of her naked backside. She abandoned the thought of slamming it shut. One good kick and he'd bring her down like a cheetah on a gazelle.

That left Option C: swan-diving through the oval of stained glass. If severing an artery on the way out the second story didn't kill her, the landing would.

"I'm crushed, Rave." Laughter flickered behind his eyes. "You don't recognize me." Without warning, he reached off to one side and sailed an oversized flannel shirt through the air. "Think back."

Raven's mind raced ahead. Taking a few drunken sailor steps, she picked the shirt up off the floor, clutched the towel tight against her breasts and slipped into one sleeve. "So . . . you're not going to kill me?"

"No." His eyes turned slitty.

*Relief turned to dread.*

"Rape me?"

He barked out a laugh. Rose from the bed, and with a narrow-hipped swagger, moved from the shadows into the light.

Raven's stomach went hollow.

*Ohmygod.*

*Yucatan Jay!*

# Chapter Two

The next time Jinx opened his eyes, the sun had set. The street lamps of Cowtown glimmered through the window. He stared out, wondering if the cat missed him.

Where was Ivy, anyway?

The way he saw it, she could at least make an effort to smuggle in Chinese food before lights-out. He wouldn't be here in the first place, if it weren't for her. Between the time he saw the muzzle blast and the shock wave sent him airborne, he promised himself he'd never again dive in the line of fire to save her bacon.

Ever.

He tightened his jaw and reminded himself Ivy wasn't the only one with family; he had the Siamese to care for. Images of the destructive feline warmed him to the core. Never mind that his pet had the capacity to reduce the apartment to rubble. Gradually, he nodded off again.

He snapped awake when the water glass slipped from his hand. An unsightly vision of Harpo Marx loomed over him.

His eyes focused.

Baked potato nose. Oatmeal complexion. A hand attached to a flabby arm with skin hanging down enough to wave itself, thrust a white sack inches from his face.

"Ivy." The inclination to flinch evaporated.

Porcine eyes peered out from behind ungovernable straw-colored curls. "You're supposed to be in the bed by the door." She thumbed at the curtain. "It says, *Porter-A* and *Klevenhagen-B* on the nameplates outside. I poked my head in and didn't see you. For a minute, I thought I had the wrong room. I had to ask at the nurses' station to get to the bottom of it."

He knew he was in bad shape when his lonely ears welcomed the resonance of a hillbilly twang that usually annoyed him five days a week. And it made him excuse the dowdy clothes he felt certain came from a thrift store set up to support battered women. Ivy was big on causes.

She took a breath. "Seems they mixed up the names. No telling how many people might've left without visiting you."

Reality put a grimace on his face. They both knew better. At times like this, he could count the friends on one hand. And employees didn't factor into the equation, especially when being hooked up to gadgets happened to be their fault.

She seemed to read his thoughts. "You saved my life. I wouldn't even be here if you hadn't jumped in front of me."

"Won't happen again."

"That bullet had my name on it. Most people wouldn't have your courage."

"Forget it. This isn't one of those Japanese skin-saving traditions where I have to take care of you the rest of your life." His thoughts turned to the Siamese. "Who's feeding Caesar?"

"I been meaning to talk to you about that," she announced cheerily, "but for now, why don'tcha try to enjoy the milkshake I smuggled in?"

Ivy flat wore him out. For the moment, he gave up on news of the seal point. "Where's my Szechuan? I always have garlic prawns on Wednesdays."

"It's Saturday, not Wednesday. You slept through

Wednesday, Thursday and Friday. And most of Tuesday."

She handed over a chocolate malt. Two sips later, he could almost feel the milk curdling in his stomach.

"What's wrong, Jinx?"

"Feel real bad." He closed his eyes and willed the nausea to calm.

"You're lucky." Ivy gave him a blank stare. She picked at the lint on one frumpy sleeve. "I heard the doctor say another millimeter, and *Goodnight Irene*."

She scrunched her face and shuddered.

He closed his eyes. Let them roll back in his head. Blackness gave way to a flash of colors.

*Gray steps. Green screen door hanging by a rusty hinge. Stepping off to one side, his right fist poised to hammer the alligator-rough paint of the doorjamb. Tattered curtains parted. The deadly eye of the .380 trained on Ivy.*

*Get down!*

*A blast of orange, then a view of the sky and not a cloud in it. And the weatherman had predicted a gully washer.*

Relentless tapping forced him to open his eyes. Droplets of rain sluiced down the windowpane in rivulets.

He shifted his gaze to the Rangers game. Bottom of the ninth, bases loaded. Then, he remembered . . . early October, Rangers fighting for the pennant.

Ivy hadn't budged. In a voice full of melancholy, she blurted out, "I don't know what we'd do if you died."

"Commissioners Court would appoint a new constable and he'd fire you."

"You're mad because I talked you out of partnering with Mickey, aren't you?"

"Tone it down. I'm trying to watch my team."

He wasn't about to tell her he was frothing at the mouth, all right. Not at her. At himself. For not trusting his gut and for pairing-up with an idiot. If she hadn't left that note on his desk the afternoon before, complaining he didn't treat her the same as the guys—

—if he hadn't gotten the idea she might be fixing to file some half-baked sexual harassment claim so she could retire early with a nice chunk of change to see her into old age—

—he wouldn't have made her show up to serve the state penitentiary's white warrant in the first place.

Fad lawsuits infuriated him. They put ideas into the vacuous minds of impressionable women like Ivy and Georgia, the secretary. He caught himself glaring. Ivy dropped her hefty form on the bed and a shot of pain went through his arm. Jinx winced.

"If something should happen to me, I wouldn't want anybody but you to finish raising Amos."

The idea made him cringe. After Ivy tricked him into baby-sitting the miniature Unabomber a few years back, he knew better. "If you ask me, that's reason enough to take a bullet."

"Amos is a good boy. He asked about you. I almost brought him in with me—he got kicked off the bus again."

Jiminy Christmas. The very idea she might haul that Ritalin-ingesting lummox in to visit, numbed him to the marrow. "I'm here to get better, not worse."

"Quit griping. I left him out in the patrol car. He wanted to play with his Game Boy."

"Is that what he's calling it now?"

Humor fell on unappreciative ears.

Ivy said, "I had some new pictures taken—"

"Maybe you can talk the booking desk into giving you wallet sizes of his first mug shot."

"Amos could use a father figure."

"That's what wardens are for."

Ivy persisted. "It's in my will. You get first crack at raising him."

"If you want to leave me something, leave me alone." What in the world would make her think he'd be interested in bringing up that surly, prepubescent serial killer? Hulking blob ought to be on a leg monitor. Probably out hot-wiring Ivy's patrol car right now.

When he glanced at the TV, the picture went off. Game over, and he didn't have a clue who won.

He fixed her with a hard stare. "Who's feeding my cat?"

Ivy's hand-held police radio crackled to life.

The dull monotone of a 'troped-up juvenile came over the air. "I'm fucking miserable."

*Amos.*

The sheriff's dispatcher barked out a demand. "Unit transmitting, identify yourself immediately."

"I said I was fucking miserable—not fucking stupid."

Before Jinx could launch into a scathing lecture, an unexpected beam of light swept the room. He turned his head in time to see the curtain ripple. The homely nurse with eggplant-colored hair reappeared.

Her unflinching stare centered on Ivy. "It's after hours. Clear out. And, don't be sneaking in any more free world food for that guy. He's on a special diet."

Jinx screwed his face into a practiced, dammit-to-hell expression. Ivy slid off the bed and grabbed her tote bag.

"One last thing," she said in a way that warned him he was about to reach a new low-water mark. "I forgot to tell you. Fort Worth PD found a blood trail in the house; Marble-Eye was gone."

On the way out, she exchanged " 'Scuse me's" with the nurse.

He never did find out about his cat.

The last time Raven saw Yucatan Jay, she was accompanying her aunt and uncle to the Amtrak station where they'd packed him off to military school. It was either that, or drop him off at a boys' ranch; Aunt Wren and Uncle Jack thought either alternative would look better on their son's résumé than a year's confinement in kiddie jail.

"What do you think?" He spread his arms and flexed his muscles.

What she thought was that she looked better, now, seated in her glazed-leather wingback, dressed in blue jeans and a button-down flannel tartan, than she did cowering buck-naked, behind a skimpy bath towel that barely obscured her headlights. What she said was, "Don't you know breaking into houses could get you killed?"

"Been doing it for years."

"Ohmygod." She clapped a hand to her mouth. "I knew you'd turn out to be a criminal."

"Not a criminal." He opened the bottle cap on his fourth Heineken with his teeth. "CIA. So, how long have you been a constable?"

*Only way he could know about her law enforcement background was by rummaging through her stuff.*

"You expect me to believe you work for the Central Intelligence Agency?" The revelation stopped her cold. "Last I heard, you were living on a horse ranch in Montana, breaking mustangs."

"A cover. I had to go to language school. Actually, I've been in and out of Libya a couple of times. Once, in Liberia —but that didn't turn out so hot. Almost got my ass shot off. After I complete this mission, I'm supposed to be in Equatorial Guinea. There's a political figure—he's not very nice—

we thought we'd try to find a replacement for him." Yucatan Jay sauntered over to the cowhide sofa, dropped with an easy free fall and made himself at home. "You speak any foreign languages?"

*"Ur-shay."*

He corkscrewed an eyebrow.

*"Ig-Pay atin-Lay."*

"You don't have to get snotty. I only asked because I thought maybe we had that in common, too."

"What do we have in common, Jay?"

He gave her a one-shoulder shrug. "I work for the government, you work for the government—"

"Used to work. I worked for the county. It's not the same."

"County, state, federal . . . what's the difference? We're all superheroes on a different playing field, Rave." His mouth tipped at the corners and he went on in a velvety voice. "You put on your little cowgirl costume and go out and save people . . . I put on my disguise—whatever that happens to be—only difference is I have better toys. You read the global section in the newspaper?"

Slow nod. She didn't believe a cotton-pickin' word, but he scored high on imagination points.

"Recall that assassination last month in the Middle East?"

Raven widened her eyes. He favored Uncle Jack. Had his winning smile and the dark auburn roots at the base of his processed blond hair; weird gray eyes like hers and Aunt Wren's proved they were cousins. But CIA? No way.

"You're asking me to believe you assassinated a world leader in the Middle East?"

"Not me—another operative. I got the wife."

Raven clutched her chest. "You murdered a man's wife?"

"Bedded her. That's how the other operative was able to take him out."

"What?"

"You don't believe me." He took a swig.

"How'd you get in my house?"

"If I told you, you'd fix it so I couldn't get in next time."

*Next time?*

One of them should be on Thorazine. She thought it should be Yucatan Jay.

"The Titan's a good burglar system. Takes about four seconds to defeat instead of two. It's fine for Cowtown, though. You shouldn't worry. Probably never happen again as long as you own the place."

"Why're you in Fort Worth?"

"New mission."

"Really." Said without enthusiasm.

He downed the rest of his beer and stared through glazed eyes. "I'm only telling you because we're family." Long pause. "There's no one else I can trust." He seemed to be assessing her ability to keep a secret. "I picked up a tail at DFW and had to abort my connecting flight. I had no place else to go. I'll be outta here by ten Monday morning, but for now I'm bunking with you." He gave the room an admiring once-over, and his dark mood seemed to lighten. "Nice digs. Did you buy these antiques with the money you made off your novel?" He thumbed at a walnut, drop-leaf secretary with a first edition of *The Lonely Constable* on display.

"My finances are none of your business."

Relaxed humor filled his face, but his gray eyes remained level and unyielding. "How long've you lived here?"

Raven gave him an aristocratic sniff and ladled up sarcasm. "Wouldn't a CIA operative know that?"

"Just making conversation." He gave the room another

visual scan, paying particular attention to the window shutters. "You bought it in 1994. Renovated in 2003 and protested the property taxes every year but one. You didn't want to spend the money your granddaddy left you, but you did because you thought he'd want you living in a nice, safe neighborhood—and he would've."

"I don't know about the safe part. You're here."

"A minor inconvenience. This'll probably never happen again in your lifetime. Have you thought of adding a panic room? With all this worldwide terrorism, it probably wouldn't be a bad idea."

"I hadn't thought of that," Raven said for effect. But she was thinking, *Fuck it. After this, I'm moving.*

"You may not realize, but the American dollar's going to shit." Unexpectedly, he stopped talking. Cocked his head. Rolled his eyes toward the ceiling and listened to the right. "Monday morning, nine o'clock?" His voice dropped to a whisper. "We're going to the bank to convert my money into gold Canadian Maple Leaf coins."

Raven's internal alarm system activated. Red lights and sirens went off in her head.

She wanted Yucatan Jay out of her house.

"You can't stay here."

"You don't believe me." His mood darkened, along with his eyes, and the easy smile he tried to charm her with disappeared. "I'm sorry to hear that."

*Oh shit. He's gonna kill me.*

"Step away from the window." He rose from the sofa. "I didn't want to have to do this. . . ."

A lump formed in her throat. This was how it happened. A psychopath breaks in, next thing you know, your throat's slit and you're hanging from a meathook like the Polled Hereford Grand Champion from the Fort Worth Stock Show and

Rodeo. She slid her hand to her waistband, to the .22 caliber five-shot she smuggled out of the underwear drawer before she hiked up a pair of fresh panties.

Three strides closer and Raven pulled her gun.

"Freeze! Or I'll drop you where you stand."

# Chapter Three

"Lights out, gentlemen." The nurse reached for the drapery pull and closed off Jinx's view of the outside with a muffled zip. Shoe soles squeaked against the linoleum as she breezed around the curtain, out of sight.

Sid spoke up. "How 'bout a sponge bath? I'm filthy."

"Tell me about it, pops."

"Peel back the sheets and see for yourself."

Jinx suppressed a contented snigger. If he had to be a captive audience, at least Sid was a character.

"Hey, where ya goin'? You're supposed to make me comfortable. How 'bout a mustache ride?"

"How 'bout a close shave with a straight razor?" Said with a nasty edge.

"Come back here. What'm I supposed to do with my flagpole?"

"I have an idea." Her voice oozed syrup and sadism. "Let's lower it, shall we?"

"Hold on, little missy—what're you fixin' to do? Wait! No!"

The snap of a flapping sheet brought the unmistakable sound of a fleshy thump. Sid yelped. Jinx flinched in sympathetic pain.

Seconds later, Sid's caretaker extinguished the fluorescents and let herself out. For the next few moments, the only sound in the pitch-black room came from the rush of cool air leaving the ceiling vent.

A low chuckle started on the other side of the drape.

Sid said, "Let's get back to that shoot-out."

Jinx told him all he could remember, from the time the parole officer dropped off the white warrant commanding Marble-Eye's re-incarceration, until he woke up in the midst of a surgical slice and the anesthesiologist zapped him back into orbit. Finishing with a yawn, the ensuing quiet had him figuring he must've put Sid to sleep.

He closed his eyes and listened to the deliberate rush of his own breath.

*You wore a white blouse to a raid, are you nuts? Where's your windbreaker?*

*In the patrol car. You want I should get it?*

*And give away our position? Here. Take mine.*

*You'll freeze.*

*No, I'll be doing a slow burn. Why didn't you just pin on a bull's-eye? If you forgot your handcuffs again, you're getting three days off without pay.*

*I've got my hooks . . . but, I left my piece back at the office, on the commode. Suppose I could borrow the backup in your boot?*

A coughing spell from Sid's side of the curtain roused Jinx from his snooze. Once the old lieutenant had it under control, he offered up a provocative thought.

"Mighta been shootin' at your point-man, but it don't sound that way."

"What're you saying?"

"I didn't get to be sixty-three bein' ostrich-headed."

"What's that supposed to mean?"

"Maybe that old boy was gunnin' for you."

"You're not one of those JFK conspiracy people, are you?"

"Hey, that guy wasn't just aimin' at anybody, it was you he capped."

"It wasn't like that."

"You're right, what do I know? I'm just forty years in the business."

*Crazy old man.*

Without giving the sinister slant another thought, Jinx drifted into slumber with visions of Raven.

*Still has a thing for me.*

*Could've tried harder to get past that nurse. Should've claimed to be my daughter.*

*Probably here to apologize.*

*That, or the bitch plans to bilk me out of my office again.*

For awhile, he slept. But in the midst of the silent abyss, with only the chill from the air conditioner, he awakened drenched in sweat.

It took several moments to recover from the nightmare. In the first drowsy seconds, he could recall quite vividly a muffled cry, followed by choking gasps coming from Sid's bed. He pawed at the window drape and a slit of blue light illuminated a dash of white from a pair of shoes on the other side of the curtain. In a blink, they disappeared.

But the unforgettable thrash of legs and arms had jolted him awake.

He whispered softly. "Sid?"

Then, louder. "Sid? You awake?"

He got no answer, only the sound of strong, reassuring breaths coming from the other side of the curtain.

Weird.

It sounded so real.

Must be the medication.

Satisfied, he put the nightmare to rest. Again, he dozed.

Yucatan Jay halted within six feet of the chair.

Raven clicked back the hammer. "I mean it." She grappled for her handbag a few feet away, and pulled it close. Groping inside, she felt for the cell phone and pulled it out —minus the battery.

"You want to call someone?" The soothing sound of his voice taunted her. "Who do you want to call, Raven? The police? I can't let you do that. Who else do you want to call?" He assumed the psychopathic monotone of HAL, the rogue computer from that space movie she hated, and the realization she was a hostage in her own home made her flesh crawl. "Who else, Raven? Let's get it out of your system so I can get the job done without taking any more shit from you."

"I want to call your parents." She barely had enough oxygen to speak. They weren't exactly her first choice—she hadn't spoken to them since the eighties—but no way would he allow her to dial 911, and phoning Jinx was out of the question.

"You want to call my folks?" He gave her a vehement head shake. "You don't want to call my folks."

"I'd feel better if I could talk to Wren."

Yucatan Jay made a slow move with his hand. "I'm retrieving my wireless. I'll dial the number. Say whatever you want." He reached into his breast pocket and she let him. Out came a wafer-thin phone the size of a credit card. Several thumb taps later, he flicked it onto her lap.

It read MasterCard on one side, complete with a logo of interconnecting red and yellow spheres and a sixteen-digit number with ROBERT E. LEE imprinted on it. The flip side was covered with a membrane that resembled a keypad, including a thin film that turned out to be a lighted digital display.

She narrowed her eyes into a squint. "Robert E. Lee? Confederate general? Are you kidding?"

"Answer it."

The fragile voice of a woman on the other end of the connection seemed faraway.

A lifetime of memories flooded back.

"Aunt Wren?" She paused long enough for realization to set in. Apparently, it didn't. "It's me, Raven. Your sister Robin's girl. Remember me?" A short lull, followed by racking sobs. Suddenly ashamed for not keeping in touch, Raven's eyes rimmed. "Don't cry. If you cry, I'll cry."

Yucatan Jay watched, stone-faced.

"Wren—no, I'm fine—I have to ask you something. Yes, some people say I resemble her. I have the same color eyes. Wren—I have to ask—no, Pawpaw was good to me. I couldn't have asked for a better granddaddy. He put me through college . . . Please, Wren, I need you to let me talk. This guy came to my house. He claimed to be Yucatan Jay." Raven listened carefully, watching the paranoiac soldier of fortune within earshot. Her heart skipped a beat, then revved into triple-time. A jolt of adrenaline surged through so fast she wanted to vomit. "When? I'll tell him you said so." And, then, "I have to go. I'll try to call back."

With a lump the size of a golf ball forming in her throat, she punched the off button. Her voice slipped into a monotone. "You're dead." *Gotta get outta here.* "Since '92." *Never make it out the door.* "You were confined to a mental institution for schizophrenia on an order of protective custody, and another patient strangled you in your sleep." *Have to cap him.* "Aunt Wren and Uncle Jack filed a wrongful death suit against the hospital." *Not enough firepower in this pissant gun.*

"The agency designed a cover story when they sent me to Burma. What'd you expect her to say? I can't make contact without jeopardizing their safety, and mine. You may not realize . . . a lot of people out there want to see me dead."

Raven still held the wireless.

Glanced down long enough to locate the nine on the keypad.

Would've punched 911 if it hadn't started leaking iridescent pink liquid in her hand.

"What the hell's this?"

"It's disintegrating. The sensors are precisely calibrated to the acidity in my skin. Someone else handles my phone, the electrodes foul out." And then, "Don't worry. I have a wallet full: VISA, Discover, MasterCard, The Home Depot—you name it, I've got it. Would you believe they cost six thousand apiece? I dropped one of these down an outhouse once; I don't guess I have to tell you what kind of deep doo-doo that got me into."

His eyes darted around the room like a trapped animal, but his voice remained dispassionate and even.

"I had to repair a water faucet and the hardware store wanted to charge sixty-nine cents for a washer the exact same size as a penny. A penny! Know what I did? I punched a hole in the goddam penny and saved sixty-eight cents. And what's with those O-rings on the space shuttle? It's a stinking, fucking six-cent part, and six goddam astronauts and a teacher died because NASA didn't fucking change out the goddam seals. I'm telling you, the American economy's going to shit."

*Schizophrenic.*

The word danced in Raven's head. She decided to nominate him for the Turd-of-the-Month—a little game she played with herself, to formally acknowledge people who pissed her off.

She knew she shouldn't ask, but did anyway. She'd need the information for the sworn affidavit if she ever made it to a telephone. "What'd you do in Burma?"

"Nearly got my dick bit off by a shark, that's what. The

mission went sour and I had to be evac-ed out in the middle of the night. First I had to borrow a four-wheeler—"

"Hot-wired it. Admit it. You boosted it."

*I'm sitting here, carrying on a conversation with a common car thief.*

"—the terrain's pretty rugged, and we weren't exactly invited into the country in the first place, so it wasn't like I could just run out on the beach and be choppered to safety." His face creased in a pensive expression, as if he were reliving the event. "I had to swim out into the Bay of Bengal with nothing but the moon to guide me. It's a scary business, let me tell you. That was back when my head was shaved."

*Shaved so the mental hospital could stick on the electrodes. To allow better conductivity for the shock treatments.*

Raven caught herself nodding.

Without warning, the man claiming to be Yucatan Jay ripped open his shirt, exposing an enormous tattoo of a green-feathered, vulture-like creature of mythological proportions. From where she sat, it appeared that a series of beads had been implanted under the skin, giving the crested bird a three-dimensional look. Best she could tell, the first copper-jacketed hollow-point round she cranked off would take out its eye.

"It's the god, Huitzilopochtli. From Aztec and Mayan cultures? Took on the human form?"

Raven shook her head. In the whirling confusion, she felt her mouth screw into a grimace.

"You never heard of the huitzil? It means hummingbird."

Slow head shake.

According to Yucatan Jay, Mayan lore provided for a white man with blond hair, a black face, blue eyes and blue legs to return as the reincarnated god of the Bijubi tribe, Huitzilopochtli. The Bijubis, a lost Mayan bloodline previously considered extinct, still used blowguns with poisoned darts as their weapon of choice. The Bijubis would know him as their leader by the great huitzil bird springing from his chest.

He never did say how he planned to pull off the black face and blue legs.

Yucatan Jay's eyes danced. "The agency's sending me down to lead the revolution. I even learned their language. Bijubis speak a type of bastardized Nahuatl."

"What?"

"My stature's substantially more imposing than that of the Bijubis. By nature, they're a diminutive race." He tugged at a shock of bleached hair. "A little Scandinavian Gold to process the mop, and presto. Thanks to tattoos, I have the bird. What do you think of the beads? I think they make him look pretty real."

"Him?"

"The hummingbird." He lapsed into the voice of HAL again. "I even thought of giving him a name. If you think of one you like, I'll consider it. I like to think of him as an alter ego, since we'll be together for awhile. I wasn't really gung-ho on the idea at first—wasn't sure I'd be able to get a good night's sleep—but you might say he got under my skin, and we're doing just fine. By the way, did you know Fort Worth is home to one of the greatest tattoo artists in the world?"

Yucatan Jay didn't look like a CIA operative. And he didn't act like one, either. He acted like a goofball, and she told him so. "Your eyes are gray, not blue."

"I have blue contact lenses. I was the best match the agency could come up with."

"Jay . . ."

"Call me Huitzilopochtli."

"You expect me to believe you're traveling to a third world

country to start a revolution?"

"Chiapas. Belize. The Yucatan."

"Because the CIA wants you to—"

"Fight the rebel troops and liberate the Bijubis." His face cracked into a grin.

Barely breathing, Raven went quiet and sunk into her thoughts. "Ohgod. You're a gun runner." From the light-headed tingle originating in her brain, she sensed her blood pressure dipping precariously low. "You're running guns to Central America."

"Not a gun runner. CIA. Pay attention."

"What do you want?"

"Drive me to the bank first thing Monday morning—" He dug in his pockets and pulled out fistfuls of hundred-dollar bills. "—so I can convert this money into gold Canadian Maple Leaf coins." And then, "You may not realize it, but the Chiapan monetary unit's gone to shit."

"Jay . . ."

"Huitzilopochtli."

". . . I'm not calling you some unpronounceable vulture name." She couldn't be certain, but she thought his lower lip protruded. "You're lucky I'm not calling the police." She didn't like the sideways glance he cast at the telephone.

"Don't make me cut the line, Raven. For now, I've only removed the cords. I need them to tie you up so I can get some sleep. I thought I could make you understand, but clearly, you don't trust me. I'm only here until the bank reopens, then I'll be outta your hair for another—what's it been—twenty-five, twenty-seven years?"

Carnal panic set in. "You're not tying me up."

In the split second it took to utter the words, Raven realized he must've known she'd made the decision to cap him right then and there, rather than chance being bound, gagged and tortured to death. And Yucatan Jay must've picked up on that flash of fear, because he was already on top of her when she pulled the trigger.

For a moment, he lay dazed, shot in the chest, with the bulk of his weight forcing the air out of her lungs. Half expecting blood to pour from his mouth, she wrenched her head to one side and scrunched her face in revulsion.

"Raven, Raven, Raven." A melodic and taunting whisper. "Now, that was really stupid." He wrenched the gun from her hand and rolled off.

*Oh, shit.*

*There's friggin' body armor sewn into his clothes.*

He sat, yoga-style, flipping the gun back and forth between his palms and let out a snort of disgust.

"These little *Getcha Killeds* are shit. You should really try to carry a bigger gun. You need a weapon with a little more heft to it. The one under your pillow handles pretty nice." He favored her with a forlorn head shake. "Only way you could hurt someone with this is if they let you walk up and shoot 'em in the eye."

*If I can get to the vegetable bin in the fridge, I'll remember that.*

The zip of the curtain snapped Jinx's eyes open. Sunday morning's sunlight warmed the side of the bed closest to the window.

"Let's get that blood pressure." A hefty nurse with a no-nonsense attitude and a voice rough enough to grate the rubber off a steel-belted radial came toward him with a pressure cuff. She lifted his good wrist, clamped her thumb firmly over a pulse point and checked her watch. "How's the pain?"

"Stout. How come I'm in the cardiac unit?"

"Because you almost went into cardiac arrest during surgery." She released her grip. While she ripped open the

Velcro and wrapped the cuff around his uninjured arm, an orderly slid the drape along its metal track.

Jinx grinned big. He would finally come face-to-face with his roommate.

He looked past the RN, toward the man making his hospital stay a rollicking good time. His smile wilted at the sight of an LPN stripping the sheets off an empty bed.

He jutted his chin in the direction where the brother officer should have been. "Where's Sid?" The RN tightened the cuff and fit the ends of a stethoscope into her ears. "The guy in the next bed—where'd he go?"

She seemed to lose her attention in the glass-covered pressure gauge.

This time, Jinx made a hearty demand. "Where's Sid?"

She wouldn't meet his gaze, but he did get an answer.

"Poor Mr. Klevenhagen expired last night."

# Chapter Four

News of Sid's death rocked Jinx's confidence. The idea a veteran officer could touch his life and then disappear depressed Jinx to no end. He didn't even get a second chance to pick Sid's brain. What if the lieutenant was right?

The whole shoot-out felt hinkey from the get-go.

What if Marble-Eye Turner was trying to kill him and not Ivy? A disconcerting memory nagged him. If there was one thing he'd learned, it was to pay attention to the old-time, beat cop. And the late Sid Klevenhagen wasn't just some low-ranking flatfoot. He'd been a homicide ace.

With sunlight beating against the glass, the room turned hot enough for a Realtor to drop in with the devil and hammer down a SOLD sign. After several minutes went by and nobody responded to the third press of the buzzer, Jinx wondered if he had the strength to hoist himself out of bed and drum up his clothes.

Might as well suffer at home.

One jerky move settled the matter. He felt the sting of Marble-Eye's bullet all over again, and sank, dizzy, against the pillows. While waiting for the furniture to stop swimming, he noticed the remote control, newly positioned on his nightstand. With considerable effort and a sharp pain zigzagging up his neck, he locked his hand around it in a death grip. He pressed the power switch and flicked through TV channels until he landed on CNN. Jinx watched, spellbound, until the voices outside the nurses' station competed for volume. He fantasized ways to have Chinese takeout smuggled in, and decided a fat kleptomaniac in a trench coat full of false pockets could pull it off.

A spirited squeal vanquished the thought.

In a voice loud enough to peel back the skin on a frozen chicken, the drill sergeant head nurse shouted, "Do what?"

Jinx's ears pricked up. He powered off the TV.

"It's true." Outside the door, a breathless LPN with an exaggerated Southern drawl flapped her hands and delivered bad news. "Mr. Klevenhagen's daughter showed up to claim the body but it's gone. She's on her way up here, right now. We'd better get the director on the phone, stat."

"You're killing me. It took me fifteen years on night shift to get a transfer to evenings, and ten more to work my way up to days. I'm not about to perform euthanasia on myself by alarming the director of Our Lady of Mercy until we're absolutely certain."

"Honest, ma'am. Somebody stole Mr. K."

"Oh, for crying out loud. Is everyone here an idiot?"

Jinx's eyes rolled in their sockets.

The head nurse lowered her voice. "Go down to the basement and make sure they didn't just misplace him."

"No way. I'm not going near a bunch of stiffs."

"It's your job."

"Dead people give me the heebie-jeebies."

"Then why the hell'd you go into nursing?"

"So I could marry a doctor."

"They're all gay. Now, get your ass downstairs and bring me back some good news."

Throughout the ensuing chaos, Jinx thought of Caesar. He wondered who got the plum role of feeding him, and why he hadn't gotten a straight answer out of Ivy the night before. His haunches had gone numb hours ago, and his shoulder burned as if someone had seared it with a branding iron. Finally, when he'd stood the discomfort all he could, he reached between the bed rails. With the push of a button, he summoned a nurse.

He got more than he bargained for. An RN of immense proportions and swollen ankles lumbered into the room. Urine-colored braids, twisted into coils and pinned at the ears, resembled a Viking helmet. And, a crop of dark silky hair on her brutish forearms eclipsed anything remotely feminine about her.

"What's the problem?"

Jinx cleared his throat. "Could I get a painkiller?"

"Does it hurt, Mr. Klevenhagen?"

"No, it doesn't hurt Mr. Klevenhagen. Mr. Klevenhagen's dead." Sarcastic.

Her lips thinned to a blue thread.

"Is it too much to get a little Darvon?" He didn't like the way her jawbone torqued. "Vicodin? Sawed-off shotgun?"

An eyebrow arched over a glittering eye.

"I don't suppose you realize how short-staffed we are, do you?" She scowled. Severe creases, weighted by the corners of downturned lips, lined her face. "Ask for help and what do they send us? A new-hire who couldn't find a vein with a road map, a landing beacon, and a miner's helmet. Last night, I asked for bedpans, and without so much as a kiss my bohonkey, he lit out of here like somebody placed him under the witness protection program—and now you."

The silence between them grew long.

Jinx unclenched his jaw. "Let me try again. Could I get something for the pain?"

Tension drained from her face. A cruel smile took its

place. "Certainly, Mr. Klevenhagen." Her voice dripped battery acid. She pivoted on a rubber-soled heel and squeaked toward the door in a spirited rush.

"I'm not Klevenhagen," Jinx called to her disappearing bulk.

Damned HMOs.

Then, it hit him—the screwup with the nameplates.

What if Sid didn't just die? What if somebody killed him in a vicious twist of mistaken identity?

He dismissed the idea with a painful shudder.

They were on the cardiac wing, for Pete's sake. The old man's ticker probably played out. When the nurse squeaked back in, he molded his mouth into a question. He wanted to ask how Sid died, but the sight of a hypodermic needle caused his eyes to widen and his mouth to go slack.

"Pull up your gown."

"I'm not Klevenhagen."

"Of course you're not." Facetious.

"I'm *not* him. Check my chart before you juice me up."

Grudgingly, she complied. Upon close inspection, the fake smile disappeared. "So, you're not Klevenhagen. No sweat. This is an all-purpose trank."

"Hold it . . . what're you doing? The last nurse stuck it in that tube."

"Do I look like the last nurse?"

He wanted to apologize for rankling her feathers. To assure her it wouldn't happen again. To admit it had been oafish on his part, to inadvertently mistake her for the previous nurse. To tell her he should have immediately noticed she was much uglier than her colleague, who happened to be grotesque in her own right.

Instead, he said, "Why can't you let it mix with the stuff in the bag?"

"We could do that." The sugary tone suggested that hell froze, and the devil had a going-out-of-business sale. "But you seem to be in a great deal of pain, and this is ever so much faster."

Their eyes locked in a murderous bent. Before he knew what hit him, she zeroed in on his rump with what had to be a square needle. Stinging heat raged beneath his skin. In the time it took him to ball up a fist, she was gone.

At the nurses' station, two legions of hell came together in battle. Jinx leaned forward to glimpse the force that had driven the nurses into a corner in a collective herd. He couldn't see past the doorjamb but it didn't much matter. The harpy's shriek made the few strands of hair topping his head stand at right angles.

"I'll make you sons of bitches wish you were stillborn. You incompetent hacks don't have a clue who you're fucking with."

"We're not deaf, Miss Klevenhagen." The head nurse kept her voice low and calm. "I know you're upset. Let me get you something."

"Get me my daddy back."

"We're working on that. May I offer you a chair while you wait? Something to drink? Water?"

"Only if it's enough to drown you sons of bitches in."

The elevator bell chimed. As the doors slid open, Sid's daughter lobbed another verbal missile.

"Emotional distress." Her voice became a frightful roller-coaster of superior knowledge and emotion. "You bastards caused plenty. I am not accustomed to shopping at funeral parlors, ushered by men in ill-fitting suits, who need massive doses of Vitamin D. Thanks to you cocksuckers, my life'll never be the same. But then—" Her voice dropped to an eerie calm, deadly enough to prickle the stubble on Jinx's face. *"—neither will yours."*

A man stepped off the elevator. He moved close enough for Jinx to glimpse the high-dollar suit and weasel-like profile of his face.

"You must be Miss Klevenhagen." He bowed low, and offered an outstretched hand.

A reed-thin woman with dark hair and pale skin that glowed like an opal under the harsh light of the nurses' station stepped into Jinx's line of vision. He grappled for his mangled wire-rims.

The lieutenant's daughter stiffened with resolve. "Who the hell are you? The undertaker?"

"I'm Mr. McAnaulty, hospital director."

"I demand to know the whereabouts of my father."

"It seems there may've been a slight mix-up. On rare occasions, these things happen. It's possible the corpse was picked up by Texas A&M University by mistake."

*"The corpse?"*

Her words grated on Jinx's ear like rusty barbwire on a flat surface. But the contempt Sid's daughter showed for the haughty little man left Jinx breathless with admiration.

"I sincerely beg your pardon. I meant your late father."

"He's late all right, you wormy son of a bitch. He's so goddam late he's not going to show up at all, is he? And what's this A&M shit?"

The director cleared his throat. In a furtive move, he adjusted his crotch, and Jinx suspected he did so to move his artillerymen out of the line of fire. "We have an occasional situation where the family wishes to have their loved one's remains sent to the University—"

"To A&M?" Her voice climbed an octave.

"—to be donated to science."

"Agriculture and Mechanics? A school for shit-kickers?

For what possible purpose? Do they have a sheep shortage?"

Nervous titters erupted from the LPNs, but her lethal presence killed their giggles.

"Stillborn," she hissed.

Then, she was gone. Jinx could tell by the way the gray faded from the attendants' faces, and from the lingering hands, clutched against their chests in relief.

His tongue began to thicken and the familiar taste of copper filled his mouth. Hooded eyelids weighed heavy over dry eyeballs. Before his lids closed completely, he wondered, again, about the Siamese.

And about Raven.

And whether yesterday had been a dream.

# Chapter Five

A few minutes shy of nine that morning, a mahogany-skinned orderly, androgynous in face and frame, floated in and slammed a food tray down on the bed table. Jinx stared at the dishes and sniffed at the metal lids. The odor of disinfectant masked the smell of what hopefully might turn out to be a decent meal.

The orderly slipped out, leaving him to study a three-course meal of gray pablum, bran muffins, and something green and watery. Next to a muffin was a coarse, dark hair; Jinx suspected the thin crust coating the fork tines was petrified egg yolk. The spoon was either filmed in soapsuds or had been used so often the finish wore off. Either way, he was down to a knife and the petri dish of vile green fungus.

He switched on the television and settled in. The Rangers game would take his mind off the crappy food and the dull throb in his shoulder.

Polishing the spoon against the bedsheet returned some of its luster. Jinx was about to play a quick game of "Name That Food" when an intimidating gunslinger straight out of the 1800s stalked in looking ready to draw down. A dark mustache drooped over a forlorn mouth, and even with the brim of the black felt Stetson shading his face, his eyes had the focused glint of a hawk.

"Mickey." Jinx grinned big. "And, Dell." Dell Teague, the brooding Aryan walking behind Deputy Constable

Mickey Van Slyke wore a straw Resistol over his sandy curls. Aqua eyes narrowed into the terminal stare of a mass killer. "Grab a seat. Make yourselves comfortable."

Pulling their chairs near the foot of the bed, they exchanged knowing looks, giving each other the go-ahead with their eyes. Then, they removed their hats. Balanced on top of their heads, were wax cartons of Szechuan.

Jinx dropped the spoon into the bowl of radioactive waste. "Remind me to give y'all a raise."

"Scalp's been burning ever since we climbed on the elevator," Mickey said.

Dell, who could work an eight-hour shift on less than ten words, nodded.

While Jinx ripped open the chopsticks, Mickey did the talking.

"We had a little excitement Thursday. But, I reckon Ivy already told you."

Jinx frowned. "She wrecked her patrol car again, didn't she?" He nudged aside a pepper strip and harpooned a shrimp before Mickey could kill his appetite.

"Nope. Remember that trash can across the hall next to the chaplain's office?"

Jinx nodded. He tilted one corner of the carton to his lips and scraped in a mouthful of rice.

"Somebody blew it up. Good thing everybody'd left for the day—explosion took out a couple of bricks on the south wall and shattered the glass door to our office. The SO's looking into it."

Jinx's eyes flickered over where Sid should have been. "Suspects?"

"Nope."

"What about Marble-Eye? They arrest him yet?"

"FWPD put out an APB. Matter of fact, there's a manhunt directed at all the hospital emergency rooms in the Metroplex. The local television stations said their sister affiliates in the adjoining states carried the story, too. I imagine if he goes for treatment within a five-hundred-mile radius, we'll know soon enough."

Jinx gnawed the inside of his lip. He reflected on sixteen years of paperwork stored in metal file cabinets back at his apartment. The most important stuff, he carried in a briefcase. Now more than ever, he wanted another look at Marble-Eye's three-by-five mug shot.

"I need my briefcase."

Mickey said, "We'll have someone bring it."

Someone meant sloughing the job off on Ivy.

"My apartment manager can let her in. If he gives her any guff, have her call me."

Mickey fidgeted uncomfortably. Dell sat inert and barely breathing, with his eyes seemingly fixed and dilated on Mickey's profile. The eerie sight tensed Jinx's neck muscles.

"What's the matter? There's something you're not telling me. Is this going to up my blood pressure?"

Dell turned to Mickey. "We might ought to hold off 'til he's better. His face's like a thermometer tip."

Mickey scanned the room. Avoided eye contact, and measured his words. "Jinx, something's going on. For the last three weeks, every raid we do turns to shit." His voice tapered off, but he wore the furtive expression of a man dedicated to finding an escape hatch.

"Gets worse." Dell's tongue slithered across his lips.

Mickey used his sleeve cuff to polish the National Rodeo Finals belt buckle holding up his starched Levi's. Color leaked out of his face. "We lost another one, Jinx—" He cast his gaze to the floor. "—Odie Oliver got away."

Jinx's nerve endings went tight.

Odie "Straight-Eight" Oliver spent time in the pen for wounding a homeowner and killing her husband in a surprise burglary. A week after the Texas Department of Criminal Justice paroled him to Fort Worth, home invasions went up a hundred percent. Before Jinx set out to apprehend Marble-Eye that fateful morning, he saw the active blue warrant issued on Straight-Eight Oliver for a parole violation: dirty UAs. Any hood rat who couldn't pass a urine analysis had to be financing a drug habit. And that meant crashing in on old people in the middle of the night, raping the occupants and making off with money and jewelry.

"You checked the attic?" As soon as he asked, Jinx was sorry. If anyone knew the work of Mickey and Dell, he did. His deputies went through Oliver's shack like the Mongolian hordes.

"Ransacked the closets, between the mattresses. No Odie. Gone."

"Gets worse." Dell's cement rottweiler expression cracked. His lips thinned into a slight smile, as if he relished watching Mickey wince.

A new wave of pain rolled across Jinx's shoulder. But the physical torture was nothing compared to the mental pressure building behind both eyes. Listening to Mickey parcel out disaster was like watching a head-on collision. He wanted to look away, cover his ears and pretend no carnage occurred at the accident scene. Yet, he stared with the transfixed gaze of a rubbernecker, and waited for Mickey to finish.

"Yo-Yo Behrens took off on us, too."

Edgar Behrens, nicknamed "Yo-Yo" in keeping with his violent mood swings, ran whores out in Stop Six. Behrens's escape had more to do with pride. A bipolar black pimp with a gimp foot, who could outsmart his deputies made Jinx sit straight up.

"Gets worse."

A surge of pain with the kick of a mule put him down. He choked back the bile rising to his throat.

One quick look at Dell curbed his appetite. He stared at his chopstick as if he had just speared a rat and it died twitching in his hand.

Mickey nodded soulfully. "The Irish travelers disappeared on us."

Jinx writhed inwardly. The gypsy-like band of thieves had fleeced Mozelle Gratten, his biggest campaign contributor six months before. And Jinx knew part of the reason the Commissioners Court appointed him to replace Raven was because Gratten, a barbershop and hair salon baron, put the squeeze on them. His wasn't the only political coffer getting a big, fat donation. The county judge expected Jinx to have them all jailed within the week, and after swearing him in, as much as said so.

"Gets worse."

Mickey wore the same doomed expression he had on the time his new bride called to tell him her pet ocelot chewed his hand-stitched ostrich boots. Easing back into his chair, he casually loosened a shirt button and looked everywhere but at the bed.

Jinx felt like he'd just stepped off the platform and into the path of a locomotive.

Smoking mad, he shifted his gaze to Dell and assessed the problem aloud. "You think someone in the office is leaking information." He sank deeper into the mattress, secretly glad he didn't know the whereabouts of his service revolver. He closed his eyes until his imagination became too vivid. When the swell of anger brewing inside levitated him bolt upright, his lids popped open. "What's your take?"

Mickey spoke. "It's like they knew we were coming. There had to be a tip, especially Straight-Eight Oliver."

An Oriental girl wearing blue scrubs, with a boyish haircut and the kind of fragile bone structure generally associated with hummingbirds, rushed in chattering in the staccato gibberish of her native tongue. It didn't take an interpreter to translate insults.

"This not Grand Central Station," she said tartly, flapping her arms to shoo them out. After running off the deputies, she turned to Jinx with malice in her slitted eyes. "You no get Chi-nee food. You get Our Lady of Mercy food."

"*Sisters of Perpetual Suffering* is more like it."

She picked up the hospital tray and studied the uneaten muck. "You feel real funny, two in morning. Big Chi-nee dragon snort fire in stomach, you no think plain food so bad."

With the precision of a foot soldier, she pivoted and took off. He upped the TV volume to the cheer of Rangers fans. Home run, top of the seventh, Rangers ahead by three.

*They had something in common, him and the Rangers: they were both still alive in the race for the pennant.*

Life should have felt good.

He dozed off wondering about the cobra in the henhouse.

A blood-clotting scream awakened him.

Inside the door to Jinx's room, stood an old piece of rawhide, drenched in sweat with his hospital gown on backward. And pointing like a turret through the shredded print fabric, was a raging hard-on.

A nurse clapped a hand to her mouth. Her face went white as she melted into the wall.

"Tickled to see you, too, girly," said the old man.

At the sound of a gravelly voice, resuscitated, Jinx let out a whoop. "Sid?"

"None other. How ya doin', hoss?"

The LPN slumped to the floor with a thud. Jinx gave the lean, weathered man the once-over. Salt-and-pepper hair arced up out of his scalp into a waterfall. A luxurious silver mustache matched a set of brows overhanging ball bearing eyes, and his leathery skin showed the patina of a well-rubbed saddle.

The lieutenant stepped over the girl as if she didn't exist. He gingerly settled his rump against the edge of the empty bed.

Still blinking in disbelief, Jinx struggled to a sitting position.

*Imagine.*

*Sid, alive.*

*And rigor mortis only set in one of his appendages.*

"They told me you died."

"Damned near did. Somebody tried to smother me."

"When?"

"Middle of last night. Damned near killed me. The stiff on the next gurney bloated up from the stomach gasses—corpse sat plum erect and moaned so loud it woke me up from the dead. When I opened my eyes, I had a sheet draped over me and it was about thirty degrees. Froze my dick like a popsicle."

Jinx stared, intrigued.

"Well, sir, all of a sudden, one a-them funny boys reached under my sheet and tried to perform an intrusive procedure on me."

Jinx experienced a perverse exhilaration that came from not having exchanged places with Sid. "What'd you do?"

"Put him in traction." Indignant, Sid rubbed his bony hip. "Whaddaya think I did? I did what any red-blooded Texan would do—kicked his ass."

Admiration turned to reverence. Sixty-three, freshly risen from the dead, and the guy's alter ego looking permanently embalmed. It was something to shoot for.

"I think it was you they wanted to kill," Sid said without a trace of bitterness. "This makes twice. Next time, if you're not careful, they might just getcha."

"What do we do now?"

"Well, first, I'm gonna revive this little lady with a few chest compressions and some mouth-to-mouth. Then, tonight at shift change when the employees thin out, I'll go down to the parking lot, locate me a tire iron and finish rupturing Mr. Funny Boy's spleen."

# Chapter Six

*Crazy Jay.*

Raven sank deeper into her pillow and reflected on the past twelve hours. Thanks to an unsuccessful escape attempt during the night, Yucatan Jay handcuffed her to the brass bedposts. Now, as she listened to the thin snore coming from the man snuggled up to her, with his relaxed hand resting on the gun pointed at her head, she lay painfully still and barely breathing.

*Insane Jay.*

Caught up in a delusional world of spies and drama, she almost felt sorry for him. He still carried a hint of boyish charm, and she had to remind herself of the reasons his parents packed him off to military school. She reassembled the memories and ticked them off in her head.

First, there was that unfortunate explosion in the high school chemistry lab. Aunt Wren and Uncle Jack blamed the teacher for leaving the door unlocked; but Pawpaw said horse-puckey, he saw Yucatan Jay reading a Houdini book, and the boy did have a perverse fascination for living on the edge.

Then, he "borrowed" the next-door neighbor's Bentley and sailed it over the dam. Aunt Wren and Uncle Jack argued the neighbor should've slapped a Club on the steering wheel; and when Pawpaw said nuts, Yucatan Jay was an adrenaline junkie, the boy's parents said, screw it, they never liked that neighbor much anyway.

And, finally, the straw that made the burro swayback: the dissection and evisceration of a pet boa constrictor after it pushed through the mesh screen on the aquarium cage and tried to squeeze Yucatan Jay's neck 'til his head popped off.

The kiddie shrink told Aunt Wren and Uncle Jack the behavior was consistent with a sick and demented mind. That a young man of Yucatan Jay's uncommon genius might benefit from a para-military structure in his life. That a defiant, out-of-control teen such as Jay would require more than anything Manitou Springs, Colorado, could offer if they expected him to turn out right—preferably a facility out-of-state—and recommended placement at the Marine Military Academy in Harlingen, Texas. And when they balked at sending him so far away, the psychiatrist told them summers in the Texas Valley weren't really all that bad, considering there were hotter places. He even suggested Yucatan Jay might as well get used to 118-degree heat, since it got a hell of a lot hotter where he was headed.

Leading Pawpaw to conclude that even though it might not be fair to keep Raven away from the only living relatives on her mother's side of the family, the decision to place her in the trajectory of Yucatan Jay's warped mind would constitute a bull's-eye for disaster.

Lax supervision, Pawpaw said, and besides, the parents were crackpots. It didn't make sense how the father paid for such a hoity-toity house on a pharmaceutical salesman's salary unless he was raising marijuana on the side. It wasn't until Raven turned eight, Pawpaw changed his tune.

Pouring over photographs in the family scrapbook one Christmas, Pawpaw slid a new picture postcard of Yucatan Jay and his family into place. Your Uncle Jack's a real stand-up guy, he said, staring at some distant point. He apologized to the wall for misjudging the man; said he was sorry he ever accused the foot-washing Baptist of growing weed . . . that if he slaved the rest of his life, he could never repay Jack the debt he owed. Then his eyes teared up, and he poured three fingers of whiskey and downed it in one gulp. First impressions weren't always right, he told her. And, oh, by the way, even though she was a baby when that holdup man killed her daddy on a traffic stop, she should be happy to know the New Mexico State Police found the decomposed remains of the thug who did it. No witnesses; no suspects.

*Only a dead robber in a canyon near Raton, with a bullet between the eyes and the back of his head blown out. As if somebody hid in the mountains and picked him off with a high-powered rifle and scope.*

Raven glanced from side to side, studying the bruises on her wrists.

Yucatan Jay burrowed deeper. His hand tightened around the gun butt.

"I used to think about you back at the military academy," he whispered sleepily.

For a moment, she thought he might be dreaming of some leggy, breast-augmented blonde. But Jay rolled over on his side and opened his eyes. Pulled the gun away from her temple, slung his arm across her middle and rested the weapon, still in his grip, on her abdomen.

"Mom and Dad sent me a snapshot of you in your cheerleader uniform." He favored her with a sheepish smile. "I kept your picture in my locker and told everybody you were my girlfriend."

"What was reform school like?"

"I enjoyed it. Not at first. But, in time, I came to appreciate it." He let go of the gun, flexed his fingers, then smoothed a rebel curl from her cheek. "I love this country,

Rave. I'd do anything for it. The United States of America's the greatest place in the world."

"Jay—my hands." She gave him a pleading look.

"Raven, Raven, Raven." He flopped over on his back and stared at the ceiling. "Who designed your bathroom? I like the Sistine chapel idea. What'd you do, commission some big-shot artist to paint it?"

"A college student from TCU. Jay—"

"You're thinking if I release you, you'll liquify my gonads."

She marveled at his ability to predict her thoughts.

"Someday I'd like to be with a chick like you."

*Uh-oh.*

"Don't worry. I'm celibate until my return from Belize." He hoisted himself up on one elbow and held her in his gray gaze. "Is it illegal for cousins to get it on in the state of Texas?"

All plans expended, Raven decided to cry. It started with a few crocodile tears and a bit of an irritating whine; but seeing how Yucatan Jay seemed unmoved by her misery, she went into a guts-out wail. Teetering on the brink of exhaustion, she tried being nice.

"I love this country, too. I won't run if you let me go. I'll be good. Please, Jay. My hands hurt and I'm tired. You can lock me in this room, if you like. There's a key on the dresser. Tomorrow, I'll drive you to the bank and you can be on your way. Please, Jay. I'm so tired."

He got up and angled over to the chest of drawers. Found the key inside a music box and pocketed it.

"That was pretty impressive, Rave, the way you can fall apart—" He snapped his fingers. "—like that. Do you think about sad stuff as a catalyst to get you going? Because I've always had a hard time crying. Well, except for the time my snake died. That was sad. Did you know snakes continue to move, even after the head's lopped off? It's like two independent activities going on: the mouth opens and the tongue flicks out, while the rest writhes around waiting for directions." And, then, "I'm going to unfasten the cuffs in a few minutes. I'm going downstairs to make a sandwich. Would you care for anything?"

She gave him a defeated head shake.

"What about a book? Would you like to read?"

"That'd be nice."

*He's really not so bad.*

"I read your new *Architectural Digest* that came in yesterday's mail. Would you like me to bring that? There's a fascinating story of the Rothschild mansion I think you'll enjoy."

*Except for the handcuffs, he hasn't hurt me.*

Raven bobbed her head. "On second thought, I could use some cheese crackers and a Big Red."

"How about a bag of Famous Amos cookies?" Yucatan Jay headed for the bathroom.

He left the door ajar, and if she craned her head just so, she could see him whipping out—

—Ohmygod—

—the biggest one she'd ever seen that wasn't attached to a porn star.

It pleased her when he lathered his hands and toweled them dry instead of heading straight downstairs to handle food.

He returned to the bed with a handcuff key pinched between his fingers. After releasing the cuffs, he massaged her wrists. At first, he rubbed softly, then with more force. And he did this little tongue thing by pulling her arm to his mouth and gently sucking the bruised area near the bone.

The maneuver left her covered in chills.

"Works every time." He winked. "You should see what else I can do—oh, by the way, don't even think about going out the window. Know what C-4 is? Plastique? It's like dynamite. I stuck some on the catch. You so much as shake the glass, you'll go up like a bottle rocket." He rose and sauntered to the door, grinning by way of good-bye. "Want a pickle? I love bread-and-butter pickles. Mom used to make them. Used to put up corn and pickled okra in those big Mason jars. Once, she even tried her hand at pickled peaches."

While Raven sat on the bed, nodding obediently, with the right side of her brain thinking, How thoughtful, the left half was a teacup ride, spinning out of control, trying to slam some sense back into her—

*Ohmygod, this is it.*

*I'm developing Stockholm Syndrome.*

Around eleven o'clock Sunday morning, Ivy poked her head through the door. "Hi, Jinx—you busy?"

"Shit."

Amos loomed behind his mother in a great hulking mass of teenaged hormones. "What'd he say?"

"Nothing. It's a bowling term." Ivy locked gazes with Jinx. "Look who I brought by to see you." She steered Amos on in. "I thought you two could visit while I run down the street to the Payless. They've got a two-for-one sale and I—"

"You're not leaving him here."

"Amos, see what Jinx thinks about tattoos. And Jinx, thanks a million. I'll be back in an hour." Ivy ducked out before he could protest further.

Sullen, Amos lumbered over with a dull glaze in his gimlet eyes. "Hey, Jinx. Howzit slingin'?"

Marilyn Manson T-shirt, pants hanging below his hips and steel-toed boots with the laces untied. Unkempt hair drooped past the junior Unabomber's eyes in oily strings. The dirty-brown color seemed darker and he had a mild case of acne. Ivy's mongrel son flopped into a chair at the end of the bed and hoisted a portable appliance onto his lap.

Jinx cleared his throat. "How's it going?"

"My mama says your hemorrhoids came back."

"What?"

"My mama says that's how come you're here. 'Cause you read the newspaper in the bathroom."

"Oh, she said that, did she? I see." But he didn't. Now Jinx wanted to wring two necks.

"Got any tattoos?"

"Amos, don't do it. The police'll be stopping you every time you turn around."

"They already do."

*I'll bet.*

A sense of professional obligation made him feel the need to talk Amos out of it. "All it does is scar you . . . make you look like a convict. Where'd you get such an idea?"

"Lotta kids had 'em at the encampment."

*Encampment?*

Jinx thought hard. As an alternative to juvenile hall, Ivy'd sent the junior Unabomber to a boys' ranch. In Utah, no less. Supposedly to rough it. Which turned out to be complete and utter bullshit.

"How was the boys' ranch? Did you have a good experience?"

"I got expelled."

Jinx raised an eyebrow.

"Nobody saw me strike that match. They only pinned it on me 'cause I caught those two counselors grubbin' in the woods when me and some dudes snuck out to make s'mores." Eyes narrowed into a squint reminiscent of serial killer

Edmund Kemper, after he strangled his mother and ripped out her vocal chords. "So, Jinx, about that tattoo—what should I pick?"

"A lock. For your mother's door, for when she finds out." He studied the flat square in Amos's lap. Curiosity got the better of him. "What's that?"

"DVD player."

It didn't take Jinx long to examine a hot horseshoe. "How'd you come by it?"

"Got me a paper route."

"Oh." Then, "Good for you."

The boy punched a couple of buttons with his sausage fingers, then stuffed the mini-earphones into his ears.

"What's on?"

"You're like a daddy to me, Jinx." Amos never glanced up from the screen. "But I'm trying to watch this Freddy Krueger flick, so why don't you just lay back and button it?"

After Raven slicked her hand under the pillow and found the Lady Smith gone, then went through the closet and confirmed the Mossberg missing, she positioned herself off to one side of the bedroom door with her ears tuned to receive the high-frequency clink of flatware. She listened as Yucatan Jay ascended the stairs with a food tray. When she gauged him to be a few steps from the top, she lifted a gilded French slipper chair and hoisted it overhead.

She could feel his presence when he reached the landing. Sensed movement behind the door. Even swore she heard him breathing.

"Raaaaaaaaven." He uttered her name softly, as though he had composed a lyrical measure made up only of half notes. It was as if they were children again, playing a quick game of hide-and-seek; only this time, the sound of her name sent a chill through her heart.

She felt the burn in her arms, and stood on unsteady legs trying not to betray her position. Tiny needle hairs prickled beneath the flannel shirt, and when she glanced down at her toes, she saw they had curled into the carpet for traction, whitening at the nails.

"Raaaaaaaaven."

She listened for any sign of him setting the food tray down. A quiver started in her arms, and she willed herself to hold out a little longer. The key slid into the lock, and her breath caught in her throat. With an eye riveted on the doorknob, watching for its twist, she endured stings of pain shooting down her shoulders.

"Raaaaaaaaven, where are you?"

An involuntary twitch started near her elbow. She blinked back tears, sensing him smiling on the other side of the door, knowing she couldn't hold it together much longer.

Yucatan Jay's next words came down on her like a velvet hammer.

"Raven. You're such an idiot. Do you really think I don't know you're waiting for me? Tell you what," he said with an air of good sportsmanship, "I'll slide this little mirror under the door to vector your location. If you're waiting to bash my skull in, I'm going to kill you. But I won't just kill you. I'll handcuff you, strip your clothes off and drag you into the bathroom. You're probably thinking, *Why would he take me into the bathroom? Why wouldn't he just do me on the bed?*

"Well, Raven . . . two reasons: first, the cleanup's easier; second, you can watch what happens in the mirror. I want you to see the expression on your face because the finale'll be timed simultaneously with the moment I slit your throat. I'm getting out my little mirror now. I'm sliding it—"

Whatever else he said, she didn't stick around to hear. She

put down the chair as gently as possible, considering she was in the throes of a complete breakdown, and dashed for the bathroom.

She was hugging the commode, dry-heaving battery acid, when Yucatan Jay brought the food tray into the room.

He cast a sideways glance at the chair and said, "Howzit going? By the way, we're out of carrots." By the time she flushed, he had laid out a checkered cloth and two fresh fruit plates on the bed.

The only weapon Raven spied among her toiletries was a can of hairspray—which she could've converted into a flame thrower if she'd had access to fire.

She stepped out of the bathroom to find him shuffling a deck of Dogs Playing Poker cards.

"How 'bout a game of Old Maid?" he asked with a quick, unreadable smile. "I'll let you win. . . ."

# Chapter Seven

For Kamille Porter, steering clear of the Château Du Roy apartments hadn't been a difficult task since Jinx first moved in twenty-three years ago. As she and her husband, Dan, sat idling in front of the circa fifties eyesore in their late-model Mercedes, she concluded that she would rather perform a root canal on an alligator, given the choice. Unlike herself, the Château hadn't aged gracefully. Taupe-colored paint coated terra-cotta bricks, and the wrought-iron staircase showed signs of rust beneath chipped enamel. Palm trees rose up from the ground like split ends under a microscope, while rosebushes on three trellises died in botanical crucifixions.

Kamille thought her son lived in a swill pit. Worse, she suspected he stayed there because he wanted to—not because of his claim that he had to reside in the precinct in order to keep his elected position.

She opened her lizard handbag, pulled out a compact and checked her hairline. Perfect. Every strand of spun platinum in place. With a manicured hand, she freshened her Paloma Picasso lipstick, then snapped the powder case shut and faced her husband.

"How many people do you think are murdered here, annually?"

"Some're probably just killed the old-fashioned way."

Her eyes crinkled in confusion. Then, she tightened her

jaw. Did the old coot really think she'd spent fifty-eight years without being able to tell when he was trying to turn the conversation to sexual innuendos? With an aristocratic sniff, she reached for the handle to let herself out, rocking the Benz with a slam of the door.

"Let's just go, shall we?" Halfway into a courtyard of blistered St. Augustine and wilted perennials, she stopped dead in her tracks. "Did you bring the gun?" Dan cleared his throat, trying to buy time, the way he always did when he knew she wouldn't like the answer. "Oh, for God's sake." She clutched the silk scarf knotted at her neck. "How do you plan to defend us?"

"We'll be fine, honeybun, it's still daylight." He raised a hand as if to adjust his eyeglasses, but Kamille suspected he wanted to shield his lying eyes.

She shot him a withering glare and strutted to the manager's office, leaving him running a hand through faded red hair, and a look of confusion settling across his brow. In no time, she returned with a key.

With the grace of a ballerina, she glided to the steps knowing her expensive fragrance and the flash of a well-turned ankle would torment him as she passed. For spite, she intended to turn in early when they got home. And if that didn't deter the old goat, she felt a headache coming on.

Migraines worked wonders with oversexed fools.

She stalled at the foot of the stairs, revved her rpms until her cheeks heated up and pointed a fingernail painted Beverly Hills chic. "Upstairs. I guess Jinx never heard of a first-floor apartment."

"Second floor's safer. Less chance of getting burglarized."

Kamille whipped around. With the top of her poofed hair barely reaching her husband's chin, she stared up his six-foot frame. "I'm sure this is equal opportunity housing. Everybody gets a shot at being robbed." She took off, kicking up grit in her wake.

"Not robbed, honeybun. Robbed is when a crook points a gun and says, 'This is a stickup.' When they rob houses, they're called burglars."

"Thank you for that informative nugget, Dan. I feel ever so much safer. Can we get on with it?"

They hauled their aging bodies up one flight of steps. At the landing, they stopped for a breather and glanced around for a reference point.

"The manager said it's around the corner."

Dan nodded. "That's the one."

While watching him adjust the tie against his tartan plaid shirt, Kamille's clenched fist went straight to her hip. Well, he could fuss with his silly self until he stretched the fabric threadbare—surely, he didn't think she'd let that little gem slip by unnoticed. Guilty, he glanced her way.

"You've been here before, Dan?"

"Not really." He scuffed his foot against the decking, something he always did when she had him cornered. "Okay, once. I came by when he was sick."

"When was he sick?"

"I don't recall . . . 1979, '80. Maybe '96? I forget."

She drilled one heel into a plank, spun away and stalked off. In front of Jinx's apartment, she held out the key, stared dead ahead and froze.

Dan picked up his stride. "What's wrong?"

Hand over hand, she climbed his jacket sleeve until she had him bent down with his hearing aid inches from her lips. Her voice dropped to a whisper. "Someone's inside."

"If there was someone inside, we wouldn't need to feed the cat."

"This goes back to what I said earlier, Dan," Kamille said

with acid in her tone. She unhinged her clutches. "Jinx is being robbed."

"He's not being robbed. He's in the hospital."

"Burglarized, then. What's the difference?"

"I thought I explained that already."

"Shut up and unlock it." She handed over the key.

"You want me to go in?"

"Well, you certainly don't think I'm going—listen—there it is again."

With their ears pressed to the door, they leaned in like wide-eyed, mismatched bookends.

Dan cupped a hand to his ear and strained to listen. "I don't hear a thing."

"You're deaf."

"It's probably the cat."

"Thank you for that helpful assessment. Perhaps the cat will vacuum our house when we're old and infirm."

"Jinx has a cat?"

"Phooey—give me the damned key." She closed her eyes and shuddered. Rarely did she swear, but when she did, Jinx was usually the cause.

She opened her eyes and twisted the knob.

A gasp hung in her throat.

There in the living room, bebopping behind a vacuum cleaner to inaudible strains of music, was a long-legged tart with a strawberry blonde ponytail, dressed in a black satin tutu, with fishnet stockings held up by a garter belt.

*"¡La cucaracha, la cucaracha! Ya no puede caminar."*

"We're in the wrong apartment," Kamille said in a horrified whisper. On the wall high above the jitterbugger, hung a lighted canvas of a naked woman with a python draped over her shoulders. And, there was Dan with his feet nailed to the floor and his face flooded with rapture.

She hissed, "Let's go, you old coot."

The dancer whirled the vacuum around.

Both women locked eyes and yelped.

Only the one in the tutu had a five-o'clock shadow. And hands the size of industrial ice scoops. And a bow tie around his Adam's apple and a lace apron over his French maid costume.

He released the sweeper and clapped his hands to his mouth.

A greeting gushed out in a rushed, affected lisp, and when he spoke, his Adam's apple bobbed. "Oh, my stars, if this isn't the most exciting day of my life." Limp-wristed, he moved toward them in ice pick heels embedded with rhinestones, and yanked off his earphones.

A deep voice filtered out of the earpieces. *"Repita, por favor. El gato está dormiendo."*

Kamille darted behind her husband. "Do not let him touch me."

*"Repita, por favor. Hay muchas cucarachas en esta casa."*

"*¡Hola!* If this isn't the bee's knees—Jinx's parents. Mom, Dad, don't just stand there shivering, come in. *Mi casa es su casa.* What am I saying? Welcome to Jinx's *casa.*"

The key slipped out of Kamille's hand and clinked to the deck. She recoiled against the wrought-iron railing. Dan stared at the intruder's shaved legs.

*Horny bastard.*

Then, his gaze strayed to the humongous cleavage and the shaved chest.

*Infidel.*

But, when his attention dipped to crotch-level, Kamille tightened her fist and walloped him on the arm. He regarded her with shock.

The *maid* slinked to the recliner. A *Hustler* lay open to the centerfold, and he slapped it shut. "I'm Glen Lee Spence, Jinx's downstairs neighbor, but most people know me as Leather Devotion. I was sprucing up the place for Jinx's homecoming." Picking up a Bloody Mary with the frilly lace of a celery stalk jutting past the rim of the glass, he pranced close enough for them to get a good look. A tattoo fanned out across one beefy bicep. "Fix you a drink?"

The earpieces were still squawking. *"El perro es muy grande. Repítalo."*

Kamille regarded him with contempt.

"These?" Glen Lee glanced down. "Berlitz tapes. *¿Como está usted? Muy bien, gracias. ¿Y usted?* There's a contest at Club Toucan and the prize is a trip to Mexico. This time next month, I'll be wasting away in Margaritaville."

Kamille corkscrewed an eyebrow. "Exactly how are you acquainted with my son?"

"Jinx helped straighten out a warrant with my parole officer."

"I beg your pardon?" She dug her fingernails into Dan's arm. He flinched in her grasp. "That doesn't explain your presence."

"I offered to clean his apartment for the next twelve months —my way of saying Grassy-ass, for keeping my butt out of a crack."

Kamille's eyes hooded. Her senses filled her with a light-headed rush. She isolated a tuft of hair on Dan's arm and pulled. He shook her off and wandered on in, parking himself, smack-dab, in front of the nude picture. Off to one side, atop a bookcase, a glowering Siamese sat on his haunches, keeping a sharp eye on the players.

"My son allows you to clean his apartment?"

"Actually, he told me if I ever came near this place he'd rip off my nerf balls and stuff them down my gullet. But lots of times Jinx says ugly things he doesn't mean. And he's injured, so. . . ."

"You were in prison?" Kamille said icily.

"It was a mistake. I didn't rob that store detective—"

Lines in Kamille's face tightened like a stringed instrument.

"—I just didn't pick my friends very well, so when they asked for a ride to the bank—"

"You drove the getaway car?"

The merry maid gave up. "Please come in." He extended a fish belly–pale, manicured hand.

Kamille's legs turned to granite. She stopped him with her most scalding *Don't touch me* look. Glen Lee took a backward step. "We are here—" She pronounced each word with such authority Dan's shoulder involuntarily hunched. "—to feed that cat, and to pick up a briefcase."

Glen Lee seemed to melt two inches in his heels.

"Oh, dear." A hand fluttered to his lips. "Did you . . . want the stuff in it? Because if you did, I sorted through it. A horrible mess . . . lots of pictures of ugly men, some of them dating back to the eighties. I threw most of it out." He sliced a hand in the direction of the briefcase. "Now he can snap it shut."

Kamille huffed hard enough to make vapor form. "I'm certain I don't know the contents. Jinx's deputy merely asked us to retrieve it."

"I'll get it. Won't you step in out of the chill?"

"Certainly not," she snapped. "Dan, do you think you could tear yourself away from the pornography? There's a crowd gathering. Look—down in the courtyard."

While Glen Lee wobbled off after the briefcase, Dan shuffled to the door.

A woman with Mardi Gras eyes, dressed in a sequined

gown, hobbled across the sidewalk holding a cigarette holder, wand-like, in one gloved hand. An old crone being walked by a Yorkie wandered about, seemingly without direction. But, it was the wafer-thin, white man in a tuxedo, with a garishly dressed lady on each arm that drew Kamille's attention.

"Lord have mercy, Dan. Those women are men."

Glen Lee sidled up with the briefcase. He tracked Kamille's gaze to the scene below, and his foolish grin melted. Without warning, he dropped the attaché, took off a high heel and hurled it over the balcony.

"Harold, that's my dress." Glen Lee turned to Kamille. "He stole my dress. You stole it, you miserable shit."

Off came the other shoe. The man in the tux shook free of his trophies, cupped a hand to his mouth and shouted, "I'm Harold, you flighty bitch. Get it right."

"Gerald, you whore—" Glen Lee lobbed the footwear. "—I'll gouge your eyes out."

"You said I could borrow it."

"Like hell, *puta*."

Kamille looked to her husband for support and saw only morbid fascination with a degenerate lifestyle.

Glen Lee stomped toward the stairs.

The lively bunch scattered, leaving only the elderly woman and her Yorkie.

Dan Porter picked up the briefcase and blew off the dust.

The Siamese, a confirmed house pet—his seal-colored face and points shimmering like axle grease—slipped out the door in a blur and took off.

Kamille Porter placed a limp hand over her heart and laid blame in five theatrical words. "Your son lives with fags."

By three o'clock Sunday afternoon, Raven calculated she'd gone almost thirty-six hours without real sleep.

Yucatan Jay, on the other hand, snored like a big, lazy dog.

She reviewed what she knew about Stockholming. About the four Swedes held captive in a bank vault at the Sveriges Kreditbank of Stockholm, Sweden, back in 1973. The Swedes became attached to their captors in a robbery gone bad—even identified with the criminals—to the extent they feared the rescuers who endeavored to end their captivity. In the area of hostage negotiations and psychiatry, the effect became known as Stockholm Syndrome, and she stared at the ceiling and wondered if the strange phenomenon applied to her.

*We lounged in bed all afternoon watching Julia Roberts movies.*

*Got misty-eyed during* Runaway Bride *and he flicked popcorn at me.*

*I laugh at his stupid stories; he tells me I'm pretty.*

*He threatens to kill me but doesn't.*

*Do I like him? Hell, no . . . but he can be charming, and he looks sweet and harmless when he sleeps.*

*It isn't like I identify with him . . . well, maybe a little.*

*I want to survive more than I want to hate him.*

*Do I hope something bad happens to him? Not at all—*

*—Yep, I'm Stockholming, all right.*

The next time Yucatan Jay carried up a bottle of wine, she decided drinking herself into oblivion wasn't such a bad idea. She didn't even need to ask why he'd only brought one glass—just instinctively knew he wanted her knocked out like a fly ball.

Yucatan Jay poured.

"You have a boyfriend?"

"No time."

Two glasses later, he asked the same question.

This time, she said, "I used to—"

After a third glass, she caught him up on Jinx Porter. When she got to the part about Loose-Wheel Lucille, the lush from the corner apartment, Y-Jay seemed downright sad for her.

By the time Raven downed her fifth glass, she asked if he wanted to play a game of Mexican Sweat, and offered to let him win.

# Chapter Eight

"Once more," Sid said. "From the top."

Weary, Jinx glanced out the hospital window. He'd already told how Ivy screamed like a Comanche when he took the hit, and how Mickey and Dell abandoned their post to check on him—allowing Marble-Eye to escape out a back window. Even nuns drilling multiplication tables didn't put in this much effort. And, they'd already gone over it—what? —three times since breakfast? He visualized the patchwork quilt of residences in an area of Fort Worth called Missouri Heights; some, little more than lean-tos, intermingled with industrial buildings and railroad crossings.

He took a deep breath. "We got a tip Marble-Eye Turner was holed-up in a rattrap off St. Louis Street. Mickey, Dell and Ivy came along as backup. We got there—"

Sid raised his hand with the authority of a traffic cop. "How'd you get the tip?"

Jinx ran his tongue over his teeth and pondered how to get a tin of snuff smuggled in. This would be a long story and he could use the jolt.

*Mickey, rearing to go, snatched up the telephone receiver on the first ring.*

*Constable's office. Where? Who're you? If you want to be carried as a confidential informant, we have to be able to show the judge your information's good.*

*And then, Mickey's hand over the mouthpiece. Hey, Jinx, they say Marble-Eye's due in at five o'clock tomorrow morning.*

Jinx remembered the address Mickey scribbled on a Post-it, same as the one the parole office listed on the white warrant. He cleared his throat and glanced out the window. In the distance, a bank of clouds obscured the sun. He took off his glasses and polished the lenses, then turned to Sid propped against a stack of extra pillows, pilfered from other patients.

"I don't know who gave the tip. Mickey said it sounded muffled. Like a towel over the mouthpiece. We drove to the house. Ivy and I took the front—"

"No, no, no."

"—and Mickey and Dell took the back." He tried to interpret Sid's expression. "I'm telling you how I remember it."

Sid screwed up his face as if he'd swallowed something vile. "How many cars did you take? Did you loose-lip? Tell anyone else where you were going?"

Jinx ran a hand over his face, stopping long enough to gouge his fingers into his eyelids until he saw fireworks. Sid was relentless.

He thought back and tried to recall more clearly.

*Stop pecking that keyboard and pay attention, Georgia. When Ivy comes out of the bathroom, tell her Marble-Eye's at a flophouse on St. Louis.*

*Whatever. Can I have the rest of the day off?*

*You just got here.*

*You shouldn't make old people come in so early.*

*I can make it so you don't have to come in at all. Oh, and one more thing—call the Korean cleanup lady and tell her we need a case of air freshener. Ivy's still eating chili dogs for breakfast.*

"It's like this," Jinx said, "we packed our gear, checked our pepper mace—pit bull repellent—and headed for our vehicles. Nothing special, just another early morning white warrant raid."

"Except you'd been keeping tabs on Marble-Eye Turner for years."

"Right."

"You always go along with your people to run the white warrants?"

"Not always."

"But you had something personal going on with this guy?"

"You could say that. I've had a beef with Marble-Eye since 1981. He knifed a friend of mine in a car-jacking. Cut him up something awful. My buddy nearly lost his sight." Jinx felt the skin on his face tighten.

Pantywaist DA struck a plea bargain. The only reason Marble-Eye spent time in the pen was because, seven years into a ten-year probation, he violated his conditions by carving up a neighbor kid.

Part of the tale struck Sid as odd and he said so. "Appears to me, Marble-Eye's choice of weapon's a knife, not a gun."

"I don't put much stock in that," Jinx said wryly. "A con'll use whatever's handy."

"I'm just saying the guy was a convicted felon. Convicted felons aren't supposed to carry firearms while they're on paper."

"He was in his house, remember? The parole officer wouldn't be likely to find a gun on a visit if Marble-Eye hid it good."

"Don't those guys rummage through stuff?"

A head shake. "Civilians don't realize how lucky we are as a community to even get them to make field visits." Jinx went back to his story. "We drove down Henderson Street—"

"Who was riding, where?"

"I waited in the lot for Ivy. Her driving record, plus the

fact that she lives out of her car, tends to discourage people from doubling up with her. Mickey drove on ahead and arrived a couple of minutes early. Dell arrived in his own unit."

"Pull up next to the house?"

"Mickey waited down the block like we always do until everybody gets there. Then—"

Sid held up his hand. "What'd you and the girl talk about?"

Jinx's mouth stretched into a wicked grin. "Her kid, Amos." He shook his head, amazed. "Frankly, I don't know how she manages him. But Ivy's into this rescue thing. She saves strays from euthanasia, gets box fans for old people when it's hot, rounds up heaters in the winter." His voice trailed off to permit reflection on her accolades. Ivy had to be one of the most free-hearted people he knew.

And a real screwball.

Sid broke the mood. "What's wrong with the brat?"

"I suppose it comes with being a teenager. A couple of us put a football pool together. We're waiting to see what day he gets arrested. Costs ten dollars a square to play."

"What's the pot?"

"Around two hundred."

Sid mulled over the news. "What numbers are left?"

"No one wants the thirty-first."

Sid sat up and stretched. "How many numbers you buy in for?"

"Five."

"Got a system, or, are you the kind of man who makes random picks?"

Jinx's lips peeled back wickedly. "I looked at the calendar and chose the days a full moon fell on."

Sid flung his creaking legs over the side of the bed and

stood. With the back of his hospital gown gaping, he tottered over to the closet and rifled through a pair of Wranglers, starched and hanging on a wire. He angled over with a ten-dollar bill.

"Put me down for the thirty-first. I feel lucky." He sat on the edge of his bed with his knobby knees poking out from under his gown. "Go on with your story."

"Dell pulled up, and I sent him and Mickey to cover the back. I remember getting out of the car. Ivy left her jacket. She never wears enough clothes. Don't give me that look, I pay her ragamuffin ass plenty. She could buy proper clothes if she wanted to."

"I didn't say anything."

"She was shivering." He rethought the scene. "Her teeth were chattering like the snare drum intro to 'Wipeout.' " Sid stared, unfazed. "Forget it. Just an old song from high school days. I gave her my jacket, threatened to fire her—"

"Maybe she shot you."

"—and we bolted up to the porch. The rest's pretty much a blur. I saw orange." For a moment, Jinx went quiet and sank into his thoughts. "Ivy didn't shoot me. I threaten to fire her at least once a week. She's the Joe DiMaggio of Tarrant County for all-time career car wrecks. Ivy's always pulling shit."

"What about Amos? Where was he?"

"Getting ready for school, I expect."

"He drive?"

"Not old enough. He's around thirteen."

"Yeah, but can he drive a car?"

"I don't understand how your mind works, Sid. Are you saying he might be trying to kill his mother?"

"I'm not saying anything yet. You never heard of gettin' all the facts?"

"You're saying I'm not a good investigator?"

"What was orange? Something Marble-Eye had on? A ball cap with Hook 'em, Horns?"

*A fireball ten feet wide, haloed in shards of glass.*

"The muzzle flash," Jinx said. "The muzzle flash was orange."

It was close to five o'clock Sunday afternoon when Raven opened one eye and tried to focus on the electric-red numbers on the digital alarm clock. Yucatan Jay was brushing her hair, taking long, deliberate strokes.

Raven rolled onto her back.

No shirt.

No jeans.

No panties.

She blinked hard. Nope, still gone.

"I'm butt-naked." Her head lolled in Jay's direction. The room blurred. "I'm gonna be sick."

"There's a trash can next to the bed. Use it."

Two empty bottles of Pierpont Riesling poked out of the wastebasket, and she figured she must've consumed them both. "Where're my clothes?"

"You're not very good at strip poker. You probably shouldn't play that game anymore."

"Did you—"

"No. I've taken a vow of celibacy until I get back, remember?"

"You didn't even want to?"

"Didn't say that."

A quiver started in her chin. "It's because I'm not pretty enough, isn't it?"

"You'll do in a pinch."

"Loose-Wheel Lucille was a drunk, and Jinx wanted her

more than me." The irony put her on a crying jag. Not crocodile tears. Big, fat waterworks. "I'm shit-faced, and you didn't even try to take advantage of me? What's wrong with me?"

He moved around to her side of the bed and sat. The jostle of movement made her stomach roil.

"Ohgod, I think I'm gonna puke."

When she finally lifted her head from the trash can, Yucatan Jay handed over her shirt.

"Great rack." He slung an arm across her shoulders.

"Stop ogling me."

With a finger stuck under her chin, he tilted her face where she could see him. "Dr. Jay thinks you've got a bad case of *sniffilis.*" She giggled. "The guy was a jerk. You deserve better."

"Really?" Vulnerable. Bordering on pathetic. "You're not just saying that?"

"No."

"Good. Because I'm gonna blow beets."

Sid was back on the phone, calling around for Betsy, when Ivy showed up at the hospital empty-handed.

"Where's my briefcase?" Jinx asked.

"I couldn't get it. I had an emergency. My next-door neighbor's house caught fire, so Amos had to give a statement to the fire marshal." She must have anticipated his thoughts, and rushed ahead with lightning speed. "Anyway, I made arrangements with your parents. By the way, they're feeding Caesar."

The news scalded him. He tensed until razor-like pain tore at his arm. "I've made it through most of my adult life without my mother dropping in. Now, you invite her to invade my privacy. I ought to fire you."

Sid laughed so hard his crossword puzzle shook. He wouldn't be yukking it up if it were his private life.

The LPN with the Southern drawl joined them, uninvited, closing in on Jinx with purpose in her step and an upraised syringe. She lifted his sleeve and stabbed with the vengeance of a serial slasher.

Before he could take a swing at her, she was gone. By the time his medication took hold and he felt himself drift off, Sid and Ivy were cutting up like spirited high schoolers at a sock hop. The last image Jinx had was an ugly visual of Sid and Ivy getting it on in the back of a '57 Chevy. He drifted off with visions of them doing animal sex, and their grotesque faces mashed against the back windshield, imprinted in his imagination.

# Chapter Nine

"We should leave. He never liked us anyway."

The abrupt shear in Jinx's dream-filled slumber came from a cosmopolitan voice he recognized as his mother's, so he did what any black sheep son would do—played possum. Kamille might be petite, but she had some pretty mechanical responses when people sprinkled sand in the gears of her day-to-day existence. Without the oil of compliance, the woman had a reputation for grinding to a complete halt. And family members in hospitals weren't regarded as a few kernels of sand—they were boulders.

And, brother, could she lay blame. Never in fifty-three years had he met anybody who could churn out guilt the way Kamille could.

He faked a snore. If he could outlast her, they might leave without him having to endure the kind of recrimination for his chosen profession they'd dished out for almost two decades. About the time he convinced himself they were about to take off, Sid butted in with a neighborly invitation.

"Drag up a few chairs and make yourselves at home."

Jinx unsealed one eye enough to take in a fuzzy outline of Sid, perched on the edge of his bed with the telephone in his lap. He punched out a number, put the receiver to his ear, and covered the mouthpiece with his hand.

"I'm phoning my daughter. She thinks I'm dead. Hello, Elizabeth? It's your daddy." A piping shriek pierced the earpiece. "She dropped the phone."

Jinx's eyelashes fluttered. Not a moment too soon, he sealed Sid's image from view.

"Come on, honeybun, why don't you set the briefcase down?"

"I think we should go."

"He might wake up. You heard what the nurse said."

"How would she know when he'll get up? Look at him. He's in a coma. They've got him so doped up he'll need a hydraulic lift to pry his eyes open."

Dan chuckled softly.

"What are you laughing at, you old coot?"

"I'm just grateful he's still here."

"I warned him this would happen. I can't imagine why anyone would want to wallow around with the lowest common denominator."

"Turn loose of that briefcase and come sit."

Jinx distinctly heard Dan pat his knee.

"Behave yourself or I'll smack you."

He stiffened to keep from flinching. His mother had a flair for drama. Even with his eyes shut, he felt those thick-lashed, jasper-colored beads bear down on him like two flame-throwers.

A grinding noise from the next bed almost brought him bolt upright.

*Uh-oh. Sid stirred.*

Submerged in concentration, quietly willing away his parents, he'd forgotten all about Sid. The very idea Kamille would meet Sid Klevenhagen was enough to make his stomach turn back flips.

Off to one side, Sid called out. "Muffin? She dropped the phone. Ain't that a kick in the stones? Betsy, I ain't dead! Take more'n a pillow over this old eagle beak to kill me. Quitcher cryin'."

"Good heavens, Dan, somebody tried to kill that man. You don't think—"

"Quit eavesdropping."

"Now you listen to me, Dan Porter. Somebody almost killed our son. What if a maniac's loose in this hospital? Jinx has an HMO, you know. I don't understand why he can't select his own doctor."

"We don't know that he didn't."

"Oh, for God's sake, Dan, do you think my son would pick a dump like this if the county had decent insurance?"

"Doesn't look that bad to me."

"Don't come right away," Sid broke in, louder this time. "I'm havin' a great time. I made a friend."

"This is insane," Kamille said in a loud whisper. "Why are we even here? You know he hates us."

"Who hates us?"

"Your son."

"Now he's my son?"

"He didn't even call. I had to see it on the news."

"He doesn't want to worry us. Sit down. You look kind of peaked."

"He never phones. And quit staring at my feet."

"Your ankles look a little thick." Dan lowered his voice to a loud whisper. "I was just thinking about those rhinestones and black stockings—"

"Love you, too, baby." Sid again. Down went the telephone receiver.

A chair scraped the floor, filling Jinx's ears with a shrillness that made him flinch.

"Did you see that?" Kamille asked. "Jinx moved. You woke him."

He tried not to breathe. His ears pricked up at the slight

tap against the floor. He didn't have to open his eyes to know Kamille was close by. The weight of her disapproval filled the air around him.

He could hear his heartbeat.

Hell, he could hear *hers*.

An unearthly scream caused his eyelids to peel back. His mother flung herself across the bed, forcing out his breath. With her hair looking like the carnival wildman, she scrambled to right herself. Horrified, they locked gazes. When his deflated lungs filled again, they inhaled Shalimar.

A flash of an arm a few shades lighter than beef jerky caught Jinx's eye, then receded beneath the curtain. Nobody had to explain why his mother's face was pressed into his crotch; Sid had goosed her.

The curtain zipped back and Sid formally introduced himself.

Kamille gave him a staggering look. Sid returned the glower with a lecherous twinkle. He seemed oblivious to Dan, setting aside a *Field & Stream* to tinker with his hearing aid.

"I don't believe this," Sid said. "I read in the *National Enquirer* where you left the country to have cosmetic surgery, but I knew it was a lie." He leveled his gaze at her breasts. "Anybody can tell those aren't store-bought."

Somebody siphoned all the oxygen out of the room.

Kamille stared, unblinking. Jinx could almost see the undertow of thoughts swirling in her head. They were like that—Sid's victims. He struck so fast women didn't know whether to take a swing, or beg his pardon.

Sid started toward her with the practiced innocence of a professional rogue. "You'll have to pardon me—" He offered an outstretched hand. "—I can't remember the names of all your movies, but I've seen every last one."

While Dan rolled his eyes and went back to more fish stories, Sid's lips bussed Kamille's fingertips.

Jinx's eyes orbited in their sockets. His mother certainly dressed as if she were waiting for the limo to pull up. But she was a shrewd piece of work. Any minute, she'd see through Sid.

"That's so sweet," she said in a voice not her own. Vivien Leigh's, maybe. Olivia de Havilland's, fine. But definitely the utterance of a starlet. Her smile turned radiant, erasing ten years from her face.

"That's my *mother*." His tone carried a twinge of betrayal. Kamille shot him a withering look. She batted her lashes at Sid's transparent flattery.

"This gorgeous diva's your mother?" At groin-level, Sid's hospital gown fluttered. Jinx dropped his gaze. Jiminy Christmas. The guy must have a bicycle pump hidden in his crotch.

He made a firm suggestion. "Have a seat, Sid."

"Don't mind if I do." Sid cozied up next to him on the bed. He gave Jinx's uninjured shoulder an avuncular squeeze. "You have an impressive son."

Kamille's eyes strayed on their own volition. She glanced down at the tent hiding Sid's alter ego, and back to the weather-beaten hand resting on Jinx's shoulder. Color drained from her cheeks. Her muscles went taut and her eyes widened with reproach.

She stalked over to her husband and gored him with an elbow. "I'm leaving."

Jinx knew the tone. He'd heard it his whole life, at least once a day, right up until 1969 when the draft board finally selected the ping-pong ball with his birth date on it.

Dan closed the magazine, placed it on the windowsill and wrangled into a corduroy sport coat. "We brought your brief-case. Your girl deputy asked us to pitch in. And your mother insisted we stop to buy you a sweat suit." He averted his gaze and pointed to a louvered door. "We left the sack on the closet floor."

"Thanks, Dad."

He glanced around absently. "No telling where your things are."

"Bagged as evidence, I imagine."

Dan's eyes misted. "I guess they have to analyze the bullet holes, huh?"

"Bullet hole. There was only one."

Kamille departed with a backward scowl. Before the door completely closed, Jinx swore he heard her say, "See? I told you there's a reason your son lives around gays."

# Chapter Ten

Kamille hadn't whisked Dan out of the room ten minutes before Jinx's doctor materialized. The HMO physician didn't just pronounce him well enough to leave, he practically ordered him gone as soon as the LPN pulled out the last needle. While scanning his side of the room for personal items, Jinx eased into new blue sweats.

"I'm downright envious." Sid hunkered gloomily at the edge of his bed. "You got your walkin' papers. I ain't seen that big old nurse since she took my blood pressure last night."

Raised your blood pressure, Jinx wanted to say, even if the curtain did shut out most of the action. He was imagining Sid with a red ring around his ramrod, and the RN with smeared lipstick and cap askew, when Sid broke the silence.

"You live nearby?"

Jinx pointed through the window. A distant matchbox rose up to touch the sueded twilight. "If you look real hard, you can see it from here."

Sid tracked the finger.

"I know the place," he said with a certain confidence. "Used to sneak in and grease an old gal's gears. Lucille. Never will forget the time I slipped over to her place. I'd barely raised my fist to the door when Lucille yanked it open and said, 'I heard you coming.' Hell, who woulda thought you could hear something like that?"

*Loose-Wheel Lucille.* Jinx kept his face carefully blank.

The smile of remembrance left Sid's face. "Lucille's dead." He plastered a wild hair down with the flat of his hand. "Reckon most of my friends are in the ground." He slid off the bed and clapped Jinx's good shoulder. "I'm pleased to have another."

The men shook hands.

"Good luck, Sid. It wouldn't have been half as much fun getting shot if I hadn't ended up in three-oh-two." He scrambled to collect his toiletries, then abruptly ditched them. He couldn't think of a single thing of the hospital's he wanted.

While wondering if the cat would be glad to see him, the door to 302 banged open.

Sid's face lit up. "Betsy."

A reed-thin woman strutted in with an attaché case in one hand and a gold pen in the other. Like whitecaps on an angry sea, shocks of silver swept back from her temples and disappeared into a thick mass of coal-black hair. Steely eyes, rimmed with sooty, spider lashes, glittered. Heavy bracelets, dripping off bony wrists, caught the glow of Sid's bed lamp enough to send gold flashes arcing out from her body. Thumbnail-sized diamonds weighted her earlobes. A sable coat stopped at her hips. Its sinewy brown color contrasted sharply with her flawless, pale skin, while the thick, rich pelts concealed her true size.

"Come on, Daddy. We're leaving this hellhole." She assumed an aura of arrogance generally associated with people who could trace their bloodline back to the royal family.

"Muffin—you can't imagine how happy I am to see you."

She slid into her father's embrace, and made a visual inspection of Jinx over Sid's shoulder. Kamille would have loved her on sight, the way she forced the corners of her mouth into a sneer of disapproval.

"Gather your things and let's get the hell outta here."

"First things first. Meet my roommate, Jinx Porter."

"I'm sure he is." Her nostrils flared with contempt.

It went like this: Betsy was a lawyer. And, until the lawsuit she filed against the hospital either made Sid independently wealthy or turned him into the new owner, her old man wasn't sticking around one minute longer. She opened the closet with a bang.

"I don't see how these charlatans stay in business." She yanked Sid's blue jeans off the hanger and pitched them onto the bed. "I did some digging. Research shows this shit sty leads the country in wrong-site surgeries. You could've told those ambulance drivers to take you to a real hospital."

"Now, Betsy, you know my doctor works here."

"Let's discuss that," she scoffed. "I don't understand why you have a foreigner taking care of you."

"Best heart surgeon in the Metroplex."

"Daddy, you're another victim. I think they roto-rootered your brain instead of your aorta. I'll find you another doctor—stop looking at me that way—I know what's best. I'll get the finest money can buy. We're never darkening these doors again." She tossed his shirt, an unassuming plaid with so much starch it seemed to rip as he forced his arms through the sleeves. "It's not like you're on an HMO," she continued, ladling out contempt. "We can afford the best medical care Cowtown has to offer—make that the world. I'm surprised someone hasn't filed a class action suit against these imbeciles." With eyes flinging daggers, she glanced over at Jinx.

It was enough to make his pulse stall.

Sid forced his feet into his wingtips, then bummed Betsy's pen and scrawled out a note.

"Here you go, hoss. My address and telephone. You need

anything, all you gotta do's holler."

The Klevenhagens were seeing who could be first out the door when a thunderous rumble brought them to a surprised standstill.

Betsy fused arms with her father. "What the hell was that?"

Sid shrugged. "Transformer?"

Jinx could give a rat. All he wanted was out. His hand tightened around the briefcase handle as he hurried into the corridor. At the nurses' station, an impeccably dressed man in a nubby-silk suit watched them guardedly while huddling with the supervising nurse.

Betsy clutched Sid's arm tighter. Under her breath, she snarled, "That little worm is the hospital administrator. By the time I get through with him, he'll be wearing polyester."

Two nurses pushed empty wheelchairs toward them, but Betsy pointed a finger charged with lethal energy.

"Do not come near this man," she announced acidly, shooing Sid into the elevator, "or you'll find yourself on the ass-end of a subpoena."

After Jinx slipped in and the doors closed the unsmiling staff from view, Sid made an unwelcome suggestion.

"Betsy, let's give Constable Porter a lift home."

"Delighted." She scowled, then slid on a pair of crystal-and-gold sunglasses like a silver screen luminary expecting paparazzi.

Outside, she left them waiting beneath the portico. An afternoon thundershower that started across the parking lot as halfhearted applause, ended up drumming the metal awning in a standing ovation. Betsy made it to the car about the time Sid dug a foil of pipe tobacco out of his pants pocket, and mysteriously produced a pipe.

"Betsy don't approve when I smoke." His eyes gleamed.

"Don'tcha hate it when other people quit their bad habits and try to foist their righteousness off on you? Got just enough time for a puff before she catches me."

They joked about missing the smell of disinfectant mingled with scrambled eggs, when a metallic-blue Lincoln with gangster-tinted windows pulled up even with the curb. Electric locks snapped open. Sid reached for the front passenger door.

"She's single," he muttered offhand.

Jinx had a notion why.

Betsy's nose twitched as Sid slid into the front seat. "I don't even want to discuss where you pirated your contraband." She wrenched the gearshift out of park and into drive.

They exited the lot in relative silence. Strains of Beethoven filtered through the Lincoln's stereo speakers, offering Jinx a thin blanket of comfort. But it was the smell of new leather that filled his nostrils and opened the closed closet doors in his brain, unlocking exhilarating memories of a backseat romp more than thirty-five years ago.

*Selma Winston.*

His parents' next-door neighbor. While Selma's husband ran the family oil company, Jinx scalped more than the old wildcatter's lawn. The woman was insatiable. Just when he thought he couldn't bring his fireman back to life, Selma pointed out another flash fire that needed dousing.

A block down the road, Betsy unclenched her jaw long enough to pose a question.

"Where do you live, Mr. Potter?"

"Porter. Know how to get to the Château Du Roy?"

"Didn't the city condemn that place?" Angelic tones of innocence carried into the backseat where he sat slumped against the window, but Betsy's riveting stare in the rearview mirror spoke volumes.

He rolled his eyes and took in the scenery. It wasn't as if he'd suggested she share a bedroll with the homeless. Or parade down the Martin Luther King, Jr. freeway wearing nothing but dirk heels and a dog collar. So what if friends opted to use the facilities at the corner gas station rather than set foot in his bathroom? Maybe they didn't understand—exposure to germs immunized the body.

They cruised Eighth Avenue in a sporadic drizzle, through the hospital district and past the south side's version of upscale eateries. When they topped the final hill, Jinx's spirits buoyed—

—and sank.

In the distance, a patrolman in a yellow rain slicker picked up Day-Glo traffic cones, then walked toward a fire truck pulling away from the curb. He tossed the pylons into the trunk of his blue-and-white, slammed the lid, climbed into the patrol car and fell in behind. That left only a white van with midnight-blue decals that spelled out *Crime Scene—Fort Worth Police* on the side. A low rumble that started in Jinx's gut, died in his throat. Sid twisted in his seat and peered past the headrest.

"Caesar," Jinx croaked. Absorbing the horror ahead, he grappled for the door handle, ready to launch into action.

"What's wrong, hoss?"

Betsy answered for him. "I hope that's not your apartment."

She whipped off her sunglasses and floored the accelerator. Above the pink indentations on either side of her nose, he could see the glaze of alarm in her mirrored reflection. The Lincoln pierced the wind, bringing the east side of the Château Du Roy into sharp focus.

Missing bricks from the face of an exterior second-floor wall lay in a jagged heap, like rotten molars in a dentist's tray.

A large hole gaped where a window used to be. Remnants of smoke carried on the breeze like putrefied breath turning to vapor in the evening chill.

Before Betsy could brake, Jinx bolted from the car. He hit the pavement in a dizzy rush.

Caesar.

Something Sid said haunted him. The theory had its flaws, but Sid had the battle scars to back it up.

*I think it was you they wanted to kill.*

He ascended the stairs on winged feet. He didn't give a hoot about the bookcases filled with first editions. The modest collection of folk art from an old flame couldn't hold a candle to the database stored in his computer. And, the PC meant nothing if it didn't have a Siamese on top to muck up the electronics with sable fur and dander, and—

If somebody killed the cat—

He sprinted past crazy old Mrs. Beale and her stupid Yorkie.

If somebody killed the cat—

Halfway to the top, he glimpsed the freakish sight of the cross-dressing Munsch twins, Gerald and Harold, anchored in the courtyard like mannequins in their Bermuda shorts, curly wigs and matching Hawaiian halter tops.

If somebody killed the cat—

By the time the ball of his foot hit the top step, he envisioned a cartoon cat silhouette blown out of the wall. Gripping the bannister, he bartered with God. Just when he struck a deal he could live with, the bright yellow tape lettered CRIME SCENE sent despair careening down on his hopes. He accepted the demise of the Siamese while simultaneously vowing the kind of retribution that carried a penalty of five to ninety-nine, or life, in a Texas courtroom.

Jinx halted in a freeze of indecision. He closed his eyes

long enough to make a childlike wish, then rounded the corner on fumes. His chest seared with pain.

He threw back his head and screamed at the heavens. "Caesar."

In the courtyard below, bystanders nudged each other. Jinx was halfway to hyperventilating when one of the Munsch brothers pointed.

A fawn-bodied cat with sable-colored extremities and sapphire eyes slunk along the wrought-iron railing. He seated himself a good three feet from the DMZ, alternately lashing his tail and sniffing boards with the dedication of a U.S. Customs agent. His mouth opened to bare a set of impressive fangs, while the chin beneath the dark mask quivered in a silent meow. As a warning, he raised a dark paw and flexed his claws. Furrows of wet hair glistened between his ears. Nobody had to tell Jinx he had a pissed-off pet.

"Caesar."

The Siamese rebuked him with a yowl.

The joy of finding his beloved pet, unscathed, took Jinx to his knees. He hoisted the cat onto his good shoulder and rose. Caesar loved elevation. Being held aloft made it easier to slash. Jinx took a step in the direction of the apartment. Twenty claws digging into his flesh, and a roomful of bestsellers rendered into confetti, stopped him in his tracks.

"It looks like somebody triggered a land mine." The whiny, effeminate voice of the Château's porcine manager came from behind.

Jinx turned. Valentine, a short man with a duck-footed walk, ambled over.

"Were you keeping explosives?" Valentine came within Caesar's lunge. The cat's claws flared.

"What the hell do you think?"

"Don't get sassy with me, mister."

The seal point tensed beneath Jinx's grasp. His heart vibrated against Jinx's hand. A paw shot out and swiped the air in front of Valentine's face. A low growl brewed in his throat. Jinx flinched at the sting of Caesar's hind claws, digging in for traction.

Raindrops dotted Valentine's bald head. He squeegeed a hand over his scalp and flicked them onto the deck of the balcony. "I suggest you buttonhole one of those policemen and tell your side of the story. They already got our version."

Jinx pressed for details. "Any witnesses?"

"None that stuck around. And let me be the first to inform you, your rent just went up."

"You can't raise the rent, I'm on a lease."

"I'll be expecting another deposit. This was a nice place until you moved in." The manager pirouetted and took off in the opposite direction.

"It's a dump," Jinx shouted. "It's always been a dump." He buried his nose in Caesar's damp fur. Poor little buddy.

Downstairs, center courtyard, Glen Lee Spence stared up, engulfed in the petticoats of a festive Mexican tap-dancing costume, cooling his cleavage with a black lace fan. Gerald and Harold linked arms and sniggered like they were competing for class dunce until Mrs. Beale's Yorkie scampered over and hiked a leg on their leather hurache sandals.

Sid sidled up with a piece of advice. "Better file a report with that detective."

He pointed to a broad-shouldered man in a blue CRIME SCENE T-shirt, standing next to the evidence collection van, writing on a spiral pad.

Numb from shock, Jinx nodded. He shifted his gaze to

Betsy. Sid's ashen-faced daughter didn't look like such a ball buster anymore.

"Attempted murder." Sid surveyed the damage with a keen eye. "I wouldn't stay here if I was you. Have maintenance board the hole up and come with me and Betsy."

She seemed to regard the invitation as a personal slight, and shot Jinx a look of utter disgust.

Sid steered him toward the detective. "We're gonna need to go over everything again, short-timer. Let's take it from the top."

The next time Raven woke up, Yucatan Jay was lounging beside her with a pizza delivery box resting on his stomach, and the TV news program volumed down low.

He gave her a casual glance. "Want some?"

He held up a half-eaten piece and a drop of neon-orange oil slid across the pepperoni, onto the glistening fat pooled on top of the cheese.

She answered by way of a lowing calf moan. A few minutes later, she warned him to stop shaking the bed.

"I'm not shaking the bed."

"Yes, you are. Quit it."

"You're drunk."

"Your fault."

"Back to bed, Sleeping Beauty. Tomorrow's a big day."

# Chapter Eleven

Jinx had no idea where Betsy called home, but if tensing her jaw worked as any kind of barometer, he could pretty much bank on the fact that the grandchildren of Fidel Castro would receive more hospitality. With a glimmer of hope—Betsy hadn't commented on the Siamese—he sat in the backseat cradling his rigid cat, and mentally reviewed the names of people who might take him in.

He started with those who should have been beholden to him for their jobs.

Dell was out. Most people couldn't be in the same room more than five minutes with his wife, Nicole, without fantasizing about ways to kill her.

Mickey was out, too. The ocelot kit he acquired when he married, had grown up. Not a day went by that Mickey didn't complain how Napoleon took over the bed, or licked his chops whenever Mickey walked through the door. He suggested the exotic cat might still be teething, but Jinx knew better. Cats of any size were serial killers. Mickey was a rump roast waiting to happen.

He could ask his chief deputy, Gilbert Fuentes, to put him up. Gil's wife made the world's best enchiladas. But the in-laws occupied the two-bedroom house with them, and Gil's wife owned a psychotic German shepherd. That would be bad for the Siamese.

Then, there was Ivy. The thought of sharing the same area

code with Amos was enough to make Jinx's chest constrict, and his forehead dot with perspiration.

That left the secretary.

Georgia and her husband might take pity and make room. But, that would mean evicting their Great Dane, Buckwheat, from the guest bed; not to mention that Georgia's attitude had soured ever since he forgot to send flowers on Secretary's Day. Okay, he didn't forget—he drew a moratorium on roses when one of the female deputies from the sheriff's office spurned him.

He expelled a bitter sigh. That eliminated the poor slobs who were obligated to him. He expanded the list to include Château Du Roy riffraff. People with mug shots and FBI case numbers.

Gerald and Harold gave him the willies. The strange brothers owned queer macaws that talked dirty, and they competed against Glen Lee Spence in fashion shows at Club Toucan.

Glen Lee Spence.

Jiminy Christmas.

Jinx shuddered. People who discontinued their sex change operations once they got boobs, gave him the creeps. Then, there was Mrs. Beale. Senile people made him check his hole card, and the Siamese would make a meal of that Yorkie.

When the Château possibilities fizzled, he dismissed family members outright. He'd been trying to kill his sister, Mimzy, since he was four and his parents brought her home from the hospital. And the thought of being around Kamille longer than half-hour increments started a brushfire behind both eyes. He moved on to names of people who didn't know him well enough to realize they didn't want him staying with them. There were none.

*Raven . . .*

Guiltily, he stroked the Siamese.

Sid twisted in his seat. "Got a picture of Marble-Eye?"

"Sure do."

He wanted to show Sid the color mug shot the parole office sent over, and coded the latches of his briefcase to open. Sick exhilaration blurred his vision. He could hear the blood emptying out of his head like the flush of a toilet.

*No Marble-Eye.*

*No rap sheet.*

Nothing but a few ballpoint pens tucked into molded leather straps.

"Jiminy fucking Christmas."

Betsy shot a glare into the rearview mirror.

He tingled with shock. "My stuff's gone." As sure as corpses popping up in a Savannah rainstorm, the son of a bitch who cleaned out his briefcase would pay.

Jinx ended up at the door of the poolside cabana behind Betsy's opulent estate, surrounded by a xeriscape of native plants and weeping willows. Lush landscape provided a shield from the harsh lighting of crystal chandeliers in the main house, a hundred yards away. Inside, he sucked in the sweet odor of high-dollar pipe tobacco and let his gaze roam the room. Nailhead sofa, upholstered in a rich, brick-colored leather. A couple of bronze Remington knockoffs graced the end tables next to the couch, and a brindle cowhide made an interesting rug substitute. It stretched the length of a field-stone fireplace and ended in front of the big screen TV, inviting winter evenings of longnecks and frolic.

"What do you think?" Sid hooked his Stetson on a walnut hat tree.

"Nice."

Jinx tightened his grip on the cat. If Sid had curtains, the Siamese would find them. With hurricane force, Caesar launched himself from the crook of Jinx's good arm and bounded down the hallway. Sid touched a wall switch; two wrought-iron candelabras suspended at opposite ends of the vaulted ceiling flooded the den with a creamy light.

Jinx settled his gaze on a shadowbox filled with WWII medals nestled discreetly against a far wall.

"C'mon." Sid cut through the dining room. Boot heels echoed off the terrazzo tile in the kitchen. "How 'bout a longneck?"

"Better not. I ought to be thinking about picking up my patrol car. It's still parked at the apartment, and I need my clothes. I'm going into work tomorrow. Maybe I can make it a whole day."

Sid angled over to the sink and stuck the caps under a wall-mounted bottle opener.

*Pfft.* Clink. *Pfft.* Clink.

Vapor snaked past the lip of each Bud Light.

"Here. Sit." Sid took a captain's chair at the breakfast table. "Who hates you bad enough to kill you?"

The call of the amber brew was more than Jinx could resist. He took a swallow, letting the icy cold slide down his throat.

"A few women wouldn't mind seeing me squirm." His voice trailed.

"Awright, out with it."

"A hairdresser once threatened to cut off my dick . . . I just considered it big talk."

Instinctively, Sid grabbed his crotch. "Where's she now?"

"Married. Lives on a big ranch two counties over." He lifted the bottle in a halfhearted toast and took a long pull.

"Any of these sweethearts know how to rig a bomb?"

Jinx's throat closed. Beer spewed out his nose. Sid reached past a pair of blackamoor salt and pepper shakers, to the paper napkin holder.

"Hit a nerve?" Steely eyes narrowed into slits. "What's her name?"

"Raven. But she couldn't have done it. Rumor has it she still loves me."

Sid shook his head knowingly. "Women are funny, short-timer. Not funny ha-ha. Funny strange. If they get it in for you, sleep with one eye peeled and the other on your gun sites." He reached over and took the Sunday edition off a stack of newspapers in the breakfast nook, then leafed past the front page, allowing his gaze to float over the contents. "Let's have it. Gimme details."

With a nose for mischief, the cat made an entrance with a low-slung body and drooping tail. After exploring the baseboard and finding nothing of interest, he bounded over and leaped into his owner's lap for an ear scratch. Jinx settled in for the long haul.

Somewhere in the middle of the sad sorry saga, a frown settled over Sid's face. The old lieutenant folded the metro section of the newspaper in half and balanced it on one knee, listening with quiet intensity how the on-again, off-again relationship soured. When Jinx got to the part where Raven walked in on him and Loose-Wheel Lucille in flagrante delicto, Sid's eyebrows shot up. By the time he finished the Clintonesque tale, Sid got up from the table and returned with a pen and a spiral notepad.

"Put her on the list."

Raven wouldn't kill him. Play up to him so she could dump him, maybe. Publicly humiliate him, sure 'nuff. But blow him to smithereens? He scratched the cat on the underside of his neck and considered the possibility.

He could almost hear her musical laughter. See a sultry smile on that otherwise angelic face. Feel the flash of betrayal in those angry gray eyes. He swallowed.

"Let's start over." Sid upended the beer bottle and pointed the empty at the refrigerator. This time, it was Jinx pulling two head-splitters out of the carton.

"I really think you're making too much of the idea Raven's out to get me. I haven't laid eyes on her in almost two years." After all their troubles, he still felt a need to defend her guerilla, get-even tactics. "It was Marble-Eye pulled the trigger."

Sid quartered the metro section and shoved it across the table. "That so?"

Jinx set the longneck aside and held the obituary column within arm's length. In the bottom corner, beneath the sub-headline proclaiming *Body found in Trinity River,* was a photo captioned with words guaranteed to prevent a decent night's sleep.

"The Tarrant County Medical Examiner's Office positively identified the decomposed remains of Newton Delbert Turner. Turner, 47, who used the street name 'Marble-Eye,' was reported missing last Tuesday by his mother. . . ."

# Chapter Twelve

Early Monday morning, Sid drove Jinx to the Château. Like common burglars, they entered through a balcony window and crunched through rubble that had once been a bedroom. While Jinx dressed for work, his new buddy hauled several armfuls of unscorched garments out to his pickup. When he came out of the bathroom armed with a razor and toothbrush, Sid made a suggestion.

"This yellow tape ain't gonna cut it. You really ought to have maintenance board up the place."

"So somebody won't steal my melted computer?" He lifted his good arm enough to sniff his shirtsleeve. "My clothes reek."

"I was thinking in terms of preserving evidence. Not to mention your book collection."

Jinx shrugged. "I'm the only one at the Château who reads anything besides the funny pages." He gave the room a final once-over, started for the front door, then stopped. Why take the long way around? He slung a foot over a heap of bricks, onto the balcony overlooking the street. "What the hell," he muttered, "this is the front door."

Sid, with his long strides, passed him.

"Hold up." Jinx darted back inside the gaping hole; he returned with a Dogs Playing Poker tie draped around his neck.

"You wear ties to work?" Sid. Slitty-eyed.

"I used to keep one at the office in case I got called to court," Jinx offered. Sid's casual head-bobbing said, Yeah, sure, but the Klevenhagen squint indicated he wasn't fooled. "It was a gift."

Sid's eyes narrowed.

"I don't know why I went back for it." He yanked off the tie. "I don't even like it."

His ramblings made no sense and he knew it.

Sid's lips angled up in a smirk.

Jinx wadded it into a ball and tossed it back into the debris. "I'll drive the patrol car if the battery isn't dead. You can follow me."

He stalked past Sid, down the stairs and headed for the parking lot. The old man caught up to him at the cruiser and pecked on the glass. Jinx slid the electric window halfway down. Before he could mash the locks closed, Sid tossed in the tie.

"You don't have to wear it," he said, "long as having it around makes you feel better." A swat on the door ended the conversation.

Downtown, with his arm cradled in a sling and Sid at his heels, Jinx strolled through the lobby of the multistory building the constable's office shared with the Tarrant County sheriff's office. Not exactly shared, since Jinx adversely possessed roughly 1200 square feet. But it was a coup, nevertheless, considering the constant bickering that took place between elected officials and Commissioners Court.

"Hands off the secretary," Jinx said in an over-the-shoulder warning. "I don't need to be fighting off a sexual harassment claim."

"Is she good-looking?"

"Who, Georgia? That reminds me—don't say anything about fat people."

"She's fat?"

"I never called her fat to her face. I was talking on Mickey's phone and she overheard me."

"Queen-size doesn't bother me."

"Married."

Sid, duded up in a white western shirt so stiffly starched it appeared to be made out of plastic, cracked a smile. "But is she hot?"

*Would Sid care if she was coyote ugly?*

"Look, Sidney, the fact she's married ought to be enough. And she's a religious fanatic."

Sid adjusted the silver handcuff slide on his bolo tie. "I used to go with a preacher's daughter. Every time we'd rut like the Devil, she'd scream, 'Oh, God.' "

"Do you ever think of anything besides sex?"

"Do you?"

A workman stenciling the last of Jinx's name onto the new glass door, stepped off to one side and opened it. A cowbell rigged overhead signaled their entrance with a clang.

Georgia, seated behind her desk, was loaded for bear. "I need the rest of the day off."

*Not, "Glad you're back; tickled you survived; hope you're feeling better; kiss my ass."*

He decided not to eliminate her from the list of suspects.

"Top o' the mornin'." Jinx narrowed his eyes. He hoped the green hue in Georgia's over-processed hair would wash out with the next shampoo, then decided it wouldn't. The scent of fabric softener caught up to him about the time he noticed the spit shine on Sid's boots. He thumbed at his side-kick. "This is Sid Klevenhagen, FWPD."

Before he could finish, an orangutan arm shot out, grabbed Georgia's plump hand and yanked her to her feet in a likely attempt to glimpse cleavage. "Enchanté." Sid's lips bussed her fingertips. "You're a looker."

She turned her head aside as if modestly savoring the compliment, then ticked off ancient high school achievements, crowned by a reign as Cantaloupe Queen. Jinx rolled his eyes. So did the deputies.

Georgia pulled free. She tugged at the Ace bandage being passed off as a skirt, which kept riding up hail-dented, grandmotherly thighs. A pair of loop earrings the envy of the Flying Wallendas rattled from side to side.

"Come to think of it," she said, dropping her brusqueness, "I can stick around awhile." Her smile hinted an element of mystery while Ivy's angled up in a sneer.

Jinx noticed the eleven-by-fourteen of Buckwheat, displayed on the desk in a gilt picture frame, where a computer monitor with Georgia's prized aquarium screen-saver should have been.

He said, "Where's the computer monitor?"

"It quit working."

"Did you call Data Services about getting it fixed?"

"Of course I did. You ask me, I think Ivy let Amos play with the computers again." Georgia looked at Sid. "I miss the fish. Besides, there's nothing to do here. Which reminds me, I need the day off."

Pretending not to hear, Jinx sifted through the in basket for signs of get well cards and didn't find a damned one. Out of the corner of one eye, he monitored Sid making the rounds, pumping hands with Gil, Dell and Mickey, before finally checking out Ivy's new purple polyester pantsuit with the Klevenhagen leer.

"Little lady—" Sid removed his Stetson. He gave Ivy a look to wilt a hothouse orchid. "—I'd like to have you over for lunch."

Jinx cut him off at the pass. "She has papers to serve. Help yourself to the coffee and come on back." He headed down the hall to his office.

"Not so fast." Georgia rattled a half-inch-thick document at him.

From the plastic spiral binding and the Tarrant County seal on the cover, he knew it came from Commissioners Court. The notion that the commissioners expected him to drop everything to work on next year's budget, scalded him.

Sid's breath grazed his neck.

"The budget request." Jinx handled it with a two-fingered pinch, the way he might dispose of a litter box tootsie roll the Siamese deposited on the carpet.

Sid lifted one eyebrow. "Bullets, copy paper, toner—maybe a little pocket change for long distance? Shouldn't take more than a page or two, right?"

"You don't know these numbskulls. This is their way of seeing to it elected officials don't live to draw their pensions."

Leaving Sid at the coffeepot, Jinx carried the budget request to the back office. He'd been shot at and worse, but when it came to a choice between taking gunfire or doing the budget, he'd almost rather . . .

. . . what was he thinking? His shoulder hurt like hell.

Inside the ten-by-twelve the commissioners expected him to use for an office, he stepped on the surge suppressor connected to his computer and toed the toggle switch with a boot tip. Gears ground, tones chimed, and in seconds, start-up messages flashed across the monitor. He waited for the log-on screen to appear.

*Klevenhagen. What a masher.*

He nestled against the chair back and waited. After typing in his password (SIAMESE), he used the wait time to thumb through the requisition list until he found a suitable starting point. He clicked his ballpoint pen.

*Item:*

He wrote *Toilet Paper.*

*Quantity:*

That required ciphering. *260 rolls.*

*Explanation for item requested:*

His deliberate, vertical script flowed across the paper. *People full of crap.*

*Plan for Economy:*

With lightning speed, the answer popped into his head. *Staff will be instructed to crap at home or use TP pirated from Commissioners Court restrooms.*

Satisfied, he flipped to the last page to the Wish List items.

*Item:*

He filled in the blank with a request that would make their unisex bathroom obsolete. *Women's Restroom.*

*Quantity: One.*

*Explanation for item requested: Ivy's full of crap.*

The cowbell over the front door clanged, and he checked his watch.

*Mail cretin.*

Another fine EEO attempt to hire the handicapped. Georgia thought the outpatient treatment at the mental ward made a big difference in the mail clerk's shitty attitude once she learned they were enforcing the guy's Haldol intake. What she didn't know was the third time she ran home and told her husband the mail clerk made her cry, the drunken bum actually rolled out of bed, sobered up, slapped Aqua Velva on his spider-veined face, came downtown and buttonholed the guy.

*I have a 30.06, a backhoe, and a hundred acres near Vidor, Texas. Don't fuck with my wife.*

It was true, Jinx heard him say it.

The cowbell jingled again. Mail cretin, gone.

Sid's voice rang out. "Here, good-lookin', let me help you with that."

Stalled in thought and staring at the computer screen, Jinx felt an unexpected prickle of neck hairs. Chills danced on his shoulders. He rose halfway when a thunderous report rocked the walls—

—blew him back into the chair—

—plunging the room into darkness.

The bank officially opened at nine but Yucatan Jay insisted they arrive fifteen minutes early. The two waited in the car with the stereo volumed down low.

Raven couldn't wait to be rid of him. The hangover she got from imbibing too much wine had soured her disposition, and anyone with half a nose could whiff what was left of the fermented grape juice still floating in her stomach.

She eyed his camouflage fatigues with cold scrutiny. "You should try to blend in, Jay."

"Huitzilopochtli."

She eyed the bulge at his waistband. "Where shall I drop you after this?"

"I was thinking you could run me down to Laredo . . . maybe let me out at the border."

"Run you down to Laredo?" Her voice spiraled upward. "I'm not riding in a car with you ten hours, Jay—"

"Huitzilopochtli."

*Bird Man of Leavenworth, more like.*

She mocked him with her tone. "Are you signing for the money as Huitzilopochtli?"

"Of course not. The agency provided me with a different identity until I secure the funds."

"How come the agency doesn't convert the funds for you? Why do you have to do it?"

He looked at her with undisguised pity, as if she could never fully understand the intricacies of the CIA. "That's just the way it works, Rave. This isn't Hollywood."

A tone trilled out. Yucatan Jay reached into the pocket of his fatigues, pulled out a cell phone and checked the number on the lighted display.

Before tapping it on, he put a finger to his lips as a warning. "Code Jerry." Long silence. "Roger."

"Who was that?"

"The President—what a micromanager." He returned the cellular to a pocket sewn into a pants leg.

Raven torqued her jaw, stared through the windshield and drummed her fingers against the steering wheel. "Why don't you book a flight?"

Jay shook his head. "Can't—all that gold. They'd look in the suitcase."

"Then check your bags."

He gave her a *You've gotta be kidding* look, polished off by an eye roll.

Catching movement in her peripheral vision, Raven jerked her head in the direction of the bank. A security guard unlocked a double set of glass doors leading into the lobby.

"Good luck," she said. But she was thinking, *Soon as you leave, I'm outta here.*

Yucatan Jay scowled. "You don't expect me to leave you? You're coming along."

*Not sure what the hell's going on.*

*Think he might be committing a felony.*

"I don't mind waiting."

He touched a hand to the bulge in his waistband; she had no choice.

Yucatan Jay said, "Here's how the cheese binds—you're my devoted new bride. I'm flying overseas tomorrow, out of Carswell Air Force Base."

"I'm not signing anything."

"You're here to hold my hand, that's all . . . you can't very well take off and leave me stranded if we're holding hands." His hand closed around her wrist and he tightened his grip until she flinched. "Don't even think about sprinting off, Raven. Not unless you can outrun a three hundred twenty-five-grain bullet traveling at fifteen hundred feet per second."

*Ohmygod, I'm Patty Hearst.*

The concussion from the blast knocked Jinx back into the chair, propelling him against the gunmetal desk. A shot of pain momentarily took the room out of focus. What sounded like the tinkle of wind chimes stalled time for him. He sat stricken, enveloped in the surreal specter of tragedy.

*What the hell was that?*

*Not wind chimes. Shattered glass.*

*Is it over?*

At first, he moved in a hypnotic state. Then, the reality of disaster set in. With tightness in his chest, he ejected from the chair and stumbled through the door. An avalanche of white powder rolled down the hallway, engulfing him in a snowdrift of sheetrock. He took a deep breath and held it.

Edging along the corridor with one hand braced against the wall, he felt his way toward the main room. A persistent whimper coming from the front office sickened him.

"Georgia," he yelled.

No answer.

He went through roll call.

Gagging sounds, coming from Jinx's men, made him crave a quick breath. Might as well have sucked down a snootful of powdered jalapeño. His nose stung and his throat burned, making it tough to swallow. He touched the wood molding at the entrance to the tiny bathroom, ducked inside, slammed the door and groped for the cold water faucet.

Screams from the outer foyer added a new dimension to the terror.

Instinctively, he yanked a stack of paper towels from the dispenser and drenched them. With a makeshift filter covering his nose, he made his way back out into the corridor and forged ahead.

*Sheetrock and gunpowder.*

*And . . . confetti?*

An unrecognizable voice shrieked, "Dial nine one one," followed by, "We are nine one one, dimwit."

*Bomb.*

Alien noises buzzed in Jinx's ears. Stumbling, he let go of the wall. When he reached out for balance, the paneling disappeared.

Disoriented, he moved in the direction of the whimper, calling out to his people.

The whimpering stopped.

"Jinx?" Georgia's voice had a creaky-hinge squeak to it.

*At least she was alive.*

"Pull your shirt over your face." Uncontrollable coughs came from Gil's direction. "Gilbert?"

"I'm okay," he croaked. But Jinx knew he wasn't. Gil had asthma.

"Ivy?"

"Son of a bitch, is this a rip in my new jacket? Wouldja look at this?"

Jinx plodded on, vectoring the location of his deputies. Dust thinned, providing him with a hazy view of the newly replaced door—or, rather, what was left of it.

"Dell? Mickey?"

Mickey's usually commanding voice sounded soft and faraway. "Toldja not to make the coffee so strong, Dell."

Dell responded with a derisive grunt.

Then, Ivy's voice rang out. "Dang-it, this was my birthday suit."

Jinx snorted in disbelief. There they were, the ceiling caved in on them, with Ivy bitching about her birthday suit. Sid would've made merry of that—Ivy's birthday suit. He'd have tried coaxing her into the bathroom, make her show him that birthday suit. Sid would've—

Realization hit hard. "Sid?"

Shame filled every pore. He'd never thought of Sid. Sid wasn't even supposed to be here. Wouldn't have been, either, if the old warrior hadn't badgered him into tagging along.

Wanted a fresh taste of the streets, he'd said.

Without a medical release, he couldn't return to the PD.

What would it hurt, he'd said, hanging out with a man with a lifetime of investigation experience?

He wasn't so pruned-up and dried-out he couldn't help, he'd said.

*"Sid."* Jinx's voice came out strident. "Sid, where ya at?"

Except for a few particles still dancing in the air, the snow-drift thinned to a smoky haze. With the cuff of his shirtsleeve, Jinx wiped the powdery coating off his glasses, bringing what was left of the constable's office into focus.

On all fours, behind the desk, Georgia crawled to her chair and hoisted herself up. She wrapped her hand in her shirttail, covered her nose and took a labored breath. No one seemed to care that a roll of blubber protruded above the Band-Aid skirt. Green-hued hair sprouted out from her head like the top of a pineapple. And when Jinx narrowed his eyes into a squint, he could see that the dislodged mass hanging by a bobby pin was a wiglet. For a frozen moment, the image struck him as comical.

Transfixed with horror, his eyes traveled the room. He

relaxed his hand. Soggy paper towels slid from his grasp. His mouth gaped in stunned silence.

Dell and Mickey no longer resembled hired killers out of the Old West. In fact, the entire staff had the freshly floured look of poultry. Fluorescents flickered overhead, threatening darkness and emitting an acrid odor. Dell's aqua eyes pierced the gloom. Mickey's mustache looked as if he'd gobbled down a box of sugar donuts. Gil flopped into his chair like the Pillsbury Doughboy on acid, wrapped his meaty lips around an asthma inhaler and forced a squirt down his throat.

A strange voice—a woman's—chilled Jinx back to reality.

"Somebody get an ambulance."

And, another—a man's. "Too late. He's dead."

Jinx's chest tightened.

*Sid.*

The way he saw it, he could confirm the bad news, or stay ostrich-headed. He stepped into the outermost foyer, maneuvering through a pack of uniformed sheriff's deputies.

"Hey, Jinx, you okay?" A vaguely familiar voice, but no body to go with it.

He stared straight ahead, into the boil of dust and mortar. Over the hunched shoulders of paramedics, charcoal cloth was gingerly peeled away, where a starched white shirt had once been.

*Sid.*

Jinx closed his eyes.

*Aw, Jesus.*

The lump in his throat threatened to cut off his oxygen. He swallowed hard. How could he break the news to Sid's high-octane, hard-drinking daughter that he'd killed her old man?

He took a step closer—to make absolutely sure some other six-foot-two-inch, Wrangler-wearing, silver-headed, cattle baron–hatted, Texas Ranger–looking imposter hadn't stumbled in and taken Sid's place. A young patrolman tried to shoo him away.

"I'm not too old to whip your ass," Jinx said, wiping powder off the seven-pointed gold star at his waistband.

Out of nowhere, the weight of an arm draped across his shoulder.

"Y'awright, Constable?"

He stared into the familiar face of a plainclothes detective and wondered why he couldn't place him.

In the time it took Jinx to shift his gaze, the emergency crew loaded Sid's charred corpse onto a gurney. They ratcheted it up waist-high, and, with wheels clacking, steered him out of view.

*Jesus. Sonsabitches could've at least covered his face.*

"You wanna sit?"

Jinx shrugged off the detective's arm, and his concern. On his way back into the office, he passed a couple of female police officers, huddled in the corner, tending to a man. Over feeble protests, they picked glass out of the ground meat that used to be his face.

*The stencil guy.*

Jagged glass, sandwiched between the metal frames of the exit doors, hung like guillotines. Beyond the sharp edges, emergency lights flashed near the loading dock. Jinx blinked. His heart cramped at the sight of the medical crew thrusting Sid into the meat wagon.

When the last paramedic slammed the ambulance shut, Jinx pushed past curiosity seekers and waved off questions.

"This is a crime scene," he growled to no one in particular. "Nobody comes inside."

# Chapter Thirteen

Shoehorned into a pair of Isaac Mizrahi strappy sandals, poured into a pair of aqua, flower-print capri pants, Raven's first act of courage called for stepping into the bank and screaming bloody murder.

Let God and the government sort it out.

But the moment she saw the decrepit old guard up close, not to mention a lady pushing a baby stroller, she changed her mind.

"Act like you like me," Yucatan Jay growled out of the side of his mouth.

"That should be easy." Facetious.

"I mean it. This is a matter of national security."

*My ass.*

*Oh, look at this . . . I'm on camera.*

*Next stop, six o'clock news. Shoulda washed my hair. I'll be wearing stripes. God knows how long 'til the jail guards let me shower.*

"Give me a kiss."

"This isn't an Elvis movie."

"Call me Ruben." He pulled at a neck chain until a military ID card flopped out on his chest. "I'm Ruben Garibay."

Raven's eyes darted around the lobby.

*I'm in a bank lobby, with a lunatic white guy posing as a Mexican.*

*Thinks he works for the CIA.*

*Evidence caught on camera.*

*Gonna spend the rest of my natural life, serving a day-for-day sentence in the federal pokey.*

She inventoried the players in a glance. Bank guard, off to the left, seated behind a desk. To the right, the young mother, signing in to see a loan officer. Tellers in the middle, opening their saloon windows. Three businessmen approaching the counter at a brisk pace.

"Look alive, sweetheart."

A suited man with a confident attitude left his enclosed glass office. Yucatan Jay stuck out his free hand. "Ruben Garibay, sir. And this is my wife, Beatríz."

*Beatrice?*

*Bastard couldn't even fake a decent name.*

*Could've introduced her as Aurora. Rosita. Margarita.*

*Which she could use at the moment. Frozen. Rimmed in sugar, not salt.*

Voices turned into a tinny buzz. Next minute, the room was nothing but a colorful smear. The first thing Raven realized once she could make out shapes again, was that she was sitting in a comfy leather bucket chair with a secretary shoving an iced-down, vanilla Coca-Cola at her.

Yucatan Jay did most of the talking.

"Beatríz forgot to take the pill. That's why we had to get married. Of course, I'm leaving the base in the morning. I'll be stationed in Turkey until this whole Middle East crisis is under control."

"What?" Raven's eyelids fluttered in astonishment.

"Just sit tight, honey. We'll get you back home and you can watch your soaps."

"What?" Raven sat up straight.

"Don't upset yourself. Remember, Dr. Jay said it's bad for you." He leaned in close to the desk and addressed the bank official in a stage whisper, "You know how women are. First they single you out, separate you from the rest of the pack. Then they stop using birth control, and next thing you know, they've got you by the balls."

"Are you crazy? You're telling a stranger I went off the pill? What kind of goober are you?"

"She gets a little excited." Yucatan Jay. Still talking in a stage whisper, acting like she wasn't there. "It's stress brought on by this deployment. It's rattled her cage. So . . . where's my gold?"

Jinx stepped across the threshold and acknowledged the hollow-eyed stares of what looked like snowmen on opium. Six cases of paper stacked next to the file cabinet by the door had been rendered into confetti. His people banded together beside Gil's desk, still in shock. The odor of burned gunpowder tweaked his nostrils and he pinched his nose to ward off a sneeze.

In an uncharacteristic move, Dell spoke. "What's the news on your buddy?"

A blend of pain and dread unlike any he'd known, started in Jinx's stomach, radiated out to his extremities and settled behind his blistered eyes. He barely had the energy to pronounce doom with a head shake. Propped against Georgia's desk, he thought hard. The image of Betsy Klevenhagen, ready to skin him alive, was enough to shrivel his meatloaf.

He willed himself from the grip of a shared hypnotic state and took charge. "Got any police tape?"

"Over here." Gil sailed a roll of Day-Glo tape through the air.

"I don't want these sonsabitches traipsing in before the bomb squad shows up."

An excited drone filtered in from the outer foyer. A siren

yipped abruptly, then faded into eerie quiet. Sheriff's deputies swarmed the halls, vulture-like, but no one dared to violate the POLICE LINE—DO NOT CROSS warning Mickey slapped up in latticework strips across the entrance.

Ivy dreamed up a ball buster. "Somebody wants you dead, Jinx."

"It could have been me." A selfless comment from Georgia.

"Coulda killed us both." Ivy again.

Mickey's eyes sparked indignance. "Coulda killed us all."

Dell and Gil exchanged knowing glances, then lowered their gazes in unspoken thanks.

Without warning, a ghostly silence swallowed up the auxiliary voices. Even the interlopers, loitering beyond the thin, plastic barrier, made no noise.

Jinx's heart drummed.

A renewed sense of urgency overtook him. He pushed himself off Georgia's desk and reflexively unsnapped his holster.

Nothing could have prepared him for the ghastly apparition filling the doorway. His breath rushed out and he yanked off his glasses and blinked. A grisly hand pawed down the flimsy barricade.

Jinx's spirits soared.

"Sid!"

"You're insane."

Raven pulled away from the curb, half-expecting the front wheels of her restored BMW to lift off the pavement, judging by the weight of the gold Canadian Maple Leaf coins in hard-shell suitcases stacked on the backseat.

Yucatan Jay's words came out in a rush. "That was so great, Rave, the way you threw up. You should consider a job with the CIA. It kind of had me worried for a second when he examined my documents, but you . . . well, you distracted him. Purple puke'll do that." He pulled the automatic from his waistband—

*Ohgod. I'm dead.*

*No reason to keep me alive.*

*Jinx'll never know I still love him.*

—and positioned it near her headrest. He swiveled his head, seemingly in a desperate search for signs of a tail.

"I don't think we're being followed, but you never know 'til you hear a bullet zing past your head." His mood lightened. "You looked pretty funny walking out of there with a wet paper towel over your face."

"I'm dropping you off at the bus station."

"That's not a good idea, Rave. I think I'll just take your car."

"You're stealing my car?"

"Borrowing it. Or, you could drive me to Laredo. Whichever you prefer."

It took Raven under two seconds to think things through. She twisted in the seat to see him better. Injected her voice with false cheer. "You're right. I could do some serious shopping across the border."

"Thattagirl." Yucatan Jay reached across the headrest, took a handful of her long, dark hair and flicked it over her shoulder.

"First we stop for gas."

"Don't try anything stupid."

Raven swallowed hard.

Sooner or later, he'd have to take a leak. When he did, she'd take off like a Jack Russell terrier.

At the first gas station, a mile from the bank, she pulled beneath the overhang and coasted up to the gas pumps. With the BMW still rolling, Raven bailed out onto the dirty pavement, rolled in iridescent fluids, scrambled to her feet and took off in the opposite direction, rending the air with a rebel yell.

# Chapter Fourteen

In typical fashion, a team of FBI agents took one look at the catastrophe and told the boys from the Bureau of Alcohol, Tobacco and Firearms, "If you want it, it's all yours."

No small wonder, Jinx thought.

He'd never known the Feebs to jerk the rug out from another agency unless they knew beyond a certainty they could solve the crime and hog the glory. And the FBI guys were the world's worst when it came to claiming credit for another agency's work. He ought to know; they'd butted heads before.

Bunkered out in flak jackets and toting a Judgment Day arsenal, the boys from ATF fanned the perimeter in record time. Rocking one foot in front of the other, a clumsy-looking fellow in a lead suit and space helmet headed into the gaping hole. A slim, dark-haired agent with olive skin and limpid brown eyes that drooped at the corners, shook Jinx's hand and took him aside.

"We told the sheriff's men to take a hike—that we have jurisdiction—but we need your cooperation. Have your people clear the building so we can do our jobs. Collect evidence." He ran a hand across Jinx's field of vision. "Constable, can you hear me?"

"We're the evidence. Besides—" Jinx pointed to Sid, "the scene's already contaminated. Sid and I were in and out."

"Makes it harder for us to do a proper job." The agent

pointed to the robot-like figure. "That's Jeremy. He's here to check for explosives."

"Who the hell would want a job like that?" Sid asked.

"Jeremy was a tunnel rat in Nam." As if that explained the wild gaze, visible through the face shield of his helmet. "His shrink says guys who take bombs apart are like the guys who make them—nuts."

Jinx agreed. Bomb suits only kept the victim in one piece so he'd have a better corpse. He balked at being run off. "If we leave, who knows what kind of evidence we'll track outside and lose forever?"

He made his point, but the agent issued a stern warning. "We'll leave paper booties by the door. If you leave, you have to put them on when you return. Until we're through, nobody handles anything. And turn off your radios—that goes double for the base station."

Georgia swept a clean spot across the desktop.

"Don't be moving stuff." Jeremy. In a disembodied voice. "Everything's a bomb 'til it's not a bomb." He glared through the face shield. "You could be handling the Saturday Night Special of explosive devices without knowing it. Break the circuit, it'll go off in your face—and frag the rest of us."

She sniffed at the rebuke, then opened her singed copy of the *Star-Telegram* and went straight for the obituary section.

Jinx beat her to the punch. "Forget it. You're not taking in any funerals today. You're sticking around long enough to give a statement."

Her eyes drifted over the page. "Here's one," she announced with the usual sorrow, tempered with a touch of sadistic glee. "It's the man who owned the gas station down from the house where I grew up. I knew his son before Enco became Exxon." She clicked her tongue in a tsk-tsk-tsk. "Imagine. Ninety-seven years old."

"A life cruelly abbreviated."

"Lose the sarcasm." She slapped the paper shut and reached for her sweater. "Well, that's it for me."

Jinx stepped into her path. He folded his good arm across his lame one, secretly relieved things were slipping back into routine. "Just because the county gives funeral leave doesn't mean you can flit off. The rule was designed to give employees time off to attend services of family members."

"Where does it say that?"

"In the handbook."

Georgia puffed up. "No, it doesn't. It says we get funeral leave; it doesn't put limitations on it."

Dell spoke. "Funerals are rude."

Chatter stopped. Everyone turned in a collective shift, including the ATF evidence boys.

"They are," he said evenly. The ATF boys blinked. "Death ought to be left up to the individual. Folks ought to be able to decide for themselves when their number's up, then pass out notices so their friends can take off without it becoming a burden on their fellow employees. It's bad form to just up and die."

The notion appalled Ivy. "You're saying invite people in advance?"

"Yep." Dell braced his arms across his chest. A thousand-yard stare formed in his eyes.

Her mouth dropped open. "That's stupid."

Dell's glare deadlocked on Ivy. The ATF boys went back to bagging evidence. Sid retreated down the hallway. Jinx followed close behind, marveling at the snow tracks imprinted on the carpet by his resuscitated friend. He caught up with the lieutenant in the bathroom; Sid was examining his singed eyebrows in the mirror.

"I thought you bought the farm."

Sid turned on the faucet and ran the water. He caressed a red splotch on the left side of his face. "Reckon some ointment would take the fire outta this brand on my cheek?"

"Want to go to the hospital?"

"So them sonsabitches can do me in?" The old lawdog scowled. "I reckon not." He brushed away the last of the burned hairs and concentrated on a blackened Brillo pad, matted at the hairline. The touch of a finger sent it into the sink bowl, and he regarded the unexpected bald spot with a curious mixture of interest and disgust. "The top of my head looks like a putting green. Think I'd look good with my head shaved?"

Sid had to be putting him on.

"I ain't wolfin'. You seem to do all right with women." He returned his attention to his blistered scalp. "Except for that gal, Raven . . . the one who wants you dead."

"It's not Raven." Their eyes locked in Sid's mirrored reflection. Jinx favored the old man with an easy smile. "I have my reasons."

"Sooner or later you'll own up to it, hoss. She's the prime suspect."

"Gratuitous violence isn't her style."

"No?" A spirited challenge.

"No. Besides, she came to visit me at Our Lady of Mercy but the nurses wouldn't let her in."

Color drained from Sid's face. "The nameplates on the room were switched. Somebody nearly killed me. I think she was after you."

"You're wrong. This is a woman who decided to turn my life upside-down in the way it would hurt me the most. To give you an idea how her mind works, she got the richest woman in Fort Worth to back her for constable and ran against me in the last election."

"Either you tell the ATF boys or I will."

Jinx changed the subject. "What do you remember about that package?"

"Bulky. Lotta tape. Had your name on it."

"What did the writing look like?"

"Before—or after—it blew up in my face?"

"Dainty writing?"

"Block print."

Jinx had a reason for wanting to be by himself.

He ducked Sid's steady eye, and took a deep breath of acrid bomb blast. "How'd you keep from being blown to smithereens?"

"I dunno. The mail guy brought in three or four boxes. Your secretary had her hands full, so I took 'em. Last thing I remember, the one on top—the one wrapped in tape and the one underneath it—slid off."

Jinx rubbed a powdery film off his watch. "If you're sure you don't want to go to the ER, then let's head for the Ancient Mariner. It's a bit early to start on a bender, but we've got a lot of territory to cover and this may take time."

An unearthly scream of the damned pierced the zombie-like aftermath.

It came from the direction of the front office.

Jinx barreled in with Sid on his heels. Ivy and Dell had frozen in mid-action, and Gil and Mickey plastered themselves against the wall. The ATF boys, with their wide-eyed gazes fixed on Georgia, appeared to have pulled in a deep breath and were holding it. Georgia was white as an aspen and quaking. Haunted eyes bulged at the telephone receiver dangling over the side of her desk.

Jinx moved to her side. Touched her shoulder. "What's the matter?"

"My mother's dead." She broke into sobs.

"For God's sake. When does it end?" He depressed the button for speakerphone. "Hello?"

A thick-tongued voice at the other end, "Who is it?"

"Constable Jinx Porter. Who's this?"

"Swillie."

"What's going on?"

"Sombitch's dead."

"What does he mean, 'The bitch is dead'?" Georgia wailed. "Mama's a saint."

"Ol' piece of crap, you know that's true. Surprised the damned thing lasted this long."

Georgia wrung her hands. "How can this be?"

"How do you know this?" Jinx demanded.

" 'Cause it was me, opened that ol' thing up."

"Opened her up with *what?*"

"Big ol' flathead screwdriver."

Georgia shrieked, guts-out. The ATF boys took in the drama in their silent, watchful way. Gil, Ivy, Dell and Mickey banded together in one corner.

"You opened her up with a *screwdriver?*"

"Umm-hmm. Just tore in, ripped out the guts. Sombitch's dead."

Georgia fainted. Keeled right over.

"Why would you do that, you sadistic son of a bitch?"

The voice on the other end of the line, bowed up, angry. "Whatchoo yellin' at me? Was Miz Georgia herself axed for somebody to fix her up good."

Jinx stared at the dead weight, limply sprawled over the chair with her eyes floating in her head. "Fix who up?"

"Her mon'tor. The mon'tor. Miz Georgia herself the one that called earlier. Said come get her mon'tor. Said somebody fucked with her computer. Said you'd bitch to high heaven 'cause she couldn't get her work done.

Whatchoo want me do?"

"Who'd you say this is?"

"Swillie. In Data Services."

The jigsaw puzzle pieced itself together.

*Way to go, EEO. Another mutant hired by the county.*

"Georgia's mama's not dead?" Jinx leaned over and shook Georgia's shoulder. With a great suck of air, the secretary came back to life.

"Whatchoo mean, dute? I ain't ever laid eyes on Miz Georgia mama."

She looked up expectantly. Mascara clumped above her cheeks like burned rubber on a racetrack. Before Jinx could say anything, she buried her face in her hands and unleashed an anguished groan.

"Maa maaaaaaaaa." Sobs racked her shoulders.

Jinx gripped her elbow and squeezed. Maintained eye contact. Enunciated each syllable. "Simmer down, your mother's not dead. It's your computer monitor."

Georgia sucked in a great gulp of air.

"Your mother's alive."

Georgia blinked. The last of the gray drained from her face, then percolated back to the top in an angry shade of crimson. "That rips it." She shoved a meaty arm into her sweater, pulling at it enough to wiggle into the other sleeve. "This is a hostile work environment. I'm taking the rest of the day off."

Slinging her bag over one shoulder, she stormed past the Day-Glo streamers, around the corner and out of sight.

Ivy and Dell picked up their lively discussion. The ATF boys exchanged bemused looks. They went back to work operating helium-cadmium lasers, trying to fluoresce whatever invisible fingerprints still existed on a piece of brown wrapper.

Jinx replaced the dangling receiver. In doing so, he caught sight of a hideous, powder-coated nest. Curiosity got the better of him. He grabbed a pencil off Georgia's desk and started for it.

Across the room, an agent barked, "That hasn't been photographed and tagged yet."

Jinx felt his face contort in revulsion. "What is it?"

Ivy swelled up. "A Dolly Parton wig. I ordered it for Georgia's Christmas. I'm having all my mail-order Christmas presents sent up here so Amos won't open them."

"It's barely Halloween."

"I wanted to make sure everybody's bought for. I hate malls."

The lead agent with the bedroom eyes tweezed a piece of paper embedded in the acoustical ceiling. "Just as I thought . . . it's the classic playing card–clothespin–fishhook device."

The deputies narrowed their eyes.

"Ace of spades," he said with authority. He slid the evidence into a glassine envelope and flipped it over with care. The inflection in his voice intrigued Jinx's staff.

An ATF officer with carrot-red hair spiking out from under a police ball cap, moved close enough to see. He turned his unsmiling face to his colleague. "I had a deck like that when I was growing up. Dogs Playing Poker."

The first officer leaned in for a closer inspection. "Where do you see that, Rusty?"

Rusty pulled a pen out of his pocket and pointed. "Right there. That's the bulldog's ear. I used to love those things."

"Photograph it first. Then fume it if you think you have a print."

Gil spoke in short breaths. "What clothespin trick?"

Rusty explained. "Aluminum strips against the clothespin

teeth. Attach the contact leads, which are wired to the device. Sandwich a piece of cardboard between the clothespin to break the connection. In this case—" He gestured to the transparent envelope. "—a playing card. *Voilà.*"

The lead ATF agent seconded him. "Compression, plus fragments, equals ground meat."

Ivy's eyes filled with rural cunning. "How come the fish-hook?"

Rusty scoured the desktop. He peeled off a Post-it note for a prop. "The fishhook attaches to the playing card, and to the box lid. If the lid's opened—or, in this case, disturbed—it pulls the cardboard away, and the contacts connect."

"Dogs Playing Poker?" Gil took another shot of his inhaler.

Rusty nodded. "I'd recognize that pattern anywhere."

Mickey blurted, "Jinx collects pictures of the dogs."

Dell nodded.

Ivy came up with a brainstorm. "Somebody's trying to send Jinx a message."

Mickey slapped his thigh. "You think?"

Dell scowled. Mickey and Gil exchanged facial expressions that challenged each other to come up with the name of somebody goofier than Ivy.

Across the room, an ATF agent held up an object for everyone to see. It appeared to be a polished mahogany cucumber.

"Here's what took the brunt of the blast, but I don't think it's supposed to have ticklers on it."

"Gimme that." Ivy stormed over in a huff. She tried to wrench the oblong object from his grasp but he held it aloft. "It's mine."

"It's evidence."

"Looks like a medieval torture device," Gil said. "Like a

mace, only longer. Skinnier. Almost like a—" He stopped short.

"Sex toy," said the hired killers in stereo.

Ivy turned to Jinx. "It's mine."

"It has nails sticking out of it."

"They can be removed."

Jinx gave the agent the go-ahead. He dropped it in a bag and tagged it.

"Thanks a bunch for embarrassing me, Jinx." Her mouth drooped in a serious pout.

The ATF boys favored each other with some confidential eye rolling and went back to work. Ivy headed to her desk.

She turned to Dell and revisited mortality. "So you're saying people ought to commit suicide?"

"It's the polite thing. That way, people can schedule around it."

For a moment, Mickey sat lost in thought. "I think Dell's onto something. Georgia could let her friends know when she'll be on vacation. That way, if they wanted to kill themselves, she'd be able to attend their funerals and we wouldn't be left in a lurch."

The olive-skinned agent with fathomless eyes pried nails from the wall while offering an unsolicited, over-the-shoulder opinion. "Y'all are sick."

"No," Jinx said, motioning Sid to follow him, "we're alive."

# Chapter Fifteen

Raven made it to the Trinity River and flung herself down the embankment without a backward glance.

Yucatan Jay couldn't very well gas up the BMW using gold coins for payment without calling unwanted attention to himself. As much as she loved that old car, it would probably end up over at the Will Rogers complex, where Yucatan Jay could have his pick of trucks to hot-wire, and throw the hard-shelled suitcases into the bed.

She jogged toward the criminal courts building to find Dell.

Dell could drive her to Our Lady of Mercy. Could make the nurses let her in to see Jinx.

Then she could tell him she was sorry.

That now she understood his identity was tied up in being constable.

She could tell him about Yucatan Jay and the missing Beemer.

Jinx would give her good advice.

Even before she cut through the county parking garage, red and blue strobe lights flashed across her field of vision.

A couple of police officers had sealed off the parking area behind Jinx's office with yellow CRIME SCENE tape, and were milling about near an ambulance when she angled across the lot.

A deputy sheriff called out her name.

Her vision tunneled. Her hearing went fuzzy.

In a strange ventriloquism whose source she could not locate, another voice commanded her to halt.

She broke into a sprint and burst through the Day-Glo tape like the winner of the fifty-yard dash.

Jinx's office lay in rubble. She made it inside the building, and screamed out his name.

Galloping footfalls echoed through the lobby as a dozen deputies surrounded her.

Jinx emerged from the jagged opening covered in powder.

Raven barely noticed the hands tightening around her arms, lifting her on tiptoes, preventing her from reaching Jinx Porter.

He headed over, grim-faced.

"Jinx, you're alive!" She clapped a hand to her mouth to squelch a hysterical laugh.

"Not quite what you expected to see, is it?"

"No." And it wasn't. Deep down, she wanted a shy grin, maybe even a stiff hug for a greeting.

Instead, she heard him say, "You're under arrest."

"What?" Her knees liquefied. She went limp in the restraining grip of the SO boys.

Her voice went shrill. "You think I did this?"

His expression suggested that's exactly what he thought.

"Have you lost your mind? I just got here."

"Where were you twenty minutes ago?"

She didn't want to tell him she was at the bank with a charlatan who, in the uncanny brilliance of a genius, perceived himself to be James Bond. He seemed to regard her silence as an admission of guilt.

"You're under arrest for seven counts of attempted murder."

"Ohmygod. You really think I did this?"

"Care to make a full statement accounting for your whereabouts?"

"No, thanks."

"Exactly what I thought you'd say."

Raven's eyes misted. She knew Jinx's MO on arrests, and didn't like to think what was in store for her. "If you believe I'm capable of something this evil, then you don't know me at all." She stifled a sniffle, squared her shoulders with pride, stood tall and presented a new challenge. "If you're so sure the evidence pointing to me is incontrovertible—" Her voice dissolved to a whisper. "—then do your job."

Jinx's handcuffs rested in the small of his back, tucked into his belt at the waist. He pulled out his hooks, snapped one on Raven's left hand, spun her around and ratcheted the other to her right.

He began the criminal's litany. "You have the right to remain silent. If you give up the right to remain silent, anything you say can be used against you in a court of law. If you need a lawyer. . . ."

Jinx left the booking desk with Raven's expression of betrayal seared into his brain.

Only one other time had she looked so horrified—when she caught him with Loose-Wheel Lucille.

She didn't do it.

So she stole his job.

So she had access to the office files, the computers, their schedules.

So the ATF boys found the Dogs Playing Poker card.

That didn't mean she masterminded the aborted raids, the shoot-out and the bombing.

After the short walk back from the Tarrant County jail, Jinx found Sid outside under the breezeway simulating a sex act on the stem of his pipe with his tongue.

"She didn't do it."

"You can worry about that later, hoss. I'd get inside if I were you. Shit's hit the fan."

"Meaning?"

"Meaning no matter how bad things are, they can always get worse."

On the strained hope the ATF boys packed up and went home, Jinx stepped through the jagged hole in the wall. Agents freeze-framed in position. They cut their eyes at each other knowingly.

It didn't take a cartographer to map out the connection between the spit shine on Georgia's desk, and Georgia lugging a cardboard box to the door with purpose in her step. The skin around her eyes was raw and swollen, and the cockeyed, chartreuse hairpiece still dangled by a pin.

Jinx blocked her exit. "Where do you think you're going?"

"Home. I'm too old for this bullshit."

His eyes bulged. Georgia rarely cursed.

"You have to leave the booties." Rusty dropped his fingerprint brush on Gil's blotter and trotted over with a paper sack. "Evidence."

He knelt at her feet and tugged at the elastic band while Georgia wrangled each shoe free, then dropped them in the bag, whipped out a black marker and scrawled Georgia's name, the date and time, and initialed it. She stood, mesmerized, while he placed the sack in a large plastic container with the rest of the evidence.

Jinx broke the spell. "When are you coming back?"

"When the Devil sells popsicles in hell." She took a step.

Jinx rested his good arm on top of his sling.

*She wouldn't leave. She couldn't leave.*

"By the way," she said nastily, "I changed your computer

password to *Fatty*. Capital F-A-T-T-Y." Her eyes flashed with sadistic glee, cementing Jinx's suspicion she still harbored ill will.

"If you're gonna eavesdrop on my conversations, I'm not responsible for your hurt feelings. Besides, I wasn't talking about you and you know it."

"Well, if you're going to make fun of heavyset people, you should do it where those of us with Rubenesque figures can't overhear."

"Now, look. . . ." He narrowed his eyes in an effort to intimidate.

"I mean it." Georgia glowered. "My weight shouldn't be a problem for anyone other than the six pallbearers who have to carry me—"

"Twelve." Dell, muttering.

"—from the First Baptist Church to the hearse—"

"A baby grand'll fit in a hearse?" Mickey to Dell.

"—and that's not any of you ingrates."

With the panache of a mime, Mickey wiped invisible sweat off his brow and flicked it into the air.

"I've got an office to run." Jinx tried to keep the panic out of his voice. "You can't leave."

"No? Well, I've got a life, and I'd like to keep it." Her eyebrows arched. "Which reminds me, somebody phoned earlier hoping you were dead."

The lead ATF agent snapped his head in Georgia's direction. "Why didn't you say? Who was it?"

Her eyes welled. She drew in several catch-up breaths. "Don't you think I'd tell you if I knew?"

"Simmer down." Jinx gave her a fraternal squeeze, but she jerked free. "What am I supposed to do without a secretary?"

"You'll find the answer in your own question. *Do without*." Her eyes cut to the hole in the wall. "My husband's here."

The nose on Georgia's rheumy-eyed mate still glowed from his morning bender; he nodded by way of hello.

Jinx wanted to take her into the back office. To ask her to stay, and maybe even apologize. He'd acknowledge being insensitive. Maybe explain he'd been under considerable stress what with the office going to shit and all. But the sight of Georgia pushing past, crunching glass underfoot and padding down the hall out of sight, siphoned off the last of his energy.

She couldn't walk out. Didn't she realize?

*He needed her.*

He headed back to his office when the sweet whiff of freshly burned pipe tobacco turned him around.

Sid said, "Was that Georgia's husband?"

"As a matter of fact, yes."

"Boy, am I embarrassed. That old wino pulled into the disabled space. I was about to jam one of my boots up his boxers when I caught sight of his license tags. Would you believe it? Sombitch got a Purple Heart in The Big One. Ain't that a banana up the tailpipe?"

A light mist bathed passersby, marking the end of another scorching day, and everyone wore a smile on their face but Jinx and the grim-faced ATF boys.

The phone rang, and Jinx caught it on the second jingle. While the agents packed up the last of their gear, he instigated a lively discussion with the county's personnel director. The conversation reached its most feverish pitch when Jinx questioned the man's parentage, and climaxed when he slammed Georgia's phone into its cradle with enough pounds per square inch to crack the earpiece.

Dell gathered his briefcase, butted his haunches against his desk and waited for the verdict.

"They say that quack Georgia sees cleared the way for her to take emergency family leave," Jinx explained.

Dell remained stone-faced. Maybe he didn't get it. Jinx shed light on the predicament.

"We can't get a replacement secretary until her leave runs out." Two lines lit up at once. Jinx kept talking. "It runs out in ninety days."

Dell's face went from a healthy shade of tan to red. The veins in his neck plumped up like garden hoses.

"Jiminy Christmas, how in God's name are we supposed to operate three months without a secretary?" Jinx looked to Sid and sensed encouragement in his glance.

All five lines glowed. Dell leaned across the desk and lifted the receiver. One by one, he punched each button, extinguishing the lights. With the extensions disabled, he walked to the door, tugged off the paper booties, and dropped them into a grocery bag Rusty placed at the exit. There, he waited for Mickey the way he did every afternoon at quittin' time.

Sid offered a solution. "Assign Ivy to answer phones."

*An idea worse than not having a secretary.*

Rusty filed out with cardboard boxes filled with evidence.

The lead ATF agent caught Jinx's attention. "We're loading up. Everyone needs to clear out so we can seal the place off."

"Gimme a minute. I need to make a couple of calls."

"We'll be back, early morning." The agent stepped into the exterior hall with the oversized tackle boxes. "Don't jack with anything." He took a few steps and whipped around. "One more thing—if the media corners you and wants a comment, here are your options." He ticked off the choices on two fingers. "You can either say the device functioned as designed, or it didn't function as designed. That's it. You don't disclose how the bomb was made."

"So I should say it functioned as designed?"

A perturbed look played across his face. "Obviously, it didn't function as designed or some of you would be dead."

"So it didn't function as designed."

"Of course it did. It went off, didn't it? Tell you what, Porter—anybody asks you for the particulars, you say 'No comment' and refer them to me."

The ATF boys stepped out in the hall and waited.

Beleaguered, Jinx said, "What am I supposed to do without Georgia?"

Sid brainstormed. "You could play secretary and let me patrol. Help your shoulder mend."

He fought off an apocalypse—Sid, putting a cheap move on an innocent voter. "Thanks, but I want to get reelected."

Sid tilted his hat enough to expose the Klevenhagen squint. "You could defy the sombitches and hire a temp."

"What?" Jinx wasn't sure he heard right, but Sid's head bobbed like a spring-loaded Chihuahua in the back dash of a low-rider.

"Get some minimum wage wench from a temporary agency. That way, it won't hurt as much if you end up paying her salary out of your own pocket."

Atlas took the world off his shoulders.

Euphoric, Jinx grinned. "Great idea." He dug the yellow pages out of Georgia's desk, released a line, and dialed. The phone purred.

Dell spoke. "Get one who'll work."

Gil, examining his mangled sleeve, crunched through broken glass and angled over to his desk.

Mickey came out of the bathroom. He let out a low whistle. "What happened, Gil? Fall on a pitchfork?"

The chief deputy rolled up his cuff and exposed a couple of angry, red puncture wounds. "My wife's dog mauled me when I stopped in for lunch." He picked at the bloody spots.

"Want me to knock out his teeth with my Maglite?"

Gil shook his head. "I already did that. Cost me two thousand dollars. My wife took him to the doggie dentist for new porcelain fangs. Take it from me—the old teeth were better. Not as sharp, and they didn't go as deep. These are like ice picks." He rolled down his sleeve. "My wife likes that dog better than me. She's probably at the vet's, making sure Blackie doesn't contract rabies."

Dell cleared his throat. In his unique, abbreviated manner, he caught the chief deputy up on Georgia's departure. "We're getting a new-hire. Georgia bailed on us."

The third ring trilled through the earpiece.

"Get one without kids," said Mickey. "Kids get sick."

"Get one who can type." Gil.

On the fourth ring, the agency answered.

Across the room, Sid bellowed, "Get one with big tits."

With a wave, *adiós,* and a "Meetcha back at the house," Jinx left the hole in the wall and walked over to the Tarrant County Corrections building.

No Raven.

Probably already remanded into the custody of the jailers.

With his pulse throbbing in his throat, he approached the bond desk. Caught the officer's attention.

"How much is Raven's bond?"

"Minimum, fifty thousand dollars. But the judge may raise it once she's arraigned."

"How much down on a fifty-thousand-dollar bond?"

"Ten percent."

Jinx reached into his back pocket.

"Take a personal check?"

★ ★ ★ ★ ★

Raven had barely removed her clothes for the strip search when the intercom buzzed and a disembodied male voice boomed over the speaker.

"Bring Raven downstairs. Her bond's been posted. We're doing a walk-through on her."

She wanted to cry and willed herself not to.

Thank God for friends like Ben Jennings. If it took the rest of her life, she'd see to it the lawyer had home-cooked meals three times a week, plenty of Crown Royal for Christmas and a lifetime supply of sheepskin condoms.

She processed out in a filthy mood, then power walked across the street to the PD to report her BMW stolen. Counting the wait, it took over an hour to give a report to the detective. When she finished, she tried Ben Jennings's office and got a busy signal.

Fuck it, she thought, envisioning the five-mile walk home.

It would take that long to get beyond her fury at Jinx Porter.

# Chapter Sixteen

Once Raven arrived home, she remembered the C-4 Yucatan Jay molded to the window latch in her bedroom. She trundled up the stairs and stared at the glob for a good ten minutes before deciding what to do.

Yucatan Jay was nice enough to leave the telephone cords on top of the dresser. She found her handguns inside the top drawer. The Mossberg ended up between the mattress and box springs. With all the firearms accounted for, she plugged in the bedroom phone and dialed Information.

The operator answered. Raven said, "I need the number for the CIA."

She copied it down, released the line, and collected her thoughts.

Hi. I'd like to talk to y'all about a CIA agent named Yucatan Jay. You know the one: dresses like a ninja; has a big-ass, 3-D, hummingbird tattoo on his chest? Yeah, that's the guy. Get me his supervisior.

Hi. Do you have an Internal Affairs division? I'd like to file a complaint.

Hi. I'm supposed to call this number and say Code Jerry. Does that mean anything to you? Roger.

Hi. I'm a lunatic so none of this story'll make any sense.

By the time she figured out what to say that wouldn't make her sound like a freak show, the office had closed and she was treated to a recorded menu selection.

Next, she tried the number for the local FBI office, and was routed to the voice mail of Special Agent Longley. A shrill tone signaled her to leave a message.

"Yes, hi. I'm calling because I couldn't reach the CIA. One of their agents broke into my house over the weekend and held me hostage. I believe he left a wad of plastique on my bedroom window, and I thought maybe you guys could come check it out." She took a deep breath and realized how bizarre she sounded. "You're probably thinking this is a crank call. I know it sounds weird—a CIA agent? How many times does that happen in real life? Would he even tell me he was CIA? I thought the whole point of being CIA was to keep it secret. Does that make sense?"

*Screw it. It doesn't make any sense to me. Why should it make sense to the FBI?*

*Raven, are you just trying to get yourself locked up again?*

*They're gonna put you in the booby hatch.*

*Hang up.*

*What the hell's wrong with you?*

*The little voice in her head screamed loud enough to jar her eyes permanently open.*

*Hang up the fucking phone you idiot.*

"Okay, well, never mind. Good-bye."

But a wad of plastique close enough to blow her to glory was enough to frighten her back into action. She dialed 911.

"Police operator."

"I filed a police report on a stolen car earlier this afternoon. Someone broke into my house over the weekend and took my car. I just discovered a strange device in my bedroom, and I'd like you to send the EOD team over to have a look at it. I think it may be some type of explosive device."

The dispatcher verified her name and confirmed the address. "We'll send someone by."

With a profound sense of relief, Raven sank onto the king-sized bed. Glimpsing herself in the bathroom mirror triggered an eye roll. Filthy clothes, broken sandal strap and a nest of hair so snarled it needed traffic flares. She was about to hop into the shower when the scream of approaching sirens brought no less than half a dozen cops and a fire engine full of sparkies fanning out across her yard.

She thundered down the stairs as the doorbell chimed.

In under ten minutes, Raven felt like the biggest fool in Cowtown. There would be no rendering-safe procedure. No total containment vessel. No track-driven robot, running on a tether, with an arm and a claw and TV cameras and sound equipment to see and hear.

Yucatan Jay didn't stick C-4 on her window hardware.

As best the Explosives Ordnance Detatchment could tell when the bomb K-9 loped upstairs with his sniffer hot-wired for explosives, Raven's cousin stuck plain old, Big Red chewing gum on the catch.

She wanted to thunk her head against the doorjamb until a big knot plumped up.

Stupid, stupid, stupid.

Yucatan Jay was no CIA agent.

Yucatan Jay was nothing but a con man, acting out some stupid part in his schizophrenic head.

Matter of fact, as best she could tell, the only good that came out of today was when one of the uniformed officers informed her the police found her car.

Yucatan Jay had left the BMW exactly where she predicted he would.

Only he didn't leave it at the Will Rogers complex, in a parking space where it wouldn't be found for days.

Oh, no.

Psycho-prick left it in a no parking zone, next to a fire

hydrant, where it would be found almost immediately.

Which meant the police towed it to the police auto pound.

Where it accrued storage fees the moment the wrecker hooked up.

And where a dozen people, no doubt, left fingerprints on it since ten o'clock that morning.

Yucatan Jay was a gentleman, all right.

If she never again thought of that asshole until it was time to confer the Turd-of-the-Year award, it wouldn't be a moment too soon.

And, the nicest thing for the recipient meant that the winner didn't have to be present to win.

The tribute could be given *in absentia.*

At the cabana, Jinx and Sid changed clothes.

Several hours later, they left the Ancient Mariner with Sid exuding his own essence of barroom.

Jinx offered to be the designated driver. "Where to now? Cosmo's is still open. We have time to stop off for sliced brisket."

"Time's exactly what you don't have." Sid held him in his falcon-eyed gaze. He slurred out some advice. "Keep your friends close and your enemies closer."

"What're you saying?"

"You think this Raven gal had nothing to do with this? Fine—have her come work for you. Best way I know to keep her under wraps until the investigation's concluded."

"Hire her? Are you nuts?"

"Sound crazy? It should. Especially since she tried to kill you."

"There's no money in the budget."

"Then, make her a reserve deputy constable. By the time the investigation's over, she'll either be cooling her hocks in jail, or she'll be cleared." Sid scratched the itch of suspicion. "Let's go have a talk with your little bombshell."

The old man made a good point.

He offered Jinx the use of his cell phone.

Jinx tapped out Raven's number and hoped she wouldn't answer.

He recognized the sultry voice as soon as she picked up.

"Raven . . . it's Jinx."

"I know." Long pause. "I have a little voodoo doll right here—after I ripped out its hair, looks just like you. Does your head hurt?" Dead silence. "What do you want?"

"Somebody tried to kill me. Three times. I had you pegged for it."

Another long pause. "What can I say, Jinx? Apparently I'm not the only one who thinks you're a grade-A son of a bitch."

He didn't phone to rehash their relationship, merely to vector her location. "What're you doing right now?"

"I'm about to snip off your pecker. Oh, look—there it goes. Feel that?"

"That's enough, Raven. I want to talk to you."

"You know where I live."

The click of a dead connection stung in his ear.

On the drive to Raven's, Jinx wondered whether Georgia walked out for good. When the time came, he bounced his worry off Sid.

"I can't imagine what'll happen if I don't get her back."

Sid gave him the Klevenhagen squint. "Raven?"

"Georgia." He turned off the main drag, and slowed at a sharp bend.

"Thought you said she was a bad secretary."

"She is."

"Then, let's celebrate her departure with a twelve-pack."

"I'm just like every other male in Cowtown. I don't like change."

Sid wasn't buying it. "Is that why you fooled around? Because you didn't like change? Face it. Every man alive likes stray booger. I had a gal pal once—let me tell you that open marriage, free love, free sex mentality takes the sport outta cheatin'. I had to trade my first wife in on one of those clingy types. Then, cheatin' was fun."

Jinx caught himself nodding. "I made a mistake. I had an old friend . . . we'd get together on a regular basis. She didn't have anybody—" He glanced over at Sid and got an ugly visual of Loose-Wheel Lucille gobbling Sid's goober. "—least I thought she didn't have anybody. Then, Raven came along."

*So, Jinx Porter . . . you're not in a relationship? Because I wouldn't want to step on any toes.*

*None to step on.*

*When's the last time you had a girlfriend?*

*A year ago. You want to go out, or not?*

*Not if you're on the rebound.*

"I knew Raven was the one for me. I just couldn't find a way to let the other woman down."

"That's a crock." Sid got missile lock on him. "Face it, hoss, you're just like the rest of us heathens. We're gonna get poontang wherever we find it."

"Did you ever care for someone enough to take a bullet for them?"

"Still love her, don'tcha?"

Silence.

Sid pushed the seat back and stretched his legs as far as they would go. "How much longer?"

"Two seconds."

But he was thinking, *Not long enough.*

# Chapter Seventeen

Holy smoke. Raven surveyed the mess.

She'd need a dragline and a Caterpillar to straighten the living room; it half-surprised her kudzu hadn't started twining itself through the furniture. In the end, she grabbed a heavy-duty garbage bag, raked the unwashed breakfast dishes off the dining table, and hurried to the back porch. She hid the sack among the rest of the trash bagged for collection, along with a couple of glasses Yucatan Jay touched.

Those, she kept for fingerprint comparison purposes.

Outside on the patio, Lupita, the Guatemalan housekeeper who showed up for a few hours each Monday afternoon, scrubbed patio furniture.

Raven shucked off her jeans and T-shirt, balled them up and stuffed them into the hamper. She cranked on the hot and cold water, testing for the right combination, before jumping into the shower. She caught her reflection and moved in for a closer look. Wiped the steam off the mirror and scrutinized her face. Tiny laugh lines had formed near her eyes, and the dimples she had as a child were barely visible when she smiled. Until today, Jinx Porter—that emotionally defective son of a bitch—hadn't seen her up close in almost two years. And when they finally ran into each other, she looked like she'd been rolled.

*Why do you care what that asshole thinks?*

But she knew. With that first introduction, she'd programmed her internal autopilot on a one-man course to self-destruction.

Not now, though.

Now, she saw him for what he truly was. A twenty-four carat, gold-plated turd.

Jinx Porter had won the Turd-of-the-Week award more than any other contender. After fifty-two weeks, he was the odds-on favorite for Turd-of-the-Year, ranking right up there beside a couple of lawyers. The only decision left to make was determining who got inducted into the Turd Hall of Fame.

She gnawed a hole in a sample packet of Lolita Lempicka bath gel and slathered the fragrant goo all over.

What to wear?

Too early for the black strapless cocktail dress that made men's necks snap. Jinx would know she didn't have a date after being in lockup most of the afternoon.

That new sweat suit from Land's End?

Too casual.

In the end, she settled on an ice-pink cashmere turtleneck and a pair of camel hair slacks that said, *I'm fashionable, successful and men lust after me; do you still troll the personals looking for dates?*

She'd barely broken out the Lancôme and powdered her nose when she heard the crunch of tires against gravel.

*Jinx.*

"Lupita!"

No answer.

She corraled her breasts, shrugged into the sweater and hurried to the window.

"Lupita, the door!"

At the curb of Raven's old Astrid Street address, Jinx took

in the sight. Gone was the 1920s bungalow. Gone, too, was the stained glass window of purple and yellow bearded irises recessed in the gable. In fact, the entire façade had been re-bricked, stuccoed, and another level added to the former three-bedroom house. Raven lived in a Tuscan villa.

*The Lonely Constable*—that little tart noir she wrote that still had Ivy stewing in her own juices—must've done all right in the bookstores.

Jinx jammed Sid's truck into park, unfurled the Dogs Playing Poker tie and knotted it around his neck. He gave it a good snap, then cut the engine and wrangled out from behind the steering wheel. A floral breeze grazed his cheek, bringing with it an unexpected moment of dread.

His heart picked up its pace. "This is bullshit. Let's hit the road."

"Not 'til we talk to her."

He let out a resigned sigh and headed for the house. In a way, coming here was worse than what happened at Marble-Eye's. When dealing with Raven, there was more than one way to get shot down.

With a clench in her chest, Raven separated the wooden blinds and watched Jinx angle across the lawn. The low-voltage sexual current running through her hit the breaker switch the moment she saw the old geezer trailing him.

The man with Jinx—a rough-cut, handsome, Texas Rangers kind of guy—looked tougher than a two-dollar steak. She sharpened her vision into a squint. Jeez Louise. He was the spitting image of that notorious PD lieutenant, Sid Klevenhagen.

Once they reached the archway to the porch, Raven knew for sure.

It didn't take her long to tell shit from shinola. Having Sid

Klevenhagen appear at the house meant wearing stripes.

Realizing the gravity of Jinx's visit, she snatched up the cordless phone. He really did think she tried to kill him. She pressed her thumb against the keypad, located Ben Jennings's number, then hit speed-dial.

She got his voice mail and spoke in a hyperventilating rush.

"It's Raven. It's an emergency. Call me back. If I don't answer, meet me at the jail—and bring plenty of money because you'll need to post my bail again."

"Ring the bell, hoss."

Jinx didn't budge; he cocked an ear to listen.

Sid pointed out the fly in the ointment. "Caught her watching us from upstairs." He touched a blistered finger the size of a ballpark frank to the buzzer.

Jinx felt his throat close. He bathed his tonsils with a hard swallow.

Through thick panels of leaded glass, a shadowy blob shaped itself into human form. A snap of the dead bolt left a knot in Jinx's stomach. The massive wood door parted a sliver to expose a chain latch. A wondrous eye the color of melted chocolate peered out.

*"Sí?"*

Sid took charge. "You speak English?"

*"¿Cómo?"*

"You got a señorita whatchacallit—" He snapped his fingers close to his ear. It seemed to jog the cobwebs loose because he said, "*Cuervo*. Raven." He folded his arms into wings and flapped.

*"¿Cómo?"* Flat stare.

Jinx studied Sid's face. "You know Spanish?"

"Little bit. *Poquito*."

"Well, I've seen you in action enough to know that if you start trying to communicate with this woman without knowing what you're talking about, we're probably going to end up as defendants in a criminal trespass suit."

Sid reared back, hurt. "I didn't say a damned thing except to ask about your gal—"

"I meant—"

"—and if she don't like it—" Sid thumbed at the mousey girl behind the door. "—let's call *la migra* and let them wring it out of her."

A rusty hinge, south o' the border, *Aaaaeeeeeiiiiii* pierced the air, followed by a staccato string of foreign speech that carried all the earmarks of profanity. The door slammed shut. The shape dissolved into the unlit interior.

"Jiminy Christmas, why'd you go and mention Immigration? Now we'll never find out anything."

"Somebody's coming," Sid said coolly.

"Why'd you insist—"

A shadow reappeared behind the leaded glass. The unmistakable sound of a chain sliding out of its track froze the words in Jinx's throat.

Sid growled, "Look alive."

The door opened wide.

Raven.

For Raven, departing Jinx Porter's bedroom two years before signaled the end of an error.

But when she opened the door to reveal the unsmiling faces of two lawdogs, and saw the birthday tie she'd given him, she didn't know whether to laugh, or knee him in the stones with her soprano maker. Without the extra coating of sheetrock, he seemed a few pounds lighter. He wore the expression of a man who dove off a high bridge and had the oxygen forced out of his lungs on impact.

The fearsome-looking, leathery-faced lieutenant kept quiet, but recrimination swam in his eyes.

Jinx broke the awkward silence. "This is Sid Kleven-hagen."

"Pleased to meetcha." Sid. No handshake.

Raven acknowledged him with a nod. She stepped aside and let them in.

"How's the Siamese?" It was a good way to begin the con-versation and in no way reflected the emotional skirmish breaking out inside her.

"Caesar?" Jinx grinned. "He's the best. Still cantan-kerous. I had to pay for new blinds . . . the apartment man-ager said the way the cat customized them looked ugly from the street."

"I'd offer you a drink but you're not staying," she said with fake cheer. "So, what's on your mind?"

"I guess you heard about the shooting," Jinx said.

"I wouldn't know. I was in New York until last Friday."

She slid Sid a sideways glance. A large oil painting of a lady in Gothic dress, posed in an English garden, hung over the fireplace, ensconced in an elaborate gilt frame, and the old man seemed to be taking in the details of the breathtaking canvas. His eyes flickered momentarily to the floor, where rich Oriental rugs stretched out to touch the ball-and-claw feet of fine antiques.

Jinx spoke. "How long were you in the Big Apple?"

"A few days. Who got shot?"

"Me."

"Well, you look all better now."

His jaw tensed. "You came to the hospital."

"You must be delirious."

"I heard you." Jinx gave her a pointed look, locking her in

his invisible force field.

Sid said, "A woman driving a Mercedes did donuts over her husband awhile back. When she finished mowing him down, she parked on top of him. Of course, I ain't saying you'd do something like that . . . you're more into guns and bombs, aren't you?"

*Securing Klevenhagen a spot at the top of the Turd-of-the-Week list.*

She wanted to tell him she understood the woman's desperation—that she knew how it felt to be rejected in favor of an inferior—that she'd walked in on Jinx getting a tongue lashing from that lush in the corner apartment, and almost dropped dead on the spot. She wanted to tell Klevenhagen she would've acquitted the Benz owner and maybe even pinned on a medal if she'd sat on the woman's jury—because she'd have done the same thing. That if it had been her driving that big-ass luxury car, the only thing she would've done any different after she parked the car on top of that cheating scoundrel, would be to swallow the key.

*Men shouldn't do mean things to the women who loved them.*

She caught Sid ogling her breasts and folded her arms across her chest. Like beads of water on a hot skillet, fury sizzled behind her eyeballs. She turned to Jinx, and keyed in on the strange look in his eyes.

Her heart skidded in her chest. "You came to rearrest me?"

*Catapulting him into the vacant position for Turd Emeritus.*

Jinx cut his gaze to Sid and back. "You're the best investigator I had. I'd like—for old times' sake—if anybody can figure out who's behind this, you can—"

"What're you saying?"

"You could start tomorrow. Check in with Personnel and get your paperwork done. Then report to the office."

"Let me get this straight. You're asking me to come back to work for you?" Bewildered by his suggestion, her eyes darted over the room. "You want *me* to work for *you?*"

"Just a thought."

"That's what you came to ask me?"

"Are you coming back or not?"

"You're not here to haul me downtown?"

"No."

He looked at Sid, still inventorying the room with his gaze, and said, "Excuse us a minute," then pulled her farther into the house. They ended up in the kitchen, a large room with pale, candelight-yellow walls, frescoed in a burnished glaze. A cook's rack of copper pots hung from the ceiling above the stove. The granite-topped island in the center of the floor showed no sign of cutlery previously on display before Yucatan Jay's visit.

She spied the little snub-nose from the vegetable bin, near the spice rack on the counter.

Jinx broke into her thoughts. "It's an inside job. Whoever wants me gone works for me. You supervised these people. Did any of them ever act like they had an axe to grind?"

Raven let out an unamused chuckle. "There's a wax buildup of negativity around you, Jinx. You're asking me who wants you gone? You may not know this, but you're a prick. Which leads us full circle. Why should I help you?"

That bought her a few seconds to consider her options.

"Because they like you. You're probably the only one who can get close enough to figure out who it is—and why. Frankly, I think it's your boyfriend."

She scrunched her face. "What boyfriend?"

"Dell. I've seen how he looks at you. He'd screw your brains out if you gave him half a chance."

"He's a friend. Nothing more, nothing less. Not that it's

any of your business—"

"Aw, bullshit. Don't act like you don't know. He practically sniffs your crotch—"

"—so don't even think you can tell me who I can and cannot hang out with, and besides, Dell's married and I don't date married men—"

"—ever since he laid eyes on you. He wants me out of the way so he can have you for himself."

"—unlike you, Jinx Porter, who could care less about commitment."

*This is what frustrated her.*

*Talking in circles; not making a lick of sense.*

*Dell? Hot for her? Nah . . .*

The very idea made her laugh. Made her want to ball up her fist and take a swing at him. To shake him 'til his head rattled and his teeth chattered.

To pound his wounded shoulder until he explained why he porked Loose-Wheel Lucille. No, she didn't have anything to do with him getting shot, but she could sure as hell understand why someone might want to empty a magazine into him.

"The only reason my friendship with Dell would bother you, is if you wanted a relationship—"

"I don't."

"—and that's never going to happen, Jinx Porter. Not in a million years." The heat of fury scalded her eyes. "And leave Dell outta this. If anybody wants to kill you, it's probably Ivy."

"Now you're trying to start some shit."

"Ha! Everybody knows about the time she got drunk and you got laid. The guys said—"

"Never happened."

"—after a shift party, Ivy got so plastered she had to bum a ride home from you—"

"Totally made up."

"—and you screwed her—"

"That's enough."

"—with Amos in the next bedroom."

From the heart of the living room, Sid intervened. "Cut the crap or I'm gonna come in there, give each of you a steak knife, stick you in opposite corners and give the command to run at each other."

Raven hissed, "That's why you keep her around when you should've fired her after she wrecked her tenth patrol car." Three years of pure, unvarnished anger bubbled to the surface. "You locked me up!" Pressure built in her head. "I was halfway to a strip search by some bull-dyke jailer when they called up and said Ben Jennings bonded me out—"

"Ben Jennings?"

"—and let me tell you, if you think I'll forget that degradation anytime soon—"

"Jennings didn't bail you out."

"—you can kiss my—"

"I did."

*Huh?*

# Chapter Eighteen

Around five-thirty Tuesday morning, Jinx dressed minus the sling. Within the hour, he left Sid snoozing. If all went well, they'd link up around eleven after Sid finished his doctor's appointment.

On the walk to the car, he stopped in the pungent air of the gray, velveteen dawn. Near the lush landscape that obscured Sid's cabana from the main house, he took in a deep breath, savoring the herbal scent of freshly raked leaves. With his gaze, he scaled Betsy's exterior wall to the only lighted window on the second floor.

Beyond the bathroom's glass bricks, a feminine silhouette, amply endowed, came into view. He wondered if his memory was playing mind tricks, or if the glass bricks distorted the attributes of Sid's willowy daughter. Her arms reached high, and when she made the slow rotation beneath the shower-head, a profile of ponderous knockers threw his beating heart offtrack.

Within the dense cover of the hedge, he felt a jolt in his groin and guiltlessly envisioned himself transmigrating into Betsy's bath. He told himself she wasn't that bad. That he felt drawn to spirited women. That he wanted to throw her down, to paw her—

Jiminy Christmas.

The unexpected appearance of an intruder cold-cocked his fantasy right out the upstairs window and back into the thorny bougainvillea. Helplessly entranced, and hopelessly pissed, he continued to watch.

The second body had door buzzers, not knockers. And, boyishly short hair. Before his voyeuristic eyes, the women fused together. As living art, they became a free-form sculpture, wrapping themselves in each other's pleasure, meshing body parts, entangling limbs, and locking lips.

*Betsy digs chicks.*

The sight made his retinas pulse. He found himself unable—or unwilling—to tear his gaze from their mating ritual. Only when they sank below the windowsill, did the show fade to the creamy glow of an incandescent bulb.

Poor Sid. No wonder he tried to fix up his maladjusted only child with a real man.

Jinx made his way to the car, fired up the engine and headed to Georgia's frame house on the north side to make amends. If it took bribing her with a raise, he'd do it. If that didn't work, he'd throw in two funerals a month, *gratis*.

A block away, he checked his watch. Seven-o-five.

The simple clapboard house had a magnetic appeal that grew out of old-world pride of ownership. As he walked up the sidewalk, it pleased him to see a light on in the kitchen. Maybe she'd cook him a ham and cheese omelet. They'd sit at the table . . . she could apologize for walking out . . . he'd give her an extra half-hour to get back into the office where she belonged.

Swaddled in a terry cloth bathrobe, with the hint of a flowered housedress peeking out at the neck, Georgia opened the screen door. Minus the pineapple-stem hairpiece, her head appeared smaller, her jawline squarer, and her eyes almost swollen shut. She offered a grudging greeting devoid of enthusiasm, but the weight of her judgment settled in her stare.

"Mind if I come in?"

She did an about-face, flip-flopped down the hallway in her slippers and left him standing at the threshold. He regarded the silent treatment as an invitation.

The house was barely more than a cracker box, with a few dismal pieces of secondhand furniture stained dark and livened up with doilies, and a handful of area rugs scattered about to warm the maple plank floors. But, the detail in the ceiling's crown molding retained an exquisite patina next to the watercolor paint job coating the walls.

Georgia disappeared at the far end of the hall. A Trojan horse–sized dog came in from a side room, his tail drooping and a look of intelligence settling across his furrowed face. Jinx recognized him from his picture. Buckwheat goosed him with a cold, wet nose, speeding him into the kitchen.

The game of follow-the-leader ended at an aluminum table with marbled yellow Formica and ice cream parlor chairs covered in matching vinyl. Georgia stood at the Roper range, with her back to him, boiling water for cocoa. Buckwheat took his place in the doorway and watched the goings-on through luminous brown eyes.

Jinx made the first overture. "Where's the man of the house?"

"Right there." Georgia gave the dog a pointed glance.

"I meant your husband."

"Shut in with the flu."

Jinx bobbed his head, agreeably. "When can you come back?"

"You must have a brain tumor."

She hovered over the stove and poured. Somewhere between the time he whiffed the aroma of cinnamon cookies and the time he realized Georgia wasn't going to offer him any, Jinx gutted up and got down to business.

"We need you."

"Don't start." She placed a full mug in front of him and seated herself across the table. "Somebody's willing to kill the rest of us because they want you dead."

The statement came as an accusation. She watched him through angry eyes, as if he should do the noble thing and die so that others might live.

"The sheriff's putting an extra man at the building entrance."

"Big hairy deal. There were three deputies on duty while you were in ICU, the day the trash can blew up."

She could have dashed cold water on him.

*Whoever blew up the office didn't have any problem getting past security.*

He wanted to reach across the table and sandwich her fat face between his hands—to jerk her close and plant a kiss on her for being right and not even knowing it. They'd all had trouble with the mail cretin.

He made a mental note to notify ATF, and said, "They're tapping the phones," to raise her comfort level. "They'll be able to tell who calls."

"High time." She used a take-no-prisoners tone, and it startled him.

"Was yesterday's caller male or female?"

"I'm not sure." She took a sip. Her raised mug lingered close enough for steam to snake up her nostrils. "They had one of those neuter voices." The words trailed off. She stared at the froth forming at the edge of her cup.

"Georgia, I know it's not the easiest job, but we need you." Shrouded in silence, the truth became oppressive. "I need you."

There. He said it. It wasn't even that hard once he realized she had his balls loaded into an automatic baseball pitcher.

She drained the chocolate and gripped the cup with both hands. "I'm not coming back, Jinx, and you can't make me. The doctor says I have a weak heart."

*Weak, my ass.*

"I'll ask the commissioners to approve a raise." Her brow twitched and he thought he detected a bit of mild interest. "Two pay grades," he added, before she could ask.

"Make it five."

"Five?" he practically shouted. "There's no way they'll approve that."

"Oh, well," she said through an exaggerated sigh, "I guess I'll just have to take early retirement at three-quarters pay. How sad for me."

She looked like she'd won the lotto, and he knew by the added eye roll, she must be reveling in his misery.

"Three," he countered sternly. "And you're not to discuss your salary with the others, you hear? Especially Ivy."

But Georgia drove a hard bargain. "First, you get the raise approved; then, I'll tell you if I'm coming back. Otherwise—" She picked up a napkin and fanned herself. "—bad ticker."

The ATF boys had come and gone by the time Jinx straggled in. The place still had an Abominable Snowman feel. Even as the maintenance crew stepped aside to let him past the raw edges being prepped for a new door, he never expected bad news waiting only inches away.

A woman six ax handles wide, with alabaster skin and fire-engine red hair arranged in short coils, sat at Georgia's desk reading the latest *Cosmopolitan* through a pair of cat's-eye glasses right out of the fifties.

She admonished Jinx in a piping soprano. "This place is off-limits. No one gets inside without credentials."

He could see she stood around five-two. He suspected she weighed over 250.

She wrangled out of Georgia's chair. "This is Constable Porter's office. No one's allowed in without going through me."

"I'm Constable Porter." He moved the flap of his sport coat aside, displayed the seven-pointed star.

"*Ha.* Anyone can get a badge." She held out her palm in demand. "Show me some ID."

With his good hand, he pulled his badge case from the hip pocket and flopped it open.

She leaned in for a closer look, then fixed him with a gimlet-eyed stare. "Nice try, mister. I happen to know for a fact, Constable Porter's dead. Who the hell are you?"

Heat crept up his neck. The shrill pitch of her voice grated on him, and he could almost feel the capillaries in his eyes constrict. Plus, she'd caught him staring at the steel-toed boots just below the hemline of her cheetah-print skirt. His cheeks tingled with the sudden surge in blood pressure.

"I told you. I'm the constable."

"I'm calling the law." She reached for the phone, stretching her sleeves to capacity.

Jinx depressed the mechanism as soon as she snatched the receiver from its cradle. "I *am* the law. Who're *you?*"

"I happen to be the secretary."

"Georgia's the secretary." But he liked the way the redhead said it—with pride—as if being his secretary brought honor, not shame.

Her lips tightened in a smug, crimson line. "Shows how much you know, Mr. Imposter. Georgia was the secretary."

He kept his tone even and metered. "What's your name?"

"What's it to you?"

"I just want to know what name to book you in jail under."

She folded her arms across her broad expanse of bosom, and for the first time, he noticed the delicate bone structure of elegant fingers, each one ringed in gold nuggets.

Her eyes narrowed into slits. "Lemme see your driver's license."

She meant business.

She eyed his DL with icy calm, and tapped a lacquered fingernail against an incisor as if she wanted to gnaw at it. "Might be fake."

"Why would I go to the trouble to fake a driver's license?"

"Same reason you faked your ID."

"I didn't fake my ID."

"Sure did. Which makes you a dumb bastard. It ought to say Lazarus on it because you're dead."

"I assure you, madame, I'm alive and I'm pissed."

"Which is your given name?"

"You're a real smart-ass."

"Better than being a dumb ass. What's your Christian name?"

"What's it to you?"

She pursed her lips and lifted one shoulder in a give-a-damn reply. "Looks like we've come full circle. I think I'll have you arrested for impersonating a peace officer."

Sometime during the contest of wills, Jinx decided he might find it in himself to like her. Georgia believed in heaven and hell and let people use her for a doormat. All this woman needed was a wart on her nose and a broom with a turbo prop. He'd even dole out a few extra bucks for perfume that didn't scream jasmine, if that's what it took.

She called herself Dixie.

The temporary agency sent her.

And what time was lunch anyway?

She made sure he didn't get any ideas that she fetched. He

could get his own cotton-picking coffee and donuts, and he damned well better bring enough for her while he was at it. And, for that matter, he could retrieve his own papers from the clerk down the hall. She had more important things to do. After all, she was the secretary.

Dixie caught him staring at her hands. "What's the problem?"

"You have a lot of rings. Georgia didn't wear much jewelry. Said it made her hands swell."

"I'm not Georgia. I happen to like jewelry. Especially jewelry that can double as a weapon. And, until they legalize brass knuckles, I'll keep wearing what I want, thank you very much." She sank her fists into ample hips and sounded off again. "Besides, I never saw so many pistols in my life."

"What did you expect, hot glue guns? We're law enforcement. Didn't the agency tell you?"

"I don't like handguns."

"You would if you needed protection."

"Oh, yeah?" Dixie snorted in disgust. Looked him over from head to toe as if he were covered in green slime. "You're probably a Republican."

No pushover, he decided. But, if she had a future in his precinct, she'd need a sense of humor. It was Gil's nature to test a victim's mettle with practical jokes—even though Jinx warned him to cut it out. The last thing he needed was a hostile work environment complaint.

In the sanctuary of his private office, he got back to the business of wracking his brain, narrowing down a list of people who might want to see him dead. With his head resting against the loose-weave chair back, he let his thoughts drift.

The whole damned mess started with Ivy. These days, it seemed everything that spiraled straight to Fort Worth's water table, started with Ivy or that brat of hers, Amos. Somebody ought to lock him up.

Somebody probably would.

He allowed his mind to free-associate.

Raven hit the nail. Each afternoon, at quitting time, the staff fled like rats out of a burning building, making the most dangerous place in Cowtown, the parking lot, behind Ivy's car. He should've gotten rid of that idiot eighteen years ago—after she wrecked her first patrol car. And he would have, too, if she hadn't been so good at handling the prima donna doctors in the hospital district. After all, he was an elected official. An elected official with an at-will doctrine. Nitwit ought to thank her lucky stars she had a job.

Only a twit locked the keys in the car at least once a week. Ran out of gas once a month. Wrecked a car twice a year. The county garage had even stopped counting the number of shredded tires and bent rims—replaced at county expense—all on account of Ivy's refusal to change her own flats.

The more he thought, the madder he got. If Ivy's brain were a neighborhood, at least half of it would consist of vacant lots. Idiot didn't even have sense enough to wear a jacket on a cold morning . . . like when they went after Marble-Eye.

He sat bolt upright, electrified. The hair on his legs stuck straight out.

What if Marble-Eye was gunning for Ivy?

Ivy was at the office the day the trash can blew up.

Still . . . it was pitch-black when he took that bullet. And, he'd offered his jacket, a midnight-blue windbreaker with CONSTABLE spelled out in yellow letters on the back. He checked his watch. Sid had a way of cutting through the fat better than anyone he knew.

Except for Raven.

Jinx gave Sid ten more minutes, then left the office and

headed for the cabana. The doctor probably put the old guy under house arrest. Sid never mentioned just how bad his heart was, but it had to be serious to land on the cardiac floor. And, he'd never been formally released. Betsy shanghaied him.

Fifteen minutes later, Jinx wheeled the patrol car onto Betsy's cobblestone drive. He rounded the crescent of native plant beds, only to see the three-car garage open and Sid's late model pickup, nose-in.

He fumbled in his pocket for the spare key and let himself inside. The aroma of ham hocks and pinto beans filled the house. By the time he spotted the cast-iron skillet of jalapeño cornbread on top of the stove, his mouth was already churning out enough spit to form a man-made lake.

The sight of Sid at the kitchen table with six empties lined up and his eyes at half-mast, surprised him. Perched atop the table, rigid, Caesar stared intently, playing his favorite game of Blink.

Clearly, the cat won.

Jinx gave his host a gentle nudge. "Hey, pod'nah, what about that lunch?"

"Drank mine." Sid looked up. His eyes lolled with the distant glaze of unfocused misery.

Jinx could tell nystagmus had set in by the involuntary jerkiness of his retinas; he grabbed a chair and scraped it across the floor. He had to know what would make an old geezer knock off a six pack so early in the day.

"What happened at the doctor's?"

"He said I'm gonna die."

# Chapter Nineteen

Raven finished up at Personnel around ten-thirty and walked back to the criminal courts building. First, she'd find Gil Fuentes. The chief deputy could catch her up on the office goings-on, and she could get a better feel for who might be the sellout.

Inside, she was treated to a view of a large woman applying fresh lipstick, and a room layered in powder. A wooden nameplate with rough-cut letters carved out with a jigsaw spelled DIXIE, and Raven assumed this was her. The woman seemed to be assessing her through shrewd eyes.

She realized she'd scrunched her face into a mask of disgust, but Jinx didn't mention how bad it was. She'd given considerable thought to selecting the black gabardine slacks, houndstooth Chanel jacket and black Bally loafers; she hardly wanted to end up looking like a dust cloth at the end of the day.

"This is horrible."

"We had to fire the decorator. Nobody liked the Olympic cross-country theme." Dixie checked her reflection in a compact mirror, then smacked her lips together and drew a fingernail across her lipline to erase a smudge. "Can I help you?"

"Where's Georgia?"

"I imagine she's on a five-day cruise by now. In any event, she's not at this dump." She snapped the compact shut, her hand disappeared below the desk and came back empty. Compared to the size of her body, Dixie's fingers were delicate in appearance, and they meshed together like slender cogs for a perfect fit. "State your business so I can get on with mine."

"I'm Raven."

"Me, too. I've been a raving maniac ever since I walked through that opening." She unclasped her hands. "What do you want?"

"Let me start over. I'm Raven." Dixie blinked, so she said, "The new deputy constable." No reaction. "Today's my first day."

"Nobody told me."

"I'm telling you."

"Well, this I don't know for sure. Break out some ID."

Raven stared, incredulous. Dixie looked over her driver's license and screened Personnel's paperwork with the intensity of a hawk.

Dixie returned the badge case. "It's a battlefield, hon. There's no place for you to conduct business in this squalor, so figure out which one of these shitheads you want to piss off and exert squatter's rights. From here on out, you're on your own." A couple of phone buttons lit up and the ringing commenced. "Get that, will you?"

Raven sauntered over to Mickey's desk and picked up the receiver. A man identifying himself as Mozelle Gratten asked for Jinx, ranting about a traffic citation he received in Dallas.

She was jotting down Gratten's number when she overheard Dixie say, "Ivy's not here. What do you mean you have her kid? Uh-huh. Is this a ransom deal? Because if her kid's a teenager, she might not want to pay . . . hold on."

Dixie twisted in her seat. "You want to take this? The

police have Ivy's son."

Raven got rid of Gratten and punched the blinking button. She listened intently and took good notes. When she ran out of questions, she put her hand over the mouthpiece. "Get Ivy on the radio. Tell her to drop what she's doing and come back to the office."

According to the caller—an airport police sergeant—Amos had finally provided a phone number for his mother after considerable strong-arming. He wasn't exactly in custody, but a couple of airport policemen had detained him at the Delta terminal.

*In North Carolina.*

"We're all going to die." Jinx pulled a chair close to Sid and slid in for the long haul. "It starts the moment we're born. The good thing about it is we don't know for sure when it'll happen."

"Is that s'posed to make me feel better?" Sid harrumphed. "My appointment with Saint Peter's so close the doctor suggested I skip lunch to go pick out a nice set of threads."

Jinx thumbed at the neat row of dead soldiers. "Is booze the answer?"

"You'd do the same if you needed a transplant and couldn't get one." Sid cocked his head and snorted. "It's not so much that I'm not a good candidate. I'm not a candidate, period. Doctors have to be practical. Why waste a heart on an old toilet like me?"

"Tell you what, Sidney, if I end up dead first, you can have mine." He solidified the offer with a fist to Sid's knee.

A silver picture frame slipped out of the lieutenant's hand, traveled the length of his outstretched leg, and smacked the floor, facedown. Jinx retrieved it. A softer version of Betsy, with honey blonde hair and a June Cleaver dress, stared back through sepia tones.

"Your wife?"

Inert and rheumy-eyed, Sid swallowed. "This's my Raven."

Jinx's heart almost clunked to a stop. Unexpectedly, the natural order of the universe made sense. It didn't matter how big a masher Sid was, or the number of women he gave free rides on the Klevenhagen Express. The lady in the picture was his Raven; without her, he was doomed to a lifetime of indiscriminate searching.

He took another glance and handed it over. "She's pretty."

Sid's head bobbed. "Damned beautiful."

A little girl clutching the woman's skirt had Sid's fearsome glare, and a lean look that foretold trouble. Betsy.

"How long were you married?"

"Forty years. Now she's eternally resting under a big oak out at the cemetery. Margie loved to garden. I guess that's where Betsy gets her love of nature."

Jinx said nothing. Sometimes, listening did more good.

"I thought I was doing her a favor, shadin' her the way I did, but birds collect on the branches and leave droppings on the marble angel." Sid swiped his eyes with the back of his hand. "Reckon I ain't such a hotshot, after all."

If Sid hadn't figured on bird droppings, there wasn't much point bringing up the idea of tree roots.

But, whatever knowledge Sid lacked about cemeteries, he made up for in police work. Jinx was about to tell him what he'd learned through Georgia, when the Siamese alerted. Caesar sprang from the table and disappeared from the room.

In walked the village scold.

Betsy glided to the countertop balancing a chocolate pie topped with real whipped cream in one hand, and a slim cigarette in the other. A rich leather belt with interlocking gold "C"s kept her tweed slacks from sliding down her bony hips, and a blue cashmere turtleneck softened her bustline to the point of nonexistence.

She caught him staring.

Steely eyes, heavily rimmed with black pencil and filled with disdain, locked on Jinx. Then, she spied the empties on the table, took a long pull on the filter and held the smoke deep inside. After a slow exhale, she asked a pointed question that made her fleshy lips less inviting, and exploded the lusty image of lean, hungry bodies, silhouetted in the backlighting of her shower.

"How long will you be staying, Mr. Potter?"

"Porter."

"Yes, of course." She clipped each word. "Will you be here much longer?"

She had a clever way of inflicting verbal right hooks to his self-esteem. Fortunately, Jinx didn't have to answer. The cat slunk in with mistrust in his unblinking eyes. His presence started a sneezing fit that took Betsy right out of the cabana.

Sid cleared the table and headed for the sink.

"Don't mind Betsy," he said. "I think she's got it bad for you."

Instead of setting Sid straight, Jinx relayed his conversation with Georgia. By the end, Sid's eyes lit up with a sudden burst of clarity, and the glassy-eyed fog from five minutes before seemed to lift.

Only Sid had a different take when it came to defeating security. "Get a roster of the sheriff's new-hires for the last three months."

"That won't be easy. In case you haven't been keeping up, there's no love lost between the constable's office and the sheriff."

"Give the job to the ATF, or let me handle it." He lifted his arm and pumped up a bicep. "I got this old gal up there who'd bark like a dog for a flex of the ol' Klevenhagen muscle."

For somebody on his last legs, Sid looked very much alive.

Close to eleven that morning, Ivy ambled into the office with her hair in a tangle. She slung her oversized leather bag beneath the kneehole desk, eyed Raven warily and flopped into her chair. "What's this about? I have three papers left to serve. I want to get off early today so I can pick Amos up from school and go home in time for a soak in the hot tub before my bingo group starts."

The last thing Raven wanted was to piss off Ivy. It wasn't as if they were friends; they didn't particularly work well together, and Raven thought Ivy's motherly instincts left a lot to be desired. When it came to filling her in on how Amos boarded the red-eye for Disney World that morning and missed his connecting flight, she thought it would be better if Ivy got the details from the airport police on her own.

She walked over to the desk and handed her the phone number.

"What's this?" Ivy snorted. "The principal's office? Because if it's the principal again, Amos is entitled to receive an education. It's not his fault the teacher can't keep order in his class."

"It's the airport police. In North Carolina. They want to talk to you."

"Is this about a paper? Because I don't have any out-of-state papers."

"Just call it." Raven looked at Dixie for support. She didn't get it. Dixie had managed to log onto eBay through the county's internet system and seemed to be caught up in a bid-ding war for cat toys. When Raven glanced back at Ivy, the woman had the telephone receiver pressed to her ear and was picking at her gums with a toothpick.

"This is Ivy from the Tarrant County constable's office. I'm returning a call." Seemingly startled, she pulled out the toothpick and positioned it like a dagger. "On his way to Disney World? Not my kid; my boy's in school until three." Long pause. "My son's name's Amos." Longer pause. "Describe him." Ivy's mouth angled up in a polite smirk. "*Ha*. Shows how much you know—Amos doesn't have a tattoo of Anna Nicole Smith."

Dixie looked up from the computer screen and rolled her eyes.

Raven whispered, "Bet it's on his arm. Amos's arms are a little on the pudgy side."

"I heard that, Raven." Ivy shifted her gaze from a cork wallboard featuring photos of Amos from birth to present day. "Amos is not fat. He's big for his age." She returned her attention to the phone. "Yes, Amos has a backpack, but—yes, it has a picture of that train wreck of a woman on it. No, I did not buy it for him, he painted it on there himself. How should I know? He probably copied it out of *Playboy*." She sat up rigid. "No, I do not buy them for him. It's that kid, Stevie, down at the trailer park. That rascal steals them from his father."

Dixie logged in a bid and sniggered.

Ivy snapped, "I heard that." After a long pause, she said, "If that kid you've got in custody is mine, I'll kiss your ass on the courthouse steps. Put him on the phone . . . Amos?" Arrogance disappeared, replaced by horror. "What the hell are you doing in Raleigh, North Carolina? Did you get a tattoo?" Short pause, then, "If it's not the kind that washes off with soap and water, I'm gonna skin your peter!" Another pause.

"Put the sergeant back on the phone."

Ivy's eyes darted over the room. She stiffened in her chair. "You put that kid on the first flight back to DFW or I'll have your ass on a platter. Don't you get smart with me, mister. Those Delta people are at fault. They never shoulda let him get on that plane in the first place without an adult. He does *not* look eighteen. Gimme your name and badge number. We'll see about this shit."

She slammed down the phone and snatched up her purse. "You—" She pointed a cocked finger at Raven. "—come with me. We're going to DFW. I'm gonna get my boy back, and you're gonna be my witness when I sue the airport."

# Chapter Twenty

A few feet from the new door—the one with CONSTAB stenciled on, and the manufacturer's sticker still on the glass—Jinx wondered if the chemistry between Dixie and Sid would be explosive. After all, hiring a temp was Sid's brainchild.

"By the way," he said, "the temporary agency sent a replacement."

A lurid grin appeared on Sid's face. He cupped his hands a foot from his chest. "Thirty-eights, or forty-fives?"

"B-fifty-twos." Jinx wagged a finger in a no motion. "Until Georgia comes to her senses, I want you on your best behavior. Besides, I don't think the new gal's your size." He winced.

*Type. He meant type.*

They were already inside before he realized he hadn't extracted any promises from Sid.

Dixie sat behind Georgia's desk, wrapped in a leopard-print shawl, with her face concealed by an open copy of *W* and a telephone receiver rooted to her ear. They paused nearby, waiting for her to hang up. Instead, she dropped the magazine, covered the mouthpiece with her hand, and dismissed Sid with a cut of the eyes.

"Who's Van Slycke?" she asked.

Jinx pointed to the empty desk off to her right. "Mickey Van Slycke. One of my deputies. Why?"

"It's some guy Mickey stopped on traffic. He's carping up

a blue streak," she said in a loud whisper.

Jinx glanced over at Gil, sporting a mummified arm from the dog bite. "You're my chief deputy. You handle it."

Gil gave Dixie the go-ahead and she routed the call.

Gil listened in silence. He rocked his head from side to side, did an eye roll at the ceiling and picked at the tape securing the gauze bandage. Abruptly, the pantomime ended.

"Appreciate your call," he said cheerily. "We'll fire him." He hung up and relaxed.

Jinx grimaced inwardly. They were a big, dysfunctional family: two gunslingers with nonintegrated personalities, a crash-test dummy, a secretary with Munchausen syndrome, and a guy who shared his wife with Cujo. The only thing keeping him from lumping in the police lieutenant with a dick longer than his own lifeline, and the temp whose cat's-eye glasses sparkled with rhinestones, was that Sid planned to return to the PD as soon as they received his medical clearance, and Dixie wasn't a permanent employee.

Thank God these misfits had a normal leader.

He turned his attention to Dixie. She and Sid were sniffing each other with their eyes with such intensity he half-expected them to start circling the furniture and hiking legs.

Sid broke the silence. "You on safari?"

"Are you being funny?" Dixie's eyes narrowed enough to spell trouble.

"I've got a bearskin hide you might be interested in checking out."

Jinx jumped in before Sid could say anything that might get them in dutch—before Dixie could figure out whether the hide Sid spoke of referred to his old leathery skin, or Yogi's. And before Sid's double entendres had a chance to root an unappetizing vision of Dixie, wallowing naked on a rug, into his brain.

"Weren't you about to gather some intelligence from the SO?"

Sid ignored him, pointing to her flaming tresses. "That hair don't look like one of nature's colors. It's pretty, but there is a way to tell for sure."

Crafty-eyed, Dixie measured Sid until he left under her watchful glare. She chewed several times—enough for a formless shape of rubbery pink to slide across her tongue like a towel in a clothes dryer—and said, "I want more money."

Jinx addressed a pet peeve. "I hate people who chew gum."

"I understand completely." The fearsome lift in her right brow, offset by the squint of her left eye, told a different story. She paid close attention to his lower lip. "I hate people who dip snuff."

"You're not getting more money."

"We'll see about that."

"Lotta people're unemployed. You ought to be glad you've got a job."

"It's you who ought to be bowing to the east when I come in. After all, I'm the secretary."

She did it again. Said, "I'm the secretary," like it was something to be proud of, not an affliction. He drew up a chair, flopped down and continued the verbal chess match. Smarty-pants needed direction if she was going to work out—plus, she left her queen exposed.

"Get it through your head once and for all, I'm the one who signs your paycheck. County employees? Feel free to vent your spleen with those pricks. Be nice to the public. Them, and me. Why's that? *Because I'm the boss.*"

*Knight to queen.*

The tilt of her chin suggested she was about to throw a clod in the churn.

"You were in the hospital for what, a week? And, the place kept functioning just like it always did the whole time you were gone?" She punctuated the statement with a curt nod. "Then, you come back, and the secretary lights out of here like somebody set fire to her britches; and while you're without a secretary for one afternoon, the place turns into a sewer. Based on this information, which of us would you say is the most important person in this office?"

*Check.*

Gil chuckled. Jinx silenced him with a glare.

Something in her genetic coding made him want to smack her silly. And the pins-and-needles tingle starting in his bum shoulder was growing worse by the minute. Should've taken the prescription pain pills, but then he couldn't drive. In the office, he'd be a sitting duck.

"Look," he snapped, "everybody here knows things are off kilter. We're trying to make the best of the chaos. If you don't like it, you can trot yourself back to the temp agency and have them send somebody else."

Dixie let out a wild cackle. "You think people are lining up to work for a dead man?"

He reinforced each word. "I'm not dead."

"They don't know that."

"Remember who signs your paycheck."

"I'm sure it'll be more than the gross national product of many third world countries." An eye roll. Followed by a ho-hum sigh.

His payroll hand wanted to ball up a fist and silhouette her against the next building. "If it weren't for me, you wouldn't be here."

"Let's not go that far." She had nails like bear claws, and

whipped a large nail file out of her purse to sharpen them. "But, since we're stockpiling grievances, I don't like the way you spit tobacco in the trash cans."

"Keeps the janitors from digging into my business."

"You're paranoid." With her free hand, she reached across the desk and turned on a small radio he'd never seen before. Dixie listened to sixties music.

That, he liked. "Lots of people would love to have a job to come to each morning."

By way of illustration, she sliced the nail file through the air. "Oh, sure, there are people who're dying to have their oxygen supply choked off, working in what amounts to a big sand dune. I recall seeing pictures of Kuwait during Desert Storm. The only thing missing here is birds falling out of the sky."

"You should've called Maintenance and demanded they send somebody."

"That's the first thing I did." Fingertips rippled against her jaw to the tempo of Gary Lewis and the Playboys.

"Has Raven checked in?"

"Yeah. She left with Ivy."

His eyes flickered to Gil, staring in fascination at the bottom of Dixie's desk. He assumed the chief deputy was checking out her combat boots.

The ringing phone shifted his attention.

"This'd better be Maintenance." She stabbed the lighted button with her shiv. Her hostile demeanor evaporated. The schizophrenic singsonged a cheery greeting and reached for a notepad. "Constable Jinx Porter's office. No, dumplin', your mama's not here. Would you like me to give her a message?"

Her jaw dropped. Her mouth rounded into a rictus. She slammed the receiver down with a bang and confronted Jinx, florid-faced. "He called me a bitch."

"Welcome to the precinct. I see you met Amos."

Dixie held the nail file as if debating whether to impale herself.

Gil chuckled. "He usually says, 'Put my mama on the phone, you bastard.' "

Dixie unwrapped a cellophane and jump-started herself with a peppermint. "That's exactly what he said. Only, he called me a bitch." She cut her eyes to Jinx and glared. "I will not be disrespected. You're the boss. Do something."

He gave her the universal, palms-up, what-the-hey?

Gil continued staring at Dixie's feet. "What's under your desk?"

Jinx craned his neck.

The air thinned.

He came up out of the chair. Dixie pushed back from the desk for a look-see. The warning slo-mo-ing in his brain, deadlocked at the back of his throat and cut off his words. Immobilized by surprise, he watched the color drain from her cheeks. Fright suctioned out her breath.

A possum-sized rat, bisected at its middle by a huge trap, lay at her feet.

She let out a scream, a real plaster-cracker. Turned the nail file into an instant dirk. Clutched it to her bosom and ejected from the chair. Wide eyes riveted on the rodent.

The carpenters froze in place.

Across the room, Gil fueled the fire. "Is it moving?"

Her fingers whitened against the nail file. Rat legs twitched. Dixie bolted with a shriek, scattering subpoenas and leaving the scent of jasmine in her wake.

Down the exterior hall, footfalls thundered.

Jinx shouted to the repairmen. "Call 'em off."

Three deputy sheriffs appeared with Glock .40s drawn. They dropped into combat stances.

"Code Four. Holster your weapons," Jinx hollered, signaling the all-clear. They stood, inert, wide-eyed and unblinking. "She saw a rat."

They left hangdog, clearly miserable they'd been deprived of a kill.

Jinx flopped into the chair. Across the room, Gil gasped for breath. Dixie had him locked in a stranglehold, with the nail file close enough to carve out an eye.

Beneath the desk, the rat convulsed at well-timed intervals.

"It's a joke, okay?" Gil pried her fingers loose. "It's battery-operated. It won't hurt you."

It dawned on Jinx she might have grounds for a lawsuit. Finger-slashes of red streaked up her cheeks as if she'd slapped war paint on them. Mesmerized by the mechanical rodent, she studied it with what appeared to be a kinky mixture of revulsion and fascination.

She propped her rump against Gil's desk. Her eyes danced. "We could hide it under Ivy's desk."

"Wouldn't faze her. She's got bigger ones than this out at the house."

Short of bobbing for eels or flossing the teeth on a great white, Raven couldn't think of anything scarier than riding shotgun with Ivy. For one thing, she suspected Ivy's record-holding for the most car crashes was due to more than needing a tune-up on her prescription wire-rims. Ivy had to be on mood-leveling meds to put up with Amos; Raven figured the woman spent half the time mellowed-out, and the other half strung tighter than a banjo.

Ivy sailed through a signal light that had been red at least two full seconds. Raven gripped the door panel, digging her fingers into the padding until her nail beds turned white, then jammed her foot down until the imaginary brake pedal on her side of the car went straight to the floorboard.

"Forgive me, Father, for I have sinned . . ."

"I didn't know you were Catholic."

". . . I'm not, but at this point, anything helps. Ivy, what the hell are you doing?"

Ivy slammed on the brake, propelling the patrol car into a sideways skid. "Outta my lane, cheeseball. Yeah, you, butt-hook. Read my lips."

"Pull over. Let me out."

"Relax. Everything's under control."

"Let me out," Raven yelled.

Ivy whipped the big Chevy off the road, skidding sideways against the guardrail. "What the hell's the matter with you?"

"I'm not riding with you."

Ivy slung an arm across the back of the seat. "Why the hell not? I missed that truck by a good foot."

Raven's gaze flickered out the window, where she searched the skies for an answer. "No wonder you're the laughingstock of Tarrant County. Jinx ought to put you on a permanent walking beat—make you serve your papers without the use of a patrol car."

"If you can't stand the heat, get out of the kitchen."

"Speaking of kitchens, what do you do—live out of this car?" Raven kicked at a pile of empty fast-food wrappers on the floorboard. "This is gross. Did it ever occur to you to clean up this mess?"

"It's not a mess—"

"There's dried-out chili spots on the dashboard, and I don't even want to know what this white, crusty stuff is on the seat. Let me drive."

"No. Besides, we're almost there."

Raven pinched her eyes shut and screwed up her nose.

"We're nowhere near the airport. We're not even headed in the right direction."

"We're going by my house first."

Raven had always wondered where Ivy lived. Now, she was about to find out. She sat back and gave her seat belt a firm yank. With horns blaring, Ivy jerked the steering wheel hard left, and shot back onto the freeway. In under five minutes, she turned onto a rocky driveway and crunched to a halt.

Not a bad house for a single parent. Depression era. Sixty, maybe seventy years old, clapboard siding with dentil molding edging the trim, and tree trunk–sized columns holding up the overhang on the wraparound porch. Could use a touch-up coat of Dutch Boy in a nice Wedgwood blue, but other than that, the place appeared sturdy and built to last.

"Wait here. This'll only be a minute."

"Can I come in?"

"I'm having work done on the house."

"So?"

"Fine. Suit yourself. But I don't want to hear any criticism outta you."

Practically giddy, Raven slung out a leg. When they reached the porch, the boards creaked under their combined weight. Two beady eyes peered out of a hole where dry rot had ravaged one plank.

Raven sucked air. She pinched Ivy's sleeve. "There's something alive under your house."

"Did it have scales?" Ivy fumbled for the keys.

"I don't think so."

"Then, don't worry about it."

"But there're vermin under your house. . . ."

"Look, Miss Priss, if I have rats, it means I don't have snakes."

"Huh?"

"If I had snakes, I wouldn't have the rats. Get it? Jeez . . . you may be book-smart, but you got no common sense." Ivy unlocked the door and left her standing inside the living room.

Raven gave the room a quick once-over. Overstuffed couch with a red velour bedspread tossed over it. Permanent butt-prints molded into the cushions. Torchère lamps on either side. Coffee table with *Better Homes and Gardens*, *Fingerhut*, *Lillian Vernon* and a *Frederick's of Hollywood* catalogue opened to a page with crotchless underwear that sent a creepy shiver up Raven's back. Big-screen, hi-def TV, a fifty-two-incher at least. DVD, VCR with an ejected *South Park* tape popped out.

She bent at the waist, craning her neck for a better view of the bedrooms. Her eyes widened at the sight of handcuffs, clicked onto a post of an old brass bed.

Ivy stormed in before she could jerk herself upright. "What're you looking at?"

"Nothing. Nice place."

"It's a fucking dump. Let's go."

"Did you get what you came for?" Raven looked past Ivy's shoulder, through the dining room to the cluttered yellow kitchen, where a week's worth of dishes had piled up in the sink.

"My credit cards are gone."

Answering the question of how Amos paid for the plane ticket.

Raven stuck out her hand, palm-up. "I'm driving."

"Over my dead body."

That's what she was afraid of.

# Chapter Twenty-one

Dixie and Gil were still watching the mechanical rat twitch when Dell strolled in with the Korean cleanup lady in tow. Since no one knew the woman's real name, Jinx had nicknamed her *No Damned Way.*

He glanced over at Dixie. "Maintenance."

No Damned Way sucked in a horrified breath. Slanted eyes rounded into huge spheres. The tiny woman held a vacuum cleaner hose against her smock as if it were a bayonet.

No Damned Way spoke in tongues. She flung her arms and wielded the vacuum attachment. Finally, she ended the exorcism with, "Dust bad for lung. I no clean. No damned way."

Jinx sat erect. The rat tail wiggled out from under the desk. His gaze darted to No Damned Way. If she saw it, they'd never get the place back in shape. Somebody ought to kick it out of sight. He stepped forward.

Dixie swelled up. "I'm not working here until this sheetrock gets hauled out, and somebody Hoovers these floors."

"T'en you no work becaw I no clean. T'is DMZ."

"We can't breathe."

Jinx made it halfway to the desk before the convulsing rat vibrated out, trap and all.

The custodian jumped straight up, unleashing a scream

that climbed in direct proportion to each vaulted inch. She landed in a powder cloud, wielding her bayonet with rapier speed.

Dell folded his arms across his massive chest and took it all in from the corner of the room.

"I no clean. No damned way."

"It's not what you think." Gil started her way. "Here—I'll show you."

"No damned way." She distanced him with the nozzle, a two-foot piece of cylindrical plastic with an angular opening designed to suck dust bunnies out of corners.

On the other side of the door frame, repairmen exchanged whispers.

Dixie lifted her brisket off the desk. She issued a bleak reminder. "It's your job."

"T'is job for National Guard."

"Then, get some help."

"You get help." Slanted eyes thinned into gashes. "You the one need psychiatrist."

The Korean stalked out, leaving deer tracks in the powder, and linear stripes from the wheels of the canister vacuum.

Gil picked up *Rodentia gigantica convulsiva* by its rubbery tail and dangled it in midair. Its magnetic pull brought Dixie and Dell over for a closer look. Dell gave it a visual scan and grunted admiration. Dixie wanted to touch it.

Jinx thought she might work out, after all.

If Georgia didn't come back by next week, he might even offer her a permanent job.

Ivy was slumped over, asleep in one of the Delta terminal's molded plastic seats, with drool coming out of the side of her mouth, when the 747 taxied up to the jetway. Raven stood near the boarding area, hoping to spot Amos first. She didn't have to wait long for Ivy's kid to deplane. She would've recognized him, even without the airline captain and a flight attendant attached to each arm.

Misshapen blob. Baggy ghetto pants hanging below the waist. Ozzy T-shirt and steel-toed boots with the laces untied. Holding a half-eaten, king-size Snickers that wouldn't do much to clear up the mild case of acne popped out on his chin and cheeks, in one hand, and a mini-disc player in the other.

Raven badged them.

"What's up?" Amos said with a sullen leer. "Hey, I know you. You're Jinx's girlfriend."

"Used to be Jinx's girlfriend." She looked the captain over to see if he had prospective date potential, saw a wedding band and rejected him on sight. "I'm Raven. I'm one of Jinx Porter's deputy constables." She jerked her head in Ivy's direction. "I'm here with his mother."

The captain spoke. "This young man caught the red-eye to Disney World. Would've made it, too, if he hadn't deplaned in Atlanta. Flight 224 went to Florida; flight 242 went to Raleigh."

Raven whipped out her handcuffs and dangled them close to Amos's nose. "I'll take it from here."

"You're not puttin' your hooks on me." Amos, with a hint of defiance.

"You'd better hope I cuff you. It may be the only thing that keeps your mother from beating the tar outta you in front of all these people."

The captain spoke. "We have to turn him over to his legal guardian."

Raven twisted her head. "Ivy. Get over here. The prodigal son returns."

Ivy lifted her groggy head. Swiped a sleeve across her

crusty mouth and shook off the last remnants of sleep. She seemed to realize where they were, because she jumped from her chair and flew at them. Raven stepped in front of Amos.

Unbelievably, Ivy veered around them and went for the captain. "You stupid sonsabitches charged my credit card. You'd better credit my account for this joyride because it's your fault my son was able to get on this flight in the first place."

After No Damned Way left, Dixie went back to her copy of *W*, Dell gathered citations up off the floor, and Gil inspected his rat for damage. Sifting through a stack of in-mail, Jinx wondered how Caesar would react to Gil's latest purchase. The thought of the Siamese gave him an idea. If he got the seal point off Betsy's property, he might stretch his visit into another week.

"I'm thinking about bringing Caesar to the office."

Dixie lowered the magazine. "Who?"

"My cat."

She closed the magazine. "I have a cat."

"That's nice." Unenthusiastic.

"Why can't I bring my cat?"

"Because there's only one office cat. And, since we're living in Sid's cabana and his daughter's allergic, it's Caese-the-Siamese."

Dixie set her jaw, folded her arms across her bosom, and played Blink. "My cat, Buster, wants to apply for the job."

"What job?"

"Office cat."

"No."

She slapped the magazine onto the blotter. "That's discrimination."

"Live with it."

"Buster's black."

"Sue me." He took a few steps in the opposite direction.

"I might. This is a hostile work environment."

Jinx stopped. "What is it with you women—always plotting lawsuits?"

"Don't look at me. It was your idea to sue."

"My idea? What the heck are you talking about?"

"Oh, sure," she bristled, "act like you don't know. You've been a white man all your life, and you don't know what it's like to be a black cat who's been discriminated against. Here comes this Asian cat with connections—that's nepotism."

"Are you out of your mind?"

"We're contacting EEO, and then we're going to get us a lawyer and sue you and your slant-eyed cat from Thailand, and kick both your tails in court—me and Buster, just you wait."

"Let's get something straight. This is my office. If I want to bring my cat up here, it's my decision." As an afterthought, he bragged about his at-will doctrine. "I'm an elected official and the head of my department. Those working for me serve entirely at my pleasure."

"Speak English."

"Meaning, if I don't like their leopard-print clothes, cat's-eye glasses, their liberal Democrat ideas or catty tone," he thumbed at the door, "they can ship out."

Dixie appeared undaunted. "Keep thinking that way, mister—sooner or later, you'll have to pay for the sins of your father and put a black cat in office."

"This is getting out of hand."

"It's time somebody stood up for the rights of the downtrodden."

"Jiminy Christmas," Jinx groaned. "What brought this on?"

Dixie looked up, expectantly. "So, does he get the job?"

"Who?"

"Buster. Does he get the office cat job?"

Jinx sighed. "I'll give him an interview."

"That's all I ask." Dixie popped a peppermint in her mouth and picked up her magazine. "Just give him an equal opportunity."

She had an engaging smile. Not one of those piano key smiles, but one that lit up her face and made those around her want to return the favor.

The phone bleated.

"This better be Maintenance. I'm not coming tomorrow unless they vacuum. I've seen ski slopes with less white on them." On the second ring, she picked up a pencil, punched the telephone button with the eraser tip and singsonged a greeting. Her smile evaporated, pulling the flush from her cheeks. An odd, distant look appeared in her eyes. Pinpoint pupils locked on Jinx, and her voice dropped to barely a whisper. "Who's calling?"

Her tongue darted out of her mouth, nervously bathing her lips. She swallowed hard. Momentarily, she returned the receiver to its cradle.

"What's the matter?" Sid's home-cooked beans sank in Jinx's stomach.

"You own a bulletproof vest?" She gave her gold rings a nervous twist. "If you do, put it on."

# Chapter Twenty-two

By the time Sid returned, Jinx was giving Dixie the third degree.

She didn't recognize the voice.

There was definitely noise in the background, but she couldn't describe it.

She remembered an interruption—the blip of a tone—like the one that notified the party on the other end of the line of an incoming call.

And, the caller was definitely female. No question about it.

Unless they were queer.

Or, knew how to disguise their voice.

But it was probably a girl.

Unless it wasn't.

Sid listened intently through the grilling. "Any chance it was the new gal—Raven?"

Jinx answered in a low voice meant only for Sid. "You're on the wrong track. From now on, unless you see Raven walking through that door with red-dot primers in one hand and a sack of galvanized nails in the other, leave her out of it."

The phone rang for Jinx. After hanging up, he passed along the bad news.

"That was the ATF. They did some preliminaries. The only identifiable prints recovered came from Ivy's sex apparatus. They managed to get some partials off the wrapper, but there aren't enough points on any of them to make positive ID. And, the palm print they found is smeared."

Sid checked his watch. "Let's get going. The chick from the sheriff's department promised to smuggle us a copy of the new-hire list. Meantime, we've got research to do."

They called it a day, leaving Dixie to oversee what was left of the office. By the time they reached Sid's place, Jinx ticked off the names and number of stars for the last five women he'd unceremoniously dumped. Not a one raised Sid's hackles. Not even the hairdresser with the wicked pair of shears.

"What about ex-employees?" Sid set a couple of iced teas on the dinner table. He ambled out to the barbecue pit and returned with a platter of ribs. He crumbled a handful of bacon into a bowl of diced, boiled potatoes, threw in a couple of dollops of mayonnaise, mustard and parsley, and generously doused it with vinegar.

"I treat my employees fine," Jinx said. "They have me to thank for their jobs."

Sid's expression begged for details.

"A Mexican kid named Castro ran against me in the last election." He reached for the spoon and dished up a healthy glob of Sid's hot German potato salad. "He planned to bring in a bunch of thugs and throw out my deputies as soon as the county judge swore him in."

He reached for a rib so tender it slid off the bone.

"At first," Jinx lifted his fork to his mouth and allowed it to hover inches from his lip, "I figured I'd beat him hands down. It's a fact, you know—that *mañana* attitude about voting—so I didn't worry. But, he had the budget of a sultan, and he got the Gay-Lesbians to endorse him, along with the Humane Society, LULAC, the Rehabilitation Center—and *wham*." The fork went in and came out clean.

Sid's eyebrows screwed up in a puzzle. "You frettin' over the queer vote?"

Jinx thought of Betsy. Sid didn't have a clue about the amazon in the shower. If he had, he'd have pitched, face first, into the potato salad.

"Losing that particular endorsement didn't bother me. I've got Glen Lee Spence and the Munsch brothers living at the apartments. And if Glen Lee hadn't pulled that robbery on account of needing to finish his sex-change operation, he wouldn't have lost the right to vote for being a convicted felon." Jinx took a swig of tea. "He did put my sign in his window, though. So, I wouldn't go so far as to say I pissed off the gays."

Sid gave him the Klevenhagen squint.

"It was the Humane Society's endorsement that stuck in my craw." Jinx craned his neck and checked the hallway for the cat. Seeing nothing, he returned his attention to Sid. "For fifteen years, Ivy collected newspapers from every swinging dick in the building. Before she served her papers, she made a run out to the pound and dropped off newspapers for the animal cages. Sons-of-bitches never even considered who gave her permission to do that."

He placed his fork on his plate. His shoulder hurt, and for a moment, he thought he might be sick.

"You had to expect LULAC to back Castro," Sid said.

"Sure. But, my office does a lot for the Rehab Center, too. Ivy bakes cookies once a month and drives them out for the patients. It's a good thing, too. That brat of hers'll end up there if he doesn't stop sniffing gasoline. Do you know he mowed the lawn three times one week, just so he could whiff fumes?"

Sid waved his hand. "Piss on Rehab. Rehab's for quitters."

Jinx chuckled. The magnetic pull of Sid's pinto beans got the best of him. He helped himself to the pan and threw in a nugget of leftover cornbread. "It hurt, that's all. You do things for people and they turn around and gut you. I don't get it." He shook his head. "Then, Raven got pissed off at me, and some matron from the ritzy west side got it in for me for serving her divorce papers—" He took a bite of barbecue. "—next thing you know, Raven's running against me for constable. Son of a gun if she didn't get my job."

Sid pushed his plate away, patted his belly and nursed his drink. "So, after all this talk, I reckon the truth of the matter is we've done a three-sixty turn back to Raven."

"I admit what's happened seems like a gypsy guerilla tactic, but I wouldn't say it gives her a reason to kill me." Chills coursed through his body, raising hairs like an icy finger.

Sid propped an elbow on the table. "What's wrong? You look like your ancestors just showed up for a family reunion."

"Nothing's wrong," Jinx lied. "Sometimes my shoulder pains me."

He wasn't up to discussing the gypsies, and how Gypsy Kos and the rest of the Balogh tribe were meaner than a basket of pit vipers. And, he didn't want to get into the trouble they'd caused him and Raven during the last election.

That would have to wait for another day.

He helped himself to more tea and hoped like hell the caffeine wouldn't keep him up.

A little after six o'clock that evening, Ivy wheeled into Raven's driveway with a spirited squeal.

"If you talk to Jinx tonight, tell him I might be a little late tomorrow." Ivy shifted her gaze to the rearview mirror.

"Why should I talk to Jinx?"

"I'm saying *if.*"

"Do your own dirty work." Raven pulled down the sun visor on the pretense of removing a lash. Her eyes flickered to Amos, caged in the backseat. He looked perfectly at home. "Do you really have a tattoo of Anna Nicole Smith?"

He pulled up his shirtsleeve. As best she could tell through the tinted glass, the tattoo was mostly breasts, with a little blonde hair and plump lips, but it did resemble the off-color celebrity and Amos seemed quite proud of it.

Ivy sped away with her threat carrying on the breeze. "If that doesn't wash off with soap and water, I'm gonna blister your peter."

Raven checked the security system, double-locking the door behind her. Before she jumped in the shower, she examined every closet and checked under her bed, including those in the guest rooms.

No Yucatan Jay.

For good measure, she slipped her hand beneath her pillow. The feel of cold steel brought instant comfort. She made her way into the bathroom and inspected the cabinets below the bathroom sink. The little snub-nose she formerly kept in the vegetable bin was right where she left it—behind the cleansers. She locked herself in and turned on the tap before realizing she forgot to check the attic.

In the upstairs hallway, she stared up at the pull string. She needed a warning device. Something that sounded like the mating call of a moose if the circuit broke. Tomorrow she'd get one.

After a few tense moments involving phantom sounds in the shower, Raven slipped into a silk kimono and headed for the kitchen. She peeled back the plastic seal on a Lean Cuisine and set the microwave timer.

The doorbell chimed.

Heading for the front door, she scanned the room for something that could double as a weapon. The closest thing she could come up with was a marble bust of Beethoven on the piano. Beyond the sheer curtain, the outline of a tall man in a cowboy hat that made him look seven feet tall, shifted uncomfortably.

Dell.

She clicked back the dead bolt and unfastened the chain. Sure enough, he stood on the terra-cotta porch smelling of Irish Spring bath soap and scented fabric softener. His face, normally a healthy tan, seemed pale in the glow of the incandescent light.

Jinx's deputy removed his hat. He stepped inside the opulent parlor and scanned the room.

She read his thoughts—that he couldn't fit into the antique chairs, and would snap the legs off the French settee with the down-filled cushions—so she led him through the house to the formal living room with a leather chesterfield sofa and matching wingbacks. He removed his cowboy hat, threaded his fingers through the crease in his blond curls and took a seat on the couch. Raven sat at the other end.

"Don't you look nice." She eyed the crisp, turquoise plaid shirt, and gave him a sly wink.

He brightened, then fumbled with his hat. Cast her a sideways glance.

"Want something to drink? I have frozen dinners. The weather's so nice we could eat by the pool."

"Gotta serve a few papers. I thought maybe you'd like to tag along. It'd give us a chance to talk."

"Can't. I have to pick up some things at the hardware store before it closes."

*An alarm for the attic and four more dead bolts. Maybe some-*

*thing that could double as a battering ram, and a rope ladder to toss out the second story.*

Dell's eyes flickered over the room. He pronounced the house outstanding. "I haven't told anyone at work . . . my divorce'll be final in a week. Nobody's business."

He changed the subject and she knew she wouldn't get anything else out of him—not without a spotlight and a dentist's drill. Dell, who wasn't much for idle chitchat, apparently said what he had to say because he got up and crushed his hat back on. Without comment, she walked him through the house and opened the door to show him out. To her surprise, he closed it.

Stared down at her with those intense, aqua eyes.

Adjusted his hat brim so it rode low on his forehead.

"Raven . . ." The silence stretched between them. "Say I invited you over for dinner one night . . . would you come?"

"Sure."

Desperation flickered behind his eyes. Probably fretting over the breakup with Nicole. He reached for her hand and she let him take it.

"You'll be fine, Dell. Everything'll work out. A lot can happen in sixty days. Some couples even reconcile." Nothing in his expression confirmed what she really wanted to know—whether the divorce was his idea, or Nicole's. "Even if the divorce goes through, living alone's not as bad as you think."

He rested his hands on her shoulders. Next thing she knew, he'd hooked her in the crook of his arm. His lingering kiss made her heart jump like a polygraph needle, and sent a shot of heat straight to her—*Ohmygod.*

Could Dell Teague kiss?

With amazing skill.

Did she like it? Evidence suggested her thong dissolved.

He let go and turned away without so much as a backward

glance. Opened the door and stepped out onto the porch. Just said, " 'Bye, Raven," then sauntered to the unmarked cruiser, climbed in, and drove off. Leaving her, rooted in place, to wonder . . .

. . . *What the heck brought that on?*

Throbbing pain kept Jinx tossing the covers, and the low-grade fever he'd come to recognize by the all-over clamminess had him thrashing to retrieve them. Finally, the cat protested with a hiss.

"Sorry, C."

Caesar's tail lashed the blanket. In the feline version of an upraised finger, he fixed his master with a glare, lifted his front paw and gave it a vigorous shake, then launched himself through the air and bounded out of sight.

Jinx eased out of bed and shuffled to the window. Sid kept the room temperature lowered to somewhere around Ivy's IQ, but that didn't stop the sweat from trickling behind his earlobes—the way it did whenever dreams of Raven invaded his sleep. He tugged at the neck of his T-shirt and moved close enough to fog the glass.

The night sky, with its gossamer shimmer and ivory tusk moon, held unspoken promises. He couldn't remember the last time he appreciated such an ethereal moment, only that he had probably spent it with Raven. He shut his eyes and remembered the good times.

Sid had to be wrong about her.

He had no idea how long he kept his eyes closed, but the sharp edge of a woman's laughter forced them open. His breath fogged the glass and he made a fist to wipe it. Voices came from the direction of the swimming pool.

A human shape, naked for the asking, swam the length of the pool. With an underwater flip, the generous attributes of the lady he'd seen in Betsy's shower came into view, wavy beneath the water's surface. She backstroked to the chrome ladder, joined by the toothpick herself.

Jinx told himself he wasn't a Peeping Tom.

That it was Betsy, taking chances.

The women cavorted at the deep end, treading water, their bodies backlit by the glow of the pool lamp. Each time a hand grazed a breast, a high-voltage current electrified his groin. About the time he conjured up the unrealistic vision of a threesome, Betsy dipped beneath the shimmering water and swam for the shallow end.

Her lady friend joined her on the steps.

Shielded by the fronds of a weeping willow, they caressed each other's faces. Jinx hooked a foot around the nearest chair and pulled it within his reach. He flopped down and positioned himself for a better view. They moved from the shadows and sank into the water. He pulled his glasses off the end table. When he returned his attention to the swimmers, Betsy had wrapped her legs around her partner's waist. She fondled the woman's tresses until their bodies became one.

What followed left him checking his hole card.

The hefty gal upended Betsy with a violent shove. Sputtering and clearly angry, Betsy went back for more. The amazon grabbed her by the hair, jerked her head back and sank her teeth into Sid's daughter's scrawny neck.

The feel of a satin glove over an iron hand grazed Jinx's leg. He tore his gaze from the bizarre lovers to catch Caesar figure eight-ing his way past both ankles. He bent down to pick up the cat, but when he glanced back out the window, the tiff seemed to be over. The women toweled each other off and headed for the main house. Disappointed, Jinx buried his nose in cat fur and watched them fade into the xeriscape.

They didn't reappear for the longest time, enough for him

to give up on the prospect of another peep show. But the moment he decided to go back to bed, they materialized, hand-in-hand, beneath the dim light of the back porch. He watched the second floor, hoping for a glimpse into the bedroom. When a night-light switched on and the amazon stood near the window, he squinted through his lenses for a better look.

She had light hair.

His breathing intensified. Betsy headed for a closet; the blonde, to an armoire. He expected them to launch into girlie rituals: blow-drying hair, nail painting, eyebrow plucking.

Boy, was he wrong.

A strobe light came on and the amazon extinguished the lamp. Choppy images appeared in snippets, vivid and memorable. A silent flick from the twenties.

Their game of bondage took on a playful flavor with Betsy trussed to a chair while the blonde stood over her, alternately teasing with the touch of a scarf and inflicting torture with her large breasts. The pulsing strobe and filtering sheers prevented him from reading their facial expressions, but the way Betsy threw her head back and writhed in her seat, he figured she reveled in it.

The tall gal dangled the scarf with the allure of a magician. It grazed Betsy's head, dropped to her shoulder, draped across her chest, and snapped away to begin the ritual again. On the third go-round, she stretched the scarf, then lowered it to Betsy's nose.

Jinx's heart picked up its pace.

Of course. She planned to gag Betsy's mouth. An absentminded thought struck him as comical. What might the defense bar think? His lips curled into a smirk.

What happened next made his heart skip.

The amazon wasn't gagging her. She tightened the scarf

around Betsy's neck.

Jinx flinched. His chest thudded.

Was it roughhousing, or murder in progress?

Betsy struggled against her bindings.

He should do something.

Every muscle stiffened. The cat yowled, propelling himself across the room using the skin against Jinx's rib cage for traction.

What if he was wrong? What if this was merely another sample of Betsy's kinked-out sexual dysfunction?

Her legs kicked wildly.

The moment he snatched his pants off the leather wingback, Betsy slumped. As he wrangled with each leg, the blonde dropped to her knees.

He should call Sid.

He *shouldn't* call Sid.

Jinx cut his eyes to the phone. A 911 call would blanket the place with blue-and-whites. And reporters.

His gaze flickered to his .38.

He yanked on his zipper and damned near spliced his cable. Blinding shock exploded through his body, leveling him waist-high with the windowsill. He continued to track the big blonde's movements through watery eyes.

Unbelievably, Betsy stood. The two embraced, their forms blurred and their roles reversed. Jinx's pants, weighted with change, dropped around his ankles.

He might just kill her himself.

The blonde crawled onto the bed and arranged herself on all fours. The scene played itself out with Betsy administering her own brand of hearty discipline. In under a half-hour, the sexual triathlon concluded when the houseguest rolled away to shut off the strobe. Betsy glided to the window and opened the sheers.

Jinx stumbled aside. His heart pounded. For several minutes she stood framed behind the glass, with nothing but the moon's reflection pouring in and her head aimed at the cabana. He knew the cabana was too faraway and too shrouded in trees to afford her a clear view inside his room. But, that didn't stop her from surveilling his window as if she'd caught him watching . . . as if she cooked up the whole sexual appetizer just for him . . . as if she meant to storm across the lawn to confront him just as soon as she detected the slightest movement.

They'd taken an awful chance, even with Sid's bedroom at the rear of the second floor. The old man could've wandered in on his way back from the bathroom, just for a reassuring peek that everything at the main house was A-OK. Because Betsy took risks, the only sympathy Jinx had for anybody named Klevenhagen, remained squarely for Sid.

Grudgingly, he stepped out of his pants and hobbled to bed. He didn't fall asleep for hours. Worse, he spent almost every waking moment beating himself up for ever having let Raven get away in the first place.

# Chapter Twenty-three

With the scent of rain hanging in the sky, the Cowtown dawn brought as much promise to the morning as Jinx could remember.

A cast-iron skillet of eggs and hash browns Sid left sizzling on the burner brought Jinx downstairs in record time. For someone who rarely ate breakfast, he found himself looking forward to Sid's cowboy cooking. Seated at the table with a paper napkin tucked into his collar, waiting for Sid to bring in steaks off the patio grill, he could hardly wait to dig in.

The front door's dead bolt snapped, followed by a slam. Betsy stormed through the cabana, calling out at a feverish pitch. She barged into the kitchen with the florid face of a hard drinker.

"Mr. Potter, I want to speak with you this instant."

Jinx rose, ill-prepared for such an unattractive shell of a woman. Her hair hung in limp sections and her brilliant-hued kimono, cinched at the waist, contrasted nicely with the faint rosy fang marks and lavender ligature line around her neck.

"Mr. Potter, you need—"

"Porter."

"—to leave my home immediately." Her eyebrows arched in severe peaks, and her eyes glinted. "You'll have to find another place to stay. Your presence here is placing me and my father in danger."

His airflow constricted. Blood accelerated to his head and

collected behind both eyes. She couldn't have seen him watching them. He made sure he stayed off to the side.

The cat, with his low-slung body and drooping tail, skulked in, sticking close to the wall.

Before Jinx had a chance to explain, Sid made his presence known. He held two cuts of beef with a meat fork over a drip plate.

"What's going on?"

"Stay out of this, Daddy."

Jinx opened his mouth to dish up an apology, then decided Betsy would have to be one slit away from chopping off his beanbags before she'd get one. At the sight of the cat, her eyes misted. She cupped her hands to her nose.

"It isn't—" She sucked in two short breaths and let out a sneeze. "—the cat, Mr. Porter." Her skin brightened to the iridescent red of squeaky-clean hide, buffed to an irritated luster.

"Elizabeth, the man's my guest."

"This is my house and I want him gone."

"Nobody's gonna bust into my digs and order people outta here."

"I have my reasons." She stood toe-to-toe, matching Sid shout for shout.

"And, what might those reasons be?"

She turned to Jinx with frustration in her stare and a warble in her voice. "You have to leave."

Now, Jinx was sure it had to do with Esther's Follies and the underwater gay ballet.

She sneezed again. "Immediately."

"That's not good enough," Sid said. "He's gonna take the cat to the office."

"They're supposed to have another apartment ready in a couple of days," Jinx offered.

"Now." She primed herself for another sneeze. He recognized the flicker of fear in her eyes and knew the truth. She couldn't rat him off as a peeper without chancing he'd out her nude, same-sex romp in the pool.

Sid's lip twitched. "You'd better spit it out, whatever's the matter. I won't tolerate any more of this nonsense."

Without warning, Betsy did the unthinkable. She went from screaming meemies, to the blurry-eyed, snot-producing, slaughterhouse hysteria common to pig-rendering plants. The walleyed fit climaxed when she flailed her fists and sent a vase of daisies on the kitchen countertop, airborne. It cracked against the wall and she let out an eye-popping scream. Betsy darted from the room.

Jinx couldn't remember the last time he felt so cheesy.

The front door banged shut, leaving the two men to stare at each other and blink.

With his appetite dulled by Betsy's fury, Jinx reclaimed his place at the table. "She's right. I need to check at the Château Du Roy and see when the spare apartment'll be ready so I can get out of your hair."

Sid wrestled with his shirt collar until his napkin hung like a big white diamond over the front of his shirt. "I've begun thinking in terms of your constituents." His eyes demanded a response.

"My constituents?"

"Yep. The voters themselves. Folks who might want to cancel your ballot. Any crazy people live in the precinct?"

"Jiminy Christmas." The thought was ludicrous and Jinx showed him so with an exaggerated huff. "Dements make up the third largest block of voters—right behind old folks and government employees."

Sid pulled back in surprise. "Really?"

Jinx nodded. "Insane people vote."

"They do?"

"With alarming regularity."

"Anybody got a beef with you?"

"If you stayed in that office full-time—" Jinx glanced at his watch. "—you'd see at least one character a day. Never fails." He pushed away from the table without so much as a bite. "I'll stop by the Château before I go into the office." He grimaced inwardly. Dealing with the apartment manager would be about as enjoyable as a kick in the gonads. "If you want, you can join me down at the precinct around nine."

"No way. I'm hitching up with you." Sid spent the next five minutes wolfing down his chow. Then, he looked up, incredulous. "What the devil's wrong with you? That's a T-bone."

"I'm not hungry."

"Not hungry?" He sliced the air with his knife. "You think I stood over a hot grill for nothing? Pick up that fork, or I'll show you how it feels to be force-fed."

Jinx didn't want to insult his fellow Texan. One bite, and the char-seared meat had spit pooling in his mouth. Sid went back to eating and, in no time, Jinx found himself gnawing the bone. Afterward, Sid cleared the table, scraped the scraps on his plate into the trash compactor and set his dishes in the sink.

"Want help?" He hoped Sid didn't, but he sensed encouragement in the lieutenant's glance and carried his plate to the countertop. While Sid rolled up his sleeves, grabbed the soap bottle and filled the sink with suds, Jinx reached for a towel. The last time he dried dishes—except for that unfortunate stint in the Air Force during the Tet years—he was sixteen and his mother threatened to puncture all four tires on his Torino fastback with an ice pick if he didn't.

In a matter of minutes, they were through.

"Wonder what got into Betsy?" Sid muttered. "I think she

took a shine to you."

"I overstayed my welcome. It's time the cat and I headed home."

The thought of moving into an apartment sandwiched between Glen Lee Spence and the Munsch twins revolted him. Living above the Munsch brothers didn't stop strains of Ethel Merman from filtering up through the carpet, but nasty shag was a heck of a better buffer than wafer-thin walls.

And then there was Glen Lee.

He despised that nail-polished, hair-bowed mutt Glen Lee called Pookie, not to mention the constant trail of androgynous friends that paraded through like the cast party from *The Rocky Horror Picture Show.* A really bad day with Glen Lee and company took on a *Blue Velvet* meets *Deliverance* theme.

By the time Jinx and Sid headed downtown, he had signed a new lease. Even though the first droplets of rain splattered the windshield, and the apartment wouldn't be ready for three more days, the promise of moving out of Betsy's line of fire made the inclement weather seem glorious.

Raven dressed in raspberry-colored jeans and cashmere pullover, matching suede jacket and Justin Ropers. She spritzed the air with a cloud of Lolita Lempicka, walked into the settling mist and came out smelling like a cross between an English garden and a child's birthday party. By heading downtown an hour early, she planned to snoop through the desks of her colleagues in the scant hope of finding something that would link them to the aborted raids, and ultimately, the attempts on Jinx's life.

The surprising sight of Amos, decked out in Tommy Hilfiger clothes and Pumas with the laces untied, torpedoed her plan. Upon seeing the boy seated at Mickey's desk, her eyes cut to Ivy's oversized leather handbag on top of her blotter. A black blazer hung over the back of her chair.

Ivy wasn't one to dress for success, nor dress to impress.

Probably wore nice clothes for that jerk, Sid Klevenhagen.

"Where's your mother?"

About the time Amos answered, "Bathroom," in a sullen monotone, Raven heard the commode flush. The door banged open, and Ivy ambled in hiking up her black britches and tucking in her white blouse. She'd obviously spent extra time on her wheat-colored, taser-styled hair this particular morning, since it lacked the usual hay-bale quality that had become her signature do.

"You're not riding with me today," she said with an air of formality. She snagged her jacket and slipped it on. "I already have a rider."

Raven's eyes narrowed to a squint. "Are you wearing lipstick?"

"What if I am?"

"It looks nice. Who's your rider?" She shifted her gaze to Amos, doodling on a phone message pad and wondered if Ivy had placed him under house arrest and ordained herself warden.

"Not that it's any of your business . . . Sid mentioned he'd like to see what I do during the day. I figured I'd drive him through the hospital district while I serve my papers."

"Lovely."

"Now, if it's all the same to you, I need to collect newspapers for the Humane Society. I'll be about fifteen minutes. You don't mind watching Amos, do you?"

Amos piped up. "I don't need watching."

Without awaiting an answer, Ivy lumbered out of the office. Raven slid into Gil's chair. From the opposite corner of the room, she could monitor Amos with the intensity of a science experiment.

He stared in defiance. "What're you lookin' at?"

*Sullen shit.*

"Do you still have your tattoo?"

He answered by way of stretching his T-shirt sleeve up over his freckled arm, exposing the busty caricature of Anna Nicole Smith.

"Did you get in trouble last night?"

"What's it to you?"

"Just making conversation."

Bracing his foot against Mickey's desk, Amos pushed his bulk against the chair back and rolled out into the center of the room. He spun around to face her. His eyes took on a speculative gleam, and locked on her cleavage.

"Are your tits real?"

In the unguarded moment, Raven bowed up. "That's very rude, asking personal questions."

"Are they? Because they don't look real."

*Oh, trust me, they're real.*

She fixed him with a hard stare.

"If they're real, let me feel 'em."

Amos needed a good paddling.

"Tell you what—" Startled into honesty, she came out of the chair and perched on the edge of Gil's desk with her arms folded across her chest. "—I'll answer a question if you'll answer a question."

His eyes narrowed. His lip angled up in a smirk. "Shoot."

"Whose bedroom is that with the handcuffs hooked to the brass bed?"

"Mine. Are your tits real?"

"Yes. Why are there handcuffs hooked to the bed?"

"To keep me from sleepwalking. Can I touch 'em?"

"No. How'd you get out to the airport to catch the red-eye yesterday?"

"Called a cab. If you don't let me touch them, I won't believe they're real and you'll have to show me." He ignored her heavy eye roll, and his expression shifted from melancholy to euphoria. "Would you go out with me?"

"No. How'd you pay for the cab?"

"My mama's credit card. Did you ever give Jinx a blow job?"

The question jarred her. "Game's over."

"But I still have stuff I want to ask."

"Tough."

Unexpectedly, Amos jerked to attention. His hand darted beneath his shirttail, and when he pulled it out, she saw that he held a pager.

"My beeper went off." He concentrated on the display.

"*Beepers* are for drug dealers. *Pagers* are for legitimate use."

Amos mumbled something unintelligible, inviting closer scrutiny.

"How old are you anyway?"

"Thirteen. You?"

"Never mind about me. Why do you need a pager? I didn't need a pager when I was your age."

"What's it to you? I get calls just like anybody else."

"What kind of calls?"

"My mama calls. Hey . . ." he said in a drawl of realization. A conniving glint replaced the dull gleam in his eyes. ". . . are we playing the game again? Because if we are, I've got another question."

While Ivy ran Amos out to school, Raven sat pondering the strange relationship between the mother-son duo. Very weird, that they would be umbilically and electronically joined.

Dell, Mickey and Gil strolled in and fanned out to their respective desks, leaving Raven to head for Ivy's. Until Jinx commandeered a desk for her, they'd all end up playing musical chairs.

Since Ivy had left her computer on, Raven logged in under her own password, and began a search on the internet for the Laredo newspaper. When the online version of the *Laredo Morning Times* popped up, she scanned it for fresh headlines. She didn't notice any photo spread of Yucatan Jay on the front page, nor buried inside, either.

Dell appeared behind her and touched her shoulder.

"Ride with me."

"Sure."

Halfway to logging off, she noticed a small story that raised the hairs on her arms. An unknown subject who popped up at the border had attracted the interest of the U.S. Treasury Department, the FBI, the local chief of police, and the Mexican Federales by spreading gold Canadian Maple Leaf coins around Laredo and Nuevo Laredo. The article didn't articulate the problem in so many words, but the implication was plain: the Laredo economy was going to shit.

*Yucatan Jay.*

# Chapter Twenty-four

Dell drove south on Eighth Avenue with Raven riding shotgun. She stared out the window, through a light drizzle, letting her mind free-associate with memories of Yucatan Jay. Dell took a right on Felix, into a residential area where property values plunged into a deep decline, before she realized the paper they were en route to serve wasn't just any paper.

Still consumed with thoughts of her cousin, she looked out the glass at a red-tagged house marked for demolition. "Where're we going?"

"Ivy got a tip this morning. Turns out Straight-Eight's got a new girlfriend on Southside—a stripper—get this—she's a headliner at Ali Baba's. Goes by the name Barbie Dahl."

Raven blinked. The little hairs on her arms bristled. "Do we have enough people for a takedown?"

"Gil and Mickey are right behind us."

Raven glanced out the side mirror. Two white Chevys switched lanes and fell in behind them.

"What about Ivy?"

Dell snorted. "We don't want her along. Let her dick with Amos. That'll keep her out of our hair."

She checked out his determined profile, and the strong grip on the steering wheel. She thought of his kiss, soft and tender at first, then hungry and consuming. An involuntary shiver zipped up her legs, lingering near her shoulders, until she drove the image from her mind with replacement thoughts of Yucatan Jay.

It didn't work for long.

Yucatan Jay only excited her because she thought he was dangerous.

Dell inflamed her smoldering emotions because she knew he was.

Would the man sitting next to her turn traitor?

No way.

Jinx Porter was wrong.

Could she prove it to his satisfaction?

Not yet. But she planned to make every effort to exonerate him from suspicion.

Down at the precinct, Dixie was shaking raindrops off her faux rhino-hide coat and reeking of magnolia blossoms. Dressed in a zebra-print smock and matching harem pants, she carefully folded the wrap over her chair back and flopped, out of breath, into her seat. A selection of candles in various sizes and pastel colors lined the desk.

Jinx surveyed the room in a glance. When he looked back at the secretary, she was lighting the wicks with what appeared to be a small derringer.

"What're you doing?"

"What does it look like?" She snapped the hammer of the mock pistol and the flint went out. "These are my aromatherapy candles. The green ones are for energy. I'm lighting the lavender ones for tranquility. This place is depressing."

"Lotsa luck. Have we heard from ATF?"

"No."

"Anybody from the PD call?"

"No. But you did get a message from some guy from Risk Management. He wants to talk to you about Ivy's wrecks."

She jerked a pink slip off the phone pad and thrust it at him. "They want to stencil a warning on her patrol car—*Don't like my driving? Dial*—with a number to report reckless driving." Her lips angled up in a smirk. "I suggested they use: one-eight-hundred-SCREW-U2."

"Fine by me . . . long as they don't call here." He crumpled the paper and tossed it into the trash can, then pointed to the carpet. "The floor got vacuumed."

"You bet it did. And, if I have my way—and I will—those lazy bums'll be back to haul out the rest of this debris by the time I go to lunch."

Sid, in the usual Klevenhagen style, asked the question they both wanted to know. "What's got you panting like a dog in heat?"

She eyed him warily through enormous red eyeglass frames studded with marcasite, then shifted her gaze to Jinx. In a voice piping with irritation, she addressed her latest grievance from the corner of her mouth.

"I walked over to the justice of the peace's office to pick up papers. In the rain." She spit her bubblegum into a tissue and geared up. "By the way, I want a key to the next building so I don't get wet."

Jinx nodded. "You and everyone else."

"What's that supposed to mean?"

"It means they won't even give me a key and I'm an elected official."

"We'll see about this shit." She opened the top drawer and pulled out a spiral notebook, hunkered over the tablet and scribbled something down.

"What's that?" Jinx asked.

"A hit list. I'm putting a contract out on everybody on it. There are a few things around here I'm not willing to put up with. Dirt's one. Rain's another. I want a key for a shortcut, I don't care who I have to neuter to get it."

"Good luck."

The belch of the coffeemaker caught Sid's attention. He ambled over to Dixie's desk with two steaming mugs and placed one on her desk.

She regarded him as if he were beneath contempt. "If you think this means I'm going to start schlepping coffee, you're mistaken, mister."

Sid's eyes widened. "I thought you might want a cup."

The look on her face said she had no expectations of people. That she wasn't prepared for folks doing favors for the sake of being nice.

She craned her neck to peek over the lip as if she half-expected something vile floating on top. "If you're going to get it, get it right. I take cream. Lots of it."

Sid mocked her with a bow, but returned with the mug of fog-lifter considerably lightened.

Dixie scowled.

"Now, what's wrong?"

"I have something to discuss." She cut her gaze from Sid to Jinx, and dripped acid. "When I was at the justice of the peace's office, I asked to borrow a pen to sign for the writs and citations. They refused to loan me one." The phone rang and Dixie emitted a low growl. She ignored the blinking light. Color percolated behind her cheeks. "I got in a catfight with the supervisor. I'm sure this is them wanting to complain." She allowed it another ring. "I told that old venereal wart I didn't know of any law that said I even had to come pick the damned things up, and if she didn't give me something to write with, she could tote them over herself."

The bleating persisted.

Sid had the uncanny ability to predict a good fight. His grin went all the way from Fort Worth to Dallas.

Jinx pointed. "Answer it."

Dixie purred out a cheery greeting. The caller doused her smile. She offered the phone with a malevolent thrust and a nasty, "It's for you."

A thorny-voiced woman Jinx recognized from the JP's office heated up the earpiece. To distribute the abuse, he extended a finger and pressed speakerphone. He handed Dixie the receiver. Everyone listened.

"That new secretary of yours was just over here giving my girls a hard time."

"Is that so?"

Dixie shook her head. Her eyes caught fire and she braced her arms across her bosom in a double-dog-dare-you pose.

"This isn't the Mont Blanc factory, Constable. We don't hand out pens to any swinging dick that wanders in. Besides," she whined, "people take our pens and don't return them. We're not in the business to be furnishing office supplies to every psychedelic heifer in this building."

Sid's grin stretched from Beaumont to El Paso.

Jinx's skin started tingling from the inside out. Somebody was trying to kill him and the pickax-nosed crone at the JP's office wanted to bitch about pens. He could hear the faint squeak from Dixie's teeth grinding.

He leaned over the speaker so there would be no mistaking his words. "What do you want me to do about it?"

"Get her under control. My girls don't appreciate being talked down to."

Jinx studied Dixie's drill-bit gaze, then looked at the Boston-to-LA leer emanating from Sid's face.

"Sounds to me like it was your girls doing the bullying."

"That woman needs Prozac."

"Tell you what." He massaged the sting in his shoulder. "Your girls don't want to loan my secretary a pen to sign off on the citations, you can either trot the damned things over and she'll sign off on them with her own pen, or you can keep 'em until they collect mold and turn to penicillin."

"I beg your pardon?" Words clipped.

"You heard me. And, if any of these lawyers call up because their writs aren't served, we'll just tell 'em to call y'all directly because we don't have 'em. And one more thing." He took a deep breath. "Don't ever fuck with my secretary again."

He disengaged the line.

Light glanced off Dixie's teeth like thirty-two beacons, and just for a second, he thought her eyes welled behind the goggle-like specs.

"Piss on 'em." He motioned Sid to the back office.

He hadn't taken more than a step or two when a baritone voice asking for Dixie turned him around. A man dressed in a plaid sport shirt and Levi's dangled something shiny.

"I'm Dixie." Said with the air of a generous benefactor. "I'm the secretary."

"I'm head of Building and Maintenance." He took a step closer. "You asked for a key to the building next door? Here you go."

She snatched it from his grasp and dropped it into an alligator purse.

Jinx cut his eyes to Sid. "I can't believe I've been here almost long enough to retire, and they never handed me a damned thing—including most of the stuff I'm budgeted for. It's enough to harelip the governor." He couldn't resist casting an admiring glance her way. "She's been here two days and she's got a key to a building the county doesn't even own."

Sid shared his thoughts. "If I ever decide to put a contract out on somebody, I'm consulting her first."

thought a skinny chick could have so much cellulite? Jinx snorted in disgust.

He made it all the way through the Es when Sid staggered in looking like a soup sandwich. With his forehead dotted in perspiration and his armpits ringed in sweat, he tossed a paper, rolled into a cylinder and rubber-banded, onto the desk.

"What took you so long?"

Sid let out a sigh of exhaustion. "Sex-crazed vixen tried to kill me. Made me do her in the men's bathroom before she'd give me the list." And then, "You mind if I ride with Ivy today? She says she'll show me places I've never been before."

Five miles from the precinct, after another bust gone sour, Dell wheeled the Chevy onto a pebble driveway next to a clapboard house painted buttercup-yellow, trimmed with Victorian spindles and gingerbread cutouts.

The brawny German cut the engine. "I don't get it," he said in a strained voice. "Straight-Eight's side of the bed was still warm. I can't believe he wasn't there. After the stripper tells him we kicked in her front door, I bet he won't come near the place. How could he know we were on the way?"

"I don't know. Where are we?"

"My place."

They entered the spartan living room and Raven scanned for a place to toss her jacket. Once she learned of the Teagues' separation, she figured he'd rent an apartment and stock it with rent-to-own furniture. Instead, it pleased her the place had a woman's touch, and she privately complimented his wife for helping him decorate his new bachelor pad.

"I don't get it either." She flopped into Dell's recliner, spread her fingers and raked them through wavy hair, made wilder by the humidity. "We should've nailed him."

He gave her a casual look sideways. "Weren't you with Ivy this morning?"

"Not for long."

"Did she say anything about Straight-Eight?"

A head shake. "Ivy doesn't much care for me."

Dell removed his cowboy hat, hooked it on a bentwood hat tree near the door and walked toward the kitchen. "Coca-Cola?"

"If you're having one."

He gave her a one-shouldered shrug. "Sandwich?"

She caught him staring, and noticed her cashmere pull-over had ridden up to her midriff. Smoothing it back down, she shook her head no, thanks.

Beyond Raven's view, Dell projected his voice. "How'd Jinx talk you into coming back to work?"

A strong pulse thudded at the base of her throat. She thought her heart would beat right through her chest. "It happened so fast I'm not really sure."

"I came by your house a couple of times last week, but you weren't home."

"Should've left your business card. I would've called you back."

"It's probably better that I didn't. Nicky and I were having so many problems it would've just complicated things."

"Why'd you leave her?" she said, testing his reaction.

He stepped into view. The contours of his face hardened. "She accused me of having a mistress."

Raven's mouth curled into a pout of disappointment. If there was one constant in her world, it was knowing at least one man existed who could be faithful to his wife. Dell.

"You cheated on her?"

"Only in my head." He brought in two Coca-Colas and

handed one over, then reached for the remote atop a wooden produce box turned upside-down for a makeshift coffee table. At the click of a button, the TV came on and he switched it to the local broadcast. "I thought we could catch the news. Talk. Or listen to George Strait. I know you like The Cranberries. I bought one of their albums."

"What should we tell Jinx about Odie Oliver?"

"The truth. That we lost him."

"He's gonna be furious."

*Probably call it a cluster fuck, and blame Dell.*

From his own recliner, Dell glanced over. Words came out in tentative bursts. "I have an idea. We could set up on the house again tonight. If we don't catch him, we can come back here. You can stay the night, we'll get up early and hit it fresh." Deep breath. "What do you think?"

*Poor Dell. Still trying. Well, she had no intention of dating anyone on the rebound. She'd learned the hard way . . . back when she used to date Jinx and found out he kept a string of women on the side.*

She retrieved her jacket and slipped in an arm. Dell almost passed out, ogling her breasts when she arched her back and maneuvered into the other sleeve. She peered down the hall, to an open bedroom door where an air mattress floated on the hardwoods.

"Come on, Dell . . ." she said with a wink, "how could I get any sleep? You don't even have a real bed."

# Chapter Twenty-five

The very idea an old man with a bad heart would suggest riding in the same car as Ivy had the effect of a wrecking ball against Jinx's ears. The only thing keeping him from launching into a tirade was Dixie, screeching through the intercom.

"You'd better get in here," she said with an agitated lilt.

"Not now, I'm busy." He unfurled Sid's list.

"Get un-busy. Gilbert just brought in a wild man."

Jinx tossed the list on the blotter and headed for the front office with Sid in tow. A scruffy, broad-shouldered Mexican sat in a chair next to Gil's desk with his hands cuffed behind his back.

"Got me a good bust here," Gil said.

He winked, then cocked his head in Dixie's direction. She sat immersed in her *D* magazine, lost in a world of Dallas couture and high fashion.

*Probably envisioning her head pasted on a skinny waif's body.*

Jinx sauntered over with Sid close behind. "What'd you arrest him for?"

"Burglary of a hab." As in, habitation. Cop-speak for domicile. "I was out serving papers. One of the neighbors flagged me down. I caught him crawling through a window with a TV."

"Good lick."

With a fraternal lean in Jinx's direction, Gil whispered, "This is my buddy from the barrio. Teaches drama at

Northside High. We were Golden Gloves together."

It took a moment to soak in. When Dixie arrived on the scene with a smart mouth—before he developed a kernel of admiration for her—Jinx didn't much care whether Gil broke the monotony with his shenanigans. Now, he wasn't so sure.

"I don't know," he said under his breath, "maybe we ought to call it off."

"C'mon, Jinx, she's as nutty as Ivy. It'll be fun." With his face full of hope, Gil looked more like a kid reined in from opening Christmas presents than a fun-loving Hispanic, a half-century old.

He tried reason. "If we prick with her she might quit. You gotta admit she's a good secretary."

"She's a card-carrying cock mangler."

Sid caught on. He sauntered away with a twinkle in his eyes. His evil grin broadened when Dell and Raven walked in, sopping wet from the outdoors.

Dixie ignored Raven completely, and greeted the brooding German with a scowl. He returned the compliment with a glower and a modest tip of his Resistol. A raindrop hit the desk and she flicked it off and went back to her magazine.

The fake burglar spoke in an exaggerated accent, straight out of the *colonia*. "Joo better loosen these cuffs."

Gil stayed in character. "Keep your shirt on."

Jinx cut his eyes to Dell, settling in at his desk. "Is he in on this?"

Gil nodded.

Dell jumped to his feet and cornered Raven on the way to the bathroom.

"What about Ivy? We can't have her cranking off rounds."

"That gynecologist who's been ducking her? Right now, she's staked out the surgery room, waiting to serve that

asshole his divorce papers."

"And, Mickey?"

Gil shrugged. "Don't worry. He knows Craig."

*A Chicano named Craig?*

"Yeah, Jinx." The husky man looked up. "He knows me."

"Do I know you?"

"You don't remember?" The Mexican frowned, hurt. "I'm the one who picked up your donation for the high school boxing tournament two years ago."

"I remember." He hoped his face didn't betray him. "Good to see you."

The phone rang.

Foul-humored, Dixie slapped her magazine on the desk. By the time she lifted the receiver to her ear, she trilled out her cheery-greetinged, sugar-coated, put-a-diabetic-into-insulin-coma, public self.

Jinx wasn't sure he'd ever get used to that piccolo voice.

Dell angled over. "I like her," he growled.

Dell didn't like anybody.

Gil said, "She's vicious. Have you heard the way she talks to people?"

"I don't care how nasty she gets." Jinx kept his voice low. "Long as she gets along with the public."

"Today's her birthday." In one collective shift, their eyes moved from Dixie to Dell.

Gil picked up a pen and pretended to fill out a report. "How do you know?"

Dell said, "I ran her criminal history."

"Jiminy." Jinx turned to Dell. "Anything in her history I should know about? Did she knock over Fort Knox? Take a sledgehammer to Mount Rushmore? Wanted for the cyanide poisoning of a succession of husbands? Maybe some public lewdness charges?"

Dell shook his head. Big shakes. "Clean. I like her."

Across the room, Dixie dripped sympathy. "I know how you feel, you poor thing. You think you've got problems, I go home each day to a drunken husband and a juvenile delinquent." She picked up the magazine, flipped the page, studied it, then leafed on through. She turned the magazine at an angle and screwed up her face. "No, shug, the constable's never too busy to talk to you, but I don't see him right now."

The men and their "prisoner" exchanged looks.

Jinx liked the way she used her copy of *D* to shield him from view. And the way she refused to lie for him.

"Yes, ma'am, I'll have him call as soon as I hear from him."

"She's efficient," Jinx whispered. "And Dell likes her. Let's call it off."

Abruptly, Dixie hung up.

"Too late." Gil regained his professional demeanor. "Lights, action, camera."

Sid loitered near her desk and ogled the temp's forty-fours. Dell ambled back to his corner, distancing himself from the action.

Jinx asked, "Who was that on the phone?"

"That old venereal wart from the justice of the peace's office." With her elbows on the desk, she rested her face in her palms. A healthy flush brightened her cheeks.

"Do we really want to refer to people as venereal warts?"

"You're right. That was the old puss-boil from the JP's office."

Gil took over.

"You're going to jail, my man," he announced in a loud voice.

*Barrio vato,* as Jinx had come to regard Gil's *amigo,* slid to

the edge of his seat. Jinx stepped off to one side.

"Joo poot these cuffs too tight." He twisted in the chair and made eye contact with Dixie. "Whatchoo lookin' at, lady?"

She stared without expression and balled her fists reflexively. Reluctantly, Dixie went back to work.

"All right, stand up," Gil barked. "I'll loosen the cuffs, but if you so much as twitch when I unlock 'em, I'll kick your ass. *¿Comprende?*"

The boxer rose and turned his back to Gil. With one handcuff released, the chief deputy slipped something into the man's hand.

"Make it look good," he whispered.

"Not too good," Jinx rasped.

*Barrio vato* took the first swing.

Dixie let out a blood-clotting scream. Gil made a defensive block and came back with a right hook. Gooey red liquid squirted from his hand.

Jinx jumped the Mexican from behind. He put him in a mock stranglehold with his good arm. Another arterial spurt came out of nowhere, spattering Jinx's face and right shirtsleeve. Pain sliced through his left shoulder. He relaxed his grip and let go.

*Scratched from the lineup.*

With an intimidating gait, Dell stalked over to the donnybrook.

No one expected to see Dixie lumbering toward them, wielding her umbrella like a skewer.

"Whoa, missy—" Sid wrenched it from her hands. "No need to lop off heads. You're not a reincarnated Cossack from the Decemberist movement."

Gil spun *barrio vato* facing Dixie and cuffed him. She yelped at the sight of blood saturating their clothes.

Jinx turned to Dell. "Keep the sheriff's men out."

Dell hurried out into the hall.

Breathless and still playing his part with the range of a Shakespearian actor, Gil said, "You're gonna fry."

"I gonna kill you, first chance, *méndigo*. Then, I'm gonna kill everybody else."

"Kiss my ass, *pendéjo*."

*"Joto."*

"I know what that means," Dixie piped up with confidence. "My son says it to his little gangster friends."

No one paid her any mind.

Jinx just wanted it over. "Get him outta here."

Gil grabbed him by the handcuffs and steered him out the door. Dixie, suitably impressed, went back to her magazine. Sid propped the umbrella in the corner and flopped into Mickey's chair. Before he could get comfortable, Jinx motioned him out into the hallway.

They waited beyond Dixie's line of sight.

"I feel kind of bad about this," he whispered.

"Aw, let the boy have his fun."

"Somebody wants me dead, and all these people think about is pranking with the secretary."

With one handcuff around his wrist and the other dangling, the blood-soaked boxer sauntered back into the office alone.

Dixie let out a scream. With a satanic leer, Gil's pal braced his hands against the desk. Dixie shrank in her seat. Her face paled, chalky-white.

"I said I was gonna kill everybody. That included you, too. I came back . . . to say, Happy birthday, Dixie."

Jinx stepped into view with Sid on his heels. Gil followed, drenched in the fake blood from the capsules from Ye Olde Magic Shoppe. Raven came out of the back.

Dell handed Dixie an oversized envelope. "Happy birthday."

Her eyes misted and her jaw dropped. The phone rang and she singsonged a greeting.

"What about the sheriff's deputies?" Jinx asked Dell.

"Told 'em she saw another rat."

Dixie's smile evaporated. "This is the fifth time you've called today. And for the fifth time, I'm telling you, your husband's not here. He's in the field serving papers. I don't know when he's coming back. I gave him the other messages. I don't know why he hasn't called, and, here's a new one—I don't give a flying flip."

Jinx sighed. Poor Mickey. Every twenty-eight days, his wife developed a case of trust-a-phobia. Georgia never uttered a peep about the barrage of calls. Everybody else bitched to high heaven. He had a feeling Dixie was about to put her foot down.

"Quit calling here. We've got a business to run." A chicken squawk ripped through the earpiece with such a fury Dixie held the phone aloft. When it finally died down, she put the receiver back to her ear and lit into Mickey's wife with a vengeance. "The rest of us can't help it if you're insecure, honey. Get a prescription for PMS and take it." She slammed the phone down, hatchet-like, killing off the squawk at the other end of the line. All smiles, she dovetailed her porcelain fingers together and faced them.

"Which one of you people brought cake?"

# Chapter Twenty-six

Things went back to normal—normal, being what was normal at the precinct. Dixie shamed the deputies for not bringing cake, and when she suggested they take her to lunch, Dell hightailed it out the door with Raven hot on his heels. Before Gil and his boxing buddy could beg off, she was on the phone to her drunken husband, gushing over her birthday scare and talking about the Benito Juárez enchilada plate she planned to order once they got to Betty's Café.

By the time things settled down and Jinx remembered the sheriff's new-hire list curled up on his desk, in hobbled another boil that needed lancing.

Thomas "Red" Stumblingbear, Vietnam veteran and Purple Heart recipient, teetered in on crutches, wearing a flannel lumberjack shirt and one pants leg folded up and pinned at the hip. Carrot-colored hair now streaked with silver, porcupined out from beneath a Rangers ball cap; doughy skin, formerly the shade of watered-down chocolate milk, had faded to an unhealthy yellow. Given the pockmarks, Stumblingbear's complexion resembled a lightly toasted wheat bun.

Jinx favored the character du jour with a weak smile. He glanced at Sid and did a little eye roll. He always went out of his way to help the man; after all, it could've been him tripping that land mine. Not to mention the guy routinely hammered down a yard sign at election time. And, he made it a point to go to the polls to connect the ends of the Jinx Porter arrow on the ballot. To be sure, Red Stumblingbear was a nice enough fellow—having inherited his laid-back demeanor from his Native American ancestry, rather than the Irish temper from the bloodline of his fiery-haired mother. But five minutes of conversation with the Silver Star recipient with the interminable stutter, flat wore Jinx out. Rude as it was, he found himself finishing the man's sentences to keep the conversation from bogging down.

"Hi there, J-J-J—"

"Jinx." He offered his hand and Stumblingbear shook it. "How ya doing, Red? What brings you downtown?"

"I n-need to ask a f-f-f—"

"Favor?"

The Vietnam vet nodded.

"Sure, Red, what can I do?"

"I'm getting m-m-m—"

"Married?"

A hearty nod. "And I want you to r-r-r—"

This time, Jinx couldn't help. They stared at each other intently, as if telepathy might work. Red got it on the fourth try.

"—run a background ch-check on my g-g-g—"

"Girlfriend."

"—to see if she ever s-s-s—"

"Stole anything?"

"Y-y-you got it."

Dixie looked on with a squinty-eyed glare. Jinx ambled over, wedged himself between the temp and the computer, and punched up the Tarrant County screen.

"Name and DOB?"

Red furnished the details and Jinx entered the data. The war hero hovered nearby, anxiously digging the rubber tips of his crutches into the carpet while the machine ground out the information. *Not Found* flashed in iridescent green letters, and Thomas "Red" Stumblingbear hobbled out of the office grinning like a leopard at a tea party.

Dixie broke the quiet. "Who the hell was that?"

"A voter. One of the few people, I'm sure, who's not trying to kill me."

She gave him a bored blink. "What happened to his leg?"

"Blown off in Cambodia."

"Cambodia? We didn't have troops in Cambodia."

Sid jumped in with both feet. "That's what them sombitches wanted you to believe."

Dixie gave a haughty sniff. "I don't think that's true."

"Well, if we didn't have troops in Cambodia," Jinx said, "why'd the government send Stumblingbear a check for fifteen thousand dollars when he came back?"

Dixie perked up. "That's his name? Stumblingbear?"

"Hush money," Sid said. "The gummit paid hush money to hush them kids up."

Jinx nodded. "While everybody else was buying brand-new Ford Mustangs with their checks, Tom Stumblingbear said, 'Up your leg,' to the U.S. government and framed his."

"So, he's a war hero?" For several seconds Dixie sat lost in thought. "Were you in the military, constable?"

"Yes."

She eyed him with newfound respect. "Did you get any war wounds?"

"A few." He examined his fingertips before thrusting them inches from her face. "They came with the draft notice. You can still see the scars from the splinters when the FBI pulled me off my porch."

Her eyes narrowed. "So, you don't have any bullet holes?"

"Just the one." And it was thumping like a metronome.

"Reckon they'd still honor that check?"

Ivy straggled in with her hair askew, and a paper silhouette target and a large tote digging into one arm. Even from a distance, he could smell the cordite on her clothes.

"Where've you been?" Dixie asked.

"Like I have to clear anything with you," Ivy snapped. Jinx shot her a wicked glare. "If you must know, I went to the range for firearms qualifications."

Everyone except Dixie knew Ivy recycled the best target from the trash after each qualification, and hung it on the wall next to her desk to rehabilitate her reputation as a bad shot.

Dixie ripped a pink slip off the phone pad and shoved it at her. "Here y'go. Your son called."

Ivy kept walking. "I already know about it. Amos got sent home early from school. They're claiming he beat up the special ed teacher. They're always blaming him for stuff. He's an easy target because he's bigger than other kids."

Gil showed no mercy. "He's bigger than the other kids because he's thirteen and still in the fourth grade."

"Sixth grade." Color raged up Ivy's neck.

Dixie wasn't one to hide her light under a bushel. "I'd brain him."

"Amos is a good boy." Ivy pitched the tote in her desk drawer and slumped into her chair. "Why, just this morning, after they kicked him out, he called to tell me the next-door neighbor's house caught fire again. The Lord works in mysterious ways. Thank God he was home to call nine-one-one. They sent an arson investigator out to talk to him. Naturally, he's got no idea who set the fire."

Jinx and Gil exchanged knowing glances.

Leafing through her magazine, Dixie casually asked, "What's in the bag?"

Ivy flushed beet-red. "I don't really think I should say in mixed company."

Sid alerted with the enthusiasm of a drug dog. Gil rolled his eyes. Jinx had his suspicions, but kept quiet. Dixie goaded her on.

"I want to see." She pushed away from the desk and started across the room. "Is it something for me? Is that my birthday present?"

"It's personal." With eyes downcast, Ivy planted a clod-hopper firmly against the drawer.

"What'd you do? Buy yourself another hundred-volt Erotica-Vibe and a backup generator to replace the one the ATF took?" Gil, unable to help himself.

"I've given up on battery-operated appliances," Ivy said with a snort. "From here on out, I'm getting something that plugs into the wall."

Dixie hooted. "I'd hate to get your electric bill."

Ivy tried to incinerate her with a glare.

Sid's hand slipped conspicuously into the pocket of his Wranglers.

Jinx stood quietly puzzled. It had to be a woman thing. Ivy didn't cotton to Georgia or Raven, either. And, Dixie was already warring with the girls at the JP's. Like Siamese fighting fish, he'd about decided a second X chromosome meant no two women could swim in the same tank.

"I'm sure Jinx isn't paying you big bucks to poke your nose into other people's business." Ivy again. Trying to start some shit.

"Listen, sister, he's not paying me big bucks at all. I'll have you know I make fifty times this much back at the agency." She pulled out her nail file and raked it against her thumb-nail.

"Fifty times?" Ivy narrowed her eyes. "Then, why don't

we get the manager on the phone? Let's see if we can't just give you a lift right back to your old stomping grounds."

"Now, wait a minute." Jinx rose halfway, prepared to drop a lid on the grease fire.

"Stay out of this, constable." With an amused glow, Dixie turned to Ivy. "The manager's on assignment."

"Mighty convenient," Ivy snarled. "Then, get me the owner."

"I'm the owner."

"What?" Jinx came up out of the chair like an invalid at an Appalachian church revival.

"You heard me." Dixie punctuated the disclosure with a curt nod. "I'm the owner."

Sid's eyes bugged.

Ivy said, "I don't believe you. If you're the owner, why'd you take a crappy job like this?"

Jinx felt his temperature heat up.

"For your information, it's not exactly standing room only, working for a dead man. When my girls found out the building blew up, they demanded combat pay. I had to take this gig myself." She reclaimed her magazine and opened it to a centerfold of pavé bracelets from Tiffany's.

Everyone waited in stunned silence. Sid's hand came out of his pocket.

Jinx tapped Dixie on the shoulder. "Are you finished with your work?"

"Certainly." She flipped a page and gave it her full attention.

"It always took Georgia until at least—"

"I'm not Georgia."

"Let's go." Motioning her back, Jinx started toward his office. When Sid gripped the chair arms to push himself up, Jinx waved him away. Once inside, he closed the door. "Sit."

She took a chair, crossing her thick legs at the ankles. "I see you took my advice and wore your bulletproof vest."

"Dug it out of the trunk, first thing this morning."

"How come you keep it locked in the trunk instead of wearing it?"

"Body armor's hot and heavy and uncomfortable."

"I bet a hole through your gizzard's pretty uncomfortable, too."

"Why didn't you tell me you owned the agency?"

She lifted her chin in a dignified tilt. "There's nothing wrong with being a secretary, constable."

"Call me Jinx."

"All right." She tried his name on for size.

"Can you afford to be away from your company for three months?"

Dixie's chest swelled, and when she let her breath out, her irritation for Ivy seemed to go with it.

"Constab—Jinx—I've got a business to run. Ivy's right, but don't tell her I said so. Nobody wanted this crummy job. Where do you think I'd be if I had to turn down clients every time my temps didn't want to work?"

"But you said there's no money in it?"

"That's for damned sure."

"So, why do it?"

"It's not always about money. My business was founded on reputation. Which means I have a job to do, shitty though it may be. And, if it's all the same to you, I'll get back out there and do it." Without awaiting an answer, she got up, opened the door and stepped out into the hall, leaving him to scratch his head in wonder.

*I like her. I really do.*

He followed her out, prepared to put Ivy and anybody else who didn't care for her in their place. They stepped into the common area, as Dell, Raven and Mickey walked through the door, grim-faced.

"I'm glad you guys are here," Jinx said. "Take a seat. I have an announcement."

"I think maybe it's you who'd better take yours," Mickey said, his mustache unable to conceal the nervous tic at the corner of his mouth. "Dell has bad news. Go ahead, Dell."

"You tell him. You're the one found out."

"Which means, I did my part."

The pep talk he was about to give, about Dixie being the second most important person in the office, stalled in Jinx's throat.

With the cold hard look of an executioner, Dell spoke.

"Ivan Balogh. The convenience store cashier claims he came in to buy lotto tickets."

Dixie perked up. "Who's Ivan Balogh?"

Jinx made a stop payment on his reality check. It would have been tough, he thought, choosing between having Ivan Balogh on his ass, or having 925 cranking amps hooked up to his testicles.

He swallowed hard. It was important not to scare the help. "When did all this happen?"

The exchange of looks between Mickey and Dell created an electric force field no one wanted to disturb. Finally, Dell shifted his eyes. They settled on Jinx like a double-barreled shotgun.

"Two weeks ago."

# Chapter Twenty-seven

The startling news about Ivan Balogh's resurrection cast a death-like hush over the room. It meant the sheriff's new-hire roster took a backseat to finding out what the Prince of the Gypsies had been up to since his funeral two years ago. Jinx didn't need to look on the booking screen to find Ivan Balogh's address. He knew it well—assuming Ivan wasn't in the cemetery plot where Raven last saw him.

"Let's go," he told Sid, and they headed for the car.

On the way to Stop Six, a predominantly black enclave southeast of downtown, Jinx filled Sid in.

"Three years ago, Ivan Balogh put a contract hit out on Raven. Then the newspapers reported he died. But Raven wanted to see for herself, so she and Gil dressed up in costume and sneaked over to the funeral home. He was there, all right, only Raven claimed she saw him climbing out of the grave after everyone left."

"How's that possible?"

"Beats the shit outta me. That was a reputable funeral parlor until the gyps showed up."

"What does Balogh have to do with you?"

"When the gypsies couldn't touch Raven, they came after me. Gil called it payback for hiring her, but I don't think so."

He stopped at a red light and took inventory of the surroundings.

He didn't want to get into the part about stumbling onto

one of their gypsy scams. About how the air-conditioner repairman who serviced the Château Du Roy—in cahoots with Balogh to perpetuate insurance fraud—rented a two-bedroom apartment and stocked it with Provençal furniture belonging to Balogh. They threw a party and memorialized the apartment's contents with photos of guests draped over objects d'art; and when the place was burglarized and the furnishings disappeared, the A/C guy put in a sixty-thousand-dollar insurance claim. Balogh expected him to split it. He didn't.

That's where Jinx fit in.

After a late-night quickie with the Baldwin sisters in the parking lot of a gentlemen's club, he rolled up at the Château Du Roy and noticed furniture being loaded into a panel truck. He wouldn't have thought much of it—rats jumped ship from the Château each summer when the A/C went out —but he had the misfortune to be in the laundry room at the same time Glen Lee Spence was filling the Munsch brothers in on the burglary in Apartment 104.

Sid said, "Why don't we stop by and talk to the funeral director?"

"Because they went bankrupt shortly after Balogh's service."

The signal turned green and Jinx pulled away from the intersection. Having Sid along kept the stomach acid down to a low rumble. And talking about Ivan Balogh kept him from dwelling on Dell stealing Raven right out from under him.

Jinx wheeled the patrol car into a driveway littered with fancy cars put together with cannibalized parts. Gypsies were like that . . . all glitter, no substance.

Sid's eyes twinkled. He slid out his pipe. Tugged at his tobacco pouch and worked the bowl until the results satisfied him. Sucked on the stem. Talked out of one corner of his mouth.

He finally got his pipe lit. "So how do you propose we do this?"

"Ring the doorbell and ask them to send Ivan out. Either way, the jig's up."

Sid keyed the car mike, gave Jinx's call sign and spoke between puffs. "Hold us out at Ivan Balogh's."

By backing the patrol car into the garage of the red-tagged house on Felix Street, Raven and Dell were able to set up on Barbie Dahl's house a half block away. During their two-hour surveillance, they took turns watching the house with a single pair of binoculars Dell pulled out from beneath the seat. When nothing of interest happened, Dell made a suggestion.

"Come to my house. I'll cook dinner."

"Can't. My maid's husband is supposed to help me install some more dead bolts."

"You've got a good security system. Why do you need so many dead bolts?"

*Because an intruder broke into my house the other night.*

*No, that won't do.*

*Because my cousin's a sociopath.*

*Hmmmm, better not get into genealogy.*

"Because I don't feel safe."

The visit to Ivan Balogh's turned out to be a bust. For one thing, Jinx couldn't tell if the milky-green snake eye peering at him through the prohibition peephole cut out of the front door belonged to Ivan or one of the other inbred members of his tribe. For another, he didn't have a good enough reason to kick in the door to find out; so when the homeowner refused them entry, they had no choice but to meander back to the patrol car and leave . . . after Jinx jotted down license plate numbers to run a check for stolen.

Jinx dropped Sid off at the hospital district with Ivy, promising to return to the cabana by six. He stopped at the mom-and-pop, bought himself a Coke—the hoopskirt glass model—because despite what the deliverymen at the Coca-Cola plant said when they only left cases of canned drinks, there was a difference in flavor. He ended up parked against the curb line in front of Dan and Kamille's.

With each sip, he reviewed his options.

Sleep in his old room and eat whatever the maid cooked. Camp out in a cheap motel and eat on the fly. Install a dead bolt in the spare bedroom of his blown-up apartment, and sleep there until the holdover tenant vacated the two-bedroom Valentine promised him. Go back to Sid's and steer clear of Betsy.

Jinx sighed. Somebody wanted to kill him, but he'd almost rather push in the patrol car's cigarette lighter and set himself afire than ask his parents for a handout.

The formidable appearance of the moss-covered, brick and stone Tudor remained unchanged since the last time he'd visited—back when he'd humbled himself long enough to ask if they'd let him hammer one of his yard signs into the fastidiously manicured grounds, last election—an act his mother gravely discouraged, and his father went along with to keep the peace. By daylight, the Porters' two-story Rivercrest mansion evoked visions of animated cartoon birds and a mice-drawn pumpkin. But, with the echo of thunder, and lightning bolts on a rainy night, vine-covered walls and alpine-slanted gables conjured up images of moldy-skinned corpses and organ music in minor chords.

On the verge of hyperventilating, he walked past the brick columns with the rampant griffins perched on each sandstone cap. He punched in the security code and went through the wrought-iron gate. After lingering at the door, waiting for his heartbeat to slow, he lifted the heavy door knocker.

The massive leaded-glass door swung open, permitting the escape of boeuf bourguignon fumes. Dan, dressed in golf clothes and cap, stood with his arms outstretched, and a half-empty wineglass in one hand. Clearly, the old man was bright-eyed with more than just excitement.

"As I live and breathe. Come in, son. I'll get your mother."

Jinx looked past the marble foyer, past the Baccarat chandelier overhanging the long walnut dining table, freshly set with Kamille's bone china and sterling candelabras.

"Wait, Dad, don't call her just yet—"

"Kamille," he hollered. "It's Jinx."

"—I need to ask you something first."

"Mimzy's visiting."

Jinx found the mule-kick of his sister's presence as crippling as a right roundhouse to the stones. The announcement rendered him frozen at the entrance. People who didn't hate their only sibling could never understand such a relationship.

And the cola he'd just downed seemed to go right through him. Hastened by the discomfort of a full bladder, and teetering on chickening out, he blurted out the request.

"I need a place to stay for a few days until my apartment's ready." That doused the old man's smile. "But first, I need to use the bathroom."

Dan's facial expression bordered on grotesque. Jinx took a step toward the pink marble bathroom. Mimzy's bathroom. He never got past the Grecian statuary.

"No, no, no. Don't do that." Kamille strolled in, elegant in her black silk slacks, low-heeled Ferragamos and gold silk charmeuse blouse. Mimzy moved in her shadow. A carbon copy of their mother except for the honey-blonde hair, thirty-year age difference and a bad case of rosacea, Mimzy linked arms with Kamille and got missile lock on him.

"Hello, Jinx."

*Snotty bitch.*

She squeezed Kamille's arm in a way that transmitted a unique, unspoken code that could only be understood by mothers who played favorites, and daughters with an eye for inheritance.

Kamille said, "We've left everything exactly the way it was."

*Before Mimzy married and moved out.*

The wineglass shook in Dan's hand. "Jinx has something he wants to ask you."

Mimzy arched an eyebrow.

Kamille stiffened. "What is it?"

"My apartment won't be ready for three more days—"

"Good. I'm sure you've worn out your welcome at that man's house with that cat of yours."

"—and I was wondering—"

"Nobody likes cats, Jinx. They shed, and they're destructive."

"I just thought maybe I could stay—"

"Here?" Kamille's eyes bugged. "Horrors, no."

"—in my old room."

Her arms flailed in a no motion. "We converted it into a sitting room twenty-five years ago. If you came around more you'd know that." She looked to Dan for support. "We have everything just like we want it, don't we, Dan?" Mimzy pursed her lips. Kamille eased close to Mimzy's ear and spoke in a ventriloquist's voice. "Somebody tried to blow up his apartment."

Dan drained the last of his wine—a move that seemed to

flush some courage back into his system. "The boy'll be safe here."

"They could blow us up."

"He's our son."

"We have a daughter, too, Dan. Just because your son wants to live in the crotch of Fort Worth and consort with known criminals doesn't mean Mimzy's life should be jeopardized. And what about our granddaughter? What's little Gigi supposed to do when she comes in from boarding school next week? No, no, no. Out of the question."

He'd become anesthetized to his mother's verbal pricks. It was enough she denounced him as her son, but, for now, what he wanted most was to sock the smirk right off Mimzy's face. And during family moments like this, he often reminded himself how he screwed up by not knocking her off the monkey bars back when he had a chance to make it look like a case of accidental death. Or, locking her in the toy box in a game of Niagara Falls–in-a-barrel, and pushing her off the diving board, into the neighbor's pool.

Dan shifted his stance. "He said three days, honeybun. Right, son? You'll leave after three days?"

"I won't have that animal in this house." Kamille's voice climbed an octave.

Jinx wasn't at all certain she meant the cat.

"That's okay, honeybun, he can stay in the garage. It'll be like old times having Jinx home again."

"That's what I'm afraid of."

He didn't stick around for more abuse. He decided then and there, that if Dan and Kamille wouldn't put him up, he'd check into a motel. The thought depressed him, but he tried to look on the bright side . . . Caesar loved climbing curtains.

By the time he left, it was dark. On the lonely walk to the car, he imagined strains of Rachmaninoff filtering out of the parlor. With his mother's words replaying in his head, he did what any self-respecting, disowned son would do.

Unzipped his fly and relieved himself on the front lawn.

# Chapter Twenty-eight

Back at the cabana, Sid hunkered over the stove cooking chicken-fried steak and mashed potatoes with gravy. Wrapped in a plaid flannel bathrobe, and reeking of after-shave, it was clear the old man planned on going out.

"I'm catching a late movie, hoss. Don't wait up."

"You expect me to believe you're going to a late movie?"

"Well, if you ain't the fly in the milk. I was tryin' to spare your feelings. Truth is, I'm drivin' Ivy out to Eagle Mountain Lake. Gonna get me some poontang by the light of the silvery moon."

"Bring her here if you want. I'll keep to myself with a good book."

"Didn't want you to feel a failure on account of you're too run-down to chase booger."

"Worry about yourself. What if your heart gives out while you're in the throes of passion?"

"Then the undertaker won't have to embalm my dick."

Raven popped a pan of Ghirardelli brownie batter into the oven, and was setting the egg timer to go off in thirty minutes when the bell chimed.

Dell stood on the front porch, lugging a tool kit and cordless drill.

"Somebody call for the *Honey-do* man?"

"That depends. Do you take brownies for payment?"

"Always."

He came inside and set up shop. Pawing through her sack of dead bolts, trip switches and battery-operated alarm devices from the hardware store, a light seemed to click on in his head.

"What gives, Raven?"

She fisted the shirttail of an oversized checkered flannel shirt. "I found the door open the other day when I came home. I decided not to take any chances."

He pulled out the attic alarm and scrutinized it. "You don't think this is overkill?"

*Not for Yucatan Jay.*

"I'll sleep better if I know it's on there."

"If you get scared, all you have to do is call. I'll come at the drop of a hat."

When the egg timer sounded, Dell was running the hand vac, cleaning up sawdust by the front door. Raven invited him to stop for a glass of cold milk and brownies a la mode, but he turned her down and kept working. Eventually, she settled onto the couch and turned on the TV for the nine o'clock news.

Lots of wrecks from the inclement weather.

Multiple homicides in the Woodhaven area. Drug deals gone sour, according to the FWPD spokesperson.

A ten-K run scheduled for the coming weekend to benefit breast cancer.

Raven sank deeper into the pillows and closed her eyes.

Dell would make the house safe.

Dell would make it so she could sleep again.

The next vignette had Raven sitting bolt upright.

A dark-haired reporter of Latin descent stood before an Aztec archaeological site near present-day Mexico City. A band of Chiapan cutthroats started an uprising that left thirty dead.

A cold shudder rampaged across Raven's torso and radiated out to her fingertips. She watched, spellbound, as a photograph of *el americano negro* flashed in the top right corner of her television. Wrapped in a white, towel-like loincloth, with his legs painted blue and his hair flecked with gold, a man in blackface with Anglo features stared back through blue eyes.

Yucatan Jay.

Federales were called out to quell the riot, but the rebel leader managed to vanish in a hail of gunfire. A profound expression of mystery and superstition settled over the petite reporter's face. Using a voice-over in English, an unidentified translator made an analogy: She compared the disappearance of *el americano negro* to the grotesque figure Nanahuatl, when he threw himself into the fire to become the god of the fifth sun, Huitzilopochtli. The reporter's name flashed below her image, along with the block-print call letters of the Mexican news station.

Raven realized she must have let out a hysterical yip because Dell took the stairs in twos. He bounded into the room with the cordless drill and a drill bit bigger than some anatomically correct parts.

"What's wrong?"

"Would you believe the Chiapan monetary unit's gone to shit?"

"Come again?"

She jumped up from the sofa, threw her arms around Dell's waist and hung on for dear life. "Do me a favor?"

He crouched low enough to set the drill on the coffee table.

"Anything." With one hand cupping the back of her head, and an arm slung across her shoulders, he pressed a kiss into her hair and returned her embrace.

"Stay with me tonight. Don't ask why. Just be here."

After Sid's truck lights receded into the night, Jinx showered and dressed for bed. In briefs and a T, with an old Richard Bachman paperback about gypsies resting in his lap, he monitored the goings-on in Betsy's house with periodic glance-overs. By the fifth chapter, his eyes tired. He clicked off the lamp, returned the book to Sid's bookcase, parked himself in a chair by the window, beckoned the cat, and waited.

The metronome tick of a chinoiserie hall clock worked its hypnotic effect. His eyes closed.

He awakened to the Siamese digging his claws in for traction. Hissing and spitting, the cat launched himself through the air. Jinx sat up and took another visual scan of Betsy's house. A light illuminated the back porch; the rest of the house was bathed in the pale glow of the street lamp. He tossed back the covers, rose, walked to the window on unsteady legs and glanced past the empty pool, across the cobblestone drive to his unmarked patrol car.

Everything seemed fine. But the Siamese, slinking to the window for a second opinion, reinforced the eerie prickle of hair on his neck.

Only two more days and he'd have his own place.

Amen.

Then it hit him.

Now that he and Raven were on speaking terms, why couldn't he ask to stay at her place? Worst that could happen, she'd say no.

For a long time, he stared at the phone, wondering if he should call ahead.

Denying his request would be harder with him standing on

her doorstep, holding his 'Looms in one hand and a fistful of flowers he plucked from Betsy's garden in the other.

He checked the clock. Ten 'til midnight. Still early by Raven's standards.

With the decision made, he removed fresh clothes from the drawer and dressed.

In retrospect, Raven realized it was ridiculous to expect Dell to stay in the spare bedroom. Especially once she dozed off and the empty soft drink cans she'd taken to stacking in front of the bedroom door came crashing to the floor.

She grabbed the Smith & Wesson, rolled off the bed and used the mattress as a barricade. Half-asleep, she was still in the middle of her dream—*helping Yucatan Jay return fire on the Federales.*

*Holy smoke.*

*She was helping Yucatan Jay?*

*Now the family black sheep had invaded her dreams.*

The electric readout on the alarm clock flashed midnight.

"Raven? You okay?"

"Dell?" Groggy, she shoved the Smith beneath her pillow, got off the floor, scrambled back under the covers and scrunched the down comforter under her chin. "Something wrong?"

"I couldn't sleep."

He shoved the cans aside with his foot and rounded the bed. In the blue light of the street lamp she saw the outline of his Jockeys, the contour of his muscular legs and brawny shoulders. When he stood directly in front of her, she tried not to look, but her eyes dipped to his—

*Cocked forty-five.*

—and she wondered why Nicole Teague couldn't find a way to salvage her marriage.

"What's going on, Raven? What scared you?"

She shook her head, unwilling to tell him about Yucatan Jay.

"What do you think about going back over to Barbie Dahl's house?" He seated himself on the edge of the bed, where she tried not to look at his package.

"Maybe early in the morning."

"Want me to stay in here tonight?"

Her willpower reasserted itself. "You're still married."

"I'll stay on my side."

*Yeah, right.*

*Just because she didn't major in science didn't make her unfamiliar with the laws of physics.*

*It wasn't Dell's pop-up toy that bothered her as much as what it would take to get it to go down.*

"I'll be a perfect gentleman . . ." He grinned. ". . . until you don't want me to be."

"Right now, we have nothing to regret."

"There is one advantage to letting me stay in here." He reached out and brushed a lock of hair from her face. "Whoever you're scared of will get me first."

He made a compelling argument.

"Deal." She flipped back the covers and gave him a sly grin. "But remember, no trespassing."

The last thing Jinx expected to see when he topped the hill overlooking Astrid Street, was Dell's Chevy pickup curbed near Raven's driveway. Watching the upstairs lights go off one by one, he sat behind the wheel for a good ten minutes with nothing but the whoosh of the defroster and the hum of the engine rumbling in the background.

He tugged a pair of field glasses from beneath the seat and peered at the front door. Dell by God better be on his way out. A flicker of movement in what appeared to be an upstairs bedroom, caught his eye. He sharpened the focus.

Son of a bitch!

Dell. In Raven's bed.

On a savage high, he dropped the binoculars on the seat, gripped the steering wheel and listened to his heart trip in his chest.

Until now, he never really believed it.

*Running alongside Yucatan Jay, with the Federales in hot pursuit, Raven dodged bullets. A few more feet, and they'd make it to the Rio Grande. According to Jay, they'd arrived at the narrowest part of the river; if they swam like dolphins, they'd reach the U.S. border.*

An arm snaked around her waist. Hot breath caressed her neck, and she nuzzled closer.

*Jinx pulled her, half-drowned, from the muddy banks.*

*Yucatan Jay was gone.*

*So were the Federales.*

His hot body pressed against her. He nibbled her neck until she rolled over and gave in to ravenous kisses. She shrugged out of her nightie. Felt his hot tongue slick across her breasts—

—linger at her navel—

"Mmmmmm."

A pyrotechnic extravaganza ignited behind closed eyes, but her mind heard Jefferson Starship.

*Whatcha doin' . . . doin' me with your love?*

Jinx never did *that* before.

"I love you, Raven. I've always loved you."

"I love you, Jinx."

*Jinx? Did I say Jinx? Out loud?*

Her eyes popped open.

She had no idea why Dell took off, only that he flung the covers aside and lit out like a striped ape. At first, she thought he was answering nature's call, and dozed off expecting his return. But when she heard him trundle down the stairs, and the alarm screamed to life with the click of the front door, she grabbed her kimono and hurried to the window. Dell smashed on his hat, climbed into the pickup and peeled off in a mid-block U-turn.

What the heck got into him?

# Chapter Twenty-nine

Only somebody high on crack would have expected to wake up to an uneventful morning at Betsy's. No sooner had Jinx stepped out of the shower and begun toweling off, when Betsy's queen-in-heat screech filtered up to the second-floor landing.

"He's supposed to be gone, Daddy."

"Well, he ain't. And I ain't askin' him to git."

"This is my house."

"It may damned well be your house, but you don't get to lord it over my head like a human guillotine."

"Daddy, listen to me." Her voice climbed in an annoying whine.

While Jinx ran for his underwear, his mind gathered speed. He was already into his slacks when he peered through the stair railing.

"I'm done listening." Sid, on the patio just beyond the screen door, waved a meat fork in her face. "*You* listen to *me*. You're the one, begged me to come live with you after I had my first heart attack."

"You wouldn't have been able to get medical attention fast enough at the ranch, and you know it."

"I agreed so you'd have peace of mind."

"If you died out in the pasture, we wouldn't have found your body for a week. Is that what you want? To bloat up and explode like a dead cow? Or have mountain lions drag you off?"

Jinx buttoned the last shirt button and reached for his boots.

"You want coyotes to pick your bones clean?"

"I'm your father, you're not my mother. If he goes, I go."

Jinx barreled down the stairs. When he reached the kitchen, Betsy's head snapped around. She came through the unlatched screen in all her fury.

The breath went out of him.

*A Kevlar vest that would stop a .357, would turn to putty against the ice pick glinting in her hand.*

"Mr. Porter, I'm begging you. Leave." Her eyes swam, iridescent. "Your presence is disruptive."

"It's probably best if I go, Sid," he said, without taking his eyes off the wicked tip.

"You're not goin' anywhere and neither am I. And what the hell's that ice pick for?"

That got her attention. She dropped her gaze and stared. Sid swooped over with the speed of a hawk and plucked it out of her hand.

Jinx sucked in a hard breath. Last time anybody pulled an ice pick on him, it had a name—suicide-by-cop—and the guy ended up in Wichita Falls on a ninety-day commitment to the state hospital.

*Where Betsy should be.*

On the way to the trash can, Sid called over his shoulder, "Get your hormones regulated." The ice pick hit the bottom with a thud.

It must have been the nasty tone of a devoted father that made her snap.

Between sobs, her message came across ineloquent, but unmistakable. "You've got—to leave—Mr. Porter."

Jinx tightened his jaw. She ought to know he wasn't going to tell her old man that she'd never produce grandkids unless some chick got out a turkey baster and a vial of donor sperm. But for the second time in as many days, she stormed out in a sniveling heap of hysteria.

While Sid ticked off excuses for her erratic behavior, Jinx went back upstairs for his .38 and handcuffs. When he descended the stairs a second time, Sid was already helping himself to flapjacks.

"She ain't been the same since her mother died."

Jinx took a seat, prepared to down a plateful of food he had no interest in. By the time he wiped his mouth clean, he'd polished off two grilled pork chops and a three-inch stack.

While Sid rinsed, Jinx dried.

At the patrol car, they both stopped short.

*Betsy punctured his tires.*

Sid ground his molars. "I never knew her to disrespect other people's property. Let me ring up an old friend. He can drop off four tires and an air tank, and we can be on the road in under an hour."

"I'll notify the county garage to send somebody after it," Jinx said.

"No. You'll be expected to make a report."

It wasn't exactly fear Jinx saw in the old man's eyes, more like a question mark.

Jinx had one of his own. "Why do you think she hates me?"

Sid shook his head. "I didn't think she did. But she's acted mighty peculiar since you showed up."

"You don't have to pay for the damage."

"I aim to."

"It's me that owes you, not the other way around."

"You don't owe me nothin', hoss. I owe you. I haven't felt this alive since—"

He didn't have to say.

"—I made Ivy bay at the moon in the bed of my pickup.

Been meanin' to ask, didja give any thought to that black market Viagra I toldja about? It's like having a pecker made of porcelain. You can spear 'em and walk around with 'em stuck on your—"

"I get the picture."

The tire-changing fiasco lasted closer to two hours, but Jinx popped three aspirin to dull the throb in his shoulder, and they sat at a wrought-iron bistro table by the pool while Sid reenacted Ivy's primal moans.

By the time they arrived at the office, the deputies were making their morning rounds. Dixie puttered over the coffee tin, scooping up grounds. This particular morning, she wore a broomstick skirt and fringed western-cut shirt. The wild eyeglasses she chose for each day's attire had become a source of amusement, and this was no different. The tortoise-shell specs overwhelming her small face matched the print in her clothes.

"Don't start with me." She nodded at the coffeepot. "I wanted some for myself or I wouldn't have fixed it. You can help yourself after I'm through."

"What about me?" Sid asked, all starched, preening, and revitalized from the late-night interlude with Ivy.

Dixie lowered her specs enough to peer over the top. "If I don't wait on my drunken husband, you'd better believe I'm not about to wait on you."

She settled in at her desk, looked up at Jinx, then eyed the telephone as if it were roadkill. "Some old biddy phoned in carping about a red tag Ivy slapped on her house this morning. What's a red tag?"

"Eviction notice," Jinx said.

"Well, she didn't have to yell."

"Put yourself in her place. How'd you like to be kicked out of your home?"

"I don't blame her for being upset. But she didn't have to scream in my ear."

Jinx winced inwardly. "So, bearing in mind that this caller is a potential voter, what did you tell her?"

"I quoted the Bible: Pick up your bed and walk."

"You didn't."

"She hollered at me."

"What'd she say?"

Dixie sank her teeth into her bottom lip, cocked her head slightly and let her gaze orbit the ceiling. "This is a quote: *What'n the fuck do you think you're doing, red-tagging my door, you stupid cow?*" Dixie folded her hands in her lap. "Nobody screams at me, constable. Nobody."

"Anything else?"

"She said she voted you in, and she could vote your sorry ass right back out again. That's a quote. And she said we got the wrong house."

"The wrong address?"

Dixie nodded as if she were satisfied with her performance. "She said Ivy stickered the wrong place."

"Jiminy Christmas."

First rattle out of the box, and he already felt like he'd spent three rounds in the ring with Gil's golden-gloved friend.

"Get Ivy on the radio and have her check the address."

While Dixie summoned Ivy over the airways, Jinx glanced over at Sid. "And, you thought this kind of mistake only happened to narcs."

Ivy's voice broke in. "Oops."

Ivy's inattention to detail made Jinx mad enough to crack marbles with his teeth. To Dixie, he said, "Gimme the mike." He squeezed the transmit button in effigy. "Get back over and apologize profusely. I want groveling."

"Ten-four."

He returned the base set to Dixie with his irritation happily purged.

She said, "After you left yesterday, that hulking ATF guy with the freckles called. What's his name, Rusty? He said he'd be down to talk to you around one. I hope that doesn't mean I can't go to lunch."

"Ivy can fill in."

"Good. My cat Buster's missing and I need time to tack up fliers."

"Of all the rotten luck. Today was the day I was going to conduct interviews for that office cat job."

"Don't start with me. Buster's gone and I'm not happy about it."

"Tell you what . . . why don't you ride out to the pound with Ivy when she delivers the newspapers?"

"Ivy has a newspaper route?"

"No. Amos has a newspaper route. Ivy collects papers for the animal cages."

About that time, Ivy burst in, doglegging enough to fling a batch of returns on her desk and lumber down the hallway to the bathroom.

Jinx checked his watch. "Like clockwork. Chili dogs, you know."

Sid screwed up his face. "She eats them for breakfast?"

"Without fail. You don't want to go anywhere near that bathroom without a canary. There's documented proof of people who got trapped back there and had to be resuscitated."

Dixie's eyes narrowed. "That isn't nice."

"Then feel free to do your work on my computer, and I'll use yours until she comes out."

"Being nice doesn't make me stupid."

The third flush rattled the walls, but the hiss of aerosol got their attention. Ivy strolled out, all smiles.

Dixie sipped from her coffee mug, then addressed Ivy. "Jinx says you'll take me to the Humane Society."

"Why would he say that?"

"Because her cat Buster's missing." Sid.

Ivy scowled. "What does Buster look like?"

Jinx and Dixie replied in stereo. "He's black."

"How long's he been missing?"

"Four or five days."

"Uh-oh." Ivy picked up the telephone and stabbed out a number on the keypad. Grim-faced, she covered the mouthpiece. "They gas 'em before nine. That's when the animal control officers start rounding up strays to take the places of the ones they euthanized." Her hand came away from the receiver. "Hello? This is Ivy at Constable Porter's. Fine, how're you? Say, let me ask you something. The secretary's cat's missing. He's black." She covered the mouthpiece again. "Is he a tuxedo cat? Does he have white on him?"

"He's solid black."

Ivy translated. "All black. Hunnerd percent. Not a speck of white. Oh, really? Okay, thanks."

She replaced the phone in its cradle. Dixie looked up hopefully.

"They gassed him."

"What?"

In a wild grab for the phone, Dixie banked the coffee cup off the wall. She scrunched the receiver between her head and shoulder. "Gimme the number."

Ivy rattled it off from memory. Dixie punched it out on the number pad. Her eyes welled and finger-streaks of red climbed her neck. It was as if Ivy had slapped her from clear across the room.

"You sons-of-bitches killed Buster," she shrieked into the

mouthpiece. "What kind of shit is this? Buster came to you for help, and you gassed him like a bunch of Nazis. I've got a lawyer and I'm gonna sue your asses off."

Jinx's mouth dropped open. Sid retrieved Dixie's cup and headed for the coffeepot. Ivy sat folding newspapers with the serene expression of a terrier. Dixie banged the phone down so hard it bounced back onto the desk. She gently replaced it, sniffed, lifted her chin stoically, and extricated herself from her chair.

Jinx said, "Look, if you need a few hours off—"

"I'm going for a soda."

On the way out the door, she all but crashed into a lanky old drunk with slick black hair, dark crescents under grossly bulging eyes, and skin the color and texture of ground meat.

The man said, "Whoa, lady," then jumped aside. "Hello, Jinx."

"Mozelle Gratten. I can't believe you took time away from the shop. I've been meaning to get by for a trim, but things've been pretty wild around here. Don't mean to cut you short but we've got something kind of urgent."

"I don't wanna be a bother." He looked at Sid through watery, suspicious eyes. "But I got me a real bad problem."

For some reason, Dixie decided to wait. She stepped back inside and wove her way around them to her desk.

Jinx sucked in a deep breath. Somebody tried to kill him. Ivan Balogh had moved to the top of the list. The sooner they found him, the better off he'd be.

But Mozelle Gratten voted. And he always leaned a yard sign against the plate glass window of his barbershop, which happened to be in the pulsing heart of the precinct. He made big, fat campaign contributions. And he drove from one end of town to the other in his lime-green 1955 Chevy pickup with a red and white RE-ELECT CONSTABLE JINX

PORTER bumper sticker stuck to the chrome.

Jinx made introductions, starting with Dixie. She fluttered her fingers in front of her nose to let him know she could whiff Moze Gratten's whiskey sour from where she sat.

"And this is Sid Klevenhagen." The two shook hands and exchanged howdys. "Sid's a friend of mine. He's helping me around the office. What can we do for you?"

Moze dug a roll of papers out of his back pocket, slipped off the rubber band, selected two, and handed them over.

"I was in Big D a month ago." He cupped a hand to his mouth and lowered his voice. "I was checkin' out one a-them nudie bars, and they gimme too much to drink. I got lost comin' home."

Jinx unfurled the papers.

A Dallas PD traffic citation.

And an eight-by-ten glossy of the back of a vintage Chevy pickup with a Jinx Porter bumper sticker slapped on the rear bumper.

"That there's a ticket for runnin' a red light." Moze pointed a gnarled finger. "And that there's a picture of my truck."

Jinx studied the citation. The grace period to pay it had lapsed. He handed the papers back.

"What's the damned deal?" Moze's eyebrows inched up like fuzzy worms.

"Looks like Dallas got itself one of those new cameras hooked up to the traffic signal. Bust the red light—"

"It was yella."

"—or fail to clear the intersection in time, they run your plates and issue you a ticket."

"How can they do that?"

"The truck's registered to you." He could see Sid out of the corner of his eye, grinning.

"Well, it may be registered to me, but them sonsabitches don't have no way of knowin' it was me driving."

"Good point. They still have to prove their case. Did you set it for court?"

"I did not."

Jinx wet his lips. "Did you pay it?"

Moze Gratten handed over two more papers and hooked a thumb through his belt loop. "I reckon what I did was send them a picture of two twenties."

"You did what?"

Dixie hooted. Sid doubled over and swatted his knee.

"They sent me a picture of my truck and demanded forty dollars, so I sent 'em two pictures of President Jackson."

"What's this?" Jinx unrolled the rest of Moze's papers. The photocopy of two twenties was stapled to another photo from the Dallas Police Department.

An eight-by-ten photo of a pair of handcuffs.

Moze lifted his crooked finger. "That's what I got in the mail today. What's it all mean?"

The barber had to have the IQ of the school zone speed limit.

"It means, if you don't pay the fine, the next picture they take is going to be of you wearing stripes, holding up a template with a criminal identification number on it."

Dixie cackled.

"Moze, tell me you didn't really send photocopies of those twenties."

"Damned sure did. They've got no right to my money when they don't know for sure who was drivin'. I coulda lent that truck to a neighbor."

"Mozelle, do you realize they could charge you with counterfeiting if they wanted to? *Counterfeiting.* And since you sent it through the mail, they could file mail fraud on you, too.

Half the people in the federal penitentiary are incarcerated for mail fraud. It's the easiest charge in the world to prove."

Without warning, Ivy rocketed from her chair and dashed to the bathroom.

"I'd call them up if I were you, and find out where to send the money," Jinx said. "I'd hate like hell to have them send me their warrant to serve."

"That's the least of my worries." Moze sported an expression of the terminally damned.

"What's wrong?"

The barber ducked his head and stubbed the carpet with the toe of his Rockports. "Don't really like to say in mixed company."

"We're all family here."

Dixie shot him a killer glare—one that said she didn't care to be lumped in with the likes of them.

"Remember that nudie bar I told you about? I tied up with an old gal and I thought maybe you could tell me . . ." His voice trailed off and came back twice as strong. ". . . How do you know whether you got *gongorrhea?*"

Sid winced.

Dixie screwed up her face. Her expression reminded Jinx of something in a jar, preserved in formaldehyde at Ripley's Believe It Or Not! She snatched up her magazine and hid behind it.

"What makes you think you contracted gonorrhea?"

"It hurts when I pee, and it comes out kinda green."

Dixie threw the magazine on the desk, got up and stalked off down the hall toward the back office.

"I think I'd see a doctor."

"How 'bout you?" Moze turned to Sid. "Did you ever get a case o' that old gongorrhea?"

Sid shook his head. "No, but I got a bad strain of clap over in Korea once, almost made my dick fall off. Liked to never got rid of it."

"Your dick almost fell off?"

"Damned near cracked the tile in my bathroom when it hit the floor."

"Jeepers—" Moze wiped his mouth with the flat of his hand. "—You think my dick could fall off?"

Sid gave him the palms-up, universal, *Who knows* gesture.

"It's kinda got a rash on it." Moze glanced around furtively. "You ever see anything like this?"

Zipper teeth ripped open.

"No, no, no." Jinx waved his hands. "You can't be doing that in here."

Another rip sounded.

Sid dropped his pants. "See this? I got this scar from a Korean whore back in 1957 when I moaned so loud my cigarette landed on her back and she bit down."

Jinx was doing his best not to listen. "Jiminy Christmas, y'all are gonna get me sued." They ignored him, comparing wear and tear on their wieners. "For Chrissakes, this is an office."

Anybody could walk in. He headed straight for the supply cabinet in search of something to throw on the pair of mangy old dogs. He yanked the door open and whipped out a traffic flare. A magnesium flame going up at 1200 degrees should do the trick. He snapped off the end and started their way.

"Sidney, Mozelle—return your firemen to their stations!"

Ivy's screech traveled down the hallway. "This is a hostile work environment."

Jinx groaned inwardly. "Ivy, Dixie—don't come in."

Dixie popped into view. She peered over Ivy's shoulder. "What's going on?"

"It's a dick dance," Ivy said.

"You girls let me handle this."

"I wouldn't handle either one of them with a ten-foot pole. Although—" Dixie gave the exposed penises a contemptuous once-over. "—it wouldn't take a pole that long. Maybe chopsticks." Like a retracting turtle head, Moze's shrank in his hand. "On second thought, tweezers."

"Yeah, tweezers." Ivy let out a hearty guffaw. "Or, those little needle-nose pliers that grip tiny nuts and bolts."

"Jeweler's pliers," Dixie echoed.

Sid's alter ego wilted.

Appendages vanished.

Zippers closed.

Sid headed to the coffeemaker with a look of practiced innocence.

"What is it about men that makes them think we women should fall on our knees and worship something as ugly as *that?*" Dixie snarled. "My drunken husband's the same way, every night, every day. 'C'mon, dumplin', just this once.' The man's a sex fiend."

Ivy hooted.

"I tell him to wait for his birthday. Then I give him a case of scotch. By that time, he's so liquored up he couldn't pull it out with an intricate series of weights and pulleys."

Tears streamed down Ivy's face. "Or, with a tractor and some rope," she said, putting the finishing touches on everyone's embarrassment.

At some point during the abuse, Moze left. Sid was still trying to blend in with the Mr. Coffee. Jinx looked at the red comets arcing out of the flare and concluded inwardly that there was nothing like the humiliation of a man's appendage to unite a couple of warring heifers.

If only the rest of the day had such a bright outlook.

# Chapter Thirty

Shortly before noon, Raven came into the office to relieve Dixie for lunch. Ivy usually manned the radio base station, but the school called to say Amos had been suspended and they wanted him gone. Since Dell offered to pull surveillance at Barbie Dahl's, Raven volunteered for the job no one else wanted.

Besides, it would give her another chance to snoop.

Alone in the office, a half-hour into relieving Dixie as dispatcher, Raven checked out each deputy's desk blotter, looking for signs that might point to information leaks.

"What's up?"

She jumped at Gilbert's voice. He caught her going through Mickey's drawers.

"I was looking for . . . correction fluid."

"Isn't that white-out on top of the desk?"

She grinned. "I guess it is." Long pause. "So, why aren't you at lunch?"

"I'm going to give blood."

"Here—take my Kel-Lite and a cup."

She might've gotten a bigger chuckle if Amos hadn't lumbered in with a scowl on his face and his mother hot on his heels. Ivy grabbed him by the shirtsleeve and tugged him over to her desk.

"Sit here and behave until I get back. Understand?"

"I don't know why I can't stay home by myself."

"Because I'm tired of people blaming you for stuff."

*People, meaning the fire marshal.*

Ivy turned to Raven. "Watch him for me. Sid and I are going to lunch."

"Oh, no, you don't. I'm not your baby-sitter."

"Amos took a shine to you." Ivy looked at the Unabomber. "Didn't you? DIDN'T YOU, BOY?"

"Yeah, Mama."

Ivy gave her a cheesy smile. "See? He likes you. We won't be gone all that long, Raven, so don't let Amos tank up on a bunch of sugar. Sugar makes him crazy."

Raven looked Amos over from head to toe . . . and experienced the trompe l'oeil of the senses. With his hair freshly washed and trimmed, the kid looked like a junior executive: Dockers and button-down oxford shirt and loafers. She turned to Gil for support.

One look at Amos and Gil remembered he had stuff to do; he couldn't leave the office fast enough.

Raven abandoned her sleuthing and returned to Dixie's desk. She was about to start an internet search for Tabasco, Chiapas, Belize and the Yucatan Peninsula when a thin melody trilled out.

Amos whipped a cell phone out of his pants pocket. "What's up, dude?" He eyed Raven with the intensity of a predator. "I can't talk now. I'm with my woman. You owe me, dude. Catch me later." He snapped the phone shut and returned it to his pocket.

Raven stared, dumbstruck. "You have a cell phone?"

"Lotta kids do. What's it to you?"

"Why do you need a cell phone?"

"My mama calls."

"Who pays for it?"

"Me."

He stared at his watch, and when she strained to listen, she could hear the thinnest conversation taking place on his wrist.

"What're you doing?"

"Watching TV."

"You have a TV?"

He lifted his arm enough for her to note the tiny screen.

"Cool. Can I see it?"

"Can I see your tits up close?"

Raven felt the potential for raw violence. Several scenarios played out inside her head, most of them involving holding Amos's head underwater until the bubbles stopped coming up. Then, Dell came in. She motioned him over and whispered outside of Amos's earshot.

"Why'd you leave last night?"

"Went looking for Straight-Eight. Barbie Dahl was home but I didn't see any sign of Oliver."

"I'll go with you tonight if you want to make another run at him."

Dell stared off into the distance. "No need for both of us to go. I'll call if he shows."

The ATF agent who called himself Rusty, showed up at one o'clock in acid-washed jeans, a polo-style shirt with the Bureau logo embroidered on the chest, and smelling of Zest. He didn't monkey around with small talk. The Bureau had information they were ready to let Jinx in on. And if they shared, they expected confidentiality.

No gossip. No leaks. No nothing.

Jinx seated the agent in the back office with the door closed.

"Here's the deal, Porter." Rusty opened an accordion file. He pulled out a supplemental report. "The evidence has been bagged, tagged and sent off to the lab in Walnut Creek, near San Francisco. As you know, there aren't enough points in what few good prints we lifted to make a match."

"None at all?"

"If we had a suspect, we'd have something to go on, but you know yourself, without the requisite number of identifiable points, it won't be allowed in as evidence."

Just because the judge might not admit something into the record didn't mean the information wouldn't be of value. Jinx eyed the report, hoping Rusty would divulge the contents.

"I could furnish you with names of a couple of possibles."

The mail cretin.

Ivan, Prince of the Gypsies.

Odie "Straight-Eight" Oliver.

His eyes flickered to the file cabinet, where he kept a copy of his employees' prints in their personnel jackets.

Raven's prints.

Relaxed against the chair back, the young man looked more like a redheaded Buddha with his paunch rising above his belt, than a federal agent. But a voice filled with confidence commanded respect, and Rusty wasted no time coming to the point.

"The person who made this device isn't a pro. Looks like our unknown subject extracted it straight from *The Anarchist's Cookbook*."

Jinx's breath faltered. "That's not exactly on the bestseller list."

"No, but it's not all that hard to come by, either. You may not know it, Porter, but we have Gothic shops right here in the Metroplex that could get ahold of an underground manual, if you ask nicely and flash enough green."

"How do you know this?"

"I'll let that slide on the off chance you didn't mean to

offend me. The fact is, I read everything about weapons I can get my hands on. That's what makes me an expert."

"What about the Dogs Playing Poker? You said the playing card was the ace of spades from a set of Dogs Playing Poker cards. That's not in the cookbook."

"No, that's personal. That's somebody's little dig so you know they know you. It's their *signature*. They're jacking with you, Porter, plain and simple. Before it's over, you'll be as jittery as a worm in hot ashes. You'll suspect your own mother."

"You obviously don't know my mother. Anything requiring manual labor automatically rules her out. She's more of a toss-the-radio-in-the-bathwater kind of woman."

Rusty wore the same deadpan expression common to other federal agents Jinx had known throughout his career.

"Your mother wants you dead?"

"I meant that as a joke."

"You never know. My brother's FBI. He worked a case in Dallas six years ago where the matriarch of the family sent all her nephews and nieces Thanksgiving turkeys laced with strychnine."

"My mother used to encourage me to play in the street. Once, when I was five, she volunteered to hit baseballs to me in the front yard so my father could go off with his friends for a round of golf. The ball kept rolling into traffic. Not to mention the number of opportunities she had to fake crib death."

Rusty's eyes widened.

Typical Fed. Couldn't graduate from the academy until the last scintilla of humor had been wrung out.

"I think you're poking fun at me, Porter."

"For years, I've pulled criminals out of attics, brought them downtown in their 'Looms, and a few I've even booked in naked. Now you want me to suspect my friends."

"These people you hauled in—most were cons, right? Well, cons have a funny way of understanding the concept of what is and is not an occupational hazard. But I can tell you with a certain degree of confidence: the greater the intimacy, the deeper the betrayal. Some of the worst crimes are committed by the people closest to the victims."

"Then you've got your work cut out for you. Anybody who's ever been in this office, or at my apartment for that matter, would know I love the Dogs Playing Poker. That could be half of the white pages."

The Buddha came alive. "You have the Dogs at your house?"

"Until somebody blew up my apartment."

The look in Rusty's eyes chilled him.

"Why didn't you say so?"

"I thought ATF knew. The PD was supposed to collaborate with y'all."

"They didn't." Rusty's freckles turned fuchsia. "You should have disclosed this, Porter. It might have made a difference."

"How?"

"I want to see that apartment." He rose, then slid the unshared report back into its file.

"Fine. I'll round up Sid."

"No extra bodies. Me and you, that's it." Rusty narrowed his eyes. They sparkled like gemstones beneath a curtain of copper lashes. "Less people, less contamination. Not that we'll find anything of interest. Hell, the place's probably totally FUBAR. You know what FUBAR means, don't you, Porter? Fucked up beyond all recognition."

"The apartment's boarded up. Sid insisted. Anyway, the police haven't finished their investigation."

Rusty whipped out a cellular phone and punched in some

numbers. He pressed it to his ear and said, "Now they have."

Jinx dug a key ring out of his pants pocket and flipped through until he found one that unlocked his desk drawer. When Rusty finished his call, Jinx pulled out a folded grocery bag and handed it over.

"What's this?"

"I'd like you to send this to the lab. See if they can recover any prints, and match them to the partials. If anybody asks what's in the bag, tell them it's lunch."

Rusty flipped the sack over. He traced his finger across a transparent strip of red evidence tape.

"And, as long as we're asking for confidentiality," Jinx said with quiet sadness, "whatever you do, don't mention this to Sid."

Rusty mulled it over. "What is it?"

"If I'm lucky, a break in the case."

# Chapter Thirty-one

It took some doing, but Jinx finally convinced Sid he and Rusty needed to tie up a couple of loose ends, and suggested things might go faster if Sid stayed behind. When the old man balked, Jinx deputized him and put him in charge of the office.

Jinx was heading for his jacket when Sid cozied up to Dixie.

"Say, Dix, did I ever tell you about the time I used to operate the breathalyzer, back when I was on patrol?"

"No," she snapped, "and don't even try to whip out your little tube and get me to blow. Besides, I'm mourning the death of Buster, so if you don't want me to pick up these scissors and perform an outpatient procedure on your little snake eggs, you'd better steer clear."

In a hearty baritone, he sang, "I wish I was in Dixie," before she fired off a verbal cannon that left the rest of the song scrambling back down his windpipe.

"You don't scare me, you senile old geezer. My whole family's fearless. You're talking to somebody whose late brother raced trains for a hobby."

Sid's eyes narrowed. "Was he any good?"

"Thirty-three wins, one tie."

Sid ducked his head in reflection. "You tie, you lose."

Everyone paused for their own internal inventory on courage.

Dixie went on. "My son got a twenty-two caliber for his fifteenth birthday. He shot himself in the ass learning to quick draw. Never even went to the doctor."

"Grazed him, did it?" Sid's eyes flashed. "Say, Dixie, did I ever show you this bullet wound I got breaking up a dice game back in '64?" He went for his zipper.

"Sid," Jinx shouted, "don't make me get another flare."

Rusty's lip curled like someone inspecting dog doo on the bottom of his shoe.

"I don't know why I'm trying so hard to save my skin," Jinx muttered on the way out. "If I do actually manage to make it out of this alive, I'm just setting myself up to fend off sexual harassment claims the rest of my term."

They spent more time getting out of the parking lot than it took making the ten minute drive to the Château Du Roy. And, when they arrived, the Château was bustling with enough activity to make Jinx cringe in embarrassment. Rusty's placid expression hadn't changed, but the condemnation in his tone when he cleared his throat and asked, "You live *here?*" said it all.

The Munsch brothers, dressed in look-alike paisley bathrobes, had pink sponge curlers protruding from their hairnets. They were on the front lawn, engaged in a tug-of-war with Glen Lee Spence over a WWII flight jacket. Glen Lee, with the heels of his over-the-knee patent leather boots dug into the ground, a black spandex skirt, red lace bra and his long hair blown back from a theatrically made-up face, seemed to be winning.

"Bitches—let go before I kill you."

Jinx wheeled the unmarked cruiser into a parking space. "I see my neighbors are enjoying this balmy weather."

Rusty grappled for the door handle. "We have to help that lady."

"That lady has a third leg. Besides, this is only one phase of an ongoing dispute I've chosen not to involve myself in."

"Those women just took a swing."

"Drag queens."

But Rusty had already bailed. Jinx jammed the gearshift into park, popped the trunk, and fished out a tire iron.

"For the plywood," he said, setting Rusty straight.

"This is a breach of the peace, Porter. Shouldn't you do something before somebody gets killed?"

"I expect when they see this tire iron, they'll scatter."

An anguished scream split the air. Jinx crossed the parking lot and hit the sidewalk.

Rusty trotted up from behind. "Holy cow. It's turning into a bloodbath. Look at that guy's nose."

"You should see when they go to biting each other."

Glen Lee caught one of the twins with a right roundhouse.

Rusty winced. "From the looks of those heels, that guy'll have a purple horseshoe on his jaw inside of ten minutes. Don't people here call the police?"

"Before the first squad car rolls into this sector, they'll kiss and make up and Glen Lee'll be scheming to borrow their Mrs. Santa costume for the drag queen fashion show."

Rusty shuddered. "I take it that's your apartment," he said, pointing to the charred cavern beyond the wrought-iron balcony.

"Yep. Home-shit-home."

The fight continued as they ascended the stairs, punctuated with an occasional yelp of pain. In the distance, a siren sounded its plaintive wail.

Jinx pried open what used to be the front door.

Acrid odors made his eyes water. He waited on the balcony while Rusty stepped inside the threshold, sucked in a plentiful breath and held it with the dedication of a judge at a wine-tasting event.

"I'll be wanting a list of every visitor you've had over the last twelve months," Rusty said when he finally let the air out of his chest.

"Easy." Jinx ticked off names. "Me, Sid, my parents, the maintenance man, the roach-killer guy, and a couple of chicks I barely remember."

"Who's the maintenance man?"

Jinx pointed to an apartment across the courtyard. "Vic's lived here twenty years."

"Who's the pest control guy?"

"We'll have to ask the apartment manager."

But Valentine wasn't in the office, and they didn't find him in his apartment, either.

On the way back to the patrol car, Rusty elbowed Jinx. "You really don't remember the names of the women you brought home?"

"Do you remember the names of all your one-night stands?"

The contempt in Rusty's answer severed any fraternal bond they had built. "I'm saving myself for marriage."

If things weren't bad enough, Jinx returned to the precinct to find Mimzy squaring off with Dixie in front of a full office.

When the cowbell jangled, Mimzy turned to Jinx and glowered. "I've been waiting five minutes," she said icily.

"What time was our appointment?"

"I'm your sister. I shouldn't need one." When he stared, unfazed, she snapped, "You need to sign these." She presented a set of legal documents, folded into thirds and paper-clipped together.

"What's this?"

"Guardianship papers. Mother and I were discussing it

when you popped in the other night. Daddy's turned into a handful. We talked it over and decided if we all form a united front—"

Jinx slapped the papers against the heirloom brooch pinned on the lapel of Mimzy's houndstooth suit. They fell to the floor and landed on her Ferragamos.

"No emasculating female's gonna put the old man out to pasture."

"You're not around to see what's happening, Jinx."

"Well, pardon me. I work for a living—unlike people on parental welfare."

"His health's declining. I didn't want to do it either, but—"

"He's not going to an old folks' home. And, if you two bitches insist on following through with this, I swear to God I'll find a way to lock y'all up."

His eyes flickered to Gil's desk. The sight of Sid slouched in the chair with his boots propped across an open drawer gave his spine the strength of an I beam. Ivy, in one of her poorly executed surveillance attempts, folded newspapers for the Humane Society, and tried to pretend she wasn't eavesdropping.

"You'd better leave while the reasons I shouldn't knock you into the next building still outnumber the reasons I should."

Mimzy's face flushed but she kept quiet. And she never took her eyes off him when she stooped to pick up the papers. When the last swatch of fabric from the kick-pleat in her skirt disappeared out the door, Jinx made an announcement.

"Families are nothing but tyrannies ruled by the most neurotic member."

Rusty's eyes had glazed over. "That was your sister?"

"Now that DNA's a scientifically recognized procedure,

I've been thinking of having her tested."

"Wasn't she in *Sports Illustrated*?"

"Not unless credit card debt is a sport."

"Is she married?"

"No one'll have her."

"Think she'd go out with me?"

Jinx dashed his hopes with a look.

Rusty's bottom lip puffed out like he'd just gotten a novocaine injection. "Why? You could set it up."

"No."

"There's nothing wrong with me. I don't smoke or drink, and I attend church."

"What color's your BMW?"

"No BMW. Ford pickup."

"You're way too good for her."

"Why won't you help me?"

"I've already got one person trying to kill me. I see no reason to make it two."

At once, Rusty noticed the others staring. He gave Jinx's shoulder a brotherly tap. "Could we talk about this in private?"

"Jiminy Christmas. Is everybody taking turns trying to screw with my life?"

"You don't mind if I catch up with her, do you?" Without waiting for an answer, Rusty yanked the door open, set the cowbell jingling and dashed into the hall.

Jinx couldn't even muster up sympathy. The man had been warned.

Later that afternoon, Ivy stormed into the office, infuriated. She smacked a fistful of unserved court papers onto her desk.

"Would somebody tell me what the devil's going on? I

couldn't serve a doggone one of these."

Jinx, sitting at Gil's desk, glanced up from the metro section of the newspaper. "Why not?"

"You tell me. Nobody's home. I leave cards and nobody calls. What'm I supposed to do?"

"Find a way."

She snorted in disgust. "This has never happened before, Jinx. Every damned paper. One, two . . . maybe. But not the whole kit and caboodle."

The cowbell clanged. In walked Raven and Mickey. Mickey stomped over to his desk, pitched the black felt Stetson onto the blotter and swore under his breath.

Raven offered an explanation. "We lost Yo-Yo Behrens again. Missed him by a half-hour according to one of his whores."

"That's what she says." Mickey's forehead creased. "Why should we believe her?"

"Once a month, she shows up at my church for canned goods and formula. If it wasn't for the food bank, that kid of hers would go hungry—and she knows it."

"What's that got to do with anything?"

Jinx wanted to know, too. He sat up straight. Put down the paper.

"What it means is that I work the food bank every fourth Saturday. If I don't authorize the donation request, she leaves empty-handed. When push comes to shove, she loves that kid more than lying to us to keep Yo-Yo from beating her up."

Dixie held the phone aloft. "Raven, it's for you."

"Take a message, please."

"It's the chief of police in Laredo. He says there's some kind of problem with a male subject who dropped your name—"

Raven paled. "I'll take it in Jinx's office."

She sprang from her chair and dashed off, leaving Jinx to wonder why a phone call from Laredo would take precedence over this potboiler of inefficiency bubbling in his office.

# Chapter Thirty-two

"Feds got my parking space." Dell stalked in a few minutes before quitting time and threw his citation returns on Dixie's desk. "They need to go get a room."

Jinx, sitting in Mickey's chair, lowered the sports section. "What're you talking about?"

"Feds." He dropped his briefcase on his blotter. "They're fogging up the windows. Tinted glass, my ass."

He'd no more flopped into his chair than a local FBI agent and female sidekick, badged their way inside. Neither made any attempt to disguise their dislike at being roused so close to dinnertime. And, judging by the fresh suck marks on their necks and the female's crooked button job, food wasn't the only thing fueling their hunger.

The suit identified himself as Special Agent Longley.

He introduced his partner as Special Agent Hough. "H-o-u-g-h. Rhymes with rough." He gave the tousled blonde a sly wink. "What's the story on the constable?"

Ivy, munching a mouthful of eggroll, pointed at Jinx and turned into the town crier. "There's been a threat on his life."

"Happens all the time," Longley said with such lackluster he could hardly conceal his boredom. "Get yourself a tape recorder and start recording incoming calls. Call us when you have something." He sneaked a sideways glance at his partner and his lips tipped up at the corners. "Let's get a move on."

"Wait a minute." Jinx came out from behind Mickey's

desk. "That's not practical or we'd have done it." His dislike festered for Hough in her fitted red skirt, and Longley in his perfectly tailored navy wool. "There are eight lines on this phone. If we recorded every incoming call, we'd have to ask the commissioners for additional funding just to pay for blank tapes."

Longley and Hough shared a simultaneous eye roll.

"What do you want us to do?" Longley's stare lingered on the gap in his partner's blouse. "Throw in a voiceprint spectrograph and a stress evaluator?"

"Y'all already tapped the line. I want you to tell us who called."

"Fine," Longley said through a sigh. "We'll check it out and get back with a printout Monday or Tuesday. Come on, Hough."

"Jinx—" Raven rushed in from the back office with the color drained from her cheeks. "—I need tomorrow off—"

She braked to a stop.

Jinx said, "This is Special Agent Longley from the FBI," and she turned whiter than talc. Raven and the FBI agent shared the same ghastly facial expression. Jinx's jaw went taut.

*They know each other.*

*Old boyfriend?*

Even Dell reacted as if he'd just met the competition and didn't like the way he stacked up.

Longley's eyes cut to Hough. "That's the woman—"

Hough's mouth gaped. "You're the girl—"

The partners finished a simultaneous thought. "—in the bank photos."

Raven edged toward Dell's desk.

Longley got missile lock on her. "Where's Yucatan Jay?"

"You must have me mistaken with someone else."

Hough said, "You don't mind if we get your picture, do you?"

Raven's eyes fluttered in astonishment. "Why would you want a picture of me?"

But Hough was already digging in her shoulder bag. Before Raven could protest, she was blinking from the flash.

Curiosity got the better of Jinx. "What's going on? This woman works for me."

"That's the only reason we're not running her in." Longley scrutinized Raven's face. "She may've been involved in a bank incident. The Bureau owns the latest in digital imaging software—we call it Faces Unmasked, Version Two —or FU-Two, for short. A photograph can be superimposed over a second picture and the FU-Two program measures the facial structure and tells us whether it's the same person."

Jinx went to the back office and fished out a copy of Raven's Texas driver's license and vehicle plate number for the BMW. He photocopied the information and turned it over to the Feds.

Raven gave him a blank stare that said, *You're helping them?*

"I don't know what this is about, but the sooner they get off this kick, the sooner they'll be able to trace those phone calls."

Longley tried to menace her with a glare. "If it's you, we'll know. And we'll be back to talk to you. Come on, Hough, let's get out of here."

He grabbed his partner's arm.

"Not so fast," Jinx called. "Aren't you even going to question these people?"

"All right." Longley reluctantly released Hough's elbow. "You knock off those two," he said to his partner, "and I'll take these."

Special Agent Longley got down to business. He conducted a cursory interview with Raven while his counterpart corralled Ivy and Dell. Hough dug a field notebook out of her saddlebag, licked her thumb, flipped to a clean page and jotted cryptic entries.

Jinx decided to hang close to Dixie. From past experience, he knew they couldn't pry information out of Dell with a tire iron. And Ivy would shower the woman with a fountain of misinformation. Besides, it was Dixie who had intercepted both calls. Dixie knew the voice.

Longley stood beside Dixie's desk. "What did the caller sound like, ma'am?"

"Which one? I had at least three lines lit up at once. It never fails. Come four o'clock, the phones start ringing off the wall."

"You said someone threatened to kill Constable Porter." He studied Dixie's jungle clothes with mild interest, and directed his next question to her breasts. "You said it was a female?"

"I think so. I answered one line—it was that old puss boil from the JP's office. I recognized her snooty voice and stuck her on hold. I punched the next line and asked them to wait, but the girl on the other end said she couldn't."

"So you talked to her?"

"No, I made her hold. Then, I went to the other one. It was somebody from the sheriff's warrant office. I put her on hold and went back to the first line."

"So the caller was a girl?"

"Who knows?" Dixie glanced at her watch, letting her irritation show.

What began as a curiosity with Longley not taking notes, abruptly caused Jinx's skin to tingle. He could sniff out a concealed microcassette recorder with the accuracy of an air-scent K-9.

The fed pressed on. He braced his hands against the desk and leaned over until he was inches from Dixie's face. "I think we can agree it was either a female or it wasn't. Can you narrow it by half?"

"I suppose it could have been a guy with somebody standing on his balls."

The room got quiet. A cruel smile formed on Dell's lips. Dixie sniffed the air and wrinkled her nose as if she, too, whiffed the leftover scent of a modern-day Romeo who had just finished swirling his swizzle stick in Juliet's blender. Stiffening to his full arrogance, Special Agent Longley found himself in the spotlight.

"Let's come to the point. What did they say?"

Dixie reached for a blue aromatherapy candle. She yanked open her desk drawer—

—drew her mock derringer to light the wick—

—and declared, " 'I'm gonna kill him and there's nothing you can do.' "

Longley's hand darted into his jacket. He whipped out a government issue automatic and aimed for Dixie.

She let out a yip and hit the floor on all fours.

"Show me your hands!"

"Don't shoot," Jinx cried. He took a step but his feet moved with the speed of cinder-block loafers.

Raven flung herself in front of Jinx.

Dixie balled up. Defensively shielded her face with bejeweled fingers. Was halfway through the Twenty-third Psalm when Longley bounded around the desk with his gun pointed at her head.

"Drop it," he shouted.

With the speed of a gazelle—a 220-pound gazelle in size thirteen D's—Dell angled across the room.

"It's a cigarette lighter," Jinx shouted, shoving Raven out of the way. "She burns candles." Longley didn't move. Words tumbled out in a rush. "It was a quote. You asked what the caller said, and she was telling you."

Dell cocked his piece, deafening the room. "Holster your weapon."

At the touch of cold metal against his neck, the fed's eyes turned into huge spheres.

Jinx tracked Longley's gaze. Agent Hough, crouched in a combat stance, trained her sights on Dell.

Jinx inwardly cursed Ivy for keeping her gun in her purse.

But, for once, Ivy acted with great resourcefulness. She went for her desk drawer, whipped something out and jammed it into Hough's neck.

"One move, and this thing goes off," she shrieked. "Tell your partner to lower his piece."

Jinx's veins iced over.

Slowly, Longley placed his gun on Dixie's desk.

Hough hiked up her hemline and returned her weapon to its leg holster.

Dell uncocked his revolver.

A low hum cut on.

It took a few seconds to register. Ivy's flesh-colored vibrator went off, jabbing itself into the woman's neck.

"Stop it," Hough snarled. "I'm unarmed."

Ivy ran her thumb along the base. Instead of cutting off, the plastic switch dropped to the floor.

Industrial-strength gears ground.

A thin, electronic rendition of "Love Me Tender" sounded. The vibrator took on a life of its own. It whacked the agent's head with a vengeance.

Hough turned around slowly. The artificial schlong writhed counterclockwise in Ivy's grip. A transparent rat the color of raspberry Jell-O jiggled near its base.

Dixie pulled herself up. She peeked over the desk through red-rimmed, mascara-smeared eyes.

Without warning, the pulsating sex toy reversed directions. After a few revolutions, it probed the air with a series of stabs before retracting.

Hough broke the spell. "What the hell is that?"

"This?" Ivy, clearly searching for the right words.

With eyes glinting, Longley moved in for a close-up. "That's the grossest thing I've ever seen. What size batteries does it take?"

"Five D cells."

Mesmerized, his eyes followed the rotating penis. "Where'd you get it?"

"Mail-order house." Then, "It's for a friend's bachelorette party."

Jinx gave her a sideward glance.

"That's downright raunchy." Longley's nose flared with raw excitement. He stuck out a tentative finger. "Can I touch it?"

"Sure, go ahead."

"It feels real. How much did you say it cost?"

"Forty-eight ninety-five with the mouse, forty-two fifty without. Music's extra. Elvis's my favorite—I mean, my *friend's* favorite. Don't get me wrong, I like him, too, but. . . ." Feeble protests tapered off.

Longley's eyes flashed. "Do women really like these? That's the biggest one I've ever seen."

"They've got ones lots bigger than this. There's an iridescent black one that glows under a UV light, but it costs a lot more and I couldn't afford it—" She abruptly shut her mouth, let her eyes loll around in their sockets. "—For a bachelorette party, you know . . . that's a lot of money for a gag gift."

Jinx silenced her with a glare. Ivy had embarrassed the office for the last time.

She got the message, but not before firing off a poignant remark. "Say what you want, but marital aids have saved more lives in this office than Kevlar body armor."

A loud commotion brought the chatter to a standstill.

The front door swung open, striking the cowbell.

No Damned Way poked her bloated face inside. Slanted eyes narrowed into gashes. She cast each one an evil glance, but Jinx took the brunt of it.

"You still here. I no clean. You people sick." She disappeared into the hallway, leaving him to explain.

He chose not to.

"There's nothing else we can do here," Longley said to Hough. He turned to Dixie with the kind of half-assed apology Jinx had come to regard as typical of the Bureau. "Damned shame about this little misunderstanding. Hope you feel better."

He grasped Hough's wrist and gave her a tug. With the cowbell hailing their departure, they all but backed out the door. "We'll be seeing you."

"Yeah," Dixie muttered, "in my lawyer's office, you big turd." The torque in her jaw hung on for dear life. "They caused me emotional distress. I'm getting a bad-ass lawyer."

Before Jinx could calm her down, the door swung open unexpectedly. Agent Hough returned. "You," she said, pointing to Raven, "will be hearing from us." She stormed over to Ivy with fire in her eyes, and ripped the rubbery device, barely twitching, out of her hand. "Assault on a federal agent carries a hefty penalty. I'm impounding this as evidence."

She stalked out without so much as a backward glance.

Silence swallowed their comments.

Dell stared at the door. Ivy started to bitch, but after a scathing look from Jinx, she shut her trap and accepted reality—without Elvis, she'd be lonesome tonight.

Jinx tried to blink some kind of logic-defying order into the chain of events. Dixie measured him with suspicion.

The phone rang. Dixie shifted into greeting mode and answered. Anxiety drained from her face. She covered the mouthpiece.

"It's for me," she mouthed without sound.

For a moment, she listened. Without warning, her mouth gaped and her cheeks flooded with color. Shuddering, she gasped for air. Realizing something was wrong, Jinx moved in.

Ivy reached for a newspaper.

Dixie broke down and wept.

Jinx came to the rescue with a steady hand on her shoulder. To whatever existed beyond the ceiling, he said, "Good Lord, now what?"

She dropped the phone. Sobbing, she clutched her hands in prayer, joyous through her tears.

"It's Buster! He's come home."

By dragging her into the bank with him, Jay didn't just leave her holding the bag. He left her holding the whole cow.

Now Raven had the FBI on her ass.

Or, rather, on her face.

FU-Two? she thought.

Well, F-U, too.

She pled ignorance when Jinx questioned her about the bank fiasco, and completely omitted the part about how the Federales were holding Yucatan Jay until she could spring him. According to the Laredo police chief, Jay gave her name as next of kin. The big question was not whether she could drive down to Nuevo Laredo, but how soon. Since Jay started spreading gold Canadian Maple Leaf coins around with such reckless abandon, the border economy had gone to shit.

Early evening, she pointed the Beemer south toward Laredo, and asked herself for the hundredth time why on earth she felt an obligation to bail Yucatan Jay out of trouble.

But she knew.

She wanted to find out why Yucatan Jay lined his *sombrero* with foil.

And she wanted to know why he lied about being CIA.

And whether she had actually spoken to Aunt Wren.

With any luck, she could get an industrial-sized go-cup of strong coffee and drive all night. Once she brought her cousin back to Fort Worth, she could call Aunt Wren and Uncle Jack and have them pick him up and whisk him back to the Rockies to have his head examined.

A thread of compassion weaved its way in.

Poor Jay. It wasn't his fault he was certifiably crazy.

Other than his parents, Yucatan Jay was her last living relative. So, having a family member who needed help—even a crazy one—trumped an ex-boyfriend with someone out to get him.

Because in Texas, the only thing thicker than blood was oil.

"You may not believe this," Jinx said, winded by the time they reached the middle steps, "but the Château Du Roy used to be a real swinging place. They had a three-year waiting list. Now, it's a freak show."

At the top, he rounded the corner to Valentine's apartment, three doors down from his own charred cave. When he glanced at the plywood nailed across his former door, a neon-red ATF sticker got his attention. So, they'd officially seized the reins from the PD.

Jinx chuckled inwardly. That must've pissed off The Blue.

He balled up a fist and pounded the doorjamb. Valentine appeared wearing a woman's red silk robe and matching scowl. A studded leather dog collar cinched his fat neck.

Jinx took the unpleasant sight in stride. "Forget the two-bedroom. I need three."

"But the two-bedroom'll be ready tomorrow."

"Change of plans. Do you have one or not?"

"Not anymore. A couple with two kids is scheduled to move in at the end of the week."

Jinx refused to put up with Valentine's effeminate whine. "I've lived here since the summer of 1979. I'm currently paying rent on an apartment I can't even occupy, and you're telling me a couple with a hundred-dollar deposit takes precedence over me?"

"Think of your relationship with the Château Du Roy like being in a bad marriage. We've already turned you into an indentured servant. Now, it's time to recruit a new mistress."

*Bastard.*

Sid didn't appear to be listening. Propped against the door facing, he massaged a toothpick between his teeth and checked out one of the bank tellers letting herself through a side door to the drive-through across the street.

What sounded like the crack of a whip, came from inside

the apartment. Sid pushed himself upright and settled his hand on his six-shooter. Jinx craned his neck for a better view. Valentine closed the door, narrowing their view to one beady eye, a sheen of silk, and a couple of graying chest hairs.

"I want that three-bedroom. If you don't give it to me, I'm moving into the Worthington Hotel and taking an offset from my rent. By the time you pay the tab, I'll end up living here rent-free."

The exposed slice of Valentine's moon-pie face, blanched. His chest swelled to its full arrogance, and between furtive glances over his shoulder, he whined, "Why so big?"

"I'm moving my father in."

Sid's expression said, Attaboy.

Valentine slammed the door. Seconds later, he returned with a new lease form.

"Fill this out and we'll put you at the top of the list."

"Put the people with the kids on the list. I'm taking the three-bedroom and that's final."

"You can't just order people around."

"Let me put it to you this way, Valentine." He made every effort to demonize his face. "If you ever plan to beat on my door at midnight expecting me to intercede in a domestic disturbance, or drug deal, or some brouhaha between Glen Lee and the Munsch brothers, you'll give me that apartment. If you don't, and you so much as disturb my sleep for any matter except to notify me the apartment caught fire, so help me God, I'll cut off your head and stick it on the gatepost as a warning to others."

"You don't have to be so touchy."

While Jinx checked the lease over, Valentine turned his simpering attention to Sid. "I'd like to welcome you to the Château."

"Thanks."

"There's gonna be a party at my place Saturday night. You're invited."

"Mighty nice of you. Thanks."

"Just want to let you know, though," Valentine said, with an air of conspiracy, "there's gonna be some drinking."

"Don't bother me none. I'm an old Fort Worth beat cop. I've had my share of choir practices."

Valentine lowered his voice. "I should tell you, there's gonna be some nudity."

"Fine by me."

"There's gonna be a lot of sex, too."

"I can handle that."

"Good. So, I can expect you?"

"Sure thing." Sid grinned.

"Great. See you then."

"Hey, wait a minute. How many people'll be there?"

"Just us."

Sid came off the wall with his fists doubled up and a reservoir of undammed profanity. The contempt he dished out to Valentine left Jinx signing on the dotted line, filled with satisfaction. With the new lease in place and a promise he could move in that weekend, Jinx and Sid headed for the car.

Valentine called out after him, "Make sure that deputy knows you're not taking the two-bedroom."

"What deputy?"

"The deputy who came by day before yesterday. The one who asked to see the two bedroom."

Jinx's heart thudded like a flat tire. "Describe him."

"Plainclothes." Valentine cleared his throat. "A black man in a canary-yellow suit and a fedora. Quit looking at me like I've got the hairs in my nose braided." To Sid, he said, "Oh, all right, I've got that genetic defect common to a lot of men. I'm color-blind."

"Did he have a goatee?"

"That is correct."

*Valentine had just described Yo-Yo Behrens.*

"What'd he want?" Jinx said.

"He wanted an apartment. I told him the only two-bedroom we had coming vacant was earmarked for you. He asked if he could view it in case one like it came up for rent. Say, you don't look so good."

Jinx's knees wobbled. "This black man—did you get a name?"

"Do you have any idea how many people I see each day?" Valentine shored up his own importance with an eye roll and a snort. "Anyway, he hasn't returned the application."

Sid spoke up. "You weren't dumb enough to let him in that apartment, were you?"

"I showed him the two-bedroom Jinx was supposed to rent, if that's what you're asking." Valentine balled up a fist and jammed it against his hip. "Anyway, Jinx bullied his way into the three-bedroom, so what difference does it make?"

"Did you leave him alone at any time?" Sid, incredulous.

"No."

The Klevenhagen squint told Jinx Sid wasn't convinced.

"Never?"

"I didn't follow him into the bathroom."

The way Sid stalked over to Valentine's door made the manager slip the chain into its channel.

He wagged his finger and spat out a warning. "This man has been shot, bombed—twice—and somebody's still out gunnin' for him. Do not let another soul into that two-bedroom apartment until we get the ATF out here to pronounce it clean."

Downstairs, Jinx defied the KEEP OFF THE GRASS sign, and cut across the spongy lawn with Valentine watching.

Inside the patrol car, Sid dug out his pipe. "You need to get hold of that carrot-topped youngster. A prospective renter could get blown to kingdom come."

"You'd be surprised how many times Château people go up in flames. Serves 'em right, anybody stupid enough to convert their bathroom into a meth lab, you ask me."

"Get that boy to run a scent K-9 through."

"Rusty had a date with my sister last night. Maybe he can bring her."

"I don't understand why you're so hard on your sister."

"She's a leech."

'Nuff sed.

Jinx reached for the car mike and radioed Dixie. Reluctant to broadcast anything urgent over an unsecured channel, he gave her the cryptic basics. Get Rusty on the horn. Give him Valentine's address. Check out the location Valentine shows him. And one more thing.

Round up the deputies and get 'em back to the office.

# Chapter Thirty-four

The farther south Raven drove, the flatter the land got.

Once she passed the Laredo city limit, the principal port between the U.S. and Mexico came alive with the smells of ethnic foods, fresh produce and cosmopolitan life. Laredo made a stark contrast to its pitiful stepsister, Nuevo Laredo, a poverty-riddled sprawl on the Mexico side of the Rio Grande River. That particular dawn, the International Bridge buzzed with a steady stream of people crossing between the two nations; and other than the feeling of inherent disgust at the undercurrent of sewage emanating from the Mexico side of the border, Raven pulled into a parking space near the bridge knowing Yucatan Jay had found the perfect place to lose himself.

Too bad he hadn't.

Idling cars bottlenecked at the gates and polluted the air with exhaust fumes as they waited to pass through U.S. Customs; border patrolmen with faces permanently creased in suspicion, whispered knowingly as she locked the Beemer and walked to the bridge.

On the long trek across the footbridge, Raven sensed an overwhelming descent into hostile territory.

Back in high school, when the Del Rio police asked for a Texas Ranger to come down and interrogate a homicide suspect, she hounded Pawpaw to let her go across to Ciudad Acuña for a pair of electric-pink, doeskin sandals from a popular boutique while he helped out the PD. But Pawpaw said, To heck with that noise, she by God oughta buy USA if she was gonna fritter away his hard-earned money on another pair of shoes, then warned her never to visit the Mexican side without an adult chaperone. When she tried to con him by saying she'd be fine in the daylight, Pawpaw said, Bush-wah, a graduating senior had no business in a border town where marauders or practitioners of *palo mayombe* could abduct her and send back body parts in a *masa harina* sack, starting with her head. He went all serious and said if anything bad ever happened to her—anything at all—he might as well lay down on the railroad tracks and wait for the Intermodal hotshot to cut him into thirds.

Once she turned eighteen and left for college, she reminded Pawpaw since she was legally an adult, she'd be making her own decisions from here on out. Pawpaw said, Fine-and-dandy—he could use a break—and, oh, by the way, long as she wanted to play like a grown-up, she could foot her own bills, including tuition. And when spring break rolled around, Pawpaw told her he'd better not catch her taking her car across the border. Best case scenario, he said, she'd risk getting it stolen. But, if she accidentally ran over one of a thousand ragamuffins darting into the street to beg money or sell little boxes of *chícle,* she could end up in a Mexican prison with no way out short of a Charles Bronson look-alike and a rope, dangled by helicopter, into the prison yard. Remember the Alamo, he shouted. Remember the Battle of San Jacinto . . . we captured that cutthroat, Santa Anna, so you wouldn't have to be there. Then he went all serious and said if anything bad ever happened to her—anything at all—he might as well lay down on the railroad tracks and wait on the Santa Fe Kodachrome to splatter him but good, since life wouldn't be worth living without her.

He reminded her if—God forbid—she defied him and went anyway, she could end up like the poor freshman who lost his life after being kidnapped by a madman, a Santa Ría cult leader outside Matamoros. He didn't raise her from scratch just so she could gallivant around the countryside never to be seen again. Swarthy lowlifes did unspeakable things to pretty coeds wandering through border town streets alone, Pawpaw said. Getting her back could take years, not to mention hundreds of thousands of dollars in *payola*. And when she laughed and said she could take care of herself, he didn't mention a word about letting the Hill Country Flyer drag him clean to the next whistle stop; or holler, pshaw, and guilt-trip her into thinking he'd wait on the cowcatcher to split him in half; he went all serious and yelled, criminently. His eyes got watery, and he flung his arms around her and hugged her tight, then made a lame excuse about ragweed season, stalked off to the bathroom and ran water for the next fifteen minutes.

Now, as she set foot on Mexican soil—a good ten years after Pawpaw died—his warnings came back as if it were yesterday.

The next thing she knew, she was sucking in a stench that felt unbreathable.

*Bienvenidos a Nuevo Laredo.*

Welcome.

You can't go to hell if you're already there.

Torn between hightailing it back to the U.S. side of the border, or finishing what she started out to do, she headed toward *el mercado,* the Mexican market, in the direction of the police station. When she got hooted at by a couple of *pachucos* propped against a building, smoking hand-rolled cigarettes, she picked up her pace.

Halfway to hyperventilating, Raven entered the stone

building marked *Policía.*

With a half-dozen swarthy men with sparse, droopy mustaches looking on, she almost didn't recognize Yucatan Jay seated inside the doorway; but once she did, it stopped her in her tracks.

His moussed, white-blond spikes were gone, replaced by the infusion of a dull brown dye closer to his own natural hair color. Dressed in baggy pants, a turquoise Mexican wedding shirt and wearing a straw sombrero with a stampede string under the chin, Yucatan Jay had assumed the demeanor of someone with Down's syndrome. The hat crackled as he turned his head in her direction, and she knew from the chief's warning, it was lined with aluminum foil. Pieces of foil protruded below the hatband like a shooter's muffler, and Yucatan Jay had molded the flaps to conform to his ears. Before her eyes, his hands seemed to atrophy into lobster-like claws, and he pawed the air and grinned like a dement as soon as he saw her.

"Hi, Waven. Still wuv me?"

She blinked hard. Beneath the fluorescent lighting of the PD's lobby, his eyes glittered as black as onyx beads.

"Can we go home now?" He tentatively rose from his chair and shuffled toward her with clumsy steps that appeared to take great effort. "How's my dog? I'm hungwy. Can Mama make me bas-ghetti? Did you bwing me a color book and colors?"

With the assumption of his new, thick-tongued speech, her retarded cousin seemed to have lost the ability to pronouce his R's.

"I'm not talking to you—yet." Said nastily.

She skirted him with the precision of a cutting horse, and headed for the front counter.

A burly sergeant tried to menace Yucatan Jay with a glare,

but Raven's cousin broke into a tune that turned "Streets of Laredo" into gangster rap. When he sprang from his chair in order to pull off a few quick dance moves, the entire room almost drew down on him.

After a short chat with *el jefe,* Raven walked over to her cousin with her heart beating triple-time.

"They call you *tonto.*"

"That must make you the Lone Ranger," Jay said through a smile.

"No, idiot. *Tonto* is Spanish for fool. How come the head honcho thinks your name's Thomas Greenway?"

"Simple misunderstanding."

But Raven didn't think so. The desk sergeant disclosed that the U.S. Border Patrol ran Jay's prints through the Automated Fingerprint Index System, known to law enforcement as AFIS; American authorities had faxed over information to verify his U.S. citizenship.

Yucatan Jay had gray eyes. Not black. Or blue.

"You're not my cousin." She could hardly get the words out. "I don't know who you are but you'd better come up with an explanation pretty goddam fast, because we're standing in the middle of a police station in a third world country and everybody in here's armed like Pancho Villa."

He grabbed her elbow and shushed her. Pulled her beyond the earshot of people entering the building in search of help, or directions.

"I lost my ID in Belize. If any police agency runs my prints, the search is diverted to a special employee section for law enforcement officials. The agency carries me as Thomas Greenway."

"CIA." She almost spat the initials. "Why didn't the CIA bail you out?"

"It doesn't work like that, Rave. If you get caught with your pants down, they disavow knowledge of you."

Raven stiffened.

Tried to back away.

But Yucatan Jay—apparently seeing her degenerate into the throes of panic—yanked her close and talked fast.

"Thomas Greenway is a pseudonym. Thomas Greenway has no police record because Thomas Greenway is dead. He was born to Hannah and Joe Greenway, and died on the day I was born."

Raven became marginally aware that her breathing had stopped. She took in great gulps of air. Jay squeezed hard.

"Stop it, Raven, before you pass out." He pressed his mouth to her ear and hissed, "I don't expect you to fully comprehend what I'm saying at the moment—don't do that, don't do that—"

Her eyelids fluttered and the room suddenly blurred.

He steered her to the chair before her knees gave way.

The odor of freshly butchered meat from the *mercado* hung in her nostrils. Jay fanned the air in front of her nose and it went away. Sounds faded to a tinny buzz.

His hot breath grazed her ear. "Come back to me, Rave. We're almost out of here. We're Americans, Raven. Don't fall apart before we cross the border."

Her eyes focused enough for her to see contact lenses floating over his irises. "Why do you have tinfoil over your ears?"

He put a finger to his lips. "To deflect the government's mind-control rays . . . so they can't penetrate my mind and steal my thoughts. Here—" He pulled a square of tinfoil from his pocket. "—put this on."

He tried to mold it over her head in a metal yarmulka, but Raven resisted. "Dammit, Jay. Stop it." She glanced around for the hard-shelled suitcases and didn't see them. "Where are your things?"

He gave her a cheesy grin, coupled with the kind of palms-up shrug that denoted terminal irresponsibility. "I got rolled in the red-light district." Abruptly, his face went serious. He cocked his head in the direction of the police sergeant and alerted. "Do you hear them? They're trying to get in using a different frequency."

"Get in where? Who's trying to get in?"

"My head," he hissed. "They're trying to tap into my thoughts. You don't hear it?"

Lookie-Lous were craning their necks to check out the problem.

The sergeant growled something unintelligible and waved them away. Raven took the gesture as the Spanish equivalent of, *Get him outta here before we lock him up.*

Jay couldn't slip into the U.S., and into the Beemer fast enough.

The Gateway City and its Mexican counterpart were tickled pink to see Yucatan Jay head north for the winter.

*Gateway to Mexico?*

*Gateway to hell, more like.*

Amazingly, Border Patrol had no interest in a white girl dressed in a skirt made of butter-soft doeskin and a matching bomber jacket, nor the Down's syndrome dement loping along behind her. As soon as Raven pulled away from the International Bridge, Jay removed his hat. He plucked ten gold Krugerrands from behind the hatband and dropped them into the BMW's ashtray.

"For your trouble, my love. And by the way, may I say how beautiful you look?" He dropped the fake Down's syndrome act, and assumed the façade and speech of an English nobleman.

"Quit trying to grease me up. I'm not talking to you."

He adopted the brogue of a drunken Scotsman. "Mi bonny lass. Don't ya be mad at your kin."

"Button it."

Stopped at a red light a mile or so from the PD, Jay pushed the electric window button and slid the glass halfway down.

*"¡Buena suerte, amigo!"* he called out, then sailed the hat into the air, to a boy on the corner with a shoe-shine kit. As the light changed and Raven adjusted her speed to the flow of traffic, Jay clicked on his seat belt, settled against the over-stuffed leather as if to favor a tender spot, leaned his head against the headrest and closed his eyes. "Good night, lover."

*Finally, the voice of an American.*

Fifty miles up the Pan American highway, his lids popped open. "Can we get something to eat? I'm hungry."

"What'd I say about talking?" Raven tightened her grip on the steering wheel, and floored the BMW. "Zip it."

"Rhymes with ticket. Which is what you're gonna get, Miss Pedal-to-the-Metal, if you don't lay off that foot-feed. I can't get you out of a ticket. Too many strings. Those highway patrolmen'll cite their own grandmothers. Hey, Rave—the speed limit's seventy. Don't you think you ought to slow down?"

Her fingers whitened. She stared straight ahead and spoke between gritted teeth. "Every time you open your mouth, I'm going to increase my speed by five miles per hour."

"You'll get pulled over."

She punched the accelerator.

"Rave, really, you need to slow down." His voice developed an edge. "THP will arrest you on the spot and take you in to see the judge, instanter."

She stomped it to the floor.

"Holy cow! Okay, okay. I'll stop talking. Raven, you can't

get pulled over for speeding. *Do you hear me? I'll stop talking.*"

She turned on the radio, tuned it to PBS and didn't speak to him again until they stopped for gas in San Antonio.

As he sauntered off to the men's room, she called, "Hurry up." She saw no reason to be together any longer than necessary.

By the time he returned, she was tearing her credit card receipt from the pump. "What kind of food do you want?"

"I'm sick of Mexican. How about Chinese? No—let's grab a burger and tour the Alamo."

"We're not here to sightsee."

"But I may never come back. Please, Rave?" He assumed the pout of a five-year-old. "Pretty please, with sugar on it? Look, there's the space needle left over from HemisFair. Can we go inside?"

"I hate you."

"No, you don't." He smiled, victorious. "You like me. A lot more than you think you do."

"You're crazy."

His eyes went dark. He squared his shoulders and straightened to his full height. "I know you're mad right now, but once I get a chance to explain, you'll understand."

"I don't need to hear your psychobabble. I know all I need to know."

"No matter how flat the pancake is, there's always another side."

# Chapter Thirty-five

Dixie sat eyeballing a *Ladies' Home Journal* when Jinx and Sid sauntered in that morning. She placed the magazine face-down on the blotter, affording them a clear view of her tiger-print smock, matching billowy slacks and eyeglasses studded so thick with Austrian crystals Jinx had to identify their true color by the earpieces.

"I don't think it's Buster." Lacing her pudgy fingers together, she laid out the problem. "He looks like Buster, he acts like Buster, but I don't think it's Buster."

Jinx said, "Did you call Rusty?"

"I did." Petulant. "He's on the way. Now, back to Buster. . . ." Her voice trailed but the intensity lingered.

"Why don't you think it's Buster?"

"I just don't."

"Does he come when you call?"

"No. But he didn't come before."

"Did you let him in the house?"

"He's got a cat door."

"What about your other cats? Do they think it's Buster?"

"They get along real good."

"It's Buster."

"You don't even know Buster." She gave her red hair an arrogant toss.

Dixie exasperated him. He wanted to wring her fat, squatty neck. Here he was, trying to offer comfort, and she was spoiling for a fight.

"If it wasn't Buster, those other cats would be all over an intruder. It's Buster."

Her face still had that hangdog expression. In the lowest, bluesiest tone her singsong soprano would drop, she said, "I dunno," then grabbed the magazine and picked up where she left off.

In the back office, Jinx culled through his paperwork until he located the sheriff's new-hire list. He mentally ran through the thirty-one names, allowing his eyes to linger on each one.

In the end, he chunked the list aside.

He started to suggest they have another look around for Ivan Balogh, when Sid interrupted his thoughts.

"Where's Raven?"

"She's on personal business."

Sid slid his haunches onto the corner of Jinx's desk. "Monkey business? Think about what's happening, hoss. If the shit hits the fan and your gal ain't around, it's prima facie evidence she's involved."

"Could be coincidence." He buckled under the weight of Sid's stare. "Nothing's going to happen."

"Did she ever work for the SO?"

Jinx scoffed at the notion. "She holds the sheriff in the highest contempt."

"Did she ever work for another agency before she came to you?"

"She did a brief stint with the PD." He figured that would put an end to it.

Wrong.

Jinx's earlobes tingled. "Why're you asking?"

"I'm trying to figure out what kind of special training she acquired since you last saw her."

"You want to know if she can make a bomb."

Dixie poked her head in, ashen-faced. "Rusty phoned. He said—and this is a quote—an enchanter device has been located at your new apartment—unquote. They're calling the bomb guy, Jeremy."

Jinx used the chair arms to propel himself out of his seat. He paced in the small space behind his desk. "I'd like to see the SO's in-service training list. I want to know if Raven ever attended a school at their academy. I want to know who the guest speakers were, and if any of them had explosives training."

Sid's eyes glimmered. "That's gonna take more than fifteen minutes."

Dixie said, "I'll call for it. I can get it faster."

"The hell you say." Sid.

"Watch me." Dixie.

Jinx waved her off and she disappeared down the hall.

"I reckon that rules out Ivan Balogh." Sid pulled out his wallet, dug out a phone number and punched it out on the keypad of Jinx's phone.

His gruff persona transformed into Texas Romeo. "Hey, baby. You've got something I want," he said in a sex-charged growl. "Meet me at our place. Men's restroom, second floor, last stall."

"You're gonna get me sued."

The notion was enough to make Sid hoot.

"Let's hope we both live long enough to see it happen."

Letting Sid pimp himself out for a current SO roster didn't seem so bad, all things considered. Crazy old Klevenhagen was always looking for an excuse to trap another hide and whip out the old pelt skinner. It also got him out of the office so Jinx could make the call to the Texas Commission on Law Enforcement Officer Standards and Education, or

TCLEOSE. If Raven received training credits from a different police academy, they should have a record of it.

It was bad enough Sid saw Raven as the number one suspect—worse, Jinx couldn't convince himself he was only checking into her work history to prove the man wrong.

In the usual bureaucratic fashion, TCLEOSE took a number—after they kept him on hold. He pushed a pinch of Copenhagen into his mouth, and poised his finger to punch up the county employee roster on the computer.

Dixie framed herself in the doorway. "Everybody's waiting up front. Mickey and Gil couldn't get any papers served, and Dell wants a word with you."

"Be right there." He performed a few keystrokes and waited for the log-on screen to appear.

Dixie stayed put. "I've decided to put an ad in the classifieds. It's not Buster."

"It's Buster."

"Buster had blisters on his nose. This cat doesn't."

"Maybe they dried up."

He punched another series of keys, but a blank screen taunted him with a pulsing cursor. "Dammit to hell, what's wrong? It won't even let me log on."

"Oh, yeah, I forgot—the computers are down."

Weary, Jinx buried his face in his hands and rubbed his eyes. Data Services suffered from Balkanization. Each employee possessed a certain number of computer skills, and whoever came on the line listened just long enough to eliminate himself from the problem before passing the baton to one of his teammates.

"Get ahold of Data Services."

"Already did." Deep sigh.

"Don't waste time fooling with some underling. Demand to speak to their computer guru."

"Did you know he has twenty-five letters in his name? That's practically the whole alphabet."

"I don't give a damn. The only thing I want to know right now is why my computer won't work."

"You're raising your voice at me for something I didn't do."

"Look, Dixie, this computer's the neurological center of this office. It has to function."

"One glaring problem is communication, Constable. The guru has a thirty-word vocabulary. He knows three phrases." She mocked him, trilling her R's in the fashion of a Middle Easterner. " 'Perhaps you are forgetting,' . . . 'Please to settle down,' . . . 'We detect a problem.' "

"I just want to know when it'll be fixed."

He mashed his fingers into his eyeballs until stars appeared. When he stopped punishing his retinas, Dixie came into focus, mournfully peering through her Elton John glasses.

"Can I ask you something? Buster's my husband's cat. If I stick an ad in the classifieds, he'll be upset. Same as my son. They say it's Buster."

"It's Buster."

"My mother says it isn't."

"Does your mother live with you?"

"What does that have to do with anything?"

"Screw the ad. If it's your husband's cat and he thinks it's Buster, why can't you leave well enough alone and just let it be Buster?"

"Would you want an imposter living in your house?"

Jinx visualized the cat. That very morning, when he picked Caesar up, he likened the taut, muscular animal to a velvet-covered anvil with razors on each paw. He could identify Caese-the-Siamese from a roomful of seal points. Blindfolded.

"I think if he wants to play like Buster-the-Cat, and live at your house and put up with you people, you ought to give him the job."

She scrunched her lip and gave it some thought, then left as ungracefully as she had appeared.

Jinx followed her down the hall, stopping long enough at the bathroom to aim tobacco spit at the commode. He found the deputies assembled at their respective desks. Dixie went back to fielding phone calls.

"I don't know if she told you—" Jinx jutted his chin in Dixie's direction. "—ATF found a bomb in my new apartment."

Multiple voices asking who and how, rumbled through the tiny room.

Only Dell seemed perennially unmoved.

Mickey twisted the ends of his mustache. "Anything we can do?"

"Matter of fact, these are your orders—"

Dell and Mickey perked up immediately. Orders usually meant getting the green light to bump up reasonable force a notch. He suspected they took perverse pleasure in inflicting pain.

"—From this minute on—"

"Put your supervisor on the phone." Dixie, who'd been carrying on a normal telephone conversation with someone from the sheriff's office, abruptly changed her demeanor. "What do you mean he's not in? I'm through dealing with you. Connect me to somebody with an IQ higher than frozen meat, if there is such a person."

Dell spoke. "Keep her."

Gil glanced over with disapproval. "I don't think that's how to get what you want."

Jinx got on with business. "From this minute on, nobody

shares my parking spot, nobody talks about what goes on in this office, and if anybody asks anything you consider way too personal about what I'm doing or how I run this place, I want to know."

Mickey zeroed in on a problem. "Where're we supposed to pull in when we drop prisoners off?"

"Park in the fire lane, I don't care, but don't use my space."

Ivy's yolk-colored pantsuit was brighter than the circuits that connected behind her dull eyes. As expected, the information skidded through, unprocessed.

She stared, bewildered. "Why can't we use yours? There's not enough parking as it is."

"Because I'm not like Georgia. I don't want to come to your funeral."

Ivy relied on Gil to translate. "Our cars all look alike. If you're parked in Jinx's space, somebody might mistake you for Jinx."

"Don't talk down to me."

A melodrama playing out at Dixie's desk, disrupted the powwow.

Her eyes gleamed stubbornly, and her shrill voice went ultrasonic. "If you don't give it to us, he'll be over there with a subpoena in no time flat. Oh, yeah? Well, you'll just think so when he comes upstairs and kicks your ass."

Jinx stared at her with a degree of censure.

"You cocksuckers think you can just push the little people around. Well, my boss can whip your boss, big shot."

Dell spoke. "We gotta keep her."

"Come on down if you think your dick's bigger than these scissors," Dixie screeched. "You'll think twice when Constable Porter locks your ass up. Or, should I say what's left of your ass? And I expect a complete list, not some half-baked piece of shit you throw together just to pacify me."

A hush fell over the room. The strident tones of a man's voice vibrated from the receiver.

Dixie formed her next insult. "Well, you can kiss mine if you can find it with your lights knocked out, numb nuts."

She slammed down the receiver, threaded her fingers together and propped her elbows on the desk.

"You know," she said sweetly, "some people might find this kind of work stressful. I find it therapeutic. Last night, my husband remarked that I'm much calmer since I took this job."

Jinx suspected the poor man was tanked.

Gil braced his arms across his chest. "I'm not sure venting your spleen's the best way to get anything from the sheriff's office."

She smiled like a big tiger, satisfied after a good meal. "He'll bring it. Or, he'll taste blood in his sleep." She shifted her gaze to Jinx. "By the way, he may want to have a chat with you. He seemed pretty hacked."

The sight of Sid strolling in, wringing wet with sweat, thrilled him until he realized the old lieutenant returned empty-handed.

"Probably be a couple of hours before we have it, short-timer," he said in a confidential growl. He pulled up a chair near Dell and speeded his recovery by whipping off his hat and fanning himself.

The brooding German grabbed his Resistol and headed for the door.

The rest of the deputies had papers to serve, but they kept manufacturing flimsy excuses to stick around for the big shit storm to come. Bad blood between the constable's office and the sheriff was nothing new, but no one could recall that anyone had ever been challenged to a duel.

# Chapter Thirty-six

After a spirited argument, Raven and Jay settled on lunch at the Riverwalk, a downtown San Antonio tourist attraction. At an open-air café, seated near the water, Jay turned into a suave gentleman.

"I'll buy." He opened the menu and scanned the pages.

"With your stupid gold Canadian Maple Leaf coins?"

"I have money."

"Krugerrands?"

"Gold American Eagles."

His hand snaked into his pocket and she stopped him.

"My treat. Think of it as a going-away gift from me to you. Once we get back to Fort Worth, I'm making it a point to never see you again."

"That's what you think, gorgeous." A waitress cha-chaed over with Crown Royal for Yucatan Jay. He raised his glass in a toast. "To us." He glanced across the water at an empty tourist boat. "Would you look at that? Swear to God, the San 'Tonia economy's going to shit."

No one quite believed it when the cowbell jingled, and the last person they expected to see walked in.

"Georgia." Ivy acted like they were bosom buddies, instead of ripping at each other's jugulars fifty-two weeks a year.

With her brassy blonde wiglet neatly curled and anchored

atop her head, Georgia showed up in a floral print dress that seemed a size smaller. And the deep frown she'd developed over the past five years had all but disappeared. Instead, her face seemed to register a permanent look of surprise. Except for what appeared to be light bruising at the hairline, her oatmeal complexion seemed more evened-out and healthy, and she was lugging a tote bag big enough to rip off Wal-Mart. Judging by the shimmery ribbons poking out, she'd brought gifts.

Georgia took one look at Dixie and her silly grin evaporated. "Who're you?"

"Who're *you?*"

"I'm the secretary." As if that settled it.

"*I'm* the secretary."

"I'm Georgia."

"You're not Georgia," Dixie said with disdain. "I saw Georgia on television two nights ago, giving testimony on the six o'clock news, when that Starving for Jesus program aired. If you were Georgia, you'd be home starving for Jesus."

"I *am* starving for Jesus."

Dixie sniffed. "You might consider cutting back on dessert."

"Of all the rude things—Jinx, tell her I'm the secretary."

He wasn't about to. And when he didn't, she fumed through his silence.

Dixie said, "The old secretary quit."

"Believe me, honey, you're not all that young."

"What I lack in crow's-feet, I make up for in typing skills."

Georgia eyed her with cold scrutiny. "I wouldn't put on airs, if I were you."

"Break out some ID." Dixie stood, snapping her fingers to speed things along.

The bag slipped from Georgia's hand. It landed on the

floor, spilling boxes wrapped in festive colors. She looked to Jinx for help.

When he opened his mouth, Dixie silenced him with a wicked glare. "I'll handle this." She snatched the eelskin wallet out of Georgia's hand, squinted, then handed it back. "You may have been the secretary, sister, but I'm the secretary now."

Jinx detected a traitorous slant in Georgia's stare. Mickey lifted an eyebrow. Gil's jaw visibly tensed. Hooking a couple of unruly curls over one ear for better reception, Ivy pretended to busy herself by scribbling on a legal pad. Dell strolled in, picked up on the tension and headed straight for his corner. He dropped his hat on the desk and plopped in his seat. With his arms resting on the chair rails, he sat, sphinx-like, and stared at a distant point on the wall.

Georgia braced her arms across her chest. Dueling secretaries exchanged laser-beam glares.

Dixie said, "If you think you'll nudge me out of this chair at the end of three months, you've got another think coming." Georgia's breasts heaved. Everyone but Ivy watched breathless from the sidelines. "This is the best job I ever had. I don't intend to give it up."

Jinx shot Gil a sideways glance. Then, Mickey. The unblinking sphinx had turned into statuary. Ivy reached into the newspaper bin, took out a handful of papers, cupped a hand to her ear and made the first of many one-handed folds.

Georgia's voice warbled. "You have no right to take my job."

"I'm not the one who left."

"I have the right to take emergency family leave."

"And I've picked up your slack. You're history. Out with the old, in with the new."

Georgia's eyes misted. She turned to Jinx. "Is this true?"

He bowed under Dixie's demonic glare. Palms-up, he shrugged.

"So now I'm the secretary," Dixie gushed with the enthusiasm of a newly crowned Miss Universe. "And you're retired."

The bashing was more than Georgia could take. Tears sluiced down her cheeks.

"Just a damned minute." Gil rose halfway.

"Stay out of it," Jinx warned.

Dixie piped up. "This is a wonderful place to work. And these are wonderful people. I have a wonderful boss and these guys make wonderful friends. If you want to be a secretary, find another job."

Georgia lost it. "That's my j-job. And my . . . ch-chair . . . and . . . I want . . . my chair back."

Dixie's eyes glittered. "You abandoned them. Now you expect them to feel sorry for you?"

"I . . . made a . . . mistake."

Inwardly, Jinx laughed.

"I love . . . my job. I love . . . my boss."

He tightened his jaw to keep from howling.

"Jiiiiiiiinx?" Georgia's voice spiraled upward.

The bleating phone interrupted the drama. Like two women vying for a parking space, they went for the receiver at the same time. Georgia won.

She spoke in a down-home, syrupy drawl. "Constable Jinx Porter's office. Yes, honey, it's me. The other lady was rude? I'm so sorry. She doesn't understand how busy you are. What can we do for you?"

Dixie turned crimson. She seemed to be evaluating how the phone cord would look wrapped around Georgia's neck.

Georgia bosomed the receiver. "Jinx honey, it's that nice Ethiopian lady from Data Services. She wants to know if the computer's working."

"Hell, no. I can't even log on."

Georgia put the phone to her ear. "Honey, he's unable to log on." She covered the mouthpiece. "She wants to know if everything else is working."

Dixie had enough. She yanked the receiver out of Georgia's hand and yelled into the mouthpiece, "The on-off buttons work. The people who use the computers work. The lights work. So, technically, everything works except the friggin' computers. I refuse to talk to a bunch of foreigners who don't know their hemispheres from a hole in the ground. I demand to speak to the maharaja. The computer guru."

Georgia's face etched in horror.

Gil's had the makings of a permanent uh-oh written on it.

Dell smiled into thin air.

It didn't seem possible, but Dixie's voice climbed another notch. "Yes, I know there's a p-rrr-oblem, but if you don't fix the p-rrr-oblem, we'll get a real computer wiz out here and send you the rrr-eceipt, shit-for-brains." She smashed the receiver into the phone set. "Well," she said sweetly, "where were we?"

The office mumblings fell silent. There seemed to be a shortage of air.

Georgia said, "You need to be nice to these people, honey. They work hard, just like you."

Dell came out of his trance. "Dixie gets things done."

Mickey parroted his partner.

"She does get things done," Gil offered grudgingly.

Georgia's eyes watered. "You're probably a real good secretary, honey, but this is my desk. And you're a lot younger. It'd be easier for you to get another job than it would for me."

"Gimme a break. I'm middle-aged." But Dixie took the plea under advisement. "Suppose I agreed to leave. When would you want to come back?"

"Now."

"They haven't caught the bomber."

Georgia flinched. "I don't care. I want to come home."

*Home.*

"Well, of course, I'd need to find another job first." Dixie touched her temple as if contemplating leads. "Naturally, I would want it to be a good job. Being the secretary is different. It's not like being a deputy. You can replace a deputy."

Mickey's mustache twitched.

"Please, Jinx. I want my old job back."

"I don't know, Georgia, things have been going really good lately."

"Pleeeeeeeaaaaasssssseeee?" Georgia's voice shot up three octaves and hung there.

Her plaintive wail made him downright mad. "Dixie doesn't attend funerals."

"All my friends are dead. Except for y'all." Georgia pulled out a tissue and sniffled into it.

"If I let you come back, are you back to stay?"

She eked out a pitiful yes.

Dixie pondered her own fate. Finally, she sighed. "I can probably find a good job in a week or so."

Rendering the tissue into giblets, Georgia picked up her tote bag and distributed gifts.

Jinx pointed to Dixie. "In my office."

Away from the chatter, he closed the door.

She flopped into a chair and made a demand. "From now on, I want to be called office manager."

"Fine."

"You don't mind?"

"You can call yourself the Baroness of Belknap Street, for all I care."

"The Baroness of Belknap," she said, testing the sound. "I like it. And I want a raise."

"Fine."

"You mean it?"

"Sure. Set it up with Personnel."

She reacted like a woman who just realized she'd been walking around town with her dress caught in the waistband of her pantyhose. "Is this some kind of a bad joke? Because I don't get paid by the county, mister. You're paying me out of your own pocket so—"

"Did you mean what you said about not wanting to leave?" He searched her face for a sign, but she displayed the flat affect of a prescription drug addict. "Because I have an at-will doctrine. I have to admit, this place hasn't run this smoothly in eighteen years."

"You'd fire Georgia?"

"In a heartbeat."

"Do you think I want her job?" A half-smile played across her lips. "You think I like it here?"

"I was going by what you said. Did you mean it when you said this is the best job you ever had?"

"Do you *really* think this is a good job?" Incredulous, now. Her tone, cutting.

He averted his eyes. "I guess the job really sucks, huh?"

"Like a big, spooling turbine." She leveled her stare. "I'd rather have my tits sandwiched between a hydraulic lift and the undercarriage of a dualley."

"Then, I suppose I ought to thank you for wood-shedding Georgia," he said without enthusiasm.

Truth was, he'd miss her and those stupid stories about Buster.

"Look, Jinx, Georgia's self-esteem problem shouldn't stem from being a secretary. This place is the absolute pits. At least you won't have any more trouble out of her the rest of your life."

He could tell by the look in her eyes, they were thinking the same thing.

*However short that might be.*

# Chapter Thirty-seven

Not long after Georgia left, a short, weasel-faced guy wearing a black SWAT jumpsuit yanked the door open so hard the cowbell flew off and clattered to the floor.

Deputies halted, mid-sentence.

The man appeared to be a few inches too tall to be a bona fide midget, even though the obvious chip on his shoulder contributed to his stunted growth every bit as much as the enzymes in his DNA bar code. When he drew himself up to his full height, the .45 strapped on his hip weighted down the right side of his pants. With the elbow of his gun hand resting on his equalizer, he raised his other hand and shook a computer printout at them.

"I am Major Skinner. Now, where's this ass-whipping constable?"

Jinx checked the overwhelming urge to laugh. He stepped into the middle of the room. "Constable Jinx Porter. What can I do for you?"

The brother officer swaggered over until he stood inches from Jinx's belt buckle. Black beads swam behind obsidian eyes. With his square jaw torqued, he pointed a stubby finger. "So, you think you can whip my ass?"

"Me? No. I'm afraid my secretary got a little overzealous."

Eyes moved in a collective shift. They stared at Dixie, beet-red and looking as if she were about to split a seam.

"Care to step outside?" The tough-talking, tough-acting,

ninja-clad lawman balled up a fist.

Ivy unleashed a donkey bray laugh. When everyone looked her way, she flailed for the phone and dialed out.

"Howzaboutit? Wanna settle this, *mano a mano,* Constable?"

Jinx didn't realize how sickly Sid looked until he glanced over and saw his sidekick's ashen face. He'd like to pound the obnoxious little fireplug down to a two-inch dowel, but he knew if he did, Sid would jump into the fracas.

The gruff-talking deputy sheriff put up his dukes. "Wanna settle it man to man?"

Jinx shook his head. "You're too much for me. I'd like to apologize for Dixie, though." Nestled comfortably in her chair, Dixie cackled. He sobered her with a glare. "She needs to work on her people skills. We're sending her to charm school."

"Well, don't let it happen again. You don't know who you're fucking with."

It took all Jinx's reserve to rein in the rollicking howl lolling around in his belly. He could drop-kick the guy clear across the parking lot, past the employees' garage if he wanted. Could dribble him out the door and sink him in the nearest waste receptacle. Pretty much the only way the sheriff's little jester could hurt him was by tickling him to death with his bullshit.

Jinx feigned politeness. "I see you have the training academy printout. I'd like to thank you for bringing it down so promptly." Still swollen up mad, the tree stump stood inert. "I'm sorry we cut into your day." Jinx, on the verge of mockery. "I'm sure you have more important things to do than drop what you're doing to help out a brother officer. May we offer you a cup of coffee?"

"Caffeine makes me crazy."

"Hot chocolate?" He almost lapsed into a fit of hysteria, glancing around to see if his deputies were enjoying the joke. The biggest cup drying on top of the file cabinet next to the coffeemaker—Dell's—was about the right size for the tough-talking squirt to prop under a cappuccino machine and use it as a jacuzzi. "Care for some cocoa with marshmallows?"

"Another time. I have an office to run. Here's your list. And don't let it out of your sight or I'll have to come back down and hurt you. Understand?" He smacked it into Jinx's hands and stalked toward the door. His parting scowl had Dixie faking a gulp.

But once he disappeared into the exterior hallway, everyone except Sid and Dell roared. Joining the hyenas, Dixie came around her desk, reclaimed the cowbell and examined it for dents.

Her grin evaporated.

Jinx felt the weight of Sid's hand on his shoulder.

The old lieutenant wasn't laughing. "Do you have any idea who that was?"

"I'm going to take a wild guess and say Grumpy. I'm pretty sure he's not Happy, Bashful or Doc."

Sid's eyes darkened. "Behind his back, they call him The Spam-maker."

"That runty little guy?"

Raucous guffaws filled the room.

"It's not funny. That's the most dangerous man I've ever known."

Jinx couldn't tell if Sid was setting him straight or setting him up. The uproar died to a few random chuckles.

"I ain't wolfin'. Good thing you told J.D. you're sorry. Those bare hands put a man in his grave."

"That wiener guy?"

Sid nodded. "I remember the time he caught one a-them

hulking steroid boys pumping iron on his wife. They were naked in his house, his bedroom, his bed, doin' the triathlon on his sheets. J.D. forgot his sack lunch on the countertop. He sneaked into the house, climbed on a chair and watched the show from the kitchen."

Tension hushed the room.

"He took off his gunbelt, looped it around a couple of times and set it on the counter. . . ." Sid's voice faded. Everyone waited in rapt silence, studying his faraway stare. "Gives me the willies just thinking about it. Casanova was on his knees, beggin' for his life. The wife grabbed a handkerchief, darted out the side door and streaked through suburbia like a white-tailed deer."

Motionless and transfixed, all ears alerted on Sid.

Jinx asked what happened.

"The grand jury called it a crime of passion. There was so much brain matter on the walls they couldn't scrape it all off. Finally had to trowel over it with spackling compound before the house could be put on the market."

"Jiminy Christmas. What the hell'd he do to the guy?"

Sid hung his head. "Lord A'mighty, I can't even talk about it."

A little past noon, Jinx and Sid were culling through the sheriff's training academy list, waiting for Mickey to drop off a couple of blue plate specials, when Rusty showed up with his shirt ringed in sweat. Without invitation, the ATF agent entered Jinx's cramped office and closed the door.

"I don't get it. That freakazoid at your apartment said the man didn't carry anything inside. How can somebody get inside with a shit-slew of explosives and nobody even sees him do it?"

Jinx turned to Sid.

"Don't look at me, I wasn't there."

"Maybe he taped the door latch open and let himself back in when the coast was clear," Jinx offered.

"I thought of that. But your fruitcake manager says he tried the lock when he pulled the door to, and it didn't give."

Sid said, "What'd the bomb look like?"

"Before or after they disarmed it?"

"Jiminy Christmas. I hope you guys got pictures."

"Two thirty-six-exposure rolls. This dude's not very smart."

Sid's interest peaked. "How's that?"

"Like I said before. Textbook case, right out of the cookbook."

Something had been bothering Jinx, and it seemed like a good time to bounce the problem off Rusty.

"I heard the cookbook was actually written by the FBI—to blow wannabes sky-high."

Rusty stiffened. "Who told you that?"

"Rumor control. You know how it is."

"No, I don't." Rusty went into his at-ease, ATF stance. "I suggest you not make things worse by spreading rumors. The last thing you need to do is compromise our investigation."

The guy had to be kidding. What was it about feds, anyway, that made real lawmen want to clean their Glocks? Jinx changed the subject.

"Did you hear anything from Starsky and Hutch, about the phone call we got here late yesterday?"

"Special Agents Longley and Hough?" Unamused. "As a matter of fact, I did. Do you realize your phone calls go through a trunk line?"

"Of course. Every county telephone does."

"Do you know who you share with?"

Jinx didn't like the glint in Rusty's eye.

Sid spoke up. "Enlighten us, Freckles."

Rusty's hair got redder. Jinx almost choked on his own spit. Right now, Rusty was their only ally.

"Every call routed through—within a ten-minute window, give or take—is on a printout in the trunk of my car. There's just one little problem."

When neither gave the youngster the satisfaction of asking, Rusty finished his own thought.

It was enough to send a sane man hurling for the bathroom.

"You share a trunk line with the sheriff's office."

# Chapter Thirty-eight

A half-hour before quitting time, Dixie had no sooner rehung the cowbell than Jinx heard it ring from the anteroom. He finished running a batch of criminal histories and poked his head into the hall to view the latest brushfire that needed hosing down.

*Jiminy Christmas.*

Amos strutted in with his hair slicked back, gold chains around his fat neck, wraparound sunglasses shading his eyes, the latest in Pumas and a high school cheerleader on each arm. From the way his head swiveled, he seemed to be taking a visual inventory of the room.

"Hey, Jinx. How's it slinging?" He turned to Dixie. "Where's my mama?"

Dixie narrowed her eyes and slapped her magazine down. "Who're you?"

Amos shook off the teenyboppers and fisted his hips. "What's it to you?"

"How am I supposed to know who your mama is unless I know who you are?"

"I never seen you before."

"Ditto."

"What's that mean?"

Mickey spoke up. "Shit. This could go on all night." He rose from the chair and crushed the black Stetson over his hair. "Your mother's still out in the field. If you want to wait for her, you can."

"You can't tell me what to do." Amos lumbered to Ivy's chair with the cheerleaders in tow. He flopped down and braced his fat, freckled arms across his chest. T-shirtsleeves rode up, and the tattoo of Anna Nicole Smith jumped out at them.

Mickey stared, dumbfounded.

Jinx stepped into the main office with a handful of computer hits. "Where'd you get the entourage?"

"Huh?"

*Your long-legged, bleach-blonde tarts, with drawn-on lips and enough makeup and mascara to pull their faces off.*

"Your little friends."

"What's it to you?"

Jinx shrugged. "Just making polite conversation."

The cowbell jingled and Gil walked in with his eyes crinkled so tight his cheeks plumped. The sight of Amos making introductions, wiped the cheeriness off his face.

Dell addressed Gil. "Why the big grin?"

"I finally got that Hummer I wanted."

Amos took an unexpected interest. "How much you have to pay for it?"

Gil angled over to his desk. "Forty-five K." He pulled a key out of his pocket and opened the top drawer, deposited his papers and locked it.

"No shit, Dude? You paid forty-five thousand for a hummer?"

"Yep."

Amos scrunched his face. "Dude, I get 'em for twenty bucks. And if you gimme a hundred, these two'll do it for fifty, plus they'll let you videotape 'em while they get it on."

A collective gasp filled the room.

Dell said, "Gilbert bought a vehicle."

"Oh," Amos said dully. "Jinx, tell my mama I got a ride home from school. They've got drivers' licenses and a new Corvette. And tell her I might not be home for supper."

But Jinx was thinking what everyone else was thinking.

*For fifty bucks you can film them?*

It was close to seven o'clock that evening when the BMW zipped past the Fort Worth city limit sign. Raven reached over and jostled Yucatan Jay awake. He winced, sat up with a bit of a struggle and rubbed the sleep from his eyes.

"Where are we?"

"Think of it as the first step to an unending journey. I want to talk to your parents. To have them come get you for a psych evaluation."

"No. I'm not calling them."

"Then I'll do it. Do you realize the FBI has pictures of us at the bank?"

"Already taken care of." He dug into his pocket. "Take me to the Amtrak station. The agency left me a suitcase," he said by way of explanation for the locker keys in his unfurling fingers.

"I'm not falling for that. I'll pull off at the next truck stop and put a bullet through you before I get sucked into anything else."

But Jay didn't say anything. Didn't spar. Didn't argue.

Just keeled over, onto the seat, with his head pressed into her lap, his forehead burning with fever and three tiny keys scattered across the floor mat.

Sid had already left to take Ivy out for supper when Jinx transferred the first load of clothes into the trunk of the patrol car. Thanks to that untimely bomb scare at the Château Du Roy, a family the U.S. marshals hid out under the witness protection program thought the hit was meant for them and took off like a pack of greyhounds. Valentine cleared the move-in. Tomorrow Jinx would tell Sid.

Jinx's shoulder throbbed with pain. On the second trip to the car, he lightened his load by half.

Down the street, the sound of an accelerating engine closed in.

Probably a wannabe drag racer, fresh out of driver's ed.

Jinx headed for the cabana, for the third and final trip.

He opened the door a crack and stuck in a boot tip. The Siamese had to be nearby; if Jinx wasn't careful, he'd make a break for it. Unexpectedly, a pair of headlight beacons swept across the cobblestones. The seal point capitalized on the momentary distraction and slid past Jinx's leg as inconspicuous as a passing shadow.

In seconds, an unmarked patrol car bounced into view. Jinx's gut clenched. No one but Sid was supposed to know his whereabouts.

He squinted, shielding his eyes against the brights. The engine went dead and the door popped open. A sturdy leg slung out and Jinx was treated to a silhouette view of his broad-shouldered chief deputy.

"Gil. How'd you find me?"

"Followed you."

An uneasy prickle of hairs stood up on Jinx's neck. The reality that he was standing in the night air with one of a handful of people he no longer trusted, chilled him.

"I tried to catch you before you left." Gil shifted uncomfortably. Stuck his thumbs in his pockets and stared anywhere but at Jinx. "I thought it'd be better if we did this without anyone else around."

An unpopular thought popped into mind.

*How'd he scrape up the money to pay for a Hummer on a*

*chief deputy's salary?*

Jinx thought of his .38, collecting dust on the nightstand, and wished he had it on him.

"I know who's tipping off the crooks." The silence between them grew long. "Raven."

*The guilty dog barks.*

"Why do you say that?"

"I've been waiting to see which deputy hasn't had someone tipped off. Ivy was the only holdout, but she came back empty-handed, too. Raven's the one person with access to all of our desks."

Jinx tossed the last of his clothes into a cardboard box in the trunk. "You managed to serve your papers."

"It's been fine since you came back, but the last few weeks Raven held that office, my targets disappeared, too. Now I lock the unserved papers in my drawer, but that's not foolproof. She could've had keys made when she worked here before."

"I'll look into it."

"Jinx—it's not just me. We all think it's her."

"Even Dell?"

"Especially Dell."

The last place Raven wanted to take Yucatan Jay was the first place she took him.

To Jinx Porter's apartment.

Ex-apartment, rather, considering the urban blight Jinx formerly called home was nothing but a gutted, charred cavity. Raven slowed the Beemer to a moderate roll. A second apartment had strips of Day-Glo CRIME SCENE tape, affixed in an X across the front door.

Jay roused himself from delirium. With some effort, he raised himself upright and looked in the direction of the

Château Du Roy . "Rave . . . where are we? This place is major fucked-up."

The hospital emergency entrance was less than three blocks from the apartment, but Jay refused to go inside.

"Take me home."

"Not gonna do it."

"You can't ditch me. I'll walk away and die. You wouldn't let me die, would you?"

"What's wrong with you? Why're you flinching?"

"Bullet grazed me."

"You've been shot?" Her voice went ultrasonic.

" 'Fraid so." His eyes pleaded with her. "Our germs are different from foreign germs. I can tell I'm running a fever. Eyeballs feel like a couple of fried eggs. Brain's sizzling like a skillet of bacon. Must've picked up an infection. If I'm gonna die, I want to spend my last hours at home. . . ." His eyes rolled back into his head. He mumbled a few unintelligible ramblings in a strange language she assumed the Bijubi tribe spoke, before switching to English and uttering a statement with perfect clarity.

"Did I ever tell you the Denver economy's going to shit?"

Raven didn't take Yucatan Jay home with her, but she didn't take him to Our Lady of Mercy, either.

She ended up on Loop 820, a few miles from the 1950s-looking tract home of the late Ivan Balogh, Prince of the Gypsies.

Gypsies didn't use hospitals. They used curses, hocus-pocus potions and homemade remedies. The only question was whether the gyps would forget the bad blood they'd shared in the past, and help her.

Yucatan Jay's head flopped in her direction. "I'm not so bad, am I?"

"I'm getting used to you."

His hand slid across the seat. He found her knee and squeezed. "If we weren't cousins, would you go out with me?" His tongue thickened through slurred speech.

"If we weren't related?" Her voice cracked. "Yes, I think I might."

*What if he died?*

She took her eyes off the road long enough to glance over. "I have an idea."

"Run it by me." A wan smile formed on his lips.

"Gypsies. They tried to kill me a couple of years ago, but we're desperate and they're all I have right now. If you won't be treated at a hospital, I'm willing to risk it if you are." She turned off the loop, onto a cross street that intersected with the Baloghs'.

"Gyps are fine. Don't take your purse inside. They'll pick-pocket. Stay with me?"

Raven swallowed hard. "Yes."

"Remember to watch the car. Gyps'll strip it faster than a pit crew." He spoke in a winded whisper. "Rave?"

"What?" She reached Balogh's street and floored the Beemer. The powerful engine roared.

"If we weren't kin, could you love a man like me?"

Her voice warbled. "See, this is part of my overall problem . . . I go out of my way to pick men who're bad for me."

"Is that a yes?"

"I think . . . yes." How would she tell Aunt Wren the son she thought was dead, actually died because she deprived him of hospital care? "You're exactly the kind of man I'd pick."

In the distance, at the top of the hill, pale yellow lights glowed through a thicket of trees. Any moment, they'd reach the home of the late Ivan Balogh.

"In case I don't make it . . ."

"You are going to make it." She blinked fast. Tears rimmed her eyes. Her heart thundered, and she drew in a gigantic sniffle.

". . . in case I don't . . . there's something you should know."

Something told her she shouldn't hear any more. That whatever confession he was about to make should remain unsaid.

"I've been smitten with you since the first time we met."

"Conserve your strength." She whipped the BMW into the drive and braked in a gravelly skid. "We're here."

He reached for her hand and she let him. "I love you."

"I love you, too." She told herself the words tumbled out on reflex.

He scooped the locker keys up off the floorboard and pressed them into her palm.

"What's this for?"

"Amtrak station. Gold American Eagles. In case I don't make it. Do something good with the money. Start a camp for wayward kids. Put them on the right track so they don't turn out like me."

"Stop it." She cut the engine. Pocketed the keys. Reminded herself she was about to deal with gypsies and stuffed them down her bra.

"One last thing—"

"Keep the doors locked, Jay. Don't open them until I come back." She ejected from the car, leaving him alone in the dark, with the haunting effect of his delirium burning between her ears.

"—I'm not your cousin."

# Chapter Thirty-nine

*Ask no quarter, give no quarter.*

Only a life-or-death matter would force Raven to seek attention from the Balogh tribe. For two years she'd tried to gather enough information to prove Ivan Balogh wasn't buried in that cemetery plot after all. But the funeral home went bankrupt within days of that hoked-up service, and the owner died before she could acquire a sworn statement to trot down to a district judge for an order of exhumation.

Now, she stood on the porch to the supposedly deceased Prince of the Gypsies' house, checking out laser eyes recessed in the door frame, staring at the pin cameras sunk into the mitred corners of the gables—

*Hi, you're on* Candid Camera*!*

—wondering what kind of hold Yucatan Jay had on her that would make her resort to such desperation.

Of course he was her cousin.

He dialed her aunt and uncle and gave her the phone.

She talked to Aunt Wren.

Only . . . maybe that wasn't Aunt Wren.

Yucatan Jay could have set up a prearranged phone call to an imposter.

Without warning, a prohibition-like peephole popped open.

Out peered a bulging green eye. "You are *gadja.*" Spoken with contempt. "What do you want?"

"I need medicine. For my friend." Raven thumbed in the direction of the car.

"Why do you think we have this?" The person attached to the large eye pulled back enough for Raven to see the delicate outline of a woman's face.

"Because this is the gypsy house. Because you don't use hospitals." Thoughts of Krugerrands flashed into mind. "I have money. I can pay."

"What else do you have?"

Raven thought fast. "A painting my grandfather left me. It's worth a lot of money."

"Bring in your friend and go get the painting."

The peephole snapped shut. Raven dashed to the car feeling drill-bit gazes and heavy breathing from shadowy phantoms concealed in the shrubbery. Even before she reached the passenger door and saw for herself, she knew.

Yucatan Jay had vanished.

The only thing Raven could think of to do after she arrived home, was to call the area hospitals.

Maybe Jay staggered out to the street and bummed a ride.

Maybe he wasn't really sick.

She described Yucatan Jay to ER personnel, but no one resembling his description had presented themselves for treatment.

Out of ideas, Raven scrunched a couple of throw pillows under her head and crashed on the chesterfield. After a brief snooze, she awakened on her second wind. In the kitchen, electric-blue numbers on the microwave clock pinpointed the time at straight-up eleven.

Raven formulated a plan. If she couldn't find Aunt Wren's phone number on the internet, she could run teletypes to

Colorado police departments. Maybe even sweet-talk them into snooping out Yucatan Jay's background.

She drove the Beemer down to the precinct. Only a few uniforms working graveyard shift angled across the parking lot at the back of the constable's office, into FWPD headquarters next door.

She intended to pull into Jinx's space. But when she whipped around the first row of cars, it was already taken.

Not by Jinx.

Ivy's unmarked patrol car overshot the painted lines, as if she'd been in a hurry to park.

Chills crawled over Raven's flesh.

Why would Ivy be here, unless . . . Ivy was the leak?

She owned a big-screen TV. Had expensive bric-a-brac cluttering the house. Plus, new construction going on in the back.

Raven parked near the loading dock, slipped up the back way and entered with a key. Someone left the metal detector on. She slipped around it and crept past the elevator, rehearsing the confrontation with Ivy in her head.

*Jinx should've fired you years ago.*

Too strong.

*Whatcha doin' here so late, Ivy? Here, let me give you a hand.*

Aw, bullshit—idiot almost caused Jinx to die. Go for the throat.

*Let me check your computer history so I can see the number of times you've pulled up information and sold it to crooks.*

The faint *ding* of the elevator sounded on another floor. Raven rounded the corner to the office. She unsnapped her purse, stuck in her hand and fisted the pistol grips on her Lady Smith.

The interior light was on in the office. No sound came from within.

Raven pushed against the bar on the glass door.

Locked.

She inserted the key with her free hand. The dead bolt snicked back with a loud click.

*Jig's up.*

Raven's eyes darted around. Ivy was either in Jinx's office, the anteroom with the teletype or the bathroom. "Ivy? Hey, girl . . . where are you?"

No sound.

Nothing but the start of a car engine, followed by the squeal of radials against the pavement.

She eased over to Ivy's computer. The metal case felt warm to the touch.

"Ivy? You in here?"

Nothing.

Without air-conditioning, the air smelled mildewy and stale.

Raven checked the rest of the rooms. No Ivy.

She returned to the exterior hallway and stared through the glass doors at the empty space where Ivy's car had been parked. Defeated, she braced her arms and butted her haunches against the secretary's desk.

Dammit.

Almost had her.

I can still have her!

Elated, Raven headed for the supply cabinet. Took out a bottle of fingerprint powder, a new brush, a stack of blank index cards and wide, transparent tape. With a dip of the brush and a light flourish, she dusted fingerprint powder on the power button, mouse and keyboard. Using painstaking care, she removed prints from each key and the on button, and applied each speciman to an individual card.

When she finished, she printed both sides of the light switch.

After a quick cleanup, she returned to the secretary's desk.

As she reached down to engage the computer's on button, the hair at the base of her neck prickled. On a hunch, she felt the metal case on Dixie's computer.

Hot.

She recoiled, slamming herself against the chair back.

"This is it," she whispered aloud. "This is how she did it."

The computer holding the most data belonged to the secretary. It was only natural that Ivy would hack into that one. Ivy filled in for Georgia during the noon hour. They probably knew each other's passwords.

Raven broke out the fingerprint powder and repeated the procedure on the secretary's computer. When she finished, she wiped off the gray powder, booted it up and began a search. Each unserved paper corresponded to the Crook-of-the-Day. She logged the incomplete busts down on a separate sheet of paper and mentally formulated her argument to Jinx.

She couldn't accuse Ivy by throwing a bunch of index cards at him without iron-clad proof. Since he kept personnel files on each employee in an unlocked cabinet in his office, she hurried back and pawed through Ivy's accordion file until she found the duplicate fingerprint card Jinx kept when he forwarded the original to TCLEOSE.

That Jinx used a magnifying glass as a paperweight, made her smile.

She slid into the boss's chair, made room on his desk, and set out to compare the first of nearly 200 cards.

Major problem—none of the prints from the secretary's computer matched Ivy's.

And the lion's share of prints on Ivy's computer didn't match the fingerprint card, either.

Raven sat up straight.

*Nooooooooooooooo.*

Morbid curiosity made her thumb through Ivy's evaluations. Jinx gave her a performance raise every year but one. Raven let out a string of colorful expletives, stomped down the hall to the office copier and made a copy of Ivy's fingerprint card. As an afterthought, she decided to poke around Jinx's desk.

What the hell?

There, in his small, vertical script, was Betsy Klevenhagen's address.

Raven's mind raced ahead. The lawyer. Sid's daughter.

The tension tightening her nerve endings for the last hour, relaxed its hold on her face.

"This is it," she mumbled. "This is where Jinx is staying."

She reassembled Ivy's file and returned it to the cabinet. Before locking up, she dug an empty cardboard box out of the trash and created an impromptu fingerprint kit to take with her.

Ten minutes later, she aimed the BMW toward Ivy's house.

She arrived around one-thirty in the morning, parked a few houses away and pawed through the police gear in her trunk until she produced a lock-jock.

Raven headed for Ivy's patrol car, prepared to confirm her suspicions.

First, she printed the driver's door handle. Then, she printed the one on the passenger side. Unless she missed her guess, Amos was the last one to ride with his mother; his fingerprints should be on the passenger's door handle.

It took some doing, but Raven managed to unlock the Chevy without neighboring porch lights flicking on. She switched off the car's interior dome light and squatted on her haunches. Keeping her head below the dashboard, she whisked the brush across the steering wheel. Then, she processed the headlight knob. As an afterthought, Raven slid into the driver's seat, slouched down and glanced at the rear-view mirror. For grins, she processed its glass and plastic case, then transferred the tape onto blank cards.

Ivy was short in stature, as well as brains.

The mirror appeared to be adjusted to accommodate someone taller.

Finally finished, Raven pressed the lock button and pushed the door to. Hearing it click shut, she gave it a little hip bump, gathered her crime scene kit and took off for the Beemer in a sprint.

A half-mile from Sid Klevenhagen's house, Raven pulled off the road, into the well-lit parking lot of a nice hotel. She checked the fingerprints taken from the inside of Ivy's patrol car against the photocopy.

None matched.

She checked her watch and noted the time. Two o'clock.

What the hell? News this big couldn't wait. Jinx should know who was selling information to crooks.

She put the comparison prints back in the box, fired up the BMW and headed straight for Betsy Klevenhagen's house.

With any luck, Jinx would be sleeping in Betsy's bed.

*Then I can let go of him forever.*

# Chapter Forty

After Gil left the cabana, Sid straggled in three sheets to the wind. Before long, he was snoring like a walrus.

Jinx's melancholy returned with Caesar's disappearance.

Alone with his thoughts, he went outside for the fifth time to stalk the cat, pausing long enough to appreciate the fragrant scent of botanicals, and the promise of rain in the air. His watch had straight-up two when he set off down the drive with a heavy heart, rattling the cat chow sack.

"Caesar." He spoke in a strangled whisper.

A rustle came from deep within the foliage. He gave the bag a vigorous shake. For a moment, he drew fresh hope that he'd coax the Siamese out into the open, but the twitch of optimism petered out when he rounded the cobblestone drive. The pool light flooded the water with a creamy sheen. Nearby, shadows danced—none of them feline.

The scent of decay hit his nose. He wandered into the native plants, miserable and short of hope. Parted the branches of a weeping willow, and spied the cat waist-high and dangling.

Marble chips crunched under the weight of a human form. He dropped the bag and went for his pocket.

Fat lotta good a snub-nose did, resting on the coffee table.

He wished he'd roused Sid before coming outside.

Jinx backed out of the thorny garden, onto a pebble side-walk that stretched the length of the pool. Lacy leaves parted like a theater curtain, announcing the first act of a bad play.

He knew now what the face of madness looked like.

It looked like a thug strolling toward him, carrying a gurgling, struggling Siamese. Caesar's forepaws were duct taped together and hog-tied to the back ones, creating the illusion of a furry purse. With each step closer, the cat bumped against his knee. At the sight of his owner, Caesar snarled encouragingly.

The vise grip of fear tightened Jinx's chest.

Some thirty feet away, the trespasser paused near the deep end of the pool. The glow from the underwater lamp illuminated his face enough for Jinx to ID him. He wasn't prepared for what he saw, and recognition rendered him speechless.

*Oh, no.*

Odie "Straight-Eight" Oliver.

Mayhem dressed in Levi's, a dark, long-sleeve shirt and Rockports with spongy soles. Straight-Eight was the only man Jinx had ever seen who appeared to be genetically engineered by artificially inseminating the Metro Goldwyn Mayer lion with the Statue of Liberty. Somewhere during the time his sluggish mind attempted to process the frightening image, he closed his gaping mouth and tried to dispel the notion that all Straight-Eight had to do was fling the cat into the pool, where he would sink like an anvil.

His surroundings came into play, rapid-fire.

The nearest neighbors had switched off their lights.

Betsy's house had an eerie darkness to it.

Sid, sleeping off a six-pack.

That left him with only his wits and the old Indian fighter, which by now had shriveled up and taken refuge behind the little hangy-down thing in the back of his throat.

"Yo, Constable. Remember me?"

He'd know that three-pack-a-day voice anywhere—emoting, uneducated and grating. "Odie Uwayne Oliver."

The cat tried another acrobatic protest. The con swatted him with his free hand. Caesar's yowl carried into the night. It was then Jinx caught the glint of a filet knife in his clench. Even in the shadows, Jinx could tell the monster's eyes filmed over with the dull glaze of mental illness.

*Stall for time.*

"How'd you find me?"

"Paid good money." Spectral shadows intensified the malice in his smirk.

"Who sold it?" He tried to sound offhand.

"For ten grand, I'll tell you."

The cretin had his cat. "Sure. Let me go inside and get my ATM card. You can draw money out tonight."

"Maybe you can get your piece while you're inside." His tone ratcheted up a notch. "No, I don't think so. I'm gonna finish what I should've done the last time you came after me." The creaky hinge voice sent a shudder through Jinx that didn't stop until it hit bone.

Jinx's eyes flickered to the house and back. "Where's Betsy?"

"Was that her name?"

His heart skipped. "What'd you do to her?"

"What I wanted to do to all of 'em. You shoulda seen her trying to talk me out of it. Cryin', blubberin'. She's queer, didja know that?" In the glow of the pool light, his eyes glimmered like hot coals. "Only queer chicks I ever knew were strippers, and women doing time. Ladies need that touchy-feely shit. Not me. Not Straight-Eight. You send Straight-Eight back to the joint, only thing he wants to feel is a man's eyeballs when he squashes 'em with his bare hands."

*He's off his chain.*

Jinx digested this silently. Betsy didn't puncture the tires.

She didn't hate him. She wanted them both out of harm's way.

The cat put up a violent struggle. Oliver tightened his grip on the makeshift handle.

Jinx tried to buy time. He needed an escape hatch for himself and the Siamese. "Why her?"

"I saw her at the hospital, when she came to pick up her old man's body." He permitted himself a diabolical chuckle. "Drivin' that big-ass Lincoln, drippin' in diamonds and gold."

"You're the one who tried to kill Sid."

Insanity shrugged its shoulders. "Fucking incompetent hospital people . . . it was supposed to be you in that bed."

The hairs on the back of Jinx's neck stood up.

The cat let out a pitiful yowl.

Jinx's heart didn't just skid, it tripped over itself. "What do you want from me?"

"Lose the warrant. I ain't goin' back to the joint."

What was Straight-Eight thinking? Surely he had to realize the Texas Crime Information Center and National Crime Information Center had everything about him but the size of his dick. And if he put a tattoo on it, or pierced it and ran a bolt through it, they'd have entered that, too.

"Every law enforcement agency in the U.S. has access to it. You're in TCIC/NCIC. It's in the computer."

"Take it out."

"It doesn't work like that."

The cat hissed. The sight of the Siamese snapping at his tormentor set Jinx's heart pounding. Oliver banged Caesar hard against his knee. The poor animal began to choke.

"Don't hurt him," Jinx pleaded. He imagined Straight-Eight in a straitjacket and wished he could make it happen. "I was doing my job. Just like you were doing yours. In your line of work, getting caught's an occupational hazard."

*Just like getting shot's an occupational hazard for me.*

The convicted felon raised the knife and carved a lazy X into the air. Frothing at the mouth, the cat went into a wild struggle.

"Put him down and walk away."

"Sure thing." Casual. Agreeable. Said with a snaggle-toothed smile.

To Jinx's horror, Odie Oliver did the unthinkable.

With a slash, the blade reddened against Caesar's taupe fur. Hellish cries pierced the night. The cat writhed in a futile attempt to break free.

The splash that followed sickened him.

Jinx no longer cared about himself. Oliver wasn't going to drown his furry old pal. Without thinking, he chased the zigzag trail of blood into the deep. It didn't matter that his pocket change turned into a cinder block anymore than it mattered that in fifty-three years, he'd never learned to swim.

The rattlesnake bite in his shoulder was just the beginning of the underwater nightmare. The rip of stitches and the through-and-through pain almost made him black out from shock. But it was the icy bath and the grave sensation from five pounds of coins and the drag of water-filled boots that put him in a panic.

Near the drain, he grabbed a handful of fur and tried to flail his way to the top, one-handed.

Boots anchored him down.

When he planted his feet against the metal grate and launched himself to the surface, they shaved off precious seconds.

He bobbed up, sputtering. With his good arm, he flung the cat with all his might, hard enough to clear the edge of the pool. Caesar landed, wild-eyed and gagging, on the grass.

A deep breath before he sank.

Clearly, Oliver enjoyed watching him drowning.

He opened his eyes to a mirage of ceramic tile border and struggled wildly. When his nose pierced the liquid veil, he took another breath and felt the strong pull of death.

His injured arm, searing with pain, floated virtually useless.

Somewhere between the time he saw the seven-foot mark wiggling underwater and his foot touched bottom, he slipped out of one boot and propelled himself above the waterline. He winced at the sting of chlorine up his nose, and flailed within arm's reach of the tile with the numeric six.

Conquered territory renewed his hope.

Submerged, he struggled with the other boot. It came off with the last of his air bubbles. With a violent push, he broke through the surface to the five-foot mark.

With toes digging into the pool's abrasive floor, he looked around.

That the Siamese had managed to defeat the duct tape on one forepaw and one back, delighted him. He experienced an incomparable thrill watching the furious cat drag himself beyond the knife-wielding lunatic. The psycho moved stealthily around the pool.

Jinx bellowed into the night. "Klevenhagen—call nine one one."

Oliver whipped around in a halt of indecision. The cat loosed another paw. He trotted out of sight on wobbly legs.

"Dial nine one one!"

Jinx continued the isometric trudge to the three-foot mark. When he reached the steps, Straight-Eight started toward the shallow end with the knife upraised.

Jinx could almost hear the monster's thoughts. He wanted to hoist himself onto the pebble sidewalk and make a break for it. But he gauged Oliver's distance and knew he couldn't outrun him. But that crazed stare made Jinx want to try.

His father's words of wisdom flashed into his mind.

*You wouldn't run from a dog that was chasing you, would you?*

Oliver closed the gap between them.

"Klevenhagen, for God's sake. Call nine one one!" A light came on in the two-story next door.

With a Comanche scream, Odie "Straight-Eight" Oliver rushed the shallow end, poised to filet his vena cava.

Jinx backed into deep water. His shoulder throbbed and his arm hung limp at his side. Distant sirens offered little comfort.

At the water's edge, Oliver said, "When I finish you off, I'm going after her."

"Who?"

"Raven. Stupid bitch almost suffocated me. When her handlers busted through the door, I crawled in the space I hollowed out of the mattress. Bitch plopped down on the bed —let's see how much she likes having the air choked out of her." He changed his voice in a way that mocked Raven. "Where'n the hell's that SOB? I'll find his ass if it's the last thing I do."

Straight-Eight cleared the last step. The water came to his waist, and Jinx knew he was close enough to lunge.

Seduced by carnal panic, Jinx screamed Sid's name.

Oliver sprang.

Jinx grappled for the edge. White-knuckled, he hoisted himself halfway out, but the force of his T-shirt, tightening against his skin, held him back. He clawed at the sharp pebbles. The wet smell of death engulfed him.

Underwater, he heard only the swoosh of the knife.

And the high-pitched cry of his name.

A muffled explosion stopped time.

Jinx felt the blade's scorpion sting. Meteor showers exploded in his head. A river of red shot from his right arm, swirling chest-high. He sucked in water and drank in his own blood.

Bubbles floated off in a white froth.

Around him, water darkened.

His T-shirt flapped free.

The madman released his grasp and floated away.

A hand gripped his waistband. Pulled him to the surface.

Footfalls pounded the cobblestones. For an instant, he thought he heard Raven calling.

Starved for air, his lungs burned. He sucked in an involuntary breath.

At first, he sputtered. Then, he banged against the sidewalk like a cast-off rag doll. Sid came into focus, standing at the water's edge in a pair of Valentine heart boxers, with a tuft of hair protruding above the V-neck of his undershirt. His arms hung at his sides, but a pistol smoked in his gun hand.

With raw intensity, the lieutenant glared.

"I want you to know that cat of yours climbed up the trellis. Came in through my window and tried to suffocate me for the last time. I got my gun to drill him. Then I decided to drill you instead. Lucky for you, he got in the way."

Pebbles gouged Jinx's cheek, but he welcomed the night air in greedy gulps. Like demons in hot pursuit, sirens screamed their arrival.

Jinx swivelled his head.

At the bottom of the pool, Odie Uwayne "Straight-Eight" Oliver lay near the drain, with his life ebbing and his shape pulsating like a heat mirage in an angry red swirl. Crimson water worked its narcotic effect. Jinx knew it was wrong but he wanted to lie quite still and hope the con would bleed to death.

Raven came into focus. She clutched her handgun, poised to fire.

Fear lined her face. Her skin looked ghastly pale in the blue glow of the street lamp.

"Ohmygod, Jinx—" She kept the snub-nose pointed at the pool. "—say something!"

Above the hush of death, he managed to speak. "How do we get him out?"

Sid answered in a gravelly voice. "Live people sue. Tie you up in court for years and make your life miserable. Dead people just inconvenience you in front of the grand jury for a couple of hours."

Raven stepped closer to the pool's edge. The dead man registered in her gaze. She whipped around, staggered over to Betsy's flower bed and heaved. Between purges, she moaned, "Ohmygodohmygod, I killed a man."

Headlight beacons made a broad sweep over the cobblestones. Still standing in a pall of smoke, Sid offered Jinx a hand. Halfway to his feet, a sickly exhilaration at the sight of the body, wavy below the surface, made Jinx's knees buckle.

Sid limped him to a wrought-iron patio table, deposited him onto a bistro chair, and took the other seat. "Is that Odie Oliver? How the hell'd he find this place?" His eyes flickered to Raven. "For that matter, how'd she?"

"Wish I knew."

Sid called Raven over to the table for a joint chiefs' meeting. "How'd you find us?"

"I snooped." Her answer came out quick and unapologetic. She moved to Jinx's side. "You're hurt." She set the gun down, threw her arms around him and buried her face in his neck.

Jinx returned a feeble embrace.

"If we can interrupt this love fest a minute," Sid growled,

"I'll take responsibility for plugging him. Agreed?"

In the hurling confusion, Raven unburrowed her head. "I shot him."

"I capped him first. Here's my advice: don't say anything unless they ask. I'll volunteer that I popped him. If the ME's office finds two different slugs, then you can fill in the blanks."

Raven appeared dazed. Trance-like, she stared through big, gray doe eyes, and spoke with the slow, dull speech of a zombie. "You shot him?"

"That cat's hurt pretty bad. He needs a doctor. You're the one has to take him." The lieutenant seemed to read her thoughts. "Either of us coulda killed him. You get the cat. I'll take the responsibility. Let's leave it at that." He jerked his head abruptly. "Here they come. Best not say anything else 'til we run it by Betsy."

*Betsy.*

Jinx's eyes flickered to the house. The unlit exterior filled him with dread.

They needed to check on Betsy.

Steel-toed boots clopped against the stones. Paramedics lugging medic kits fanned across the drive. The pain in Jinx's stab wound dulled to a persistent throb. He examined the laceration on his arm. Rivulets of blood clotted to a trickle. Raven stuck the .38 caliber into her waistband and backed away.

Jinx heard a man call out behind him. "MedStar. Somebody call an ambulance?"

Turning in the direction of the voice, the sight of Sid, slumped over the patio table, took the words right out of him.

# Chapter Forty-one

While a young Fort Worth firefighter with a nasty cold tried to talk him into riding shotgun with Sid in the ambulance, Jinx's mind reeled and his fear turned to dread. The Siamese could be bleeding to death. He was beyond shock. He hadn't seen this much mayhem since a couple of TCU coeds tried to beat a freight train.

Betsy wouldn't have stayed cooped up inside with the kind of spirited squeal two ambulances, a fire engine, the ME and a convoy of incoming patrol cars made.

The stuffy-nosed sparky peeled back Jinx's blood-soaked T sleeve. He grimaced, then whistled for assistance.

The wound wasn't lethal, but Jinx had to admit it felt like it nicked bone.

A paramedic trotted up. "Last call, Constable. You coming?"

"I have to find my cat." When the fellow seemed unconvinced, he pointed to Raven. "She'll give me a ride."

The last thing Jinx needed was a glut of medics with probing questions the DA might get ahold of later and twist. He knew he required medical attention, and he wanted to check on Sid, but Betsy might be injured or dying. He had a duty as a peace officer—and as Sid's loyal friend—to help her.

He jutted his chin at Raven to follow him. "Don't say anything until we're out of earshot."

They headed for Jinx's patrol car. He dug the keys out of his pants pocket, and removed a battering ram and two pairs of latex gloves from the trunk. Raven's eyes widened.

"We're going in that house."

Halfway across the broad expanse of lawn, a baby-faced corporal built like a double-wide, shouted at them to halt.

Jinx mumbled, "Don't turn around," then called back over his shoulder. "I live here."

"Why do you need a battering ram?"

"Forgot my key."

The sandy-haired patrolman pulled his handheld radio out of its pouch and squawked for a supervisor. It was just the kind of first-generation, mountain-people mentality he had come to expect from someone fresh out of rookie school.

"We don't have much time." Jinx pulled off his sopping socks and left them in a pile next to the doormat. "Don't touch anything."

"What're we doing? Shouldn't we knock?"

One good heave-ho splintered Betsy's back door and shattered the etched glass recessed in the wooden panels. It was enough to send her shrieking down the stairs if she'd been able, and the thought of how Jinx might find her turned his blood icy.

He propped the battering ram against the doorjamb, handed Raven a pair of surgeon's gloves, and slid his on.

"Hi, pretty boy! Mama's home!" The crackly squawk of a big, colorful parrot came from a perch near a potted banana tree.

Jesus H.

His heart raced so fast he thought it would explode. Inside, he felt along the wall for a switch, flooding the room with light. They stood inside a wicker-decorated atrium filled with a jungle of plants.

The bird let out a hearty laugh. "Who's your best friend?"

"Betsy," he shouted.

The bird belted out, "Spank me," then introduced a short repertoire of sexual profanity creepy enough to clot blood.

Raven's face lined with shock. "What the hell kind of place is this?"

He motioned her into the kitchen. A flip of the switch confirmed his thoughts.

Nobody there.

They stormed through the breakfast nook and into a large dining room. The glow of a crystal chandelier illuminated the richly flocked wallpaper and polished mahogany furniture —but no Betsy. The chandelier lit up the walls enough for him to glance into an opulent parlor. Fine French furniture lined the walls and exquisite Oriental rugs covered the floor, but no sign of Betsy anywhere.

"Betsy Klevenhagen," Jinx shouted. He flipped a wall switch and the mezzanine to the second floor lit up. "We'll finish downstairs first. Remember, don't move anything."

They hurried past the parlor, down a short hall that led to the living room.

The white room.

Two empty champagne flutes with water beading at the base of the stems, rested on a cocktail table in front of a leather sectional. An open bottle of Dom Perignon tilted to one side of a silver urn.

Jinx pointed to a foot trail in the crushed carpet. "Don't disturb those tracks." A downstairs bedroom and half-bath in pink fossil stone revealed nothing. "We're wasting time."

"That wound's pretty deep, Jinx. You've lost a lot of blood."

"You think? Come on."

They sprinted up a cantilevered staircase, careful not to

graze the curved banister. At the top, Jinx located Betsy's bedroom. He sucked in a deep breath, filling his lungs with the soft scent of citrus. He felt for the wall switch.

It looked nothing like the den of iniquity Jinx had imagined. An unmade, king-sized canopy bed draped in gauzy swags and covered with a spread made of Battenburg lace, commanded one wall. A large canvas of a nude Betsy, painted in the style of Andy Warhol, hung over a small chest of drawers next to the entrance to the marble bath.

"Stay put." Jinx moved to the master bathroom.

In seconds, a mirror outlined in small, round bulbs lit up like a marquee.

Nobody in the malachite jacuzzi.

He slid back a sliding mirrored pocket door and pulled the shimmery tassel hooked up to a chain switch dangling from the ceiling. The woman had more clothes than Imelda Marcos had shoes, arranged in a rainbow of similar hues.

Nothing appeared displaced.

At a glance, the remaining two bedrooms and spare bath indicated no sign of foul play. Sid's daughter was neat and orderly, and he wondered, fleetingly, why Sid ever thought they might be compatible.

Raven whispered behind him. "The PD's coming in."

He hurried through an arched hallway leading to a study. Another shrill whistle and an eerie, "Gimme some, bitch," made him whip around. From the mezzanine, he watched the beam of a Maglite sweep across the atrium and filter through the tropicals.

He hollered, "You fuckers keep your hands in your pockets—this is a crime scene."

He whipped around and grabbed Raven's arm. "Post yourself at the bottom of the stairs. Whatever you do, don't let those guys come any further."

"They're cops. How do you expect me to stop them?"

"Show 'em your tits. Hell, I don't know. Tell 'em to treat this house like a whore with crotch rot—don't fuck with it." He didn't like her scowl. "You have a better idea?" By her silence, apparently not. "Look, just do the best you can."

Raven hurried off.

Jinx went on in.

*Aw, Jesus. Aw, Betsy, no.*

He found her seated at a writing table, facedown and slumped over the desk. If not for the dark stain gelling around her middle, a look of surprise in her ghastly expression and a pearl-handled letter opener she used to defend herself still clutched in a death grip, she might have fallen asleep. Stepping near, he felt her neck for a pulse.

She did have a pulse—a weak one. He knew what he had to do.

*Ain't gonna make it.*

Footfalls seemed to come in surround sound.

Hurrying to the door, he shouted a warning. "Nobody comes up here but Crime Scene."

Not much time.

The house filled with brother officers.

Avoiding the shoe-print impressions behind the chair, he eased one shoulder against Betsy's rib cage. With fire burning his wound, he scooped her close enough to hoist her over his shoulder and watched her guts protrude. He stuffed them back inside and carried her out into the hall.

The first Crime Scene detective ascended the stairs like rolling thunder. "What've you done?"

"She's still breathing. I'm a peace officer. Don't trample anything."

Off to one side, Raven still held her post.

"She shouldn't be moved," snapped a burly officer with

sergeant's stripes. "MedStar's en route."

"Back off—I'm not letting her bleed to death."

He descended the steps, trying not to jolt his dying charge. "If they're not here by the time I get to my patrol car, you sons-of-bitches better move your units out of the way, or plan to appear at a collision review board."

"Yeah, but—"

"She's my friend's daughter and I live here. And, if that's not good enough, I'm in charge. You may have jurisdiction in Fort Worth but my jurisdiction covers Fort Worth and Tarrant County."

He didn't know why they let him walk out with Betsy, only that they did.

Maybe they'd made the acquaintance of the ball buster in his arms, leaking like a sieve. Maybe she'd emasculated them in court. Dangled their testicles in front of the jury. He only knew he was glad the sirens announced the arrival of more paramedics.

Once MedStar loaded Betsy in the ambulance and sped off toward the hospital district, Jinx set out to find his furry old pal.

Raven stuck close by. "You were so gentle with her." She made a tentative suggestion. "You were good friends?"

Angry, he whipped around. Narrowed his eyes. Tensed his jaw. "I'm not playing twenty questions with you, Raven. Come to think of it, what the hell are you doing here? I never gave you this address."

"I killed a man tonight, Jinx Porter," she said in a voice so soft he caught part of it lip-reading. "You ought to be glad I'm here. I saved your ass."

"Sid saved my ass."

"You haven't changed a bit. You're still the same self-centered, egotistical—"

He left her standing there and headed toward the cabana.

"—you're nothing but a back walking away."

Outside the cabana, Raven sat at the bistro table, staring at her bloodstained bomber jacket, waiting for Jinx to return. Her heart was still beating so hard she could see it through her knit shell. She thought of Yucatan Jay, and wondered if he admitted himself to the hospital, and if he did, whether she'd find him at Our Lady of Mercy.

Pawpaw warned her there'd be days like this. Gosh-a-mighty, he said, when she told him her major was criminal justice, find another occupation. You don't want to be a cop. You might have to kill a man someday. And when she told him she had a good mind to start with Billy Mack Peterson for standing her up at Sigma Chi Derby Day so he could elope with Mary Sue Turner, Pawpaw said, Phooey, it's one thing to say you can take a human life, it's another to follow through.

An unmarked patrol car rolled into sight and a tall, attractive lady around Raven's age alighted from the driver's side. She wore her shoulder-length, brown hair with the ends neatly curled under, and when she looped a camera strap around her neck, the breeze whisked back her bangs and gave her a maverick look.

Her name was Cézanne Martin.

Raven had never formally met the PD's homicide ace, but she knew her reputation from newspaper accounts of grisly murder investigations, and recognized her on sight. With an avant-garde investigation style that drove her superiors crazy, Cézanne Martin had made the AP wire numerous times, and once even appeared on *Court TV*. She exchanged words with a steroid-monger, plainclothes detective, then pulled a Maglite from her waistband and shined it over the driveway.

*Looking for shell cartridges and blood evidence.*

*Wait 'til she finds tonight's dinner in the moss rose.*

Raven noticed the plainclothes detective sauntering her way. He buttoned the top button on his suit jacket and faked a smile. She pushed herself from the table in time to make it to the cabana door.

A voice called out behind her. "Wait. I want to talk to you."

Flashing the officer her best beauty pageant smile, she yelled, "Bathroom," and threw the dead bolt. She vectored Jinx's location by the noisy cat search going on overhead.

"Jinx, I'm coming up." She planted a foot on the first step and ascended the stairs halfway.

"Stay put." He stomped past the balusters, stood at the landing and glared. "I'll be down in a minute."

"I know who the leak is," she said, her voice soft and uneasy. "That's what I came to tell you."

# Chapter Forty-two

All through the cabana, Jinx had reassured himself he did right by his friend. He saw to it the paramedics took Sid first. He did what he could for Betsy. Now, he'd follow the telltale droplets to wherever they'd lead him, and pray to God he'd find Caesar alive.

He located the Siamese beneath Sid's bed, matted in blood and distressed in his breathing. Grabbing a towel from Sid's bathroom, he lowered himself on all fours and pulled Caesar out. The seal point took a bite out of his finger.

"Sorry, old buddy." The cat showed his appreciation by raking his claws across Jinx's stomach. He wrapped the animal in terry cloth and held him close.

He considered himself lucky.

Only now, Raven had come inside, wanting to talk like every other woman he'd ever known—yap, yap, yap—and he didn't need to be listening to what she said because he already figured out to his own satisfaction she tipped off the crooks. He had no idea why she'd do such a thing, but Gil had to be right. She had access to their computers, and he'd given her free rein when he let her come back to work for him.

*Stupid Jinx.*

He'd cared a great deal for her.

Big fat lie.

Okay, he'd loved her, dammit. Loved her more than any other woman he'd ever been with. Trusted her enough to tell her personal stuff, even. Gave her a glimpse at his crappy life with Kamille and Dan, and that bitch, Mimzy. Jiminy Christmas, he'd damn near popped the question one night after a two-hour sex romp that left him so satisfied he'd spent the next five years trying to find a woman who could top it.

Would've asked her to marry him, too, if she hadn't nuzzled up and whispered those three little words in his ear—words guaranteed to scare the hell out of every red-blooded male in the universe—words that not only spurred men to enlist in the military, but had them begging to see combat.

That's when she blew it.

Instead of "I love you," she should've been saying the three words guaranteed to keep a man around for eternity: "You're damned lucky."

Given their history, Raven turned out to be a far bigger disappointment than he'd ever imagined.

Another step creaked, forewarning him she was coming up. With a tight grip on the cat, Jinx strode to the landing.

"What do you mean you know who the leak is?"

"That's what I came to tell you. I figured you'd want to know right away. I came over to lay it all out so you could decide how we'd handle it."

He relaxed his grip on the Siamese. "Come on up." He padded off to the bedroom in search of his boots and she followed him. He shoved the cat at her. "Take him."

"He doesn't like me."

"Right now, he doesn't like me, either. He doesn't have much use for people, period, unless they have curtains, or bring him grilled salmon."

Grudgingly, she took him. Caesar bared his fangs and let out a weak snake hiss, but he seemed to settle down when Raven cuddled his head beneath her chin.

While putting on his socks, Jinx issued a directive. "Take

him to the all-night vet clinic, then meet me at Our Lady of Mercy. We'll talk there."

Downstairs, only a cop could hammer the door with his fist in a way that shook the whole house.

Raven's eyes got big. "It's that plainclothes detective. He wants to talk to me."

"I'll get the door. Take the cat out the back way. There's a gate near the cliff. The zoo's right below us. Be careful you don't fall into the lion cage." More pounding rattled the windows. The PD would be wanting written statements. He shouted, "Coming," and then whispered, "Go."

"Please, Jinx, I'm worried about you."

"If they corner you, the cat'll die."

"Don't you even want to know who's responsible for the leaks?"

He favored her with a flat stare.

*Yeah. Confess.*

Her answer stunned him into silence.

"It's Amos."

# Chapter Forty-three

On the slow walk to the open mouth of the ambulance, Jinx averted his gaze from the pool. Not having a platoon of policemen crawling up his 'Looms, wanting answers, came as a pleasant surprise.

In the bed of the meat wagon, with a paramedic bent over him, he listened to his own heart race.

At the hospital, his neck muscles tightened like a stringed instrument.

Proned out on a bed in the ER, he inhaled Betadine fumes and watched feverish physicians work on Betsy.

Jinx didn't need to hear a surgeon pronounce her clinically dead.

He'd known the moment he saw the permanent look of betrayal hardening on her face.

In a far corner, a cluster of doctors obscured all but two big feet sticking out past the edge of the table; he said a quick prayer while the resident physician stitched his deadened tissue together.

*I know You haven't heard from me in awhile . . . but that old man's the best friend I've got. If You'd help him, I'd consider it a personal favor. Amen.*

Jinx said, "I know that lady over there. And that man's her father."

"It's been standing room only tonight."

Guilt got the better of him. He made another silent appeal.

*You're probably thinking: What's he gonna do for Me if I save his friend? That's a fair question. Okay, here it is: I'll stop chasing booger. Amen, again.*

The next stitch nicked a live wire. "Jiminy Christmas!"

"I can deaden it some more." The resident glanced around for a nurse.

"Forget it. It'll take too long. Can't you hurry?"

"Look, Mr. Porter . . . a week ago, some knucklehead filed a fifty-million dollar lawsuit against Our Lady of Mercy. Now, everybody's walking on eggshells. If it's all the same to you, how about letting me do my job?"

The plainclothes detective Jinx spoke to at the crime scene, arrived looking for Raven.

No, he hadn't seen her.

No, he didn't know where she went.

Yes, he'd call if he heard anything.

After clarifying a few details regarding the timeline of events, the detective bagged Jinx's bloody T-shirt, and invited him down to HQ to give an in-depth, written statement. As a professional courtesy, he set their appointment for four o'clock, then left to check on the lieutenant.

Once the doctor tied off the last stitch, Jinx took a seat on a bench near the automatic doors and waited for Raven. The only thing making the wait moderately entertaining was the presence of a man wrapped in gauze beneath the flimsy fabric of a turquoise Mexican wedding shirt. He spoke English with a thick South African accent, and tried to settle his bill with gold Krugerrands. When the cashier insisted they only accepted U.S. currency, credit cards or payment by invoice, the foreigner stormed out the exit, carping about the Fort Worth economy turning to shit.

After Raven dropped Caesar off at the all-night veterinary

clinic, she swung by her house to see if Yucatan Jay had broken in. But the sight of two people with binoculars inside an unmarked car with government tags, altered her decision to stop. Special Agents Longley and Hough were pulling surveillance.

She whipped around in a mid-block U-turn and sped off in the other direction.

At Our Lady of Mercy, she found Jinx waiting near the ambulance entrance.

"What'd they say about Caesar?"

"He'll make it. They said you'd have to leave him a few days to make sure the antibiotics work, but after that, he can come home. Oh—and the vet said he's filing a dangerous animal report. And, there's a surcharge for handling wild animals."

"Caesar's plenty domesticated."

"I'm just repeating what the vet said."

"Sid may die."

"I'm sorry." Raven cast her gaze to the floor.

Jinx looked her dead in the eye. "Tell me why you think it's Amos."

She ran down the particulars, winding up the argument that finally convicted Ivy's brat in her eyes. "He owns the latest in electronics. He can't finance expensive stuff like that on a paper route. His mother can't afford it on a deputy's salary. We discovered he was a computer hacker at age eleven; you said yourself that he broke into your personal computer that time you baby-sat him, and compromised your data files. Since you never put your foot down when Ivy brought him to the office on weekends, it doesn't take much of a leap to figure out he stole information out of our computers. He probably broke into the server."

Jinx mulled the news over.

Raven dropped the olive in the martini. "I caught him at the station last night."

"You spoke to him?"

"He left before I could confront him. But he stole Ivy's patrol car, and probably her key to the building. I took fingerprints off the computers and the light switch. Once you examine them, you'll agree they're his."

Jinx checked his watch. Six o'clock in the morning. "When do you think Amos gets up for school?"

"I doubt he went to bed. He's probably on the phone selling information, or out collecting payola."

"This'll kill his mother."

Raven patronized him with a smile. "I have an idea she'll hire a good lawyer. Knowing how Ivy enables that kid, the DA'll need an airtight case."

A team of physicians in sweaty scrubs walked toward them. The shortest assumed the leadership role. "We're moving Mr. Klevenhagen to a room in the cardiac ICU. We'll know something soon enough."

Jinx nodded gravely. "What about his daughter?"

"I'm sorry. There was nothing we could do."

Raven hatched an all-or-nothing plan.

While Jinx pronounced the idea juvenile, he conceded he had nothing better to offer. Based on assurances Raven could get the hospital's full cooperation, he agreed.

The plan called for Gil to swing by the office for a microcassette recorder and a fresh tape. He dropped them off at Our Lady of Mercy for Raven.

Jinx drove the BMW to Sid's, and slipped into clean clothes.

Twenty minutes later, he arrived at Ivy's house.

With a bird's-eye view of the front and side yards, he

waited with the engine idling. Ten minutes later, she burst through the door in a heated rush. Jinx ducked below the dashboard and waited for Ivy to start the car and roar off in the direction of the freeway. As soon as she left, the apprentice Unabomber stepped out onto the rickety porch, dressed like a cross between a pimp and the trench-coat mafia.

Jinx wrenched the car into gear.

Ivy's hormone-raging teenager started down the sidewalk with his back to the Beemer.

Jinx rolled up beside Amos with the driver's window rolled down. "Want a ride?"

"What're you doing here?"

He patted the steering wheel. "Just taking her out on the freeway to blow the soot out . . . to see how she unwinds. Want a ride?"

Amos's eyes brightened. "Is this yours?"

"Raven's." Jinx stopped long enough for Amos to climb in. "Buckle your seat belt."

"Seat belts are for sissies."

"Click it or ticket."

Amos scowled. He pulled the shoulder strap over his bulk and slid the metal tongue into the catch until it snapped. Several miles up the highway, Amos turned suspicious.

"You're driving too slow. What gives, dude?"

"You like Raven, don't you?"

"I guess."

"She likes you." Jinx cut his eyes enough to watch Amos shift his backpack over his crotch.

"Yeah?" A healthy flush colored his cheeks.

"She's all the time saying she does. Raven likes beefy guys like you and Dell. She likes 'em young, too. Not old like me."

"Really?"

Jinx turned on Raven's stereo. Strains of Enya filtered out.

Amos's face contorted into a grimace. "Dude, that's lame. Try this." He unzipped his backpack and pulled out a CD case chocked with music discs, pulled one out and slid it into the CD player. Moments later, they were treated to the soundtrack from *Nightmare on Elm Street—The Hidden Hits*, playing in the background.

"Where we goin', dude?"

Jinx took a deep breath. "Raven got shot this morning on a raid. The doctors don't think she'll live."

"Duuuuuude. . . ." The freckles on Amos's cheeks lightened.

"I figured since we're her favorite people, it's only right we should be the last ones to see her."

"She's really gonna die?" Amos's neck veins throbbed.

"I can honestly say she is."

*Someday.*

*We all are.*

His voice cracked. "Dude, that sucks."

Jinx couldn't be sure without jerking his head, but he thought Amos might be tearing up. He reached over and switched from CD to FM radio. "Last Kiss" was finishing up on the oldies station.

Jinx turned up the volume. "I wasn't a very good boyfriend back when we used to date, but I aim to do right by her now."

"Whaddya mean?"

"Gonna clear my conscience."

Amos sat up with mild interest.

"Do you believe in heaven, Amos?"

"No. I dunno. Maybe."

"I do. And when I die, I want to go there. Georgia says there's this passage in the Bible that says you can't get to heaven unless you forgive your enemies. And if they don't forgive you, too, then you're both doomed to eternal damnation."

"Huh?"

"Hell." Long pause. "I figure you can tell her whatever you want, maybe clear your conscience, too."

"Dude, I got nothing to say."

Jinx swapped lanes. Floored the accelerator and turned the other cars into a colorful smear. "We all have something to say. Like, if I were you—" He sneaked a quick peek at Ivy's lummox. "—I'd start by telling her I thought she was pretty. But I'd probably apologize for not always being nice to her."

"Do I have to tell her I filched a picture of her from your house?"

Jinx gritted his teeth until they hurt. "Why would you do that?"

"I look at it while I beat off. Do I have to tell her that?"

"She won't mind. She's dying. It'll probably give her a thrill." He stole a glance, and tried to envision how Amos's chin would look with his fist glancing off it. "She may want you to forgive her for something she did to you, too. You've gotta give her that chance. Just speak from your heart."

"What kinda stuff're you gonna say?"

"I'll ask her to forgive me for things I did back when we dated. There's a lot she doesn't know. All I'm saying is you're getting an opportunity to tell her how you feel about her. And if you're sorry for anything," Jinx explained with the patience of Job, "you can tell her now, before it's too late."

Amos nodded. He stared out the window in silence, but Jinx caught sight of him swiping his nose with the back of his hand.

When they arrived at Our Lady of Mercy, Jinx ushered Amos to the cardiac wing. An LPN directed them to the nurses' station at ICU. Jinx had no idea where to find Raven, much less how to slip past the nurses, but he directed Amos to a chair in the waiting room and sauntered off to find out.

*Shit.*

He came face-to-face with the drill sergeant head nurse.

Her eyes signaled good fortune. She greeted him with a modicum of cheer. "I suppose you're here to see Raven?"

Jinx blinked.

"Don't stay too long. There's not much time." She gave him a sly wink and pointed to a room near a janitorial closet.

Jinx motioned Amos over. "Wait here by the door. I'll go first so you can see how it's done. You come when I'm through."

Amos nodded. The pulse in his throat throbbed.

Jinx made a big production smoothing his clothes. He straightened his shoulders and opened the door to Raven's room.

Beneath the covers, surrounded by equipment, she seemed small and pale. He knew the head nurse had a hand in their plot by the gauze wrapped around Raven's head and the breathing tube taped to her mouth. With a backward glance at Amos, Jinx walked on in, prepared to give the performance of a lifetime.

# Chapter Forty-four

Raven touched her finger to the play-record button, waiting to catch Amos's confession on tape.

It surprised her when Jinx called her name and slid into the chair next to the bed. He took her hand; his gentle touch sent a thousand volts through her.

"I never thought it would end this way," he said with the passion of a soap opera star. "I brought Amos with me. We each have something to say to you."

She gave him a subtle squeeze and kept her eyes closed.

"I never should've cheated on you, Raven. You've gotta believe me."

What the hell?

This wasn't in the script. She clamped her teeth tight.

Jinx continued the soliloquy. "That romp in the sack with Loose-Wheel Lucille didn't mean a thing. You got too close, Raven. I felt like a coyote in a trap. I would've chewed off my own leg to keep from getting married . . ."

Raven tried to ease her hand away, but Jinx tightened his grip.

". . . I always knew I'd get caught. And, before that—" He let out a fake cry and dropped his head onto the bed. "—when I took that woman home from the sheriff's department—"

*There were others?*

"—It started out as an innocent lunch, but she had the biggest tits I'd ever seen in my life. When she offered to show them to me, I had to see her naked."

Raven's heart thundered.

*Gettin' a new voodoo doll. When I'm through . . . dare you to find a body part that doesn't hurt.*

A lump hardened in her throat.

"And the time the Munsch brothers' niece came to town? Don't worry, I used a condom and it was a quickie. And those sisters I met at the bar? Well, you have to give me that, Raven. How often does an opportunity to pork sisters come along?"

She dug her nails into his skin. He let out a yip and jerked free.

"Anyway, you forgive me, right? Squeeze my fingers for yes."

She crimped her hand. Up popped a stiff middle finger.

*Buck you, fuddy.*

"Amos wants to see you. Just remember I'll always love you."

Chair legs scraped back from the bed. Leather boot soles squeaked against the linoleum.

Heavy footfalls lumbered in. She engaged the play-record switch and waited.

The door snapped shut.

She could feel the burn of Amos's stare.

"Hi." Long pause. "Jinx says you're gonna die. Sorry."

More dead airtime with Amos.

"I never meant anybody to get hurt."

Raven's hair prickled.

"Is it wrong to want things like other kids?"

Raven thought back to a distant time.

*When the Ranger from Company D came to the house and broke the news Pawpaw had died.*

Seconds later, the burn of a tear slid over her cheek.

"My mama didn't know anything about it, just so you

know. They were s'posed to gimme money, and I was to tell 'em when y'all were coming. I only did it five times." He sniffled.

Silence.

Amos broke into tears. "Okay, eleven," he whined. "But a couple shouldn't count against me because I made less than a hundred bucks. And one bitch totally stiffed me. Anyway, I'm sorry for what I done."

Raven felt Amos's breath hot on her cheek. He sucked the snot back up his nose and put his lips near her ear.

"Since you're gonna die anyway, wouldja mind if I had a look at your tits?"

# Chapter Forty-five

Being proned out in a hospital bed when Amos abruptly ripped back the sheet and lifted her hospital gown wasn't what made Raven sit bolt upright and scare the living shit out of Ivy's kid.

Copping a feel did it.

Amos screeched like a parrot, but he took off down the hall like a striped ape.

Leaving Raven to spit out the breathing tube and deal with Jinx.

The boss ambled back into the room, jerking his head in time to see a patch of fabric from Amos's coat fluttering out the door. "What the hell just happened?"

"Little bastard assaulted me."

"Are you hurt?"

"Am I hurt?" The tape recorder whirred in her hand. She lifted it to her lips and checked the wall clock. "Confession concluded at nine thirty-eight a.m. Constable Jinx Porter has entered the room. No one else entered or left the room while suspect gave his confession. Interview is now terminated." She clicked off the microcassette, smacked it against his upturned palm and mentally awarded him a lifetime achievement award in the Turd Hall of Fame.

"Good lick, Raven. Hey—where're you going?"

"Where I'll be appreciated." She snatched her clothes out of the closet and stalked out of the room with the hospital gown fluttering against her T-shirt. "And don't try to follow me, Jinx Porter."

He pursued her into the hall, to the elevator. "You wanna meet at the office?"

"Don't talk to me." She stabbed the button several times, spun off in the opposite direction, and paced the length of the foyer. She took great care to avoid eye contact. Impatient with the sluggish elevator, she made a beeline for the stair exit.

"Raven, wait. Are you mad about what I said in there?"

But she was already through the fire door and taking the concrete steps in pairs.

Jinx's voice echoed through the stairwell. "Honey, that was just for show—not the part where I got upset—that was real."

The outside door banged shut, putting an end to his flimsy backpedaling. Raven stepped out onto the sidewalk and into the brilliance of a crisp new morning.

By the time Jinx reached the ground floor and poked his head outside, he could watch her fumble under the front bumper for the hide-a-key. Let the bewildered bastard get his own ride home.

Inside the car, she glimpsed him in the rearview mirror. She revved the engine, slammed the Beemer into gear and left him standing in her exhaust.

*That's what I get . . .*

Like the song, George Strait summed up the relationship with Jinx Porter better than she ever could.

*. . . I've come to expect it from you . . .*

After putting out an APB out on Amos, Jinx left the hospital around ten that morning, heartsick and afraid.

Dell wasn't his first choice to provide a lift back to the precinct; he was the only choice.

Until Jinx returned to the office, Gil and Dixie were running the show. Ivy left for DFW Airport in search of the Unabomber; Mickey got a tip on Yo-Yo Behrens and ended up in the boondocks, pulling surveillance.

The brooding German pulled under the portico and unlocked the door.

Dell said, "You sprang a leak."

Jinx climbed in. He glanced at his shirtsleeve. A spot of fresh blood had seeped through the bandage and left a stain drying on the fabric.

"Guess you heard it was Amos."

Dell nodded gravely.

The big Chevy bounced out of the parking lot and merged into traffic.

Jinx pondered the wireless phone on the seat between them. "You mind?" He took Dell's one-shoulder shrug to mean, Have at it. He tapped it on and punched out his sister's number.

Mimzy answered on the third ring, practically incoherent. She must have workmen in her home. He thought he heard hammering in the background.

"It's Jinx."

"What do you want?" Breathless.

"Did you go out with that ATF agent? Rusty?"

"Why do you ask?" Strident.

"I need to talk to him."

"About me?" Her voice went shrill.

"Regardless what you might think, it's not always about you."

She let out a groan, and the phone went dead in his hand.

Grinding his molars, he pressed redial. This time, Mimzy answered with a chipper hello.

"Mimzy, don't hang up."

"Why shouldn't I?"

"Something bad happened early this morning."

Her voice caught in her throat. "Is this about Momma and Daddy?"

"No. Do you have Rusty's home number, or not?"

"Not unless you tell me."

She let out a squeal, and he realized she had company. Not that he minded his sister getting laid. Maybe a romp between the bedsheets would improve her lousy disposition.

"Are you going to tell me why you want it?"

What the hell? No way in the world he could intercept every newspaper in his parents' social circle, and trim out the article that would certainly appear in tomorrow's edition.

"I caused the death of an innocent woman."

"Oh." Short pause. "Why didn't you say so?"

"You don't sound surprised."

"Well, Jinx—" She expelled a ragged sigh. "—the rest of us pretty much gave up a long time ago trying to figure you out."

Then, she put Rusty on the line, and Jinx realized the background noise he originally identified as sounds of demolition, was actually Mimzy's headboard striking the wall.

God bless him; Rusty lost his virginity.

God bless any man about to get involved with the most fucked-up family in Fort Worth.

Jinx pressed the off button. He stared through the windshield, wondering what to do about Raven. He'd not only let the cat out of the bag, he set fire to the bag. Now the cat was running around loose, with an *I'm an asshole* banner fluttering from his tail.

On a positive note, maybe total honesty would lay the groundwork for a new foundation in their shaky relationship.

Jinx broke the silence. "Gil said you thought Raven did it."

Dell drew in a great intake of air. He unfolded his sunglasses and shielded his eyes from view. "It's time you know . . . I love her."

"You're married." Jinx's face hardened into a grim expression. He couldn't have gotten a worse jolt if his deputy handed him a live wire to hold while he turned on the hose. "You can't be in love with her."

"My divorce will be final in under a week."

For a long time, Jinx said nothing.

"I'll take good care of her, Jinx. There's nothing I wouldn't do for that girl."

Jinx gave him a grim nod. Each understood the other's position. As they rolled into the parking lot behind the station, he threw the deputy a bone to chew on.

"May the best man win."

# Chapter Forty-six

Raven arrived home, relieved that Special Agents Longley and Hough had given up spying on her. This time, she parked the BMW in the garage, and skulked through the backyard with one hand clamping the back flaps of the hospital garment closed, and the other with a choke hold on her leather skirt and bomber jacket. After checking the security system for intruders, she entered through the back door, dumping the ruined clothes on top of the washing machine.

She made a quick sweep of the first floor. After satisfying herself she was alone, she went upstairs and repeated the procedure. Once she took a thorough shower and loofa-ed off the aftermath of the deadly rampage at Sid Klevenhagen's, she blow-dried her hair and dressed in a black skirt and pullover shell that befit an early-morning death experience.

The police would be wanting to take her statement.

In front of the mirror, she took a long, hard look at herself. In her mind's eye, she'd aged ten years overnight.

It didn't matter what Sid said. They'd both plugged Straight-Eight Oliver.

If the grand jury couldn't divine that she'd killed a man in defense of a third party, she'd spend the next six months mired in legal bills, paying for Ben Jennings's new cigarette boat.

She drove down to FWPD headquarters. It was the right thing to do.

Pawpaw would've been proud of her owning up.

At HQ, Cézanne Martin offered her coffee and a Krispy Kreme. She had a winning smile and a hospitable manner, and if Raven didn't know better, she could have easily been back at the sorority, sitting across the breakfast table with her Big Sister, confiding about that humiliating breakup with Billy Mack Peterson, the star baseball pitcher.

Raven told what she knew, reviewed her sworn statement and scrawled out her signature, then temporarily surrendered the Lady Smith for ballistics. Not until she was back behind the wheel of the BMW three hours later, did she remember the locker keys Yucatan Jay gave her.

She aimed the Beemer in the direction of the Amtrak station.

With thoughts racing, Raven turned on the stereo. The soundtrack from that Freddy Krueger movie Amos liked so much blared through the speakers.

What the heck?

At the stoplight, she pushed the eject button and pulled out the CD. Dozens of fingerprints covered the disc's surface.

Amos.

If Jinx needed comparison prints to seal the kid's fate, she could produce them.

The light turned green; she returned the CD to the player and switched to a cassette tape of Enya. Next thing she knew, she was pulling in the parking lot.

Inside, she made her way to a stand of lockers. She checked the numbers against the keys.

The first locker contained Yucatan Jay's camouflage fatigues and a blue jay feather.

The second held a journal and money bags from the bank. She took a look inside. Empty. A glint of metal caught her eye. A gold American Eagle. She dropped it into her purse and tossed the bags aside.

With a quick thumb-through, she noted entries in the first few pages of the journal—entries containing personal data about her, including driver's license information and a blueprint to her security system. The rest appeared unused.

Raven sucked air.

She tried the key to the third locker and found copies of photos from years past: a grainy picture of Yucatan Jay in military garb; his parents drinking lemonade with her on their porch; Pawpaw, balancing her on his hip, with only the point of her chin protruding beneath his pale gray, Texas Rangers cowboy hat, swallowing her head.

She fought off the grief steeping inside her.

She found Yucatan Jay's transcript from the Air Force Academy in Colorado Springs. And a battery-operated tape recorder and a series of one-hour tapes marked one through ten, labeled "Interview with Yucatan Jay, March, 1992."

And, then . . . the worst.

A low moan brewed in Raven's throat. Her skin crawled with goose bumps, and the hair on her arms stuck straight up. She flipped open an annual for the Air Force Academy and found his picture, along with a folded sheet of parchment paper.

*Noooooooooo.*

No mistake.

She must've been stuck on stupid, and passed out on dumb to ever think the man in her house was Yucatan Jay.

Similar in stature and coloring, yes.

An uncanny resemblance, yes.

But not her cousin.

Her head reeled. Blood swirled inside her veins. A high-pitched ring pierced her left ear and held on.

Now, she knew.

She unfolded the parchment—a Colorado death certificate —dated March 28, 1992.

Her eyes swam over the page.

Yucatan Jay.

Asphyxiation by strangulation at the hand of another.

Homicide.

Late that afternoon, Rusty popped in at the Château Du Roy while Jinx was boxing up the last of his books to transfer to the vacant apartment.

"Fingerprints on that ice pick you sneaked us came back from AFIS. One matched Odie Oliver's right thumbprint. The rest belonged to Betsy Klevenhagen. We figure she had no connection to Oliver . . . that her prints got there when she brought it to you. Let's grab a bite and I'll fill you in."

In a rear booth at a home-style restaurant, over the din of the dinner crowd, Rusty ran down what he knew. "The judge signed an evidentiary search warrant for Oliver's house," he said, staring at the new sling around Jinx's arm. "Oliver kept a ledger on his stolen merchandise." He looked as if he'd just eaten a lemon, rind and all. "He paid Amos with a stereo and a big-screen TV. It's all written down. That ought to nail your case.

"And something you'll like—that old couple—the county judge's relatives? We recovered a lot of their stuff."

The waitress set their chicken-fried steaks in front of them, and they ate in relative silence. When they did speak, it was about the Bureau, or the election—still a year away—or about Sid, confined in Our Lady of Mercy with a NO VISITORS sign posted at the entrance to his room. After they pushed back empty plates of homemade lemon meringue pie, Rusty relented.

"I know you won't be satisfied until you see it for yourself, Porter. Lucky for you we're through kicking tires. The guys are ready to turn the house over to Oliver's next of kin, so I don't see how showing you around could hurt. Besides," he said through a grin, "we're practically family."

Condolences seemed to be in order.

Aluminum foil covered the windows of Oliver's putty-colored A-frame—not such an oddity considering Oliver's occupation made him pretty much a day sleeper. His desk revealed a dusty outline where a computer had once been.

"We seized the computer," Rusty said. "He had an old copy of *The Anarchist's Cookbook*—the underground blueprint for bombs—nails similar to the ones we dug out of your office wall and the bedroom wall at your apartment, and duct tape. Our computer guy says the user pulled a ton of stuff about incendiary devices off the internet. This freak even grouped them according to capacity to maim. It should help when you testify before the grand jury."

The experience made Jinx wish he'd told Rusty good-bye at the café cash register.

# Chapter Forty-seven

Raven swallowed two aspirin, dead-bolted the lock Dell installed on the bedroom door, pulled the Mossberg out of the closet and placed it beside her on the bed. In time, she drifted off to sleep.

She awakened close to midnight to the aroma of oven-baked pizza.

Racking a shell in the shotgun, she quietly unbolted the door and eased down the stairs. Tiny hairs pierced the sleeves of her cotton nightie; her skin tingled with enough energy to power the West End of Dallas.

*That does it. Tomorrow I'm looking at houses.*

The table had a place setting for one. A large sausage and mushroom pizza still produced steam in its box. Positioned near a cloth napkin folded into the shape of a bird, was an unopened can of Big Red. Next to the soda pop, a half-full glass of ice, beaded in sweat. A yellow rose lay beside a bread-and-butter plate full of BBs. A small note card, folded in half, rested on the dinner plate.

With shaky fingers, she opened it.

*Raven,*

*Someday I'll explain, but now I must go. I only have a few days to visit family before I'm off again. A problem came up overseas. Sorry, but I needed a few items from the train station to facilitate my new assignment. Mbuti pygmies are being hunted down and eaten like game animals by rebel fighters in the Democratic Republic of Congo. The Congolese economy's going to shit.*

*Take care,*
*Thomas Greenway*

*P.S. Sorry about the rug. I'll buy you a new one next time we meet.*

Raven spent the next half-hour locked in the bedroom, rocking back and forth with the Mossberg in her lap.

Scrambled thoughts filled her head.

Pygmies? Cannibals? Was this guy for real?

Why would Thomas Greenway want to buy her a new rug? So, he tracked in a little dirt. She'd vacuumed up the mess with a hand vac.

The real puzzler was how he defeated the Titan, an attic siren and four new dead bolts. By the time the digital readout on the alarm clock flipped over to one o'clock, she knew for damned sure she no longer cared to spend the night in her own home.

It took forever for Dell to open the door. But when he did, she threw her arms around him and hung on for dear life.

"It's a flyspeck house," he said, pressing a kiss into her hair. "I only have one bed."

He didn't invite her in, just stepped aside and let her enter under her own steam. She glimpsed the private side of the quiet man, and a low-voltage sexual current ran through her. For a guy with eyes that could freeze water one moment, and melt pistachio ice cream the next, Dell wasn't just some ass monkey. He respected her.

In bed, with her head resting in the crook of his arm, Raven tasted his gentle kiss.

As much as she wanted, she couldn't let him make love to her—not while he was still married to Nicole. If she gave in to desire and Dell went back to his wife, it would ruin their unusual bond.

And if there was one thing Raven needed right now, it was the friendship of a stable man.

A bubble-gum sun popped up on the horizon when Raven slipped out of Dell's house and hurried home. The note Thomas Greenway left had permeated her dreams, preventing a decent night's sleep. Especially that part about the rug.

At first glance, the Persian Hamadan looked as good as the last time she vacuumed it. But on closer inspection, the pattern in the short, dense pile appeared to have a repair. Raven flipped back the rug and examined the hand-tied knots.

And that's when she found it . . .

. . . the slit in the rug, caused by the trapdoor Thomas Greenway cut out when he entered the crawl space beneath her house and sawed through the wooden floor planks.

# Chapter Forty-eight

By early Monday, Jinx yearned for familiar surroundings.

While Dixie fended off a continuous barrage of phone calls, he spent the morning holed up in the back office in the throes of posttraumatic stress. Raven must have assumed her job ended; she hadn't shown up for work that day. Now, solitude gave him an unwanted opportunity to replay the events in his head, and by mid-afternoon, he decided he could only escape by going out on patrol.

A false spring had settled across North Texas, making roses bud and flowers perk up one last time before the first killing frost set in. Instead of returning to the office at four-fifteen, Jinx prowled the south side in the obscurity of the unmarked car. First, he swung by Rosemont, a militant neighborhood of elderly whites, and turned onto Red Stumblingbear's street. Stumblingbear, lounging on the porch with a cheap brew, hopped up from his rocking chair and grabbed his crutches. While Jinx curbed the vehicle, the Vietnam vet hobbled to the gate.

"Hi, J-j-j—"

"Jinx."

"I h-h-heard you were b-b-back at w-w-w—"

"Work. Yes, news travels fast. Doing all right?"

"Yup. I s-s-started to c-c-c—"

"Call me?"

"—to s-s-see how—"

"To see how I was doing? That's mighty nice. Say, listen, I wonder if I could ask you for a favor?"

"S-s-sure."

"I know it's a little early, but my campaign signs are due in from the printer any day now, and I thought maybe you'd let me hammer one in your yard when the election rolls around."

He didn't like the silence that followed.

"Well, J-j-j—"

"Jinx."

"I w-w-would, but my g-g-g—"

"Girlfriend?"

"—found out you r-r-ran her c-c-c—"

"Criminal history?"

"Yeah. She told me, n-n-never to let you s-s-s—"

"Set foot on your property again?"

"You g-g-got it."

With his blood pressure skyrocketing, he drove off. On the drive through Worth Heights, three people shot him the finger, but veering off into the Magnolia neighborhood brought an even worse reception.

This time when he waved, Fort Worth's south-side aristocracy looked right through him.

Around lunchtime, Raven pulled out the baby book Pawpaw kept on her, along with a couple of old photo albums and scrapbooks he updated from time to time. Correspondence between Pawpaw and Aunt Wren showed the same address on all of the envelopes, the last piece being a Christmas card that came to the house the year before he died.

Directory Assistance had no listing on a phone number for her aunt and uncle, but unpublished phone numbers were common.

Regardless, whether she dropped in uninvited, Wren and Jack were the only family she had left. Even if she didn't find them in Manitou Springs, time away from Jinx Porter would be worth it.

By four o'clock, she had already packed a suitcase and made an airline reservation for Denver, when the doorbell rang.

Dell.

Standing on the porch with his back to the wall, checking out the street, always on guard.

She opened the door and he instantly brightened.

"You didn't wake me up to say good-bye." After an awkward pause, he said, "Are you coming back to work?"

"Did Jinx send you?"

"I'm asking for myself."

Raven ducked her chin. "I'm going away for awhile. I'll call when I get where I'm going, in case the grand jury's looking for me."

"Amos is in custody. The truant officer found him the last place you'd expect—at the intermediate school, sitting in class, taking notes." Dell's eyes went dark. "The ME's office faxed over their report this afternoon. The autopsy said Sid's bullet killed Odie Oliver."

A fresh shot of adrenaline went through Raven's body. Even if killing Oliver would've made her the heroine, she didn't want to be the one who did it. Didn't want to live with the notion she'd taken a man's life, even if she had sworn to uphold the law. She felt the tingling sensation of frayed nerves unraveling.

"My divorce was final today." For a long time, they stared at each other, taking a quiet inventory. "I've loved you five years, Raven."

"Dell. . . ."

"How much more time do you need?"

"I don't know. I have someplace to go. . . ."

"Wherever it is, I'll meet you." Aqua eyes pleaded.

"I'm not that easy to get along with." She drew a finger down the pearl snap buttons on his western-cut shirt. "You may not believe this, but the word bitchy has been used on occasion."

"I'll adjust." He wrapped his hand around hers, folded it back and kissed her palm.

The feel of his tongue on her skin sent an electric shock right down to her—

*God, that man was good.*

"If you're gonna disintegrate my thong again, shouldn't you should come in and close the door?"

# Chapter Forty-nine

Neither Betsy Klevenhagen nor Straight-Eight Oliver's obituaries made Tuesday morning's newspaper, but Gil showed up at work looking like his should have. This time, he raised eyebrows when he came in with both arms mangled.

"Did you ever think about putting that dog to sleep?" Jinx said.

The resident animal activist had been pretending it was business as usual, but Jinx's comment touched off a riot. Before he finished redistributing Gil's papers, Ivy stormed out.

Jinx retreated to the rear office. One glance at the calendar date encircled on the blotter reminded him he'd won the office pool. The money he'd get for predicting the correct date of Amos's first arrest ought to just about cover the co-payments for his trips to the ER.

But the best thing to happen that day occurred when Edgar "Yo-Yo" Behrens turned himself in to Fort Worth police. Word got back to Jinx—Yo-Yo told the booking desk he didn't want the constable to make the chariots swing low for him, the way he did for Odie Oliver.

The second best thing happened when the head of Risk Management phoned to say the county would no longer pay off Ivy's car wrecks. Meaning the next time she crashed a car, he could make her walk.

Good luck seemed headed in his direction until Dixie put

a call through from Fort Worth's police chief. It seemed, as a pre-Halloween prank, Gil and his brother tossed a lit packet of Black Cats through the door of a Chicano nightclub, and everybody inside drew guns and aerated the place with a hail of bullets.

Wednesday morning, Dixie went back to managing her temporary agency and Georgia retook her desk. She spent the morning calling everybody "honey"—especially the county employees Dixie put on her hit list.

By the time Jinx finished reading the sanitized version of the PD's report on Odie Oliver, he held out faint hope they might escape a grand jury investigation. He ventured out into the main office and caught Georgia staring into a makeup compact, powdering her nose and humming the melody to "This Little Light of Mine." Fresh paperwork piled up on her desk. It was obvious she hadn't done a lick of work since she strolled in late.

As for Oliver's funeral service, Jinx never once considered attending.

Instead, he chose to patrol his precinct and let Georgia field calls.

While he prepared to leave for the day, the phone rang. When Georgia didn't answer by the fifth ring, he plucked the receiver and jabbed the only blinking button.

"Constable Jinx Porter's office."

"Don't ever come to my house again. You come to my house, you die."

Jinx's blood tingled like a million grains of sand.

*Ivan Balogh, Prince of the Gypsies.*

"You'd better run like the wind, fuckhead. I'm on my way out there right now."

Early Thursday, an uninvited guest appeared in Jinx's office.

*The Spam-maker.*

He wanted to redeem his raincheck for hot cocoa. While Jinx readied the water and measured chocolate powder into Dell's coffee cup, a strange story unfolded.

Amos had befriended the little spark plug.

The spoon dropped into the mug with a clink.

Jinx faced off with the most dangerous man Sid Klevenhagen had ever known. "You admitted him into the building? But, why?"

Skinner's face flushed. "He said he wanted to join the Explorer Scouts program I run, and asked me if I'd sponsor him."

"Just why are you here?"

"To tie up loose ends. I wanted you to know I didn't have anything to do with him ratting you off the morning you got shot out at Marble-Eye Turner's house." The Spam-maker hoisted himself up onto the chair and sat back with steam coiling out of his cup. He wove a remarkable tale of a disturbed boy who gained access to the SO under the guise of friendship. "When that warrant on Turner came in, there were fifty others just like it. I had a couple of men out sick, and a couple more goldbricking. We were swamped."

"That's why you people routed it down here." The last of Jinx's anger seeped out. Skinner had real talent for letting the air out of a man's spare tire. "This isn't the first time we've had to do your dirty work."

"Here's how I've got it figured. For three days, it sat in the basket because nobody had time to serve it. I heard you had a hard-on for the guy on account of he messed up your friend. Best I can figure, the kid—Amos—took the address off the warrant while we were talking about Explorer Scouts. Then again, some questions are never answered. And some answers die with the perps."

He acted like a man who would know.

Other mysteries dropped into place, unspoken. Being Ivy's kid, Amos could come and go through the metal detectors without attracting attention. He'd swiped his mother's patrol car and keys on at least one occasion; explosives could have been smuggled in after-hours.

As for blowing up the Château Du Roy, Amos could've parlayed that address into easy cash, selling it to Marble-Eye, Straight-Eight, Yo-Yo and anyone else Jinx had a beef with. If Oliver conned Valentine into letting him inside an apartment, he probably also scammed access into the one he blew up. Either way, it would take Superglueing the mincing fairy to the asphalt, and backing over him with the patrol car three or four times to get the fat bastard to squeal on himself.

Being part of the criminal subculture, however, Glen Lee Spence would know. And he'd strong-arm the information out of that prissy transsexual the very next time the apartment complex's air conditioner crapped out and Glen Lee propped open the door for ventilation.

Not long after Skinner left and Jinx retreated to the rear office, Georgia poked her head in and waved an envelope.

"Certified mail, honey," she announced, handing it over.

Jinx checked the return address. "What in the hell does Dallas PD want with me?"

She ambled back down the hall without answering.

He slit the envelope and pulled out the contents. When he unfolded the letter, an old mug shot of Mozelle Gratten and a two-day-old teletype fell into his lap. Even before he read the request to arrest the barber, the distinct feeling he was about to lose another vote came over him.

He picked up the phone and dialed the DPD.

"I'm short of manpower. I can send it up to the sheriff's warrant office or mail it back—either way, it's your call."

It delighted him when they chose the SO. The way he figured, Skinner owed him. Mozelle Gratten's warrant could die a natural death under that big old swamp pile floating around Skinner's in-basket.

Friday morning, Ivy started in with her every twenty-eight-day blue-flu routine. By early afternoon, he figured she'd flopped in her recliner with a cold beer in one hand and the remote control in the other. He envisioned her basking in the glory of Jerry Springer reruns, watching like they were home movies of close family members.

It wasn't until everyone left for the day that Jinx found a batch of Ivy's unserved citations. Disgusted, he rubber-banded them together to carry home. Sometime before Sunday, he'd see if he couldn't manage to serve a few, then warn her if she ever pulled a stunt like that again he'd fire her.

He started in the back office, turning off lights.

Midway down the hall, he heard the cowbell clang.

Dixie waited in the foyer.

As he came closer, he noticed a skinned ermine, complete with head, wrapped around her neck, biting its tail with the alligator clip some taxidermist substituted for jaws. Her eyes were rimmed red and her face had an opalescent sheen that resembled mother-of-pearl.

"You came for your check?" The sight of her simultaneously pleased and embarrassed him. "I already mailed it."

"That's not why."

The look forming on her face unleashed an ant farm race up his legs. "Care to sit?"

Misty-eyed, she shook her head and scanned each desk, silently gazing into her memories. "For the past two days, all I've been able to think about is how I could work here and still manage my business."

"You said this place sucked."

"It does. Call me crazy, but it's the people I miss. It's *Alice in Wonderland* every day." She touched a finger to one eye. "I mean, look at Ivy."

*I'd rather not.*

"You people think she's hard up. You think she doesn't have a dime for a pay toilet since she's always poor-mouthing, but I did some checking. Do you realize she's managed to save practically every penny since she's worked here?"

"*This* Ivy?"

"Shug, that woman's got more money than I've got hips."

"Not *our* Ivy."

"When's the last time you saw her house?"

Lost in thought, Jinx cut his eyes to the ceiling. "Nineteen eighty-one, maybe '82."

Dixie nodded knowingly. "Sucker. Out of curiosity, I drove by yesterday afternoon."

Jinx wiped a hand over his face, stopping briefly at one eyebrow. Ivy was his excuse for not giving to the United Way. By allowing her to continue working for him, he made her his own personal charity.

"And Gil." Dixie misted up all over again. "He's priceless. I never knew a grown man could be so much fun. Most men I know grow up to be jaded, like—"

She stopped short, but he finished the comment in his head.

*Like me.*

The thought triggered a load of battery acid in his stomach.

"And, Mickey and Dell—God love 'em—that's who I'd want if I were in a bind. Then, there's you."

By this time, she'd worked herself into a full bawl. What was it about women, for crying out loud? Couldn't hold it together long enough for a man to key the door. Men didn't act all crazy.

"You should've told me this before Georgia returned."

Dixie, swollen and pouty, went into a stance. "I want my desk back."

"If you're serious—" He switched off the last of the lights in an attempt to herd her out of the office. "—I don't think you'll have to wait long. People drop dead every day. I'm sure by the time Georgia picks up Monday's obituary section, she'll have two or three funerals lined up."

"I don't want to substitute. I want a permanent job."

"I've never known Georgia to stick with anything."

"What about 'Starving for Jesus'? She looks better than she did on TV—and the camera adds ten pounds."

"I can't tell if she's starving for Jesus, or eating for the devil. The camera may add ten pounds, but since that show aired, she's put on ten of her own. Besides, Gil stopped by her house, midweek. Said he saw a brochure on the Formica for a deep-sea cruise. Guess she'll be cruising for Jesus, next."

They stood in the outer hallway while Jinx locked up. The dead bolt shot home.

Dixie's eyes remained fixed and glazed.

"All right, Dixie. I'll give it some thought. That's the best I can do right now."

# Chapter Fifty

After arriving at Denver International Airport, Raven spent the first two days tooling around in a rented SUV, backpacking in the Rockies. The crisp mountain air cleared her head. By the time she stopped at Golden and took the short tour through the Coors Beer factory, spent the night at Idaho Springs and made a loop through Central City, Leadville and Buena Vista, she felt emotionally ready to tackle Colorado Springs.

The last known address for her aunt and uncle didn't appear on Raven's city map, so she stopped in at the police department for directions. She headed for Manitou Springs, dashed into a flower shop and purchased a fall bouquet, and drove off in the direction of Wren and Jack's. At the base of a rugged hill, she spied their modern log cabin with plate glass windows, hanging off the cliff. When she reached the top, the address on the mailbox corresponded with the one Raven took off Pawpaw's last Christmas card.

A rustic, four-foot fence with a wooden gate surrounded three sides of the house, sectioning it off from a larger, undeveloped tract. Raven tooted the horn. No snarling dogs bounded over. No one popped out on the stoop to greet her. She gripped the flowers, unlatched the gate and walked to the porch.

Lifted the door knocker and tapped out her arrival.

Soft footfalls padded to the door. The curtain moved, and

one watery eye peered out. Fabric floated back into place, and in seconds, the dead bolt clicked and the door opened a sliver.

"Yes?"

"Aunt Wren?"

An awkward moment passed. Then realization set in. "Oh, my stars."

The old woman stepped aside and let her in. She stood around five-foot-four, bent and shrunken in her simple cotton housedress, but she had the same mercurial gray eyes as the pictures Pawpaw used to show Raven of her mother.

"I'm Robin's girl." She glanced down at the bouquet of flowers, then back at her aunt.

The withered woman turned away. "Jack, look who's here."

Wren clasped Raven's hand and led her to the kitchen. Offered her a seat at the breakfast nook and asked if she'd like fresh coffee cake. Before Raven could decline, she opened the oven and a blast of warm air carried with it the smell of buttered brown sugar.

"I'd love some." Raven placed the flowers on the red-checkered tablecloth.

"I suppose Jack's still out back. A bear came up last night and tore into the trash. Jack says they smell my cooking."

With spryness in her step, Wren bustled to the table carrying the plate. When she went back for the coffee cup, Raven noticed her hands shook.

She offered her aunt the bouquet. "I bought these for Jay."

"Honey, you didn't need to bring flowers. I grow my own. When you finish, I'll show you my garden out back." She beamed.

Raven cleared her throat. "Do you know a man named Thomas Greenway?"

"No." Her eyes darkened and her face creased with fear. "I should get Jack."

Raven clutched the gnarled hand. "You do know him, don't you?"

Wren's mouth contorted into a ghastly expression. "Of course not. Jack!"

Outside, the sound of heavy boots trundled up the steps. Through the door glass, between café curtains that parted in the middle and hung in folds secured by tiebacks, Raven glimpsed the form of a tall, lean man, bundled against the cold. He bent at the waist, brushed his hands over the front of his pants and wiped his feet.

Raven pushed back from the table as the door swung open.

She extended her hand expecting to see Uncle Jack—

—and came face-to-face with the man she knew as Yucatan Jay.

In the Saturday dawn, Jinx transferred the last of the uncharred books from his old apartment to the new one, stacking them on top of a produce crate pilfered from the complex's Dumpster, and converted into a makeshift table.

"Sorry about the spartan furnishings, Dad. Have you seen my newspaper?"

Dan Porter, proned out in one of two recliners, glowered at his son. "It's my newspaper, boy. You can have it when I'm finished."

"The paper's mine."

"No." Dan wrapped it in a protective clutch. "You always cut out the funnies before I get a chance to read them."

"That was a long time ago, Dad. And you're in my chair again. Your chair's over there, remember?"

"I like this one. It's nice and hollowed out."

"But, you'll be able to watch the ball game better from that one."

"There's no TV."

"They're delivering it this afternoon. I reminded you three times."

"Have you seen my glasses?"

"They're sticking out of your shirt pocket."

With a stranglehold on the newspaper, the old man sank deeper into the chair. Glaze-eyed, he drifted into his memories. Soon, he dozed.

A short while later, Jinx shook his father's shoulder. Dan blinked himself awake.

"I'm leaving, Dad. I'm going to the hospital to see Sid. It's the first time they've let him have visitors."

"Who's Sid?"

# Chapter Fifty-one

Jinx had to admit that away from the harpies in his family, Dan didn't exhibit the docile personality everyone on the outside found so endearing. Without a medical diagnosis, he wasn't prepared to accept the old man's behavior as a symptom of the ravages of Alzheimer's, but he couldn't recall the last time his father stood up for himself before moving into the Château.

On the drive over to Our Lady of Mercy, Jinx formulated questions for Sid.

Sid would know what to do about Dan.

Sid would help him get somebody into the apartment to care for the old guy.

Whatever was wrong, Sid would know how to handle it.

At Our Lady of Mercy, Jinx could hear the old lieutenant carrying on down the hallway. The head nurse pulled the door handle to Sid's room until the latch snapped shut.

She cut Jinx off at the pass. "Mr. Porter, if you're looking for Sidney Klevenhagen, I wouldn't go down there if I were you."

Her tone was enough to make his heart misfire. "What's wrong? He's okay, isn't he?"

Without invitation, he skirted past her, followed the sound of Sid's voice and flung open the door. A big-breasted nurse perched on the edge of the bed glanced over. Sid's hand slid off her thigh.

His eyes narrowed into a murderous glare. "You better get the hell outta here while I'm still confined to bed, you sorry sonofabitch."

The monitor went wild. The nurse fled, leaving them alone.

"Sid—"

"I never want to see you again. You're the reason Betsy's dead. Now get the hell outta here before I yank out these wires and wrap 'em around your goddam neck."

With Aunt Wren and Uncle Jack looking on, Yucatan Jay, aka Thomas Greenway, frisked her for weapons. Finding none, he took Raven's elbow and ushered her down a steeply graded hill behind the house.

"What the hell's going on?"

"Stop it. You don't realize it, but your voice carries."

"You'd better tell me where we're going, or I'll scream bloody murder."

With the speed of a cheetah, Jay put her in a choke hold and clamped a hand over her mouth. Raven's eyes widened with fright. Aunt Wren and Uncle Jack made no move to help, only clung to each other, shivering, on the porch.

"Nobody asked you to come here. You were supposed to think I'm dead."

Tears sluiced down her cheeks. A shudder of fear went through her.

"Stop it, Raven. Stop it right now," he hissed into her ear. "I'm about to remove my hand. If you so much as squeak, I'll karate chop your windpipe shut. Understand?"

She gave him a meek nod.

He let go, and she clutched her throat, smoothing her fingers over the skin to make sure everything was still in place. "Who are you?"

"Thomas Greenway. Yucatan Jay. Christopher Balzac. Adrian Wallace. Bob Lee." His eyes rolled skyward. "I can go on if you like."

"How could you leave like that?"

"I told you. I hold a rather unorthodox position with our government. I have a job overseas. When it's over, I'll retire."

She gave him a head shake.

"Don't believe me? I'll show you." He dragged her farther into the incline of trees until they came to a level area off the main path. Yucatan Jay kicked pine needles aside with his boot; the outline of a cellar door came into view.

"You want to know about me?" Agitated. "Come into my bunker."

"I'm not going down there with you."

But he broke out his wallet, flipped it open and swiped it through the air. Powered by hydraulics, the door slid back on its own. He gave her a nudge, and they descended a narrow set of steps, into an underground command center illuminated by fluorescent lights, filled with electronic monitoring equipment, a state-of-the-art printing press and flight maps of third world countries. Tiny chirps came from a nearby monitor.

*He really is CIA.*

The overhead door slid shut, closing out the daylight and sealing off escape.

"Why'd you come here?"

Air came in short gulps. "You turned my life inside out. I had to know the truth."

"You're crazy about me."

"Not at all. You make up stupid stories about pygmies and cannibals—"

"That's all changed. The Mbuti pygmies go on the back burner for now. Something more pressing came up." He rested a hand on her shoulder. Brushed a maverick curl out of her face and tilted her chin up with his finger. He kissed her on the lips, and when he removed his hand, a smile angled up one side of his face. "You love me."

She shook her head, wondering where this was all leading. "Is Uncle Jack CIA?"

"Retired."

He smoothed the palm of his hand against her face and kissed her again. This time, Raven kissed back. Logical thoughts swirled inside her head. She didn't need to be mixed up with a man like Yucatan Jay, even if that little tongue thing he did to her ear made her eyes roll back in her head and her body start to quiver. His lips turned into suction cups halfway down her neck, and when he ground himself against her, she let him.

He stopped, mid-bite. "This is no kind of life for a normal person, Rave. It takes sacrifice, discipline and dedication. Duty to country first. Everything else takes a backseat. I couldn't do that to you."

She mouthed, "I know," slathering his face with kisses as she undid his top two buttons. She slid her hand down the front of his shirt and felt a series of Band-Aids stuck to his smooth skin.

Jay winced. He sucked in a breath of air at her touch.

"Did it hurt getting those beads taken out?"

"Not as much as having to leave you."

"Did you really get rolled in the red-light district?"

"No."

"What happened to your tattoo?"

"It washed off."

Caught up in the electricity of Yucatan Jay's force field, Raven closed her eyes.

"I'm a human lie detector, Raven. You can't beat me." He

fit his palms to her breasts. His tongue slicked down her neck, and this time it was Jay, undoing buttons. "Tell me again why you came looking for me. And this time, tell the truth."

"Are we cousins, or not?"

"I'm not Yucatan Jay. Y-Jay ran into a problem in Sudan. I'm meeting him in two days."

"You mean he's not dead?"

"Not yet."

"Where is he?"

"In prison. There's some concern the Sudanese government may execute him."

Raven was still naked beneath the covers when Tommy Greenway got up to make coffee. She watched him puttering around in the kitchenette, still processing the information he shared with her just before he plundered her lips and took her to bed.

His mother was Uncle Jack's sister. He grew up in the Rio Grande Valley and played high school football against Yucatan Jay. Spent hours hunting and fishing with Uncle Jack after his mother died and his father turned to alcohol, and eventually came to live with them in Manitou Springs when Yucatan Jay came back from military school, rehabilitated. The cousins chose the Air Force Academy, and when they graduated, Uncle Jack got them jobs. Taught them everything he knew about intelligence and counterintelligence. Tommy and Y-Jay often worked as a team, but Y-Jay had a thrill-seeking gene and he kept taking unnecessary risks that compromised his assignments. Now, he was being held captive in a godforsaken country where beheadings were the norm.

"When will you be back?"

"I don't know."

"What if I never see you again?"

He brought her a cup of coffee and sat down next to her. "This is why we don't make good family men. There's always that chance."

She caressed the spot where Huitzilopochtli's wing used to be, and sparked a hunger in Greenway's eyes. They shined as bright a blue as Uncle Jack's in the incandescent glow of the table lamp, and glittered as she traced her finger down his chest to a place where the hummingbird's tail feathers should have been.

"I don't even know what name to call you."

"Does it matter?"

# Chapter Fifty-two

The Yankees were ahead three-zip when Jinx returned home to a blaring television.

Dan had found his glasses and sat happily absorbed in a copy of the *Fort Worth Business Press.*

"Listen to this, boy." He traced a gnarled finger with permanent nicotine stains across a sub head. "Our Lady of Mercy hospital is being sued for two hundred million. Think they'll get it?"

"I wouldn't know." Jinx shifted his attention to the ball game. "Who's winning?"

"We are."

"We're the Rangers, Dad. We're out of the play-offs."

A crooked smile angled up Dan's face.

Jinx wandered into his bedroom and tossed his windbreaker on a mattress, still wrapped in plastic. "Daddy, have you seen Caesar?"

"Who's Caesar?"

"The Siamese."

"We have a cat?"

He found him hiding under the new bedsprings, still nursing a grudge. The vet had shaved his fur down to the skin.

Jinx dropped on all fours and tried to coax him out. "C'mon, Caese." The Siamese hissed. Sapphire eyes turned to garnets and the fur on his tail haloed around its bony stem.

"All right, I shouldn't have laughed. I was happy to see you, that's all." The cat eased back in mistrust. His lopsided mohawk stood out at right angles. Jinx stretched his arm as far as it would go.

His furry old pal drew blood.

Wincing, Jinx flopped on the bed and rubbed the new laceration.

The world was a lonely place.

The last three weeks had taken on the tragic proportions of a Shakespearian drama.

By nightfall, the numb feeling dogging him all the way home from the hospital turned into a crushing, permanent ache. He retreated into the bathroom for a hot shower. After dressing for the second time, he grabbed Ivy's papers and sifted through them. Nothing that couldn't wait 'til Monday. He re-banded the stack and tossed them into a cardboard box.

He collected his badge case, wallet and car keys and reappeared in the living room.

Dan looked upon him with admiration. "Well, well, well . . . aren't you slickered up?"

"I'm going out for awhile."

"Where to?"

"Hey, I've got more than one friend, you know."

"Long as you're standing around, how about bringing me a Dr Pepper?"

"Help yourself. I've got something to do."

"Going to see a girl? Is that why you're all slicked up?"

"I'm not slicked up."

"Your mama didn't like that last gal you brought home. That gal you took to the prom?"

"The only girl I ever took home to meet Mother was my ex-wife."

"Nobody liked her."

"Well, that's okay. She didn't much care for us, either. I'm locking the dead bolt, Dad. I want you to stay put until I get back. And don't let anybody in."

"What if your mother comes?"

"She won't."

"But what if she does?"

He closed the door and threw the lock.

In the sanctuary of the patrol car, numbing grief gave way to despair. The only thing easing the pain was that the car seemed to drive itself. On a hill, a block from Astrid Street, Jinx did a visual scan. Raven was unloading a set of matching suitcases from the trunk of the BMW. She headed for the door and disappeared inside.

He shifted the car into gear. While he still had the nerve, he gunned the engine, pulled away from the curb and wielded the big Chevy in behind Raven's old classic. A sense of urgency filled his senses.

He didn't want her to be with Dell.

She shouldn't be with anyone but him.

Raven was wrong. He *could* commit to one woman.

He could commit to *her*.

With heart thudding and shoulders squared, he stood at her door with his fingertip pressing the bell. Beyond the window, a soft silhouette floated toward him. His knees turned to sand but the granite feet propping him up refused to flee.

A hundred bad memories took flight with the snap of the dead bolt.

He cleared his throat and swallowed hard. Carnal panic vibrated behind his eyeballs. His gut wrenched at the turn of the handle. The sound of his own blood whooshed in his ears.

He knew what he had to say.

This time, he'd say it.

The door swung open. Raven clapped a hand to her mouth and stared through haunted eyes. A blue jay feather hung from a string around her neck.

"Mind if I come in?"

She whispered his name, stepped outside and pulled the door behind her until only a dim shaft of light shined through.

"I've been missing you a lot." He reached a hand beneath his jacket, removing a set of handcuffs at the small of his back. The first, he snapped onto her wrist. The second, he clicked onto his own. "Don't pick Dell. You belong with me."

As she curled her fingers into the front of his jacket and hauled him close, the prerehearsed speech he perfected on the drive over evaporated like desert rain. He found himself uttering those three horrible words, guaranteed to make stronger those men it did not kill.

"Be my wife."

The pulse in Raven's throat throbbed against the feather Tommy Greenway tied around her neck when he confessed he'd loved her since the day he taped her cheerleader snapshot to the inside of his high school locker.

And now, Raven couldn't believe Jinx Porter had just spilled his guts. For a moment, her lungs refused to inflate. When she managed to catch her breath, she came down from the emotional high and remembered somebody else had a vested interest in her future.

Jinx slid his handcuffed wrist around her waist, pinning her arm behind her. "Will you marry me?"

"Jinx—" Her eyes welled. The first pangs of panic set in. "—why're you doing this now?"

"I love you."

With her free hand, she fisted the cloth on the front of his jacket and checked his eyes for signs of desperation.

"Come on, Raven. Can we go inside? I want to hold you and kiss you. I want to make up for lost time. I was stupid. I messed up. It took losing you to realize you're the best thing that ever happened to me."

He leaned in to kiss her, tentative at first, and she softened against his touch. Physical tension left his body as he devoured her mouth in gentle, deliberate bites. Swept into the promise of shared passion, locked in the grip of overpowering seduction, Raven's world narrowed into a single episode where Jinx Porter's strange hold over her sent desire speeding through her system.

She'd waited three years for this moment.

The door hinge creaked behind her, breaking the spell, and she realized Jinx had pushed it open a sliver. His eyes went wide and he unsuctioned his lips from hers. The flush of color left his face at the sight of Dell, dressed in his Sunday best, down on one knee with an open ring box still in his outstretched hand.

# About the Author

Laurie Moore was born and reared in the Great State of Texas, where she developed a flair for foreign languages. She's traveled to forty-nine states, most of the Canadian provinces, Mexico and Spain.

She majored in Spanish at the University of Texas at Austin, where she received her Bachelor of Arts degree in Spanish, English, Elementary and Secondary Education. Instead of using her teaching certificate, she entered into a career in law enforcement in 1979. After six years of police patrol and a year in criminal investigations, she was promoted to sergeant, and worked as a district attorney investigator for several DAs in the Central Texas area over the next seven years.

In 1992, she moved to Fort Worth and graduated from Texas Wesleyan University School of Law, where she received her Juris Doctor in 1995. She is currently in private practice in "Cowtown," and has a daughter at Rhodes, two bad Siamese cats and a Welsh Corgi. She is still a licensed, commissioned peace officer.

Laurie has been a member of the DFW Writers Workshop since 1992, and has served on the board of directors for the past two years. She is the author of *Constable's Run* and *The Lady Godiva Murder*. Writing is her passion.